FAIL STATE

A NOVEL OF THE END OF DAYS

JOHN BIRMINGHAM

GIGANTIC BOMBS CORP.

1

THE SOLDIER OF FORTUNE
SWIMSUIT EDITION

They did not make it to Montana. On the second day out, they came up against a couple of trucks blocking Route 50 just east of Aurora, a West Virginia flyspeck on the road map Rick held folded in his big, scarred hands while James drove. Sat-nav was down, and phone cover was spotty at best. However, it had been flaking out long before they'd escaped the gridlock around Winchester. Melissa and Michelle sat in the rear cabin of the Sierra with Nomi, the black labrador, lying between them, accepting ear scratches and tummy rubs as though they were only her due. The trucks hadn't crashed. They'd been arranged in a crude roadblock. Just parked across the tarmac, bumper to bumper. Armed men and women sheltered behind them, and a local sheriff's car was parked out in front.

Hand-painted signs by the side of the highway warned drivers to SLOW DOWN, TURN AROUND and GO BACK. The red and blue turret lights on top of the police cruiser flashed briefly as James's big SUV was about to come out of the woods beyond the edge of town.

"What do you want to do?" he asked, slowing down. A dense forest of black spruce and fir trees crowded up close on either side of the road but gave way to farmland up ahead, where Route 50 approached the tiny hamlet. The locals had set their roadblock out in the open, maybe a hundred yards beyond the tree line.

"Best pull up here, I reckon," Rick said.

The turret flashers stopped as James eased over, still in the gloom of the forest, about three or four hundred yards from the blockade. Nomi, sensing something was up, whimpered softly until Rick reached into the rear of the cabin and patted her.

"You want to come with?" he asked Mel. "Talk the talk?"

His girlfriend smiled.

"Cop to cop, you mean? Cos I don't think anyone up there is gonna rate my three years with the Old Bill."

"We should go," Michelle Nguyen said, meaning Melissa and herself alone. "It'll be less threatening if it's just a couple of girls. Plus, I got this to wave around."

She fetched her ID card out of a shirt pocket. The laminate identified her as a senior research officer with the National Security Council.

Rick Boreham didn't much like the suggestion, and they could all see it on his face.

Michele Nguyen softened her delivery with a smile.

"Rick, you're a cover model for the swimsuit edition of *Soldier of Fortune*, and James here looks like he's totally gonna try to sell them life insurance or a newsletter subscription. Either way, they'd be justified in shooting you both on sight. Let us go. We're pretty and non-threatening, and we tick all the diversity boxes."

Rick didn't smile. But he did think on it for a moment before answering.

"Okay, but take Nomi," he said. "People love dogs more than they do people. You're less likely to get shot with her."

"You're probably right," Michelle conceded. "Come on, girl."

"Wait!" James said. "Your guns. Are you gonna take them?"

Both women spoke at the same time.

"Yeah," Michelle said.

"No way," Mel answered.

Two beats of silence.

"Okay," James said into the stillness. "This isn't awkward at all."

"You can't go unarmed," Rick started, but Mel cut him off.

"We have to go unarmed or not at all," she said. "Look at that set-up. There's a dozen or more of them pilchards up there. Everyone is packin' shooters, for sure. These things are just gonna get us killed."

She held up a Glock 26 subcompact. They all had weapons now.

"She's right," James said.

Both Rick and Michelle turned their disapproval on him.

"You just said the two of you would be better because you don't look like a threat," he gently reminded Michelle. "And do the math. Twelve or thirteen guns, firing from cover, against two in the open. We don't want trouble. We just want to keep driving. I'll go if you want. I'm cool to go talk to them."

"You're not going anywhere, Poindexter," Michelle shot back, but he could see from her chagrined expression that she had accepted his point.

"I'll go with Mel," she said. "And no guns."

"Sorted," said Melissa.

The two women exited the car and removed the holsters at their hips. Mel took Nomi by her lead. Rick's dog gave him a single backward glance, but upon his instruction to "Protect", she put her head down and trundled off with the girls.

"They do look a hell of a lot less threatening than two guys marching up there," James said. "Or, you know, you, at least."

Rick snorted softly.

"Guess so. And you're right, James. I worked enough checkpoints to know what it's like."

He fell quiet for a moment before adding.

"I hope this is the right thing to do."

James left the engine idling, even though they needed to save gas. The price had already spiked to fifteen bucks a gallon, and Homeland Security had ordered nationwide rationing. First time since the late 1970s, according to NPR, but James wasn't so sure of that. He thought maybe there'd been some during one of the Gulf wars, but he couldn't check, not without data coverage, and they had none. That had crashed early and hard. It was frustrating for somebody whose whole livelihood was based on moving information around.

Of course, food was supposed to be rationed as well, but market forces were quickly taking care of that. They had two boxes of fresh vegetables in the back of the Sierra, bought earlier that morning from a roadside stall near Leesburg in northern Virginia. A farmer, protected by two shotgun-wielding sons, had demanded a hundred dollars for a small bag of spinach leaves and two hundred for a pound of potatoes; although James was open to barter and Mel was able to trade three packs of cigarettes for the spinach and a small punnet of cherry tomatoes.

She didn't smoke. None of them did. But Rick had suggested taking the Camels purely as trade goods. Seven cartons of them they'd looted, no other word for it, straight from the storeroom at Rick's workplace, a country club in Maryland, ten minutes drive from Darnestown and a solid three iron across the river from one of Donald Trump's golf courses.

James had wondered how that trade might have gone if Rick hadn't been standing behind her, cradling his weapon.

"What a mess," he said quietly.

Mostly, he was just talking to himself, and that just to fill the dead air space. He was a lot less comfortable with silence than Rick, who sometimes seemed as though he was carved from some ancient, living hardwood.

"Hell of a thing," his new friend agreed, inclining his head at the trucks.

The girls walked steadily toward the sheriff's vehicle and the two big haulers behind it. One was a large van, but the other had an empty flatbed in the back. James recognised it as a container trailer. A dozen or more townsfolk sheltered behind it, all of them armed as best he could tell.

"Pardon me," Rick said as he twisted around to reach into the backseat. "Don't want to get out and set anybody's trigger finger to twitching."

James awkwardly pulled his seat forward, opening up a few more inches for Rick to squeeze through. He grunted and strained, reaching for a daypack that was just out of reach. James shifted again, careful to keep his foot away from the accelerator, even though he'd put the Sierra in park and engaged the e-brake. It was enough, and Rick was able to pull the small pack into the front of the car.

He fetched out a pair of binoculars. They were well-used, in scratched and faded desert camouflage. He raised them and scanned ahead.

"Melissa?"

"Yeah, Mishy?"

"What do you think of James?"

They walked in tandem, their steps drifting in and out of sync as they advanced. Mel Baker was a good foot taller than Michelle Nguyen. She wore Nike Flyknits, which made very little noise as she advanced. Michelle's Doc Marten's made for a muffled crunch on the hard road surface. Nomi padded along between them, her nails clicking in counterpoint.

"Funny thing to ask. He's your fella, isn't he?"

That last sounded like *"Inny?"*

Michelle blew out a ragged breath.

"If I want, I guess."

"What do you mean if you want? Aren't you two, like...you know?"

Michelle's silence was answer enough.

The English woman almost stopped on the tarmac. Nomi got tangled between them, and it took a moment to sort out all the legs and leads.

"Bugger me," Mel said. "I thought you two was proper linked."

The more petite Vietnamese-American woman snorted.

"I only really met James a day or so before you did. We kissed the night of the... you know. The shooting. But nothing since."

Mel did stop then.

"You what, girl?"

The guardians of Aurora shifted perceptibly in the distance. Nomi panted happily, and Michelle nodded that they should keep moving.

"Don't want to spook them," she said. "But yeah. Status update, it's complicated."

It was Melissa's turn to exhale loudly.

"End of the fucking world usually is, eh?"

Michelle was a moment replying.

"Usually. Yeah."

They were halfway to the blockade when Nomi decided she needed to take a leak.

"Oh man, this is not the impression I was hoping to make," Michelle said as Rick's dog lifted a leg on a hand-painted sign warning outsiders to STAY AWAY.

They scoped out the townspeople while Nomi relieved herself. Individual faces resolved into unremarkable types.

"Butchers, bakers, smartphone app makers," Mel said quietly.

And a sheriff so bow-legged he looked as though he'd spent a lot more time in a saddle than behind the wheel of his old brown Crown Vic. None of them were smiling, but the lack of open hostility in the expression of the law enforcement officer at least reassured Michelle. He seemed content for them to come on and make their pitch even if their dog had just pissed on his stern warning to stay the hell away.

It was a high, fine morning, the first week of fall, but the steam press heat of a cruel summer still lingered close. Michelle Nguyen was beginning to leak sweat. Beside her, Mel seemed almost preternaturally cool, which was absurd. Her family background was Caribbean, but Melissa was pure London, and that place was cold and foggy as fuck. Even in summer, every time Michelle had ever been. She glanced over at Mel as they walked on.

Mel kept her expression pleasant and her hands where any shooters could see them.

There were plenty of shooters.

When they were forty or fifty yards out, the cop stepped forward and raised a hand. Nomi sat immediately. The man wore a pistol at his side but carried no other firearm that Michelle could see. He didn't have to. There was a whole arsenal backing him up, including the big honking assault rifle his deputy carried. That would be a military-grade, fully automatic unit, she guessed. Not some single shot, wank fantasy substitute.

The sheriff, who reminded her fetchingly of Bill Murray with his little pot belly and decidedly cherubic nose, hooked both thumbs into his belt when the two women and their smiling dog came to a halt.

"Hi," Michelle said. "I'm Michelle Nguyen. This is my friend Mel Baker."

"And this is Nomi," Mel added.

"I'm Sheriff Hughes," the cop said mildly. "Evan Hughes. And I'm afraid I'm going to have to ask you ladies to turn around and go back where you came from."

Michelle smiled, trying to look as harmless as possible. For the first time in a long while, she was suddenly aware of her tattoos and midnight blue hair. Maybe they should have got James to do this. He looked a lot more like these guys than she did.

"We came from the DC," she said, feeling as if she was somehow lying and about to be caught out in that lie. "There's no going back there. It's been evacuated. You would have heard, surely?"

Hughes nodded.

"I did hear that, yes, ma'am. Saw it on the news, too. But I'm afraid it doesn't change the situation here. We've secured the town under an Executive Order signed by the President before they evacuated him. Residents only in town, I'm sorry. You'll have to move on. It's only for the duration of the emergency. I'm sure you'll be fine."

"We'd love to move on, Sheriff," Mel Baker replied. "We're heading to Montana. We just want to get there as quickly as possible. But this is the way through, and if we could just pass..."

Sheriff Hughes shook his head.

"Sorry. I'm afraid I can't do that, ma'am. We are in lockdown. You'll have to backtrack. I suggest Route 24. I understand it's clear south to the Spruce Knob rec park and beyond."

The two women exchanged a look.

Michelle spoke up again.

"Sheriff Hughes, I'm going to take an ID card from my pocket if that's okay with you?"

His deputy shifted. He didn't put his hand on his gun, but he did get ready. Nomi's tail, which had been happily thumping away, fell still.

"Okay," Hughes said.

"I work for the National Security Council," Michelle said, pitching her voice to carry to the people behind the barrier too. She took out the laminated card, still wrapped in a bright red lanyard, and took a few cautious half-steps toward Hughes. A few of the townsfolk moved, some of them raising their weapons, but the sheriff made a placating gesture, and they stood easy again, or at least a little easier.

Hughes beckoned them forward.

"Come on here then," he said.

They walked the rest of the way to him.

This close, Michelle could see how frightened people were. Not Hughes. He didn't seem worried about anything much at all. But his deputy was sweating like the Devil's own nutsack, and the vanilla ghetto posse they'd put together at the barrier was definitively confirmed as a motley collection of up-gunned homemakers, all of them well out of their comfort zone. She wondered if the other end of town was similarly cordoned off.

The sheriff inspected her ID card and handed it back.

"Yep," he said. "That's you all right."

But he gave her nothing else. Seemed that Sheriff Evan Hughes wasn't much interested in her connection to the centre of power.

"Uhm, I need to get to Montana," Michelle improvised, "... as quickly as I can. It's a matter of national security. For the... National Security... Council."

She trailed off.

Nomi made a sort of strangled noise. It perfectly captured the frustration that Michelle felt.

"Route 24 is your best choice then, Miss Nguyen," Sheriff Hughes said. "Because Route 50 is closed to through traffic. By virtue of Executive Order 14101."

"Come on, Sheriff," Mel Baker tried. Her pleading London accent sounded weird and utterly out of place here. "You can just let us through. You know that. I used to do this job."

Hughes shook his head slowly.

"Not around here, you didn't, Miss. Around here, it's my job, and I'm advising you strongly to take Route 24."

His hand dropped to the butt of his service revolver.

Nomi started to growl.

Michelle's gaze followed the move as though hypnotised. Hughes' hand was rock steady, but it was old and liver-spotted. She stared at the grey hairs and veins that stood out from his leathery, suntanned skin. The dark wood pistol grip looked just as weathered as the hand which settled on it.

"Come on," Mel said, taking her by the elbow. "Let's take the other road."

"Good choice," Hughes nodded.

His hand moved away from the gun as though it had never been there in the first place.

Michelle found her legs did not work as they should, and she stumbled as Mel pulled her away. Turning her back on all those guns and blank faces, she tripped over Nomi and blundered into Mel. Nomi scurried out of the way, and Mel absorbed the awkward collision without fuss to carry her a few steps back up the road towards where James and Rick waited in the car. It seemed a long way off in the distance.

2

AN OLD WOMAN SPEAKS IN DOG FARTS

The end of the world had arrived. It just wasn't evenly distributed. Darkness fell hardest where the light of civilisation had burned with the brightest splendour. The crew of the International Space Station were ideally placed to observe the dying cities of the North American continent, but immediately after the Chinese cyber-attack on the US, there was surprisingly little to note. Unlike the morning of the 9/11 atrocities, no vast grey plumes soared into the atmosphere like dark volcanic ejecta.

Indeed, as the edge of darkness crept across the continent at the end of that first day, the Canadian crew member, Dan Frith, noted that the dense filigree of electric brilliance that traced the veins and arteries of urban life far below seemed noticeably brighter – a consequence of tens of millions of automobiles trapped in immense traffic jams. Second-order effects of the cyber strike, such as panic buying, creeping hunger, and eventual mass starvation, were not readily apparent from four hundred kilometres above the Earth's surface, unlike the accelerating collapse of the power grid over the following week and a half.

It would be six months before the continental United States was completely dark, save for a few hundred pinpoints of light scattered far from the ruins of the great cities. But by then, the four men and two women who had observed the petty struggles of mankind as the Gods once had looked down from Olympus had themselves perished. No NASA missions came to their rescue. The European Space Agency, like Europe itself, was taken into the maw a new Dark Age. Roscosmos, ESA's Russian equivalent, was quickly militarized with the outbreak of hostilities on the Eurasian landmass and just as quickly destroyed in the short, brutal war that followed.

Roscosmos was always an unlikely hope for salvation, Frith noted in one of the last mission logs. A quirk of the crew rotation schedule meant that he had replaced the previous Russian crew member, Cosmonaut Colonel Danya Spasojevic, when the final Soyuz docked with the space station, two weeks before the catastrophe that came to be known, however briefly, as Zero Day.

Nobody read Frith's mission log.

The ISS burned up on re-entry fifteen months, and two days after General Chu Jianguo of the 2nd Bureau, Third Department of the People's Liberation Army General Staff pressed a single bright red key to launch Operation Golden Path.

Unit 61398, the spearhead of the PLA's digital war-fighting regiments, was designated by foes in the US military and intelligence complex as an 'advanced persistent threat'. It did not long remain so.

With two fleets of the People's Liberation Army Navy heavily engaged in combat with at least four US allies in Southeast Asia, the President authorised independent operations by those US forces that survived the precision attacks on the 7th Fleet. One such asset was SSN 777, also known as the *North Carolina*, a Virginia-class fast attack submarine that had been lurking sixty fathoms beneath the Taiwan Strait when China's East Sea Fleet put out from Ningbo and Shanghai.

Appraised of the location and track of the enemy's passage by encrypted satellite burst, Captain Michael Sharp ordered Helmswoman Nicola Webster to bring the *North Carolina* around. The boat's ninth-generation nuclear reactor fed full military power into the pump-jet propulsors, accelerating her to 35 knots as she raced into engagement range with Admiral Wen Bo Xi's carrier battle group.

Seven minutes before Sharp would have ordered the release of an anti-surface ship strike package, orders arrived from the national command authority re-tasking the 777 onto a priority land attack mission. Sharp was the very model of professional restraint, keeping wholly to himself his opinion of such a strategically ruinous directive. He ordered his crew to reformat the weapons package. The sailors in the boat's payload module were every bit as professional as their commander, but they were not subject to the strictures and constraints of command rank.

As they swapped out the anti-ship weapons for a smaller flight of long-range cruise missiles, they volubly cursed the treasonous stupidity of their civilian masters. All to no avail, naturally. Captain Sharp ordered the launch as soon as the track was plotted. Six long-range cruise missiles shot from the vertical launch tubes along the North Carolina's spine, breaking the surface a few seconds later and burning away towards the Chinese mainland. They speared into the headquarters of Unit 61398 after thirteen minutes of supersonic flight time, obliterating the entire complex in a miniature supernova.

General Chu was not there. Most of Unit 61398 was not there, having been dispersed to alpha sites before launching their strike on the American foe. Eventually, more missiles would end them, but not for a little while. And General Chu was not among their number when the second, more successful strike came in.

He was at home, in bed with a cold.

He had contracted the cold, which grew rapidly worse, from his driver and bodyguard, Lieutenant Bo Min. The good lieutenant had his dose from a girlfriend, a dancer at the Flower Drum Club in Shanghai, and she, in turn, had encountered the HPAI B1 subtype virus from a contractor hired as a cutout by an agent of the CIA's Special Activities Division.

The Agency had not chosen the contractor imagining that he would deliver America's vengeance upon General Chu Jianguo. The contractor was infected because he was Han Chinese and so lacked an enzyme that worked as a trigger to kill the replicator switch in the tailored virus. He was also known to the Agency as a source of synthetic opioids, a massively lucrative business that had blighted millions of American lives over the previous decade. The Agency were not moral arbiters. They had chosen on occasion to use the contractor because he did good work. On this occasion, they chose him because he was biologically suitable but also well-placed. It was not possible to run a business such as he did without at least the tacit approval, if not active connivance, of the state security apparatus in China.

Thus, Contractor P7X-T9 was judged to be a viable transmission vector for delivering the virus directly into the social circles occupied by the highest levels of the PLA and Chinese Communist Party.

As indeed he was.

The bug leapt from the contractor to the dancer, to the driver to the general, and from them to 99.94% of everyone they encountered during the three-day incubation phase.

There were three hundred contractors.

The virus spread rapidly.

WITHIN THREE DAYS, Li Wei, a five-month-old boy in the Chinese city of Hangzhou, tossed about in his little bed, his tiny face scrunched up as he whined. He rubbed his ears, and his nose ran with clear snot. He seemed overtired and unusually irritable to his mother, Chen. She changed his nappy and was alarmed to discover a striking rash on his upper thighs. It had not been there half an hour ago. It was not a common diaper rash, and she wrung her hands as she debated calling her mother-in-law. Her mother lived in distant Fuzhou; her husband Chao's family was here in Hangzhou. Chen and Chao had met at University, and their marriage had been reasonably happy, even when Chao travelled so much. She knew he did important work for the State, although she wasn't entirely sure what. It paid the bills, however, and there were so many of them with a new baby. It seemed impossible to get ahead of them.

Li Wei squealed and writhed, and Chen put aside thoughts of her absent husband. She put a slender hand on her son's forehead. He felt very hot. Her sleek Vivo cell phone lay on the table; it was one of the rewards for a family with a sky-high Social Score.

Should she call?

She gave her son a worried glance. He rubbed his ears with his tiny fists and bawled raucously. The cry grated on Chen's nerves. Was she a bad mother to feel it so?

Enough, she thought. Enough! She reached for the phone, swiped to unlock it and scrolled down to one of her least favoured contacts, her mother-in-law. Chunhua the dragon. She had set the phone up to display a terrible fire-breathing lizard when Chao's mother rang. As she did often to berate Chen for her poor parenting and lack of wifely virtue.

Just dialing this number felt like failure. But she pressed on. The phone rang, and her son sneezed and choked.

"Hello?"

"Good morning. I have a question for you if you have time?"

Chen felt like an idiot. This was a mistake.

"Of course you do. Speak then, child."

Chen's ears burned. *Child*. She had a diploma in organic chemistry, and she would surely return to work in a few months. Child! You speak in dog farts, old woman, she thought. But Chen held her tongue and spoke.

"Your grandson is sick. He has a strange rash."

There was a pause on the phone, and when Chunhua spoke again, she was all business. "Does he have a fever?"

"Not a bad one. His temperature is thirty-eight."

"No, that is not so bad. What does the rash look like?"

"It's on his thighs; it's hard to describe."

"Does it look mottled, like lap cheong sausage?"

"Kind of, I suppose."

"Your supposing will not suffice! I need to look for myself. I will be there within the hour."

The dragon cut the call.

Gah! What had she done?

Chen paced the room. Her baby cried.

She had done the right thing, she assured herself.

Chunhua was not a good person, but she was a retired army nurse, very senior, with many commendations from the state. Chen had to trust her opinion in this matter, if nothing else.

The hour spent waiting stretched out like dry rubber. Li Wei remained restless and crabby. Chen wandered continually to the big window overlooking the city, far below. The view had once thrilled her. Now, she felt like a prisoner in a high tower.

The door chimed at last, and her diminutive mother-in-law pushed into the apartment, nodded brusquely at Chen and marched directly to the crib. She reached down, picked up her grandson and placed him on the changing table. Chunhua sucked through her teeth as the boy whimpered.

"Ai! I called a friend at the hospital, and she said they are seeing this a lot, and some patients are getting very sick." She looked over the baby, who was naked. He shivered and wailed. "This rash is one of the symptoms." She shook her head. "I don't know how widespread it is; there is nothing on the news. But sometimes that can be the worst sign."

"I'm sure the government knows about this. They will do something," Chen said.

Chunhua's expression twisted. "Yes, of course they will." She opened her mouth as if to say more. Then she closed it. She pursed her lips and finally went on. She looked at her grandson. "I have never seen something quite like this." She paused and closed her eyes. She opened them. "I don't think they can quarantine all of Hangzhou."

Chen gasped. "Quarantine! How serious is this?"

Chunhua busied herself with her grandson. "I do not know." She wrinkled her brow and looked at Chen. "I will stay and watch him. You will make tea and dumplings. I have not eaten yet."

It was not a request. But it was a concession. Chunhua famously refused to eat Chen's dumplings, even though Chao loved them. Ha! Probably *because* he loved them.

Chen nodded. She would make the dumplings if it helped her son.

As she headed for the kitchen, her nose tickled, and she sneezed.

TEN THOUSAND KILOMETRES from the bright, sun-lit eyrie of Chen Lin Li's luxurious forty-second-floor apartment, Donna Barolo sneezed too. And coughed. But she was not infected with the HPAI B1 virus. She had burned her hair trying to light a cigarette and inhaled the foul smoke from the greasy, unwashed ringlet.

Donna had been saving the cigarette, the last in her pack.

It was going to kill her. She knew that, and not in some abstract way. Donna Barolo was going to die because she had stepped into an elevator about fifteen seconds after a lieutenant in the PLA's Unit 61398 unleashed a packet of malign code specifically designed to attack the software running on the servers of four large commercial property management businesses in the US.

Donna worked for the international law firm Baker and Mackenzie. Bakers, as they were known, retained one of the four targeted businesses to provide building management services in their brand-new office tower in LA. There was nothing specifically about Bakers which attracted the attention of Unit 61398. Nothing much, either, about the property management firm they retained other than its size and market reach, which drew it into the targeting reticle of the PLA. Operation Golden Path called for maximum disruption to the urban infrastructure of America's major cities as a feint to draw the enemy's attention away from the critical strike in Southeast Asia.

Donna Barolo became part of that feint when she stepped into the fourth car in a bank of six elevators that serviced the offices of her employers on floors 33 to 39 of the 55-storey tower in downtown LA. Donna, a paralegal, needed a cigarette, and nobody was around to tell her otherwise. The senior partners were all in some crisis meeting; those who were in the office, at least. Half the lawyers and support staff hadn't made it to work because of the insane traffic.

Four, maybe five seconds after Donna stabbed at the button to take her to the ground floor, the elevator car jerked to a stop, and the lights went out.

"Shit," she muttered.

Donna clicked on the torch on her phone. She always had her phone in hand, even today, even though there had been no service since the previous day. (Another effect of Unit 61398's diligence). Donna raised the big-ass Samsung in the air before genuflecting in the hope that some stray signal would connect. It didn't. The phone's flashlight threw her shadows up the wall like a looming ghoul.

The elevator's emergency handset, which she tried three minutes later, was dead and would remain so ever after. Donna held out for just over an hour before anxiety and nicotine cravings got the better of her, and she tapped out her first cigarette. She was almost disappointed when the smoke alarms did not sound.

Seventeen thousand six hundred and eighty-two elevators went down across the United States on the second day of Operation Golden Path, the massive militarized Chinese cyberattack that became known to the survivors as Zero Day. None ever came back online again. Many people were rescued. But many more were not. Over the next week, more than thirty thousand people like Donna Barolo died of thirst in the dark.

It was what the war planners of the 2nd Bureau, Third Department of the People's Liberation Army General Staff called a 'second order effect'.

There were many of them.

3

THE BEST MONEY HE NEVER MADE

Jonas Murdoch lay in bed before dawn, thinking about that twenty-five grand. He was never going to collect the reward payment. He knew that. And not because the cops back down in Seattle would snap the cuffs on him for punching Omar in his fat face back at the warehouse. Or for stealing his roomie's mountain bike and nearly nine hundred bucks in cookie jar savings, all before fleeing the city.

Nope.

Jonas knew he'd never collect that twenty-five large because the federal government, which had offered the money as a reward for the capture of Eladio Morena, no longer existed.

Neither did Morena, as far as Jonas knew, but he could give less than one wet shit about that.

It was still dark outside, and his Spartan habits had not entirely fallen away, even as the world fell apart around him. Jonas always rose early. This morning, he woke, as he had for the past week and a half, in the best cabin out back of Big Al's Diner in the village of Silverton, nestled into the first folds of the High Cascades. A former logging town a couple of hours northeast of Seattle, Silverton had fallen back on the tourist grift when all of the old-growth forests had been worked out. The first week of Fall had come upon the picturesque little village with crisp mornings and a hint of frost, even as the prolonged, brutal summer heat threatened to creep back into the day most afternoons.

Jonas stretched luxuriously under a single blanket on the king-sized bed. He rolled over to place his half-erect penis between Tomi Yates's deliciously warm and agreeably firm butt cheeks. Like him, she was naked, and after a moment of sliding his cock up and down between those well-toned ass cakes, Tomi groaned and started grinding back into him.

After some slow-n-easy rubfucking, just to say good morning, Jonas had a rail spike boner, and Tomi guided him into her from behind. Their fucking quickly turned noisy and feral.

She came first, and Jonas flipped her over and finished on top, roaring like a bull as he shot his wad.

Fuck yeah. That twenty-five grand was the best money he never made.

Sheriff Dave Muller, who both loved and looked a bit like a glazed donut, had put Jonas in for the reward after he'd body-slammed Morena in Silverton's main street. Not the sort of vigilante action a straight-arrow like Muller would generally encourage. Still, Morena had been punching the jellied shit out of Al Barrett, owner of Big Al's and sponsor of Silverton's three junior high sports teams and, for good measure, the town's amateur landscape painting club.

It was not a mystery to Jonas why nobody else had stepped up to save Barrett's life — and nobody doubted that Jonas had done just that, least of all Big Al himself. Morena's attack had been fast, savage and calculated to dissuade any local heroes who might try and prevent him from stealing the thousands of dollars in cash Al had just withdrawn from the S&L on Main Street.

Jonas was neither a local boy nor a hero.

He attacked Morena in a blind rage because the greasy fucking bean-eater was pounding on Al in the middle of the road, where Jonas was speeding along on his stolen bike. Motherfucker almost made him crash, avoiding the fight as he came around the tight curve into town at speed. Reason enough to lose his temper. But

Jonas Murdoch was not just a bicycle thief. He was a proud All-American five-star bigot who purely fucking hated wetback assholes like Eladio Morena. He had good reason for that, but long story short, Jonas had kicked that shithead into raw taco meat when everyone else in Silverton was too paralysed by abject fear and confusion to do much of anything but stand and watch like drooling retards.

It was the day the Chinese had collapsed the banking system. Or maybe the Russians or even the ragheads.

Nobody really knew, and it didn't really matter.

All that mattered was that Jonas was no longer on the run from the consequences of his bad temper and worse choices back in Seattle. He was burrowed in tight here in Silverton. His input and assistance were eagerly sought out just because he beat the shit out of a beaner. And, of course, Tomi Yates, the hottest bitch in Silverton, had decided she could do with his input and assistance, too, most fucking agreeably in the form of the pussy-pounding pillow meal he'd just fed her from both ends.

"You don't want to hang out with me, baby?" Tomi asked half an hour later.

"Sweetheart, I just hung out with you three times," Jonas grinned as he got dressed by the bed. "I'm gonna need my breakfast if you want me to hang out some more."

He saw the way her eyes went a little wider at the mention of food.

"You going to the meeting with the town Committee?" she asked as innocently as a platinum blonde cock sponge could.

Not so fucking much, in other words.

"Sheriff Dave asked if I would. Darren O'Shannassy, too. Because your bad boy right here is a straight shooter, respected on both sides of the aisle."

Tomi shook her head, causing a couple of silver-tinted ringlets to sway in front of her eyes.

"Man, I don't know how you do it, playing referee at those meetings. Those two totally hate on each other."

Jonas smiled.

"Bringing people together, sweetie. That's what I'm all about."

"Can you bring me some food back?" she asked, getting to the nub of it. "I know they got food at those meetings. Everyone says so."

Jonas was tempted to make a joke about a little starvation being good for her figure. She was looking fucking *sculpted* since Big Al's ran out of curly fries, and like everyone else in town, she'd had to work on the barricades. But he kept a lid on it. Even with a ditz like Tomi, he had a role to play. Jonas pulled on his jeans and tucked in the black tee shirt he'd worn for three days in a row. She was gonna bitch about that any time now, and he was gonna tell her to wash it for him if it was such a big deal. And while she was at it, she could do the rest of his shit too. But he would keep it cool for the moment. She wasn't that hungry yet.

"I'll see what I can do, baby. If there's anything to grab, I'll get some for you. Here," he said, reaching into the back pocket of the jeans. "Don't tell anyone I gave you this."

Her eyes went wide for real this time, sparkling with anticipation.

He tossed her a protein bar. A good one, too. A big ass choc-fudge mofo from Musashi.

"You get this from your gym guy?" she asked, tearing the wrapper open and taking a bite.

He'd never seen anybody enjoy a protein slab so much. They all tasted like brown ass to him, with a double coating of more ass.

"Yeah, Chad kept a few back for me. Our secret, okay?"

She nodded, her mouth too full of keto-friendly whey protein isolate and sugar-free cocoa mass to speak.

Jonas assessed he was taking a risk, letting her in on that deal. There was always a chance Tomi would go straight to the source and dump him for Chad Moffat. Except that Moffat was one of your true Bros-B4-Hoes retards—like, seriously, the dude had a tattoo and everything—and Jonas was the only reason Moffat was safely inside the fortified wall that secured Silverton from the outside world. They'd been ready to run his ass off when he rolled up to the Cascade

Gate in his ridiculous fucking douche-wagon, this dusty white Jeep covered in pictures of The Chad Himself and motivational brainfarts for his personal training business.

'Your workout is Chad's warm-up.'

'Unless you puke, faint or die, Chad has failed.'

And Jonas's personal fave... *'Zumba? Bitch, please, I LIFT!'*

That one made him smile because Zumba cucks always fapped on about how hard it was, but that was just the pain of human dignity leaving the body.

He left Tomi to finish her contraband breakfast, promising he'd catch up with her later after the meeting and then doing his turn on the guard roster. All of the able-bodied men in town, from County Comptroller Howard Wetsman down to the lovable town drunk Colin McFarland, had to pull at least one rotation a day on the barricades. More than half were armed from a cache of weapons assembled in the first days after the true extent of the emergency became evident, and the President signed an Executive Order authorising duly elected municipal governments to 'take all necessary measures' to secure their towns and cities. The remainder of the sentinels in Silverton, however, had to make do with axe handles from O'Shannassy's hardware business, baseball bats from the sports department of the small local high school and, in McFarland's case, with a genuinely ferocious temper made worse by enforced abstinence.

Even the dwindling store of alcohol was rationed because empty calories were still calories.

Jonas strapped on his pistol. He could carry it openly now. Hell, it wasn't even a choice. The town's Emergency Committee had passed an Ordnance requiring all able-bodied residents and 'authorised visitors' to go armed 'in service of the common defence at all times'.

"Later," he threw back over his shoulder as he pulled the door to the cabin closed behind him. Tomi would have her own assigned chores and responsibilities to get to, but she wasn't so stupid as to turn up smelling of bootleg chocolate. Jonas walked the short distance from the tourist cabins behind Al's bar and diner, his boots crunching on the gravel path as he breathed deeply of the fresh autumnal air. The first week of September had not been kind to many people anywhere, but Jonas Murdoch considered himself blessed. Even as he turned left out of the driveway and walked up Main Street, taking in the sight of dozens of labourers working away at the freshly planted vegetable gardens on the town common, he had to suppress a smirk at how well things had turned out for him. A little over a week ago, he'd been a fugitive from the law. Now, he was the law.

Evidence of the change lay all around him. The toilers in those freshly dug fields. The raw, roughhewn timbers, cut from the dense forest surrounding Silverton and still oozing dark brown sap, lashed and nailed together into the motte and bailey style fortifications guarding the eastern and western ends of the village, the only two points accessible by road. He took in the riflemen stationed at high points along Main Street, mainly atop the rooflines of the taller buildings like the county hall and the former telegraph offices, lately occupied by a homewares and knick-knack store. Darren O'Shannassy's grocery business was shuttered, with extreme prejudice, but not from lack of produce to sell. As the major food store in Silverton, it had been designated a top priority for protective security, second only in importance and resourcing to the effort to plant and harvest a winter crop on the town common, where rows of fast-growing green beans, radishes and turnips had been planted from seed stock gathered by Jacques Loubert, high school science teacher and keen amateur gardener.

Lachie Saunders, proprietor of Silverton's only licensed marijuana dispensary and wholesale grow shop, had given over all of the space in his greenhouse to kale and lettuce and was supervising the construction of five more, much larger glass hothouses to grow as much of a winter crop as possible.

He and Loubert were supposed to address the town's Emergency Committee about hydroponics later that morning.

Jonas shivered in the early morning chill as he hurried up Main Street, nodding here and there to anybody who recognised him and waved. His heroics in saving Al Barrett had not been forgotten, but they were not exactly the news of the day any more. That would be the completion of the barricade on the northern side of town, where

Brad Rausch had towed the last car into place to close up the wall protecting the playing fields between the town centre and the forested slopes climbing away to the first peaks of the High Cascades.

Those fields were the first to be planted out, on the order of the Emergency Committee, and armed guards patrolled the boundary between the precious, newly turned furrows and the woods from which two scavenging parties had already appeared, armed with a considerable arsenal, and driven by the hunger of people fleeing a city in total collapse. Joe Wolfenden's small militia team was out there somewhere, aggressively patrolling against new incursions. The plunging slopes on the southern side of town were also patrolled, but the problematic geography there largely defended itself.

It was a hell of a turnaround from the tiny tourist village Jonas had rolled into a week and a half earlier. Silverton was more of an armed and armoured hamlet now, and he smiled to himself to think that he was in large part responsible for the change.

And for all the bodies piled up outside the ramparts.

4

MORE DELIVERANCE THAN SALEM'S LOT

Route 24 was open for all of forty-seven minutes; as long as it took to drive south from Aurora to the next chokepoint at Dryfork. In that time, they passed through open farmland, national forest and three small settlements, each larger than the one before, and none of them sealed off to outsiders.

"Jesus Christ, it's like Salem's Lot," Michelle said as they hit the edge of the first village, a cluster of mean, slumping hovels gathered around a crossroads a few minutes after the turn-off.

"More like Roanoke," James remarked, and he was pretty sure only Michelle got the reference.

He gave the gas a nudge, speeding them through the half dozen shanties hunkered down by the side of the road. They saw no sign of movement or even of habitation.

"Spooky," Mel said from the back seat.

"Well, people are spooked, I guess," James said. "Those folks in Aurora. I know the type. I grew up with them."

Michelle leaned through the gap between the two front seats.

"I don't know that you did, James. They weren't a bunch of mouth-breathing Team Jesus retards."

Mel snorted. Rick said nothing. But James protested, "Hey. Come on."

"You know what I mean," Michelle countered. "If those assholes back there were thumping the Good Book, it was the prosperity gospel, not the old testament. Can you turn on the radio? I want to try find out what this Executive Order's about. You cool with that, Rick?"

They hadn't bothered with any news broadcasts since leaving Maryland. The signal-to-noise ratio was low, and Rick found the media's hysterics upsetting.

"As long as it's not batshit crazy, I can deal," he said, turning on the radio.

Instantly, the cabin of the Sierra filled with static, and Rick punched in the next preset channel. James concentrated on driving. It took four tries to find a news radio broadcast, WXKX, out of Clarksburg, but they were hosting talkback. It was not going well.

"Oh man, this is a YouTube comment thread come to life," Michelle complained. "Turn it off. I'm gonna try to call the mothership."

She alone had a working cell. Not an iPhone or Android like the rest of them, but a satellite phone issued to her by the NSC when she evacuated DC. Michelle had orders to check in on a schedule, but so far, she'd made only one call, and it had gone through to a recorded message telling her there was no change in status and she was to check back in twenty-four hours.

"You got a signal?" James asked.

He was a T-Mobile customer. Rick and Mel were both Verizon. None of them had a single bar of connection. As best he knew, it wasn't just because they were deep in the boonies. Michelle said the cell networks were such juicy, high-value targets they would have been a priority for the Chinese and Russians in the opening moves of any hybrid conflict. She was hooked into a military-grade network, and the only sure way to take it down was with anti-satellite missiles.

"Hang on," Michelle said as she keyed in a long PIN.

They sped past a red brick church with a steep roof and a single spire. The terrain here was rumpled, and wooded hills piled up on both sides, creating a long valley, its southern reaches overlooked by the white cross of the old church.

Melissa leaned forward to join in the conversation while Michelle played with the phone.

"For what it's worth, they looked like normal punters to me. Back in Aurora, I mean," she said. "Not crazy survivalist wank-badgers or nothing. Just peeps and fam, yeah? They were proper vexed, but that Sheriff had them in line."

James frowned, thinking it through.

"Good for them, but not for us if this starts happening everywhere," he said, checking his mirrors.

"What do you mean?" Mel asked. "We can drive most of the way through to your parents' place, can't we? With just one or two stops for gas?"

James slowed to make the turn as the road swung hard right to go around a small lake. It was green and thick with reeds. The Sierra chugged through a rolling landscape of tilled fields and started climbing into a long stretch of heavily forested hill country. There were no farmhouses now. No pasture or cleared paddocks ploughed into regimented squares and straight lines. It was all wilderness again. They did pass a few cars and pick-ups going in the other direction. Local people in working vehicles, James reckoned. Faded trim. Dusty tires. Rusty panel work. He'd seen a lot of that back home, too.

Michelle announced that she had a signal, but she couldn't get through to anyone on the other end.

"Nada," she said after punching more numbers into the handset. She powered down and put the sat phone away in its case.

"We've got enough gas to get us maybe three-quarters of the way there," James explained, returning to Mel's question. "And I think we'll be able to get more. To be honest, we passed enough abandoned vehicles back in Maryland that even if we couldn't buy gas, we could probably siphon some from a stalled car. There'll be some real traffic up ahead for sure, with people trying to get out of Chicago in particular, but we can go cross country in this bad boy if we have to."

He made a fist and banged affectionately on the dash.

"But?" Rick said, almost as though he knew what James was thinking.

"But, yeah, if we have to divert or backtrack or go miles out of our way every time we hit someplace like Aurora, and if there's like hundreds of them between here and Montana..."

He trailed off.

"Thousands," Rick said. "There'll be thousands of them if this situation doesn't get better."

"Yeah," James said. "Thousands of roadblocks and detours. And millions of people on the move. Out of the cities."

They would run out of gas a long time before they cleared the Midwest. Probably before they made it out of Ohio.

They hit the next village after another twenty minutes. A place called Thomas. Population 586 according to the signpost outside the town limits. The sort of backwater where they rolled up the sidewalk at sundown, James thought. It was an old coal town, and the state highway doubled as the main street. A roadblock cut off through traffic, but this time, deputies in bright yellow vests waved them onto a side street. A detour took them and two other cars onto an unsealed gravel track that wound around the back of the local school before rejoining Route 24 near the empty parking lot of a craft brewery. Nobody said much of anything as they rolled through the back streets. There were plenty of people out on the roads here, and they stared at the brand new Sierra as James followed a straggling line of bright orange witches hats, marking the designated route through and out of town.

His eyes swept over the townspeople, most of whom appeared to be carrying stuff somewhere. Some were obviously returning to their homes from grocery shopping, but many seemed to be hauling household items like pieces of furniture or electrical goods. Unlike in Aurora, nobody here was armed, which was reassuring. They weren't about to get carjacked.

"Maybe they'd let us buy some beer," Rick said, nodding at the tall silver silos of the Mountain State Brewing Company up ahead. James pulled up at the intersection with Route 24, but if they had any ideas of picking up a few growlers for the road, the bright red plastic barriers blocking access to the microbrewery were enough to discourage them. Another lawman leaned up against the hood of his cruiser at the crossroads, waving the traffic through.

He returned James's wave with a curt nod, but he did not smile.

"Nah, it's not Salem's Lot, darlin," Mel Baker said to Michelle. "It's Deliverance."

Two minutes further on, another cop waved them past the town of Davis, a bigger settlement, maybe twice the size of the little coal town, but no more inclined to welcome visitors.

"At least they let us through," Mel said.

"Hurried us through, more like it," James added, but mostly to himself.

They tried the radio again at the top of the hour, finally catching a news break as they skirted the edge of a state recreation area. News-Radio 1170 out of Wheeling, West Virginia.

"*Chaos in Washington,*" the announcer said breathlessly, "*With mixed signals from the Pentagon and the White House in response to the sneak attack now definitely blamed on China, which continues to deny responsibility while pressing ahead with military action in South East Asia.*"

James glanced over at Rick.

"You okay with this, buddy?" he asked.

"I'm fine," the former Ranger said. "Leave it on."

Most of the headline story went back and forth between White House surrogates and the Pentagon, who seemed to be at cross purposes with each other. There was no word from the President, hunkered down in a secure and secret location, but a spokeswoman insisted he had ordered US forces to secure the home front. At the same time, the Secretary of Defense and the Chairman of the Joint Chiefs had assured allies in the Pacific and Europe that America would meet its enemies in the field.

"*NATO members voted overnight to mobilise forces as Russia menaced the borders of Poland and the Baltic states,*" the newsreader said, "*but no word yet on whether US forces will be factored into any response.*"

Michelle started to say something but then shushed herself as a report on a third day of food shortages and rationing in dozens of American cities came on.

"That be fucking right," she muttered. Then—"Hey, quiet, I need to hear this"—causing James to smile. He gave the radio a touch more volume as they emerged from a long passage through deep woodland. A small farm lay to the left of the highway, and the Sierra's wheels hummed over a low concrete bridge that spanned the Cheat River. He caught a glimpse of people fishing in the shallow rapids.

"Shelves remain empty in most urban areas, and even many smaller towns and rationing is in force, as authorities struggle to cope with a massive cyber-attack on key food distribution companies around the nation."

The Secretary of Defense was back, calling out the cyber-strikes of the previous three days as diversionary attacks designed to distract the Administration and sap the will of the American people.

Michelle spoke up in a cartoonishly deep voice, presumably meant to imitate the Sec Def, "But we will not be sapped or distrativated..." she said, as the man himself said something just as nonsensical on the radio. She insisted on quiet again, even though she was the only one talking when the reporter mentioned Homeland Security's 'urban stronghold program', but before they could learn anything of it, James slammed on the brakes and the tires bit into the tarmac with a screech and the unmistakable odour of burning rubber.

A pine tree lay across the road, but it had not come down in a storm.

Somebody had cut through the thick base with chainsaws and dragged the massive fallen log across the road with chains.

Men stood behind it. None of them in uniform, but all of them armed.

Rick was already reaching for his weapon when one of the men fired a single blast from a shotgun into the air.

James threw the car into reverse, performing a tight bootlegger's turn, throwing everyone over hard. Nomi yelped. Mel swore loudly. Michelle cried out in alarm.

Only Rick was quiet. He had braced himself with one hand and was swivelling to track the shooter as they spun around. But no further gunshots sounded as James stomped the accelerator, sending them back where they had come from. At high speed.

"So," he said raggedly when they were a safe distance away. "I guess Route 24 is closed now."

Route 24 never did open again, as far as James O'Donnell knew.

5

THE THREE RIVER REACH

They were safe. They were secure. They were fucked.

Damien Maloney studied the map in the galley of *Lasseter's Reef*, scowling at the light blue filigree of riverine trace work running west and north of their current position, moored somewhere near the centre of Franks Tract.

The Tract was a state park, 3000 acres of flooded land in the Sacramento-Joaquin River Delta. The only way to get in here was by boat, hence the safety and security. The only way out was by boat. Explaining why they were fucked.

Damo traced one thick finger up the straight blue line of the Sacramento River shipping channel, forty-three miles from the Liberty Cut to the inland port of Sacramento. Thirty feet deep and two hundred wide, it was more than big enough to offer passage to *Lasseter's Reef,* and he had intended just that when they set out from the yacht club back in San Francisco. Nine days earlier.

Damo's scowl deepened. If only they'd made the run that first night. They'd probably be in Canada by now, getting fat on poutine and maple syrup. Instead, they were stuck here in the arse end of the world, pulling their puds while they waited on... Well, to be perfectly fucking crude about it – the end of the fucking world.

He put down the thick enamel mug of instant coffee he'd been drinking and leaned over the maps again. He wasn't familiar with any of these watercourses. *Lasseter's Reef* was a big ocean-going yacht, not well suited to manoeuvring in the confined narrows and shallows of the Delta. The tips of his fingers, blunt and powerful from years in the mining industry, drifted over the alternative routes. A cursory glance at the charts suggested they had at least half a dozen options. But they didn't. He knew that not all of those rivers and streams were navigable, not by a fucking aircraft carrier like the *Reef*, anyway.

And his 'charts' were exactly as much use as a pair of fake tits on a prize bull.

Damo had a full suite of navigational maps for the Bay Area and the coast north and south for hundreds of miles. He had even more stowed away for the Great Barrier Reef back home. And the Caribbean. And the Maldives, the first place he'd taken the *Reef* and half-a-dozen mates on a surfing and drinking safari when he'd cashed out of the mining business five years ago. For the hinterland waterways of the Sacramento-San Joaquin Delta, however, he had to rely on a National Geographic road map. It had nothing to offer a pilot attempting to navigate the flooded lowlands of Franks Tract.

"Who calls a fucking lake a tract anyway," he grumbled to himself. "It's so fucking misleading as to constitute professional fucking malfeasance."

"Damo. Baby ducks on the pond, buddy."

He looked up from the table to find Karl Valentine frowning at him. And young Maxi Sarjanen grinning up a storm.

"Ah shit, sorry, Maxi. Don't tell your mum."

"Fuckin' oath not, mate," the young boy beamed in the broad, flat Australian accent he'd been practising for a week now. His eyes were alight with mischief — at least until Valentine clipped him lightly across the back of the head.

"You ain't old enough to talk like that, and if your mom ever hears you, take my word for it. You will never be old enough."

"Ow!" Maxi said, rubbing the spot just behind his ear.

Karl shooed him out of the galley, carrying two bottles of water for Jodi and Ellie, who had the watch up on deck.

"Much happening out there?" Damo asked.

He meant on the lake, not up on deck.

"A new boat came in about half an hour ago," Karl said. He gestured at the beer fridge, "You mind?"

"Only if you don't get me one, too," Damo replied. It was hot below decks. He'd stopped running the air-conditioning when he realised they couldn't get up the shipping channel, couldn't get through the port of Sacramento, couldn't do much of anything other than sitting on their arses out here in the middle of the Tract. They had to preserve fuel now, and food. But it was hot, and a beer wouldn't hurt anybody. It might even shake loose an idea about getting out of here.

Karl fetched a couple of imported ales from the small glass-fronted cooler. *Stone and Wood*, all the way from home. Damo knocked the top off his, took a long pull, burped and sighed.

"Let's go up. I'm not doing any good down here," he admitted.

He led the way out of the galley and up the short stairwell onto the deck. The sun was high overhead, fierce and bright, forcing him to squint until he pulled a pair of Ray-Bans from his shirt pocket and slipped them on. The quiet, unsettling wetlands of the Tract revealed themselves. Gently rolling hills, lightly forested here and there, boggy marsh and flooded valleys, reedbeds swaying and rustling in the breeze which rippled the surface of the water, throwing off brilliant bursts of reflected sunlight. And boats. Dozens of them, of all kinds. Only a couple of big cruisers like the *Reef*, but all manner of yachts, runabouts and fishing skiffs, too. All of them carefully spaced away from each other. Everybody keeping their distance.

"Ladies," Demo said, raising his beer to Ellie and Jodes. They were dressed for the heat in cut-off jeans and sleeveless T-shirts. Ellie Jabbarah, his former sous chef, did not lower the binoculars from her eyes. She was scoping out the only vessel that was moving across the surface of the lake. Damo followed the direction of her gaze and found the moving target, a twin-engined deck boat. White-hulled, navy blue trim. Looked like maybe four or five people on deck. Damo's eyes had been going bad for years, and he couldn't make out details that fine.

Nobody said anything as long as the boat was moving. The lake had reached a sort of nervous equilibrium a couple of days ago when the last boat from San Francisco had sailed into the Three River Reach. Literally sailed, too. That had been a single-masted racing yacht that passed through the gently bobbing armada before continuing silently north. Since then, nothing.

This latest arrival took anchorage near the northernmost point of Mandeville Island, almost as though they intended to block the channel. Not much point in that, Damo thought. Everything was blocked up at Sacramento anyway.

Still, he breathed a little easier when the anchor splashed down into the cool waters of the lake, and Ellie lowered the binoculars.

"Four men on deck," she said. "Sidearms and a couple of shotguns. But fishing poles, too."

Demo gestured for the spy glasses, and she handed them over. He scanned the new arrivals, nodding. They looked like they were setting up to catch some lunch. They were armed, as Ellie had said. But so was he. So was everyone.

"Maxi, you think you could keep an eye on these blokes?" Damo said. "While I talk to your mums and Karl. You can use the binoculars. Just let us know if they do anything besides fishing."

The young boy's eyes went wide with the thrill of grown-up responsibility.

"You be careful with those now, Max," Jody, his mother, said. Ellie had come onto the scene a couple of years after Jodie had split from Chad, the boy's biological father. The sperm donor, as Ellie referred to him. But never within Max's hearing. Damo got the lad set up on one of the rear-facing seats from which he had enjoyed fishing in happier times when it hadn't meant the difference between eating and going hungry. The adults moved in under the canvas of the wheelhouse, where they could keep an eye on Max but converse without being overheard.

"What's up, Damo?" Jody Sarjanen asked. It was an innocent question, but Damo had to check himself before he replied sarcastically. The heat, his frustration, the lack of control, it was all getting to him.

He folded his thick, meaty arms. They looked like a couple of well-cured ham hocks sitting over the top of his beer belly. He let his chin sink onto his chest.

"We can't stay here much longer," he said. "We've got plenty of food in the tucker box and enough fuel to keep the freezer running for months. But we were just lucky."

He gestured at the small flotilla around them.

"Some of these people are probably living on what they pull out of the lake. Increasingly, everyone will. And that's a finite resource. It's not sustainable."

"You got a plan?" Ellie said. She loved a plan, but she could also improvise under pressure. It made her a great chef.

"Still working on it," he smiled, without much humour. "We can't head back through the Bay. Well, we could, but that's a shit idea. Even if we got through and out into open water, we don't have enough range to get anywhere safe."

Karl Valentine made a face.

"Don't know that anywhere is safe right now," he said.

"Fair cop," Damo nodded. "I think our best bet is still north. My farm. But we gotta get through Sacramento, and I don't know how far north the river is navigable after that. I figured we could get a car or something. But that was a fucking long time ago in a galaxy far, far away."

"And a lot less fucked up than this one," Ellie said drily.

"Too fucking right," Damo agreed. "Once we get off the boat, we're in the same hole as everybody else. We got food. But no transport. And it's a fucking long and dreary walk to Canada."

"And when you get there, you're in Canada," Ellie grinned. She leaned over and kissed Jodi on top of the head.

The deck moved gently underfoot in the breeze. It was quiet enough that they could hear occasional sounds from the other boats, even though the closest was over a hundred yards away. The quiet, in fact, was eerie. No planes overhead. No traffic. No music or talk radio or electronic chatter of any kind.

"You could try Sacramento again," Ellie said. "They can only tell us to fuck off."

Damo wasn't convinced.

"Mate," he said. "They blocked everything when the Feds declared it a stronghold city. I don't see why that would've changed. They're not letting anyone in."

"Can't hurt to ask, Damo," she pushed back. "A trip upriver might be nice. We could do a spot of shopping in town, baby," she smiled at Jodi. "Get one of those martinis you like at the Shady Lady Saloon."

"We don't want to go into the city," Jodi said. "We just want to go through."

"And maybe they'd be cool with that," Damo said. "Or maybe they'd seize the *Reef*, grab our stores, and throw our arses back in the river. We just dunno, Jodes."

They had been able to monitor the emergency until about three days earlier when the last of the terrestrial radio stations fell silent. No idea why. Maybe the power ran out. Perhaps it was another round of cyber-attacks. Maybe...

Damo shook his head, annoyed with himself.

Speculating was bullshit. What they did know was this: San Francisco was under martial law. The army and police had been authorised to use lethal force to maintain a curfew. But the curfew wasn't holding. Or it hadn't been the last they knew. As Ellie had predicted, the attack on the country's food distribution infrastructure on the first day of the war wasn't just a crippling blow; it was a killer. San Francisco couldn't feed itself for more than three days, and it was not alone in that.

"Emergency broadcast system is still on the air," Karl offered. "I could monitor that for the rest of the day. See if it says anything useful."

Ellie snorted. "That'd be a first."

"Mister Maloney!" Max called out, "They're coming."

All of the adults turned in his direction. He was pointing out across the water.

The newly arrived motorboat was driving directly at them.

6

IT WAS LIKE SHARKNADO SEASON

There was only so much they could fit into her dad's trusty Oldsmobile Alero. When Tammy got her ass home from that final shift at the Dollar General, she hurried into the house and kicked everyone off of the TV. They were all glued to it; Roxarne, her roomie, and the four kids, but they weren't keeping up with the Kardashians like usual.

Rox looked at her with big, frightened eyes.

"Tammy, News 9 says there's a war with China and riots all over the place. People fighting each other for food and gas."

"Uhuh," Tammy confirmed. "Saw it myself at work. People have gone crazy, Rox. Like it's The Walking Dead or something."

The kids all turned and stared at Tammy, mouths open.

"Are zombies coming?" Bobby Jr. asked.

Tammy rolled her eyes.

Bobby Jr. was all hers since Bobby Sr. left for the fracking, but the boy could still be as powerfully foolish as his dad at times.

"No. That ain't for real, Bobby. But something has gone bad for sure. There was an honest to god damn riot at the Dollar General this morning. Over government cheese and hamburger helper, if you can believe that! One guy even shot a hole in the ceiling."

"Damn," Roxy said. "What'd Gutterson do? Shit his pants?"

That set off howls of laughter from the children.

Tammy shook her head. "Wouldn't know from shit about him. He took off, too. Left me and Wynette to run the whole store with all this other stuff going on. Didn't say a damn thing before he left."

She stopped, her jaw dropping open.

"Goddamn! I'll bet he cleaned out the safe."

She was genuinely shocked, first by the realisation and then by the fact that she hadn't thought to do it herself.

When things went to pieces, it was usually Tammy who called balls and strikes. She muted the television, which was just a bunch of politicians anyway and said, "Okay, team. Listen up. I ain't sure what's happening, but it's big and it's everywhere. So, we're gonna get the hell gone from here for somewhere safer."

"But why?" Roxarne asked. She wasn't snarking. She just wanted to know.

The four children were all charging around now, not getting any of their shit together in any which way at all.

"Roxy, folks was already beating on each other for the last box of Mac-n-Cheese. And it really was the last one, too. Wholesalers told us this morning they couldn't deliver for at least three weeks. Not just the Mac-n-Cheese. Nothing. Folks was panic buying like it was fucking Sharknado season. I'm telling you, we got to get gone."

Roxarne frowned.

"But Tammy, this is Dillonvale. Nothing happens here. Ever. If shit is happening everywhere else, ain't we better staying where it ain't?"

On the TV, a Kroger's burned somewhere. The news ticker underneath was saying crazy things about China and Russia, and Tammy read it for a few seconds without much thought of anything beyond the certainty of a stray cat that it best get the hell out of the dog pound. She clapped her hands together hard. It sounded like a whip-crack. Everyone jumped.

"You kids! Everyone start packing for a big sleepover and only bring the shit that matters. Shoes, undies. Medicines if you got 'em. Move! Now!"

The kids all cheered and ran for their room. They all shared one. And they did love a sleepover or a campout, even if it only meant sleeping on the floor watching cartoons at a friend's house while their moms pulled late shifts.

As soon as she had chased them out, Tammy took Roxarne by the arm and led her to the front stoop, where they could not be overheard.

"Roxy, I have to go. I..."

She breathed out a hot lungful of air. She was shaking.

"Rox, it was scary as. I ain't never seen nothing like this shit. Not before big storms or nothing. Peeps was fucking desperate. When I left, they were this close to a riot. Wynette sent me a text. Said this guy had shot up the damn roof. Those tiles are asbestos, too."

Roxy frowned and ran her hands through thick purple-dyed hair. She was having trouble taking it all in. "I still don't see why..."

"Roxy, I took the money from the till. All of it. Hundreds."

"Shit, Tammy! Why'd you do that?"

"I told you. Shit was getting crazy, and I just had to get out of there same way I know we have to get out of here."

"Well, we do now. You're a fugitive," Rox said. "But where can we go? Hermanstown? Ain't likely to be no better over there."

"We'll go to my brother Michael's. It's farm country; people won't be fighting each other for food there."

Roxarne regarded her sceptically.

Tammy pressed her lips into a thin line. "Well, I hope not, anyway."

She gave Roxy a little punch on the shoulder. "C'mon, time's a wastin'."

"Wait. How much money did you take?"

Tammy dug the thick wad of notes out of her pocket.

Roxarne gaped when she saw how much cash her roomie was holding.

"Shit, girl, I never seen so much green in one place. Business is good at the Dollar General."

"Was today at least."

Tammy counted the notes quickly. She had plenty of practice

counting other people's money. But even she was surprised by the take.

"One thousand, three hundred and eighty-two dollars," she whistled.

That settled it. No way she could just go back and slip this into the till. They would already have the FBI looking for her.

"We could get to Canada with this much," Roxy said, her voice soft with wonder.

Roxarne turned this way and that, seeming to comprehend the enormity of it all for the first time. She put her hands on her hips and blew out her cheeks.

"Oh man, where do we even start?"

Tammy could tell her friend was getting invested in this now. Once Roxy committed, she always jumped in with both feet.

"Just pretend like it's when we can't make the rent, and we got to get out," Tammy said.

Roxy laughed. "We always done that in the middle of the night."

"And this time, we can see what we're doing. So this time, it's different." As soon as the words left her mouth, Tammy felt a sense of finality she didn't really understand. Not in words. But this was different, for sure. They would never come home again. "And we're taking every scrap of food in this house," she said, moving to the tiny kitchenette and throwing open all the cupboards.

Roxy scrunched up her face. "The cans under the sink, too? Half of them, the labels fell off."

"If they ain't bulging real bad or rusty, yeah, them too."

"OK, when do you want to go?"

"Soon as the car is packed up." She had a thought. "Don't forget the photo box."

Roxy nodded and called out to the kids who had dispersed throughout the house. They were screeching and yelling out to each other, but in the wild, excited way that kids did when they knew adventure was calling. And these kids had already seen plenty of adventurin', thanks to both moms' consistently poor choice in men. The next hour and a half wasn't so much controlled chaos as it was just chaos - plain and simple. Stuff got dumped out of Walmart bags;

backpacks got packed, then re-packed. Possessions went to the Olds and then out into the trash. There were arguments, of course. And fights and tears. With four kids and two grown-ups, space was tight. By the time they were ready to go, Roxy's father's prized car was sagging on its tired springs.

The money she'd stolen from the Dollar General lay heavy against her thigh, and she kept looking up and down the street, expecting a patrol car to turn up at any time.

But nobody came.

Tammy and Roxarne rented an old miners' shack on the western edge of Dillonvale. The streets here were mean but a real quiet and dangerous sort of mean. She knew of three houses on their street alone where you could buy meth out the screen door straight from the cook. And if she knew that, the cops had to know too, but they never came around, so maybe it wasn't so weird that nobody had chased her for Gutterson's money.

Hell, that asshole for sure stole ten times as much.

Tammy cursed her foolishness.

Why hadn't she thought to empty the safe?

In for a penny, in for ten grand, after all.

She patted her pockets and found the car keys. The kids were all in the back, already complaining about being piled on top of each other. Roxy was leaned into the back seat, too, for some reason. The sun was high overhead, and the car had no AC.

"We ready, Rox?"

"Wynona has to pee again."

"She can wait. We're leaving."

"Mommy..."

"No, Wynona, I watched you go ten minutes ago. It's time to leave."

Her daughter started to cry.

"But I don't want to leave!"

Tammy ignored her, opened the driver's door and climbed in. When you lived with four kids in a small clapboard shack, you learned to tune out the small shit. Roxy folded herself into the passenger seat among bags and boxes and put on her seatbelt. She looked spaced out. Shell-shocked, Tammy's dad would've called it. For a brief moment, Tammy looked at her friend, and she wanted to hug her. Roxy had got her the job at Dollar General. Roxy had taken her in when Bobby Sr lit out for the fracking. Roxy was about the only good thing in her life besides Bobby Jr. and Wynona, of course.

Oh, and Jakey and Liana, Roxy's little ones, too.

She had a lot to be grateful for.

But they had to get going. Tammy turned the key and prayed.

The Oldsmobile answered. The engine turned over twice and caught. It ran with a slightly choppy idle and a "check engine" light, but it ran. That stupid light had been demanding someone check the engine since before Bill Clinton got blown in a White House cupboard. Tammy put the shift into drive and pulled away from the little house by the railroad tracks.

That first night they didn't get nowhere near Michael's place. Instead, they stayed in a Motel 6, one hundred and sixty miles west of home and maybe three hundred north of her brother's farm. Tammy had wanted to make it all the way there in one hop, but after seven hours of what seemed like a million detours, accidents, wrong turns, and traffic jams, they pulled into the motel with a promise for the kids that they could have their own room, with two big beds, and a special feed for being so good on the drive out. The children hooted and cheered.

It'd even been fun, too, that first night on the road. There was an All You Can Eat Chinese place in a little strip mall across the way from the motel, and they'd showed those Chinese guys that maybe it was not such a great idea to computer attack America and leave your buffet undefended.

Hadn't been as much fun after that.

The roads got no better. Gas was stupid expensive, and the Olds was a thirsty beast. They listened to music the first day. Letting everyone choose a song in turn from Roxy's Spotify. She had heaps of music downloaded onto her phone, which was good because they weren't getting any cell cover by then.

Soon enough though, Tammy suggested they should listen to the news radio, just for a few minutes, to figure out what was up with the traffic if for nothing else.

They caught up on that at a roadhouse, where she bought sloppy joes and Cokes for everyone. The money seemed to be running through her fingers like water, but the kids really had been pretty good, all things considered, and she wanted to keep them sweet. This road trip was looking like it might take a while.

She listened to the public radio while Roxy took the kids inside for the cool air and the food. Her dad, a union man, had always insisted on the NPR because he didn't trust the word of anyone selling news for a profit. Tammy preferred to get her daily news from TMZ, but she'd kept to her habits and her dad's prejudices, if truth be known, a long time after the black lung took him under.

She was glad nobody else was in the car when she tuned in.

At first, she thought it was some sort of prank show. They were talking about the war with China and another one with Russia and about how computer hackers had done more damage to the cities and airports and power stations than any foreign army could hope to with bombs and stuff. She might have scoffed, another thing her dad had taught her to do, had she not just had the lesson hammered into her by two days on the interstate. Dozens of cars were lined up at every gas station they drove past. Hundreds near some of the bigger towns and cities. Long lines of people snaked out of the grocery marts pretty much everywhere. It was like the Dollar General except worse.

At least the roadhouse still had supplies in the freezer on account of good timing with their weekly delivery. But those sloppy joes were not cheap.

Tammy was quiet when the others came back, full of sugar and high spirits. Even Roxy, who'd been subdued since they left Dillon-vale, was much improved in mood now they were set on their course. Tammy painted a smile on her face for the kids as they returned, excited to tell her about the treats they'd been bought, but Roxy sensed the fragility of Tammy's good cheer, and she did not press her on the issue of what she learned from the radio.

"I'll tell you later," Tammy said quietly.

Later was after dark, camped out in a farmer's field somewhere in northeastern Ohio. They were lost and hungry, but at least Tammy's cash had bought them a full tank of gas at a little rural pump a few miles back. The owner had been happy to sell her fuel at twice the posted price, plus a hundred dollars for about twenty bucks worth of snacks.

The kids had all used the restroom, which was a blessed relief. Bobby Jr. was getting way too comfortable pulling his little badger out in public to relieve himself. Tammy and Rox cleaned themselves up as best they could, too, grateful for the lukewarm water in the rust-stained sink.

"It's like a movie, Rox," Tammy said as she wiped under her armpits with a damp wad of toilet paper.

"What sort of movie is that?" Roxarne asked.

"The stupid sort with lots of shit blowing up," Tammy said testily before apologising. "I'm sorry, Rox, but I'm frightened. We're running out of money. And I don't know what we're gonna find at Michael's. He ain't so far from Akron, and the radio news said it was bad everywhere but worst anywhere big."

"Akron ain't so big."

"Bigger than Dillonvale, and that was bad enough for me."

"Well, I didn't see that, of course," Roxy frowned. "We left on your say so."

Tammy felt her temper flare, but she doused it as best she could. Roxanne was one hundred per cent right. They had left entirely on Tammy's say-so, and Roxy had been nothing but positive and bright ever since, at least with the kids.

"We did," Tammy admitted. "And I still think we did right. But we need a lot more to go right for us now, Rox. We need to get these children somewhere safe."

They were both quiet.

"Where the hell are we, anyway?" Roxarne said at last.

"Somewhere in Columbiana County, I reckon," Tammy ventured. "I sort of recognised some of it as we was driving through at the end of the day. We shoulda stopped then."

Rox shrugged it off.

"You're right, but we had to get the kids safe. Better to push on, which we will do tomorrow."

Roxy gripped Tammy's shoulder and squeezed.

They hugged and got back on the road.

The two other times she and the kids had visited Michael, Tammy had simply followed the directions on her phone. She would turn here and there as instructed, and the phone was always right. But now, when she needed it more than anything in her life, her piece-of-crap Samsung was pretty much worthless. There was no cell cover anywhere. Not even in the towns they'd driven through. And by the true fall of night, they were pulled up off in the pitch-black at the edge of some cornfield in the middle of nowhere.

She wanted to cry. Bobby Jr., being the oldest and also the man of this adventure, spoke sagely as he pointed his flashlight around their campsite.

"So I guess we sleep out here?"

"Yeah," Tammy said. "We'll put up the tent for you and your sister. The little ones can sleep in the backseat."

She could see his grimace by the torchlight.

"The Dora the Explorer tent?"

"Yep."

"But that's for little kids, mom."

"It's what we have."

A raindrop splattered on Tammy's face.

She woke up for what seemed the hundredth time around dawn, and she could not get back to sleep no matter what. She had taken the tent with Bobby and Wynona. Her back ached something terrible with the sciatica she sometimes got near her period. Her eyes felt crusted with sand, and she knew there was no coffee. She also needed to pee. The rain had stopped at some point during the night, so at least there was that to give thanks for. She turned and fumbled around in the space between the snoring kids for the roll of toilet paper. Thank God, she thought again, for Roxy. It had been her idea to steal every roll in the roadhouse toilets.

Tammy poked her head out through the tent flap, toilet paper in hand. She got out and looked around. She could see corn, the small rural road, a house in the distance, and not much else. She picked a spot to relieve herself, a small clump of bushes. When she was done, relieved no farmers or cows had come by, she stood, wiggled back into her jeans, and tried to decide what the hell they were going to do today. They absolutely had to get to her brother, but what they had seen on the road yesterday, that was not even halfway normal. It really was some shit out of a movie, she thought.

"Hey, Tam."

She jumped a little but smiled wanly. "Mornin', Roxy. Sorry, ain't no Starbucks out here."

"Yeah. So what are we gonna do?"

"Get the kids some food, then we'll look for North Georgetown. It can't be far. Hell, we're in the right county, at least. We got to be."

Roxy looked at her and shook her head. "As long as the roads are open." She paused. "I can't believe our fucking phones don't work. I just paid my bill, too."

Tammy spat. "Yeah." She tossed her head in the direction of the farmhouse in the distance. "I'll bet they know how to get there. We'll ask for directions to Michael's farm once we get to town."

They got the kids up and sorted them out. Everyone ate a little, and Bobby put away the Dora tent. He was trying to be a man like his dad. Except, of course, Tammy knew Bobby Sr wasn't much of a man at all. She prayed this would be their last night camping.

The kids ate Twizzlers and Pringles for breakfast, and Tammy fired up the Olds and drove away from the saturated field; a few minutes later, they pulled into the driveway of the little farmhouse. She took a deep breath and told herself it was all good. She breathed again, switched off the engine, and opened her door.

"I won't be but a few minutes," she said.

She left the open in case they had to get out of there, fast.

As Tammy walked toward the house, her runners crunching on gravel, she saw a curtain move.

They were watching her. She kept going, climbing the steps, which creaked underfoot. She began to raise her hand to knock when the door opened. Quickly.

Her bladder suddenly felt very tight.

A woman with a shotgun greeted Tammy. She looked like she could be anywhere between thirty and sixty. She was haggard, but it wasn't a recent thing. This woman had lived hard. Tammy had seen enough of that in Dillonvale to recognise it in the woman's face.

"No food here, little sister," she said and firmly.

"Not looking for food, ma'am."

The woman seemed surprised by that.

"Oh. Then what do you want?"

The shotgun did not waver. The big black hole at the end of the barrel seemed infinitely dark.

"I'm trying to get to my brother, but the phone doesn't work. I just want to know how do I get to North Georgetown?"

The woman lowered the shotgun, but only an inch or so. Now, she was aiming to blow Tammy's jaw into the wind rather than the top of her head.

"You follow this road north to the 400, turn right and head into town. You're not far. Could have made it last night, you just kept going."

Tammy nodded. "Thanks."

"Hope you find your brother. Family's all we got in times like this." They were kind words, sincere, too, Tammy judged, but the barrel of the shotgun still didn't waver.

She nodded, turned and walked back to the waiting car.

She imagined that big ass gun was pointed square between her shoulder blades the whole way, and it was all she could do not to break into a run. Muscles ticked and jumped up and down her back. What had gotten into people?

She breathed hard when she climbed back into the Olds.

Shut the door.

Hands shaking.

Roxy spoke before the kids could start up.

"She didn't seem very friendly."

"She wasn't. But I got directions."

Tammy steadied her breathing and put the Olds into gear. Her nerves stopped tingling as soon as the engine caught, and she pulled back out onto the tarmac road. She turned right and drove north through a patchwork of forest, farms, and tiny wooden framed houses. After ten minutes or so, they came to a T-intersection. It was the 400. She turned right and drove into town.

"Mom, can we get pancakes for breakfast," Wynona asked.

"No, I want an egg McMuffin," Liana countered.

"Are we there yet," Jakey threw in.

"We are," Tammy said, ignoring the demands for breakfast. This place was a two-horse town, and both horses had bolted. But at least there was a post office. She slowed as the brown, slatted, wooden building came into view. The streets were empty except for one car, which had apparently broken down and been abandoned. Right there. In the middle of the damn road. Who could she ask for directions next?

"Over there," Roxy said, pointing out an elderly man in blue overalls, walking up her side of the street past the Old Stagecoach Inn. Tammy eased the Olds up next to him, and Roxy wound her window down. The old fellow doffed his straw hat.

"Morning, ladies."

"Good morning, sir?" Roxarne said. "Do you know where the Williams farm is? We're looking for my friend's brother."

The man grinned.

"Is she really your friend or something else," the man grinned.

"Oh, for fucks sake," Tammy muttered under her breath, but before she could say anything or drive on, the old guy replaced his hat and went on.

"Not that I care. It's a free country, is what I say. Folks can marry who they want, I told that asshole on the phone. Course, it was a recorded message, so nobody was listening. But I knew their game. They were all into the push polling for that Portman asshole. I'm a Sherrod Brown man, m'self..."

"Sir!" Roxy cut him off.

"Yes, ma'am. Can I help you? My word, that is a whole litter of little ones you got in back..."

"Sir, we're looking for my friend's brother. Mike Kolchar. He works on the Williams farm."

"The soybean place," he nodded. "I know them. Ha!" he actually slapped his thigh when he laughed. "They went all in on Trump, you know. And he fucked them good with his damn tariffs as a thank you."

The man shook his head and spat a tobacco-brown hawker onto the ground; it landed a polite distance away. Tammy was sure he was about to launch into a long history of the soybean farmers and the former president, but instead, he pointed down the street.

"Follow Rochester Road south, go a mile and on the right, you'll find your farm."

Roxy answered. "Thank you so much, sir."

The old coot grinned, his eyes crinkled. "Anything for a pair of pretty ladies. I hope you find your brother. And happiness. Everyone deserves happiness. Except..."

Tammy floored the accelerator, and they peeled away.

She felt giddy with relief.

This nightmare would be over and soon. There would be shelter, food. They could maybe take a bath or at least a shower, stretch out, and they'd be among family and friends. She hadn't seen Mike for a couple of years. Not since the kids were tiny, but he texted her every now and then. Usually memes and shit. But he was always saying to come visit. He moved around a bit, from trailer to apartment and once into a house. But she always knew to find him through the farm. He was a foreman there. For the first time in what seemed forever, Tammy felt like everything would turn out OK. She found the Rochester road without a problem and turned south. She watched her speedometer to see when a mile had passed, but that wasn't necessary.

The Williams farm was big.

And it wasn't a farm. It was a goddamn soybean factory, and...

And it was pretty obviously closed.

The car got real quiet.

No one lived there. They could all see that. This place was all shiny steel boxes and silos and warehouses. With nothing like a charming old clapboard farmhouse or even a barracks for some poor Mexican workers to sleep in.

Tammy pulled the car over to the side of the road.

"Is this Uncle Mike's farm?" Wynona asked.

"Uh, yeah," Tammy said.

"Where's Uncle Mike?" Bobby Jr said.

"Not here," Rox answered, but she was mostly talking to herself.

Tammy turned the keys, stepped out of the car, and squinted into the fierce morning sun.

Nothing going on behind the gates. No sign of life.

Wind whistled between the silos. Sun glinted off the green John Deere robot tractors. Mikey had told her they knew where to go because satellites told them.

Apparently, the satellites had told these ones to crash into a barn and a silo and, in one case, to tip itself ass over tit into a fucking ditch.

"Well, shit." Roxy kicked at the rich Ohio dirt.

Tammy wanted to cry.

"You got any ideas, Rox?"

It took her a moment or two before she replied.

"I got some family around Elkins. I think."

"You figure they'd have us?"

"They're family. That matters."

It hadn't mattered to her brother, Tammy thought bitterly.

But she caught herself by the scruff of the neck.

They had no time for that shit.

And she wasn't being fair anyway. After all, she had just lit out from Dillonvale with two families in tow and a pocket full of stolen cash. Mikey hadn't known they were coming, and who knew what shit he had to deal with when the Chinese messed up those satellite tractors.

"Mom, where's Uncle Mikey?" Wynona asked, sounding as though she was about to lose it.

Tammy pressed her lips together and pulled the child to her. Wynona buried her face in Tammy's stomach.

Tammy looked at Roxy; she squared her shoulders.

"We need a map."

It was a long way from North Georgetown, Ohio, to Elkins, West Virginia.

7

MORAL JEOPARDY

"It wasn't an ambush," Rick said from his vantage point at the edge of the small plateau while he scanned the Canaan Valley with his binoculars. Nomi sat next to him, as quiet and still as a stone dog in a temple. "Wouldn't have been any warning shot if they'd meant to ambush us," Rick went on, mostly to himself.

"Suppose not," James conceded as he turned the grilling racks over the coals of the campfire. Five gutted river trout dripped natural oil onto the coals, spitting and fizzing and throwing off small bright tongues of flame. Late afternoon, September in the Canaan Valley was still warm, even balmy, but the heat would leak out of the day soon enough, and they would have to smother the fire before nightfall. It wasn't safe.

The first night they were there, the day they'd turned back from the roadblocks on Routes 50 and 24, bandits attacked another campsite on the far side of the valley. Rick had been adamant that they not let their fire burn through the night in spite of the chill which came on with darkness. The former soldier was right. They counted more than a dozen lines of tracer rounds snaking in on the small, flickering point of light five miles away. The industrial clatter of weapons fire reached them a few seconds later. Campfires all over the Valley had winked out in the next few minutes.

As James tended to the fish grilling over the coals, Mel Baker walked back from the tailgate of the Sierra, where she had been fussing over her contribution to their meal.

"I made a salad. Last of the greens, I'm afraid," she said. "Sorry, they're a bit limp."

"Trout's pretty much done," James said, careful not to burn himself as he lifted the grilling rack away from the fire pit. A few last drops of fish oil dripped into the coals, flaring as they ignited. The rich, heady smoke set his stomach to growling, and his mouth watered at the promise of food. It helped to think about the small things, the real things, that he could actually deal with. Like cooking their dinner.

There was a tree stump in the middle of the small clearing where they had set up camp. The ghost of a red spruce giant. The pamphlet and tourist map they'd taken from the abandoned visitor centre at the entrance to the park said the entire valley had once been so densely forested with red spruce that sunlight did not reach the ground for thousands of years. Those ancient forests were gone now, logged out before the early years of the twentieth century and replaced by a thinner covering of replanted conifers, heathland marshes, cotton grass and ferns. Canadian blueberries grew in abundance around the edge of the clearing amid starflower and marigold blossoms. It was, everything else aside, a beautiful place to rest and share a meal with friends.

The old stump in the centre of the campsite had obviously been used for many years as a picnic spot, overlooking a hundred-foot drop into the wetlands and headwaters of the Blackwater River. Hundreds of people had carved their initials into the smooth, flattened disc of knee-high tree trunk, and a few smaller logs circled it as rudimentary seating. Mel had already laid out paper plates, cups, a bottle of water and a six-pack of beer from the cooler in the SUV.

"Come get your supper, Rick," Mel said, adjusting the pistol at her hip as she took a seat on one of the logs.

"Where's Michelle?" James asked as he laid the smoking fish

down on a paper plate. The last couple of days, he found himself getting nervous whenever he couldn't see her, and the anxiety was getting worse. It was the sort of thing that might once have occasioned months of expensive counselling. Not so much now, though.

"Gone to the loo," Mel stage-whispered in her theatrically British accent. She gestured over her shoulder to where Michelle Nguyen was indeed emerging from the bushes, cleaning her hands with a medicated wet wipe. Michelle, too, wore a sidearm. She wore it so comfortably that James wondered if she had ever been more than a simple analyst for the National Security Council.

The hunting rifle, which James preferred over any handgun, leaned against the side of the tree stump. A Ruger bolt-action thirty-aught-six, it was familiar to him from his family's homestead in Montana. Unfamiliar, though, was the feeling of a vertiginous plunge into moral jeopardy he suffered at the thought of having to use it on another human being. He'd only ever shot vermin and range predators on his family's ranch. James had been a good shot, even on horseback, when it had meant protecting a newborn calf from a coyote or his mother's chickens from a wild cat, but in spite of all that'd happened this last week or so, he was still not sure he could pull the trigger on a man.

He bought the Ruger at the same place he got the two baby Glocks for Melissa and Michelle and hundreds of reloads for everyone, including Rick. A gun shop in Clarksburg, just off the 270 at the start of their westward journey.

Paid a bruising markup over the sticker price, too.

As things fell apart in the cities, demand was peaking in the personal protection market, and James had dropped a solid wedge of his remaining cash on the rifle. Apart from his facility with camp cooking and a haven with his parents at the far end of their journey, he worried that he had nothing to offer their little caravan besides money. The world had very little need for an investment advisor right now. Anyone with a functioning brain stem could see that weapons, ammunition, food and defensible shelter were the only growth stocks worth holding.

He sat down just as Michelle arrived. She took a place next to him on the log, squeezing his arm and smiling 'thanks' for cooking the fish. Her culinary skills did not extend far beyond having programmed her iPhone with voice-activated shortcuts for her favorite Uber Eats deliveries. A talent that was well past its use-by-date. Rick joined them at the tree stump, his face a relief map of worry lines. He muttered a command to Nomi, who ran off into the woods. She would bark up a storm if anyone approached the campsite down the overgrown fire trail or through the surrounding forest.

James more or less knew what Rick was going to say before he said it.

"Still don't know if we should move on or hunker down," he said.

He'd been having this debate with himself and the others for the last week.

Mostly with himself, though.

"Haven't heard any gunfire for a while," James offered. "And that was just a couple of shots. Probably somebody hunting game. There's plenty of deer down the valley."

"He's right, sweetie," Mel said. "Whoever shot up that other camp, I reckon they moved on."

Rick forked a whole trout onto his plate and looked to Michelle. The threat analyst.

She shrugged.

"Small unit militia tactics are not my thing. But Mel is right about the data points. We haven't heard a gun battle in days. Just random shots. People hunting for food. But if you think we should move now, we'll move. Your call."

Rick picked at his food, his brow furrowed.

"I just don't know," he said. "This was a good spot to lay up. We can cover all the movement through the valley. The fire trail is the only way up here, and it's easily defended, but... I just... don't know."

James felt his friend's unease. It was not far removed from his anxiety about whether he could ever shoot somebody. With Rick, that wasn't in question. The day James O'Donnell had met Rick Boreham, Rick had killed five men who'd attacked the Harris Teeter in Darnestown. And God only knew how many more he'd put under during multiple tours of Afghanistan and Iraq. But James saw his own disquiet reflected in Rick's eyes.

He was worried he wouldn't be able to keep them safe. They had been lucky, in a way, getting caught up in that armed robbery back in Darnestown. It had rubbed their noses in the brute reality of what was happening. Of what was going to happen. It was why Rick and Mel had joined James and Michelle on the long drive to Montana, to the ranch where James had grown up. They could be safe there while things shook themselves out. But now James, like Rick, was beginning to wonder if they would ever make it.

A gentle breeze wafted up from the valley floor, rustling the undergrowth on the steep-sided plateau and bending the tips of the fir and replanted spruce trees that crowded in around the campsite. James' forearms puckered into gooseflesh at the slight chill. They had been hiding in Canaan for a week, and he was still getting used to the microclimate. Even at the end of summer, the wetlands seemed to hold tight to a memory of some winter long passed. The night of the gun battle on the other side of the valley, the mercury had dropped into the low thirties, and they had all shivered under their blankets.

Everyone except Rick, of course. He'd taken himself off into the dark of the woods, patrolling the approaches to their hideout until dawn.

He would do so again tonight while the other three rotated watch at the camp.

"Good fish, James," Rick said.

He set aside the last fillet for Nomi. They had five heavy bags of kibble in the Sierra, but they had to manage her food stores as keenly as their own. Pretty much every place they'd stopped on the first part of their long drive, panic buying had emptied the shelves. And James knew better more than anyone that those shelves were not about to fill up again. He'd been the guy in Washington, warning everybody what was about to go down.

"Lot of streams on my parents' ranch," he said as he chased a small tomato around the paper plate. "My dad and I would fish most weekends we got the chance."

Rick nodded and grunted, and nobody else spoke for a while.

Nobody needed to say the obvious. James's parents might be fishing those streams out of need by now.

There was no way to know. Michelle's satellite phone was down. Or maybe, the satellites themselves. The phone worked just fine, but she said it was like the sky itself was empty.

James was just beginning to feel the weight of the silence around the tree stump when Rick spoke up again.

"You shouldn't stray too far out into the valley," he said. "It's not safe down there."

"We need the food," James said. "Once we get moving again, our supplies won't last until Montana. "

"You won't need the food if somebody puts a bullet in your back or cuts your throat," Rick said sharply.

"Baby," Mel said quietly. "Take it easy. I went with him. Michelle watched the camp with Nomi while you got your head down. We weren't gone long, and we were both armed."

She unshipped her Glock. Laid it next to the paper plate with limp salad greens and slightly burned trout. When she spoke the words came out in a deep bass, a caricature of Rick's accent.

"It's an ugly little pug," she said, recalling his demo at the gun shop in Clarksburg. *"But it's the right size for a little lady's smaller hand, and you cannot beat it for reliability. You lady folk squeeze this here trigger with even your weak little lady fingers, and it'll put a round exactly where you're pointing, even if it's wet, muddy or whatever."*

Rick closed his eyes and exhaled as though blowing on scalding hot soup to cool it. He started laughing.

"I'm sorry," he said when he got himself back under control. "I just worry, is all."

"Worry about what's coming when we get back on the road," Michelle said. "This place is quiet. Out there..." she gestured vaguely with her beer at the wider world, "it'll be getting medieval by now."

"Bad enough last week," James agreed. "Those folks at Aurora, they weren't expecting any outside help. And Dryfork looked liked they didn't want any."

Rick nodded. He'd finished most of his meal in a few bites. He started to pick through Nomi's fillet, looking for stray bones.

"We're going to have to go around them," he said as he worked. "Around them and all the hundreds of other little places that walled themselves off in time."

"Places like that aren't the problem," Michelle said. "Our problem is getting through ten million refugees in Ohio and another ten million out of Chicago. And staying ahead of the thirty or forty million who made it out of the cities back east."

That brought the silence again.

It always did when the conversation circled back here.

The fall of the cities.

8

A BIG HIT OFF THE CHEMTRAIL BONG

Brad Rausch's smash repair business lay well beyond the crude but effective fortifications securing the far end of the town. Rausch had opted to remain in place, however, insisting that he could easily defend his 'compound' and that it provided the town with a listening post in the woods to the north-west. Jonas didn't think the auto mechanic was being entirely bull-headed about it. The big waves of refugees had hit the ramparts from the direction of the city, where the blacktop curved away into the forest before switching back on itself multiple times as the road to Seattle descended from the foothills of the Cascades. Coming from the other direction, from the high slopes of the wilderness, the town's defenders received almost no human traffic after the first couple of days. Nonetheless, Jonas also recognised within Rausch a jaw-jutting, obstinate nature that had led him to exile himself from the town's polite society in the first place.

It was a short walk, maybe five minutes along Main, from Big Al's to the hastily erected timber tower and stockade just beyond Doc Cornwell's little cottage on the very fringe of the forest. Jonas took a quarter hour getting there, stopping twice to help out with heavy lifting along the way. Jacques Loubert and Lachie Saunders were trying to wrestle a diesel-powered generator off the back of a Toyota pickup, and they were fucking up a simple lift and carry job the way only a couple of lentil-eating weed-fags could. So Jonas plastered on a smile and hurried over to help them, which mostly meant doing the job himself. It was almost like being back at the ol' Amazon fulfilment centre. He then lost a few minutes rescuing Selectwoman Natalie Bochenski, who was trying to push a shopping cart full of old wooden cheese moulds and churns from Melanie Miles' Genuine Colonial Knick Knack Depository across the freshly ploughed and planted town Common to Darren O'Shannassy's Red Apple franchise.

"The direct route isn't always the fastest, Councillor," Jonas grinned as he lifted the metal shopping cart out of the muddy ditch in which it was stuck.

"Thank you, Jonas. I don't know what I was thinking," she gushed. Selectwoman Natalie was always a little gushy around Jonas, and although she wasn't his type—she was more like the Anti-Tomi—he still made time to indulge in some tactical flirting with her. She was a close ally of O'Shannassy and worth cultivating for that alone, if not for her vote on the Emergency Committee.

"Nat, a fine-looking woman like you shouldn't even have to think about this stuff when there's lug-heads like me going spare for want of something useful to do," he said, putting just a little bedroom growl into the words "a fine looking woman."

She gushed and fluttered around some more and asked if he was coming to the 'EC' meeting at nine that morning. It was a rhetorical question, mainly asked to extend their conversation a few moments more after Jonas had deposited the shopping cart back onto solid asphalt with a metallic crash. They both knew he would be there. The last week and a bit, Jonas Murdoch had very carefully positioned himself inside the machinery of Silverton's official response to The Emergency.

That's what people around here were calling it now, with a capital 'T' and a capital 'E'.

For a while, 'the national emergency' and even 'the war' or 'the cyberwar' had been preferred because it'd been all over cable news before the cable and then the terrestrial news broadcasts went dark. Nobody, least of all Jonas, had a clue what anybody outside of Silverton was calling it now. Privately, he thought of it as 'this Chinese clusterfuck' since it seemed a laydown certainty that the slants in Beijing had kicked the whole thing off, but nobody was talking much about them anymore. Nobody in Silverton, anyway. Their war had become this weird, almost medieval struggle, a bizarre sort of siege, with the town sealing itself off against all outsiders and everybody inside the barricades reduced to acting the part of muddy peasants, frantically grubbing for sustenance.

Beyond the wooden palisades? Who knew?

"Yeah, Natalie," Jonas grinned. "I'll be there with my notepad if you need me to sit in your lap and take dictation, Councillor."

"Oh, you," she blushed, pushing him away and getting a nice squeeze of his pecs in as she did so.

Jesus, he thought as he left her to deliver the antique cheese-making kit to O'Shannassy. *The things I do for macronutrients and defensible shelter.*

He resumed his trek to the gate works, or the small fort, or whatever the hell you called the structure safeguarding the town's north-western exit. The Cascades Gate was its official title. Twin to the Seattle Gate back up at the other end of Main. Jonas allowed himself a private grin. But exactly what kind of gate or fort or barricade it was, he couldn't tell you. For a guy who styled himself as The Centurion not so long ago, the last week had rubbed his nose in just how ignorant he actually was about all this shit. Even more embarrassing to admit? It had been Doc Cornwell, Moonbat-in-chief to the town's yoghurt-weaving liberal faction, who'd come up with the plans for both structures. And not just plans in a general sense, but actual fucking schematics. Her late husband, three years dead of prostate cancer, had been something of a Roman Empire nut. Most amusing of all, at least to Jonas, he'd even had a pretty popular podcast about it. And in his extensive library at home, three books on Roman military engineering. Sheriff Muller had prevailed upon the good doctor of Silverton to turn them over to the Emergency Committee after two of his deputies were injured by refugees armed with baseball bats who swarmed the much simpler crowd control barrier he'd erected on the second day of The Emergency.

The fortifications had gone up as quickly as an Amish barn. Jonas, along with most of the able-bodied men available, had helped out under the direction of Dan Meehan, a retired carpenter who'd 'come up the hill' from Seattle ten years ago to escape all of the 'hipsters and latte nerds down there". Along with the cars packed bumper-to-bumper in a great steel semicircle enclosing most of the town's playing fields, the twin forts were the most obvious expression of changed circumstances.

But not the only ones.

Every food business along Main Street and in the half-dozen little side streets that ran off it had closed. Not through lack of wares to sell or some panic buying spree, but in accordance with another bylaw passed by the Emergency Committee requisitioning 'all foodstuffs and resources for the duration of the current crisis'. Every store owner, from Darren O'Shaughnessy to Ginger McCauley, proprietor of Get Fudged, had been issued receipts for the full value of their stock – due compensation to be paid by the town 'when the current difficulties allow'. Some of the businesses, like the Red Apple, were boarded up and constantly guarded by 'special deputies'. Others had simply been closed as if for the winter. Their stock, however, now sat in three secure locations. O'Shannassy's Red Apple. The big vault of the Farmers Mutual. And the holding cells of Sheriff Muller's lockup. The only previous occupant of the county jail, Eladio Morena, had been turned out of the Seattle Gate on the third day of the Emergency. Nobody could justify feeding him anymore, and Sheriff Muller forestalled any suggestion that he should simply be hanged, given the difficulties of the current situation.

Jonas had no idea where the greasy fuck was now, but he did not doubt that Morena was still alive. Cockroaches like that would survive a nuclear war.

His stomach grumbled as he approached the soup line for those workers who had taken the early shift tilling the Common. He estimated that about thirty people were waiting on their bowl of barley and corn broth. A similar line snaked away from an open fire out on the playing fields. There was heavier work out there, he knew. And a better breakfast, with some bacon and potato chunks added to the broth. Jonas had done his fair share of labour out in those fields and on the long arc of automotive steel and glass twinkling in the morning sun.

He'd been a little surprised at how quickly everything had come to evoke a frontier theme. Not just through the obvious imagery of the two mini-forts but the open-air cooking, the haphazard market gardens, the constant din of carpentry and even ironmongery, and, of course, the weapons. Everybody with access to a firearm now carried it openly. Those without handguns or hunting rifles or the guards assigned to internal strongholds like the three food stores most often carried improvised clubs. As his boots crunched up the tarmac of Main Street and he took in the details of the early morning all around him, Jonas could not help thinking that people did not look nearly as frightened and confused as they had in the first few days after everything went sideways. The faces in the soup line smiled as people chatted to each other, waiting for their handout. They did not look like the bums you saw or used to see waiting for handouts in the city. The guards at the parapets and walking the boundary secured by the long curve of bumper-to-bumper cars glowered at the outside world, but their expressions softened when they turned to anybody within the town limits.

Made sense, he figured. These people were slaves two weeks ago. They didn't know it. They thought themselves free. But they weren't. They were owned by the banks, the government, the media, the big corporations, the whole shitty fucking system. Now they were free. Was it any wonder they were smiling? Even if they didn't know why.

As he approached the Cascade Gate, he watched a small hunting team breaking down a deer carcass, stripping off the hide and opening the stomach cavity to empty the guts for a couple of dogs that had joined them on the hunt. There was good game to be had in the forests around Silverton, but previously only during short official seasons, determined in the state capital, and strictly so. The Emergency Committee had waved away all that bullshit about five minutes after Doctor Cornwell had testified under oath that even with rationing, the town did not have enough food to sustain itself through the coming fall, let alone the winter. Jonas didn't know any members of the hunting party, and they were too busy to bother with the usual courtesies as he passed by, but in spite of the gore and the sight of their dogs tearing at the deer's entrails, he found himself drooling at the prospect of fresh meat.

He shouldn't have. He was almost certain all of this protein would be salted, vacuum packed, or somehow stored for the coming months. In the same way, all of the milk in town, which really meant whatever milk was left in O'Shannassy's little supermarket, was being turned into cheese, and the local baker had given up on artisanal loaves for the tourist trade, instead converting the last of his flour into hardtack.

The Cascades Gate loomed over him, looking a bit like set dressing for a B-movie. It was not a fully enclosed fort, of course. More like a log palisade raised to support a firing platform. The logs, the first of which had come from Silverton's main tourist attraction, a long-defunct sawmill turned into the town's Forestry Museum, sank their footing deep into the road surface. Road maintenance workers from the County Council had jackhammered a trench clear across Main Street to provide a structural foundation. The primary construct consisted of a tower, very obviously moved from a kids' playground, the firing platform, and a rudimentary gate system that looked like it had once been somebody's garage door. The palisades ran into the forest on the right, all the way down to a steep fall, and on the left, ending at a natural rock formation where another rifleman kept watch. Both guards on the firing platform had their backs to Jonas, and he called out to them as he approached.

"Yo, guys. Jonas Murdoch going through to see Brad Rausch and Chad Moffat at the auto shop."

Only one of the men turned around.

Leo Vaulk. Jonas grinned.

Leo was for sure the most heavily armed man in Silverton, and he rattled with personal artillery when he waved at Jonas. They'd met a week earlier at Big Al's, where the Vaulk had taken a big hit off the chemtrail bong and was laying out an amazingly dense and complex logarithm of QAnon talking points about the real reason Hillary Clinton had invited the Chinese to attack America. Jonas started grooming him immediately.

The other guard maintained his watch on the road, even though nothing ever really came from that direction. Jonas recognised the more disciplined rifleman as the dad who had looked after his bike back on his first day in town when he had crash-tackled Morena and earned his place on this side of the barricade. Jonas still didn't know the guy's name. Maybe it was Tony.

"You are clear through, Jonas," Leo called down. "We're almost done here, man, but I'll brief the next watch that you're out in the field."

"Thanks," Jonas called back.

He walked towards the crazy-built garage door thing, which was secured with two long, thick wooden bars and lots of rope and chain. A kid was sitting reading an Avengers comic. No way he could lift those railway sleepers. It would have been a heavy lift, even for Jonas. But the kid hopped up and moved his chair aside, giving Jonas access to the wicket gate, a small door cut into the much larger main entrance. The smaller gate was secured by a couple of big modern padlocks, which the kid opened with a key. Jonas bent down, stepped through, and heard the gate closed behind him before he could turn around. Both padlocks snapped back into place with muted, metallic clicks. He looked up at the wall of the fort. From this side, it looked formidable.

9

THE HUMAN WAVE

The sun was on the rise when they came over the hill. Tammy was tired from a long night of driving. Roxarne snored quietly in the front seat next to her. The four kids were asleep in back. They all came to when she slammed on the brakes.

The Oldsmobile's tires bit into the road surface, but they did not bite hard. They'd been as bald as a baby's ass when Tammy drove out of the Vale, and she'd put some hard miles on them in the days since. The thin rubber skin of the ancient Goodyears screeched on the asphalt. The Olds started to drift across the surface of the highway. And Tammy Kolchar screamed.

They all screamed, the kids in waking confusion and terror; Roxarne because she blinked open her eyes and saw what was happening. The car slid, uncontrolled, for what felt like forever as Tammy fought the wheel and tried to remember what to do when you lost control of a vehicle.

The dangerous skid probably lasted for just a few seconds, Tammy conceded later, but it felt like they were about to fall into eternity. The road ahead was blocked — not by a stalled car or a big accident. God knows they'd seen enough of them the last few days. And later, thinking back on it, she did recall that there were, in fact, plenty of vehicles blocking the way ahead of them. But that wasn't why she hit the brakes.

She crested that hill, and even with the sunrise suddenly burning into the back of her tired, watery eyes, she could see they were about to plough into a whole damn crowd of people. These idiots were everywhere; lots of them just laid down in the middle of the damn road. She pumped the brakes, wrenched the wheel in the direction of the skid, tried not to wrench too hard, and tried to remember all of the lectures her dad had given her about what he called 'driving defensive'.

In the end, they lived, and so did the dumbasses who'd just laid themselves down on the road ahead of her. The Oldsmobile planed across the surface of the highway, tires squealing and smoking, passengers crying out in alarm, Tammy cursing fit to shame a pit boss in a coal mine, but ... they came through.

The car finally lurched to a halt, three, maybe four feet from the nearest body. Then, that body stirred and slowly lifted itself from the road surface.

"Holy shit," Roxarne whispered. "It's The Walking Dead."

Tammy's mouth hung open.

"Mom," one of the children cried out. "Mom, what's up with them?"

Tammy had no idea who said that. She was paralysed by the scene in front of her.

She was not entirely sure of where they had fetched up after a long night of driving and stopping to sleep when she and Roxy were too tired to go on safely. Somewhere in Ohio? Maybe? And not far from a big city either. She could see the high-rise towers shining in the morning sun all the way off on the horizon. A vast plain stood before the city. Miles of suburbs stretched away from the shimmering mountains of steel and glass, but the tree-lined streets gave way to open fields and farmland. Great ribbons of highway ran away from the metropolis, one heading in her direction. It was choked with traffic, none of it moving. None of it had moved in days, from what she could tell.

Tammy Kolchar dry swallowed her shock. Between the hill she had just crested and the edge of that faraway city, a great but quiet army of humanity lay all atop one another in the dirt and on the road. Some obviously dead. Others were stirring to life, possibly at the noise of her long, screeching slide. There were tents out there. Whole tent cities. And little forts made out of cars circled like wagons in a TV western. And there were people. So many people.

"Back up, Tammy, back up now," Roxarne urged.

"Mommy, what's happening? What's up with all those people?" Jakey asked Roxarne from the back.

Tammy could not back up because she was so tired and so unnerved by the sight of so many human beings just sort of lying there out under the open sky that it short-circuited all the wiring in her head.

"Back up, Tammy! They've seen us," Roxarne said, her voice rising in panic.

Well, of course, they'd seen them.

The Olds had been just about the only thing moving in that part of the world.

Except for the folks who was dragging their asses up off the ground just ahead of them. Dozens of folks.

No. Scratch that. Hundreds.

There was hundreds now that Tammy took the time and had the slowly returning presence of mind to do a quick and dirty headcount. There was easily a couple of hundred people within a hundred yards of where they fetched up, and they was all of them getting up now and pointing, and shuffling, and in a few cases even half stumble-running towards Tammy Kolchar. It was like a wave rippling over the surface of the world. A wave made of human bodies as knowledge of something happening transmitted itself back through the vast host. There were thousands, tens of thousands of people moving out there.

"Sweet baby Jesus," Tammy whispered.

Was the whole damn city camped out there in front of her? Had a million people come pouring out of those high towers and the miles of suburbs and flowed out across the plain, looking to escape the same way she had led Roxy and the kids away from Dillonvale?

Roxarne punched her in the arm. Hard.

"Bitch, move! They're coming!"

"Ouch," Tammy protested. Her arm jangled with the pain. Roxy had put the fucking knuckle in, and she was strong. Freakout strong.

And with good reason.

They was coming, all of them as could still move, and they was coming for the Olds. The only damn vehicle anywhere within ten miles that was still able to move. The nearest of them had laid hands on the vehicle when Tammy threw the stick into reverse and gave the engine some sweet gasoline. The car roared back to life, and the tires spun in the dirt. She feared they might blow out; they were so thin, but they held.

THUMP.

The children screamed as two figures launched themselves at the hood of the car, one of them landing on it with a loud bang. It was a man in a business suit, but the suit was dusty and torn, and his face was sunken and authentically mad.

"You have to help me," he cried out, his voice muffled by the closed windows.

Tammy tried not to look into his eyes as she yanked the steering wheel around and gave the accelerator a taste of her boot. The man snarled, like actually fucking snarled at her; she was sure of it. Like he was some sort of animal or something. Another loud bang sounded from behind.

She'd hit something or someone.

"Mommy, noooo!" Liana cried out.

Tammy shut her mind to everything but getting them turned around and gone. She could see where this was going to end if she fucked it all up. Hundreds of people would swarm the car in moments, pile them under and finally drag them out. Then they'd likely tear each other apart trying to get control of it. For half of a heartbeat, she saw it happen inside her mind. Saw the human wave breaking over the top of them, pulling the little ones out of the back-seat, pulling them apart in the frenzy.

Another bang and another flailing body landed on the hood. It was a younger man this time, and he started fighting with the first guy for position. Tammy jammed on the brakes, and the sudden jolting stop threw them both off the vehicle. That merely allowed her to see how many more were coming on. All of them, it seemed. They would be buried in seconds.

"Hang on, everyone," she yelled before crunching the shift into reverse and stomping the gas pedal hard.

The Oldsmobile shuddered and lumbered over a couple of bumps. She ignored the screams. It was easy to do in the uproar of more and more desperate pursuers surrounding the car. She mashed the horn. It seemed both stupid and necessary. What else was she to do?

"Fuck off all of you, just fuck off!" Roxarne cried out, pounding at the passenger side window with her fists. A grotesque freakshow of nearly inhuman faces surrounded them. Haggard, angry, desperate. Lips skinned back from teeth, spittle flying, eyes rolling.

The children screamed. The car skewed and lurched and bumped over yet more unknown obstacles. And then they were free, reversing at speed back over the crest of the hill. A few determined souls kept after them, but Tammy had the road now, and she was able to throw the car into an emergency brake turn that whipped them around in a half circle, pointing them back to where they had come from.

She poured on the gas and sped away without ever looking back.

10

THE PLAGUE

They had quickly settled into a routine, partly by design but mostly of necessity. Rick insisted on patrolling far beyond the edge of the camp all night, every night. He also insisted that while he was securing the approaches, someone remain on guard at the camp while the other two slept in shifts. It was a sensible arrangement, and nobody took issue with it. James, having lived and worked on a ranch until leaving home for college, had acquired his outdoor skills early, under the exacting eye of his father and the leading hands. He could set up and break down a campsite just as efficiently as Rick, but never having had the convenience of MREs or the luxury of an army field kitchen to call on, he was also a better-than-average outdoor cook. He took charge of ensuring they were well-fed each day, and he insisted on tidying up afterwards with a fastidiousness they were all getting used to. Mel, a city girl her whole life, nonetheless retained the practical realism gained in her previous job as a London copper. After Darnestown, it was she who had argued for each of them to carry a personal weapon at all times. And when she wasn't helping James gather food or standing her watch over the camp, she took responsibility for everyone's health and fitness, instituting a regime of strength training and cardio workouts that left James and Michelle sweating and shaking like leaves in a gale the first couple of times they attempted them. She also insisted the two 'cube farm cripples' practice basic unarmed self-defence with her for another hour each day.

With no outdoor skills to speak of, Michelle Nguyen fell back on what she did know. She gathered information, and she calculated their prospects of survival.

Sometimes, this meant talking with other travellers they met in the park. There were a lot of families camped down the Valley. Many of them refugees, or more accurately, escapees from the city, just like her little Scooby gang. Two groups of school kids had also been caught out on Zero Day. One group had driven out in their bus the morning after the attack on the campsite to the west. The other was still bivouacked around a small pond about a mile to the south.

No cops or even park rangers ever came to investigate the shooting.

Most days, she scanned the car radio, listening for newscasts, overseas bulletins, or the national emergency alert system.

The latter was the least useful, consisting primarily of canned recordings, a week out of date, reminding citizens of limits on cash withdrawals, federally mandated food and gas rationing, and curfews in dozens of eastern cities affected by food riots. Michelle knew that on the West Coast, the list of affected cities would be different, but the alert system used Specific Area Message Encoding to target the broadcasts down to the county level. There were repeated warnings about travel restrictions to what Homeland had designated as 'stronghold cities'; a dozen or more of them, chosen as best she could guess for their smaller populations, defensibility, access to reliable nutrition and proximity to significant ground combat assets.

It was all being sold with an upbeat can-do message, but to a professional realist like her, it sounded grim.

After dinner, but some time before sundown, Michelle sat in the driver's seat of the Sierra, a notepad and pencil in hand, as she carefully scanned up and down the FM and AM bands. Her take from the daily survey was getting thinner. When they'd driven away from Rick Boreham's cabin, she'd been hopeful that in spite of the wild violence at the Darnestown food market, things would not fall apart. That the centre at least would hold.

Now, rolling up and down the dial, she had no doubts about the desperate situation they were in. They had good elevation at their campsite in the Canaan, and when they'd first arrived, six separate radio stations had carried the emergency alerts.

That number had since dropped to three. A datum point that was more informative than anything within the recorded messages.

She flicked through the channels, stopping at every live signal. Most were small operations. A lot of tiny transmitters down in the Bible belt had filled the spectrum abandoned by larger commercial operators. After a couple of days listening to half-starved preachers furiously polishing their Revelation boners, Michelle had learned to flick over the religious whackjobs as quickly as she did the older emergency alert system messages. That didn't leave much. There was a rap and hip-hop station that never dropped off the air, but it was a robot operation like the EAS. No human staffers, at least not in the studio.

Still, she felt a small thrill of relief when her fingers found DJ Khaled kicking it out at 98 on the FM dial. She listened quietly to *Gold Slugs* for a little while, letting her thoughts wander. The sun had dropped towards Table Rock at the western end of the valley, throwing long shadows down the basin of the Canaan. She could see James and Rick in the rearview mirror, standing by the edge of the forest, deep in conversation, while Nomi sat patiently by her master, awaiting his command.

In a few minutes, Rick would bend over, scratch the dog behind the ear, and tell her to "Guard the house."

As far as Nomi was concerned, their small campsite was 'the house' now.

Then Rick would disappear into the trees until dawn tomorrow.

He was carrying the AR-15 he'd taken from one of the men he'd killed at the market, extra ammunition that James had bought back in Clarksburg, a protein bar, water, and a small thermos of coffee. He was dressed in dark clothes and a heavy, camouflaged jacket.

James wore blue jeans, a checked shirt, and his boundlessly sunny optimism. Her heart swelled a little at the sight of him.

Michelle tweaked the dial again. Static and white noise. Another tweak for more of the same.

The big metro stations had been dropping out with increasing frequency for days. She noted which ones had gone quiet since her last radio check.

WBBM and WBEQ, Chicago.

WBMV, Mount Vernon.

KDKA news radio out of Pittsburgh and the last of the AM shops in Scranton.

All dead air now.

WBIG in Aurora was still going strong, though. "The Big One" had pivoted from its usual fare of shopping, farm news and local sports to a solid slate of hyperlocal civil defense alerts and stern warnings to outsiders to stay the hell away or be met with lethal force under Executive Order 14101.

Ten days since the Chinese had launched their first cyber strike and Michelle still could not quite believe how devastating it had been. She understood that other hostile actors, both state and non-state, had piled on in the chaos of the opening salvos. But still... she had been tasked with threat assessment by the National Security Council, and they simply had not seen this coming. Not like this.

Who would have thought something as medieval as siege and starvation would work in a society where three-quarters of the adult population were clinically obese, and most of them morbidly so?

James O'Donnell.

That's who.

Michelle stole another glimpse at him in the rearview mirror. James was patting Nomi and smiling as he chatted with Rick, who looked like a private military contractor who'd somehow taken a wrong turn and badly lost his way. What on Earth was James smiling about? And what could he be saying to crack the granite facade of Rick Boreham's impressively stoic features? Even from this distance, Michelle could see the merest grin shining through as the deep worry lines over the former soldier's eyes faded just a little, for just a few moments.

She almost sighed.

James.

He'd warned them of the attack in the last crucial hours before the Chinese collapsed America's civilisation. Its banking and communication networks, and most critically, its food distribution systems. He warned her bosses back in Washington of precisely what could happen. And they had listened. But too late. And here they were now, hiding out in the wilderness as vast armies of starving refugees poured out of the great cities, and hundreds of millions of people turned on each other over scraps of food. And there James was with his weirdly boyish grin as if he could not be happier to be anywhere than right here, camping out with friends.

She'd thought she understood him when they'd first met. But he was not the money market data nerd Michelle had hired as a consultant to write a report on the trade war.

The fucking trade war?

Jesus Christ, things changed quickly.

Michelle had just completed another sweep of the dial while her thoughts wandered to James, as they so frequently did now. She was rolling back to check in with DJ Khaled when a crackling, far-away trace of a refined British accent caught her ear. She adjusted the tuning knob on the SUV's entertainment system, thought she heard it again, inched it back just a fraction, and there...

There it was.

"...BBC World Service. I'm... casting from emer... ...vernment pledged to restore... army authorised to... martial law..."

The connection dropped out, disappeared in a wash of atmospheric interference.

Michelle cursed silently and leaned into the console as though she might somehow drag the signal out through the speakers with her own hands. Her anxiety had focused in with laser-like precision on that far-away voice. She twitched the tuning knob one way and then the other.

Nothing but electrostatic hiss and crackle.

"Come on," she muttered, trying again.

"...reports of the Chinese Army deployed in Beijing and Shanghai as a flu-like plague sweeps through the Asia Pacific region, but with particular virulence on the Chinese mainland."

Her heart had quickened with excitement when she'd captured the fragile signal from the BBC, but now it pounded at the mention of a possible pandemic in China. Her head swam for a moment, and she lost the signal when her hand slipped on the dial.

It came back, however, clear and at full strength for just a few seconds.

"...blamed the shocking speed of the contagion and the high mortality rate in China's densely populated urban centres on foreign devils and evil adversaries. No US government spokesperson was available for comment. The Chinese media, however, has been quick to blame enemies closer to home, with many accusing the Japanese of tailoring the bird flu virus to target Han Chinese ethnic communities specifically..."

The signal disappeared again, this time for good.

Michelle fell back in the seat. She was sweating and trembling just a little.

As hard as it had been to accept just how wholly and swiftly Beijing had swept the legs out from under its American foe, she had even more trouble accepting that somebody in the chain of command above her had authorised the use of a bio-weapon in response.

This bird flu had to be a weaponised virus.

She was sure of it. Beijing would be, too.

She leaned forward and searched for the BBC signal, but it was gone. Whatever quirk of the upper atmosphere had allowed her to capture it - gone too.

Michelle rubbed at her upper arms where gooseflesh had broken out.

The valley was deceptively quiet.

She knew there were hundreds, maybe thousands of people hiding away down there and scattered along the rim of the bowl-like geological depression nestled in higher reaches of the Allegheny

Mountains. Some had been camping in the National Park when everything went sideways. Others were undoubtedly nutjob preppers and survivalist weirdos who couldn't quite believe their time had come. But most would be people like them; small parties with the good sense and even better luck to get out of the cities before it was too late.

How long did they have before the first real human wave broke over the edges of the Canaan?

More than fifty million people were living in the northeast corridor of the US. And more again if you threw in the millions of Canadians just over the border and across the Great Lakes.

How many of them were heading towards their little campsite right now?

She had no idea and no way of finding out. The satellites were dead, probably raked from the skies by Chinese or Russian missiles. It was insanely frustrating.

"Michelle? You okay?"

She jumped at the voice.

Melissa had come up beside the SUV, and Michelle hadn't even noticed.

"Sorry," Michelle said, her voice cracking just a little. "Lost in my thoughts."

"Anything on the radio?" The Englishwoman asked, nodding at the console.

Michelle Nguyen's breath shuddered out of her.

"Same old shit," she said.

She almost left it at that.

Many years of keeping the government's secrets had not prepared her for sharing with outsiders. But she forced herself to break the old habits of thought. They hadn't worked so well recently, and they could get her killed in this new reality.

"There was one thing," she said. "I think we need to talk about it. Is Rick still here?"

Mel Baker shook her head. Her teeth shone white through a wide grin. She always looked happy when talking about Rick.

"Nah, sorry, luv. He's gone. Like a bloody shadow into the night, he is. You ready to do some training? We've got an hour or so before it's really dark. I can take the first watch. You'll be tired, promise."

Her grin faded when she saw the look on Michelle's face.

"What's up, babe?"

Michelle just stared at her, searching for the words.

Finally, she said, "Things are going to get much worse."

11

NOBODY WALKS AWAY FROM THREE BAGS OF DORITOS

Not much had changed at Brad Rausch's auto shop since Jonas first called out there the morning of his second day in town. The smash repair joint had impressed him then as something of a fortress, and Rausch was not put to much trouble fortifying it further. He'd boarded up the windows of the glass-walled office out front, and the steel gate to the lot in back was now closed and chained up. But that was it, as far as Jonas could see.

"Yo Brad. It's me, Murdoch," he called out from the road, loud enough to startle a few birds from the tall pines and fir trees that crowded up to the edge of the property line.

"Jonas, bro! Up here. Check it out, man."

It wasn't Rausch.

Jonas craned his head back and to the left, following the voice to find Chad Moffat peering out over eight foot of corrugated iron sheeting, waving a shotgun in the air. A chain rattled, and the main gate screeched open.

Rausch wore a pistol at his hip, like Jonas, but he also carried an AK 47 knockoff. Or, hell, maybe it was the real deal.

"Come on in, Jonas," he said. "Don't like to have the place open too long."

Rausch did not open the gate very wide, and Jonas had to squeeze past him on the way through. As always, Rausch smelled of hand-rolled tobacco, pulled pork and sour sweat. Jonas had wondered early on whether he'd smell of lentils and potato soup like everyone else in town. But one night camped out here, knocking back a bottle of Jack he'd pilfered from Al Barrett's place set him straight on that. Rausch had a big freezer full of wild pig meat and a diesel generator to keep it going when the power went down.

The power had gone down on the fourth day.

"You're early," Rausch said.

"Got an Emergency Committee meeting later this morning," Jonas explained, looking around for Chad. He found him climbing down from something that looked like a swimming pool lifeguard tower. Whatever it was, they'd turned it into a serviceable firing platform to give them coverage of the road and forest outside the walled compound. Chad hurried over with a big, dopey grin on his face. Big and dopey was Chad's natural state of being. Jonas was amused to see he was still wearing his samurai sword. He'd never seen him without it.

"Yeah, the meeting," Rausch grunted. "You reckon they can get me some more diesel for my tow truck. I'm burning through it like a motherfucker hauling wrecks back and forth to build that stupid wall."

Jonas smiled wryly.

"I just take the notes, Brad. But I can talk with Howard Wetsman before the meeting. Or maybe Natalie Bochenski. She's in charge of resourcing."

Rausch nodded. The promise was enough for him. Jonas Murdoch always delivered.

The car lot was much bigger than you'd imagine if you could only see the front of Rausch's place. He had room enough for at least two dozen vehicles inside. The site was about half full now, and most of the cars didn't look like they needed to be in a smash repair shop.

"You picked up anything good since that Toyota?" Jonas said, seeing the answer for himself.

"Yeah, we found a Mazda CX 5 about 20 miles north of here

yesterday. Three-quarters of a tank full. Just pulled over by the side of the road, driver's door open. No sign of the occupant. Even had some tinned food and Doritos on the back seat."

"Still fresh in the bag," Chad Moffat said as he came up. "Three bags of Doritos, man. Flaming hot nacho, too. Who walks away from that?"

Jonas could see the vehicle a short distance away, parked nose-in next to a late-model Jeep Cherokee. The Jeep was pockmarked with bullet holes, and a dark brown splash of dried blood obscured the driver's side of the windshield. Jonas walked over to inspect the Mazda while Rausch chained up the main gate again.

"Nobody with half a brain," Jonas said to Chad, answering his question. It had been rhetorical, but Chad probably didn't know what 'rhetorical' meant, so Jonas answered it anyway. "What do you think happened to them?" he called back over his shoulder.

Having chained and padlocked the main gate, Brad Rausch shrugged as he joined them.

"Dunno," he said. "Maybe they walked into the woods to take a shit and couldn't find their way back. You don't know these forests, you can get lost in a couple of steps."

"Grizzly bear could've taken them too," Moffat said.

Jonas instinctively dismissed most things the giant 'roid ape said, but he caught himself in this instance.

"You reckon so?" he asked Rausch.

The mechanic shrugged again, open to the suggestion.

"Got all the big meat eaters up here. Maybe not so close to the city, but you get a little north, closer to the Canadian reserves and sure, you got your grizzly bears, your black bears, mountain lions, packs of wolves. They could all take a man. But I didn't see no sign of that. Pretty sure whoever it was, the dumbass just walked into the woods for a shit, and they're still out there somewhere."

"Finding it with so much gas was a score," Jonas nodded. "Everyone's running low or running out."

"Three-quarters of a tank," Rausch said, patting the hood of the Mazda as if it was a prize stallion. "But yeah. This is a good vehicle for a long road trip. Tiptop mileage. We should add it to the manifest. I

can take the Jeep into town and a couple of other beaters I pulled in
off the side of the tourist route to close up the gaps in the wall near
Red Man's Creek. That's if the Committee can see their way to finding
me some gas and diesel."

"Leave it to me," Jonas assured him. "What's the range on the
CX 5?"

Rausch shrugged. It was his standby answer to most questions.

"Depends. About twenty-five, maybe twenty-six miles a gallon in
the city. Not that anybody's driving in the city no more unless it's in a
fucking tank or something. Thirty-five, thirty-six out on the freeway.
But some places your freeway's gonna be a fucking parking lot."

"Yeah," Jonas conceded. "We're gonna need that gas."

He checked his watch.

7:35 AM.

"You getting much of anything on your radio?" he asked. It was the
real reason he'd come.

The mechanic's face darkened.

"Nothing good," he said. "You might as well listen for yourself."

Jonas and Chad followed Rausch back into the office. It was much
darker than it had been the first time Jonas was here. The plywood
sheeting Rausch had fixed over the windows blocked out all-natural
light. He pulled a string hanging from the ceiling to turn on a single
naked lightbulb as they entered the front office. The same racks of
tired pornography and dusty, overpriced automotive parts sat undis-
turbed, but all of the foodstuffs were gone. The Emergency
Committee had requisitioned all the Twinkies and chewing gum.
Rausch had gladly given them up as his contribution 'to the common
good.' Some of them, anyway. A much larger consignment of the
energy-dense protein mix was secured within the cells of Sheriff
Muller's county jail, but Jonas had managed to siphon off at least two
boxes for himself and his people.

He had people now. These two useful idiots. Tomi Yates and a few
of her girlfriends. And a handful of guys like Dale Juntii, the ex-
marine, and Leo Vaulk, who had the security contracts for both the
Farmers Mutual S&L and the local Wells Fargo branch.

Rausch unlocked the storeroom, flicked on another light, and waved them through. They were all big men, and it was crowded in there. The freezer, a sizeable commercial unit, hummed quietly in one corner, drawing power from the diesel generator outside. Three cardboard boxes of high-energy protein bars and two extra-large tubs of protein powder sat on top of the freezer. Rausch had boxes of chocolate bars, corn chips, cigarettes and soft drinks stacked up against one wall. The Emergency Committee might have requisitioned his supplies, same as they had with every other business in town, but with Jonas checking the inventory and making sure Selectwoman Bochenski was too distracted to notice, it'd been a simple matter to hold back at least a quarter of the stock. Having run riot through Amazon's much more closely controlled stock management system, the jury-rigged efforts of Silverton's Emergency Committee were not hard to subvert.

Rausch had even given up all the ice cream, frozen pizza pockets, and microwave burritos from his front-of-house freezer. But only Jonas, and now Chad, knew about his other stash.

Oh, and Tomi Yates.

Can't forget her, Jonas reminded himself, already regretting the moment of weakness that had led him to give her that protein bar earlier. He'd already got laid. Three times. What the fuck was he thinking?

A small table took up one corner, surrounded by the hidden boxes of contraband food. An old-fashioned radio unit sat on top of it. Jonas had assumed it was CB radio when Rausch first showed it to him, but the mechanic had laughed at the idea.

"In these hills?" he scoffed. "Nah, I wouldn't pick up nothing but the hum from the fucking freezer. No, this is a sweet little bitch I got me a couple of years ago to listen into the state troopers and the Highway Patrol, looking for work."

He'd gone on then, at tedious length, about radio frequency spectrum and wireless experimentation and a whole bunch of eye-glazing shit, and Jonas had realised that Brad Rausch was a ham radio nerd the same way Mikey Summers was a lycra-fag bicycle nerd. Chad pulled a couple of cookies-n-cream flavoured protein slabs from an already open box, handing them around for breakfast as Rausch played with his radio set. His expression was grimly concentrated but also peaceful, almost sublime. He was in his happy place, even if his happy place was in the middle of a full-on balls-out apocalyptic meltdown.

"Listen up," Rausch said. "I been monitoring these guys since yesterday."

He adjusted a couple of dials on the unit and sat back. Jonas frowned as he listened to what sounded like a conversation between military personnel. Or maybe hardcore taxi drivers.

"Delta Six, this is One-one."

They couldn't hear the response.

Rausch said quietly. "This'll be the skip that we're hearing. It's low power and in the clear."

Jonas had no idea what he meant and focused instead on the radio.

The voice spoke again.

"Six, we lost our key."

"What am I supposed to be listening to?" Jonas asked.

"Dude lost his key," Chad chuckled. "I fucking hate that."

"Quiet," Rausch said. "Just listen. Pretty much everything the army does is in FH or FH-M mode on a SINCGARS radio. FH, or Frequency Hop, literally skips the freq III times per second. And the only way the radios can talk to one another is by having a 'key,' or a set pattern issued by some higher-up that lets the radios synch up. It's an amazing system, really."

Jonas and Chad exchanged a look.

The transmission faded, the mechanic turned up the volume, and the voice came back.

"Be advised, we have secured the OBJ. One Foxtrot Kilo, we'll bring him back in the truck when we Charlie Mike."

"A Foxtrot Kilo is a friendly KIA," Rausch whispered as though imparting a terrible secret. "One of their guys got shot. Probably defending a food warehouse. They been talking about it."

Jonas leaned forward, straining to hear these snatches of chatter from the outside world. He would admit, it was strangely compelling.

The radio crackled again. The speaker sounded as if he was calling from the bottom of a well.

"...fuck was I supposed to do, Six? We were taking fire! Fucking assholes. We're trying to feed them and they lit us up."

That got his attention.

"So what, people are shooting at the army now?" he said. "Where is this?"

"Seattle," Rausch said without hesitation. Army secured a couple of wholesaler food depots. They were running relief, like in Africa or some shit. Handing out food and stuff from the back of trucks."

As usual, they didn't hear a response. Rausch lit a stale cigarette, he drew in, and blue smoke curled from his nostrils. The radio crackled one final time.

"Yeah, we got it all. The trucks are full. Exfil to base, time now."

Jonas scratched his head. "What's he talking about? Are they taking stuff back with them? Supplies? More men?"

"One-one out."

The transmission faded, and the radio went dead. Rausch shrugged.

"I picked up the first skip late yesterday. Been listening to shit go bad, like real bad. But I can't say how exactly, only hearing one side of it."

"Shit's been bad for two weeks now," Chad said, sounding almost offended that Rausch had only just noticed.

Jonas straightened his back. A couple of discs cracked loudly in the confined space.

"Brad, I know we're looking at bugging out in a month or so when the food's nearly gone, but I reckon you might want to get the vehicles ready to go as soon as you can."

Rausch made a *'How come?'* face.

"If it's desperate enough down in the city that civilians are willing to get into it with the army, and the army is pulling pack to barracks..."

"Fort Lewis probably," Rausch supplied.

"Whatevs," Jonas said. "But let's say they've either given up on holding the city together or, more likely, they got orders to just save what they can of their own shit. We're gonna start seeing big numbers coming up the range again. It's tapered off the last few days. Lot of people are already dead. But these new ones won't be like the first waves of refugees. These will be the survivor types. Type of motherfuckers aren't frightened of throwing down with heavily armed soldiers."

"I get you," Rausch nodded.

"Yeah," Jonas mused. "I wonder if anyone else will?"

12

THE HEADREACH CUT OFF

Everybody moved at the same time. Karl had insisted they practice. Jodi ran to the stern, scooping her son up and hurrying him away below decks. Damo punched the starter motor into life and fed revs into the *Reef's* powerful engines. Twin fantails of water erupted from the water line at the rear of the vessel, and *Lasseter's Reef* lurched forward, throwing everybody a little off balance. Damo hunched over the controls, every muscle in his back feeling as though it might spasm. He was exposed, directly in the line of fire.

Ellie and Karl grabbed two shotguns from the wheelhouse and hurried to the transom, each of them crouching out of sight. Damo swore as he heard the first crackling reports of gunfire. He turned to look over his shoulder quickly and swore again when he saw the other vessel driving directly at them, throwing off dirty great bow waves as it gained on them. Three men lay on the forward deck, all of them firing rifles. Bullets cracked and whispered past. A few rounds struck home, chewing through fibreglass, shattering a running light, and ricocheting of metalwork.

The lake was in turmoil. Dozens of watercraft suddenly on the move, like frightened beasts on the African veldt, all trying to flee the

sudden predator. He heard a few answering shots, but not from Ellie
or Karl. They remained hunkered down low, as Karl had taught them.
The shotguns they carried were excellent weapons. Damo could
afford the best. But they were not good at range, and neither Ellie nor
Karl were firing from a stable platform.

He pulled the wheel around to the left and then to the right.

"Port and starboard, fuckwit," Damo cursed to himself. "You're on
a boat now. It's port and fucking starboard."

Either way, he knew not to run in a straight line. Every turn, every
random tack, every unpredictable move made it harder for the
gunmen to get a line on the Reef.

Damo had one advantage. He'd been here for a week and a half.
He knew the waters. Driving hard for a channel he knew to be
bounded by a sandbank, he tried to forget about the bullets flying at
him from behind, concentrating instead on not running aground or
ramming into one of the slower, smaller vessels scattering all over the
Tract.

There was still no answering fire from Kyle or Ellie, but that was
all good. They would just be wasting ammunition at this point and
letting the pirates know that the Reef was defended.

Fucking pirates!

Hard to believe except for everything that'd happened the last
week or so. And it wasn't as though he'd never dealt with anything
like this before. Mining for copper and gold, especially in some of the
places he'd worked, was a dangerous, maverick industry with few
rules or constraints beyond those imposed by the ultimate law: profit
and loss. He'd never had to run from pirates before, but he'd dealt
with bandits, militia, warlords and mercenaries all over Africa. It was
why he could afford a boat like the *Lasseter's Reef*.

Jodi reappeared from below, holding his pistol.

"They're going to catch us," she cried out over the noise of the
engine.

"That's the idea," Damo said. "You should take that below. Look
after Maxi. Shoot anyone who comes through the door and looks like
they need it."

Jodi shook her head in vigorous denial. They'd already had this conversation. Many times. She insisted she couldn't hurt anybody like that, and when she got distraught at Damo for gently suggesting she might have to, to protect Max, he let it drop. She had Ellie, of course. And Damo knew for a sure thing that Ellie Jabbarah could put a man down, so he never got up again. But he also suspected that if it came down to it, Jodi Sarjanen would do whatever it took to protect her kid, too.

"Hold on then, Jodes," he shouted as he threw the wheel around to negotiate the curve of the sandbank he hoped was there.

He gritted his teeth as he felt the keel scrape over the soft bottom, then exhaled when they made deep water on the other side.

"They still coming straight at us?" He shouted.

"Yes," Jodi called back.

"Good."

But the manoeuvre didn't work. He had hoped the pursuing craft would bottom out on the sandbank. It didn't. There was a titanic THUMP as they struck the sand bar, but they had enough speed to clear it anyway, crashing down on the far side with a hollow, liquid boom.

"Fuck me purple," Damo roared in frustration. He'd really fucking hoped that would end the chase. But now these cunts had gained a few more yards and would soon draw level with the *Reef* in the long curving channel that led away into the more difficult narrows of the Headreach Cut-Off.

The men had stopped firing now. But that wasn't necessarily a good thing. They'd seen Jodi, and they might have wanted to take her captive. Two of them had climbed to their feet and were getting ready to throw grappling hooks.

"You better give me that roscoe then, Jodes, and get yourself down below. It's about to get a little fuckin' sporty up here, mate," Damo said. He cut back power to the engine, losing speed and returning to a more predictable course.

"Hand me that towel too, would you?" he said to Jodi, who had not returned below decks or handed over his gun. She was staring wide-eyed at the jet boat, which had closed to within a few feet of the Reef.

Karl and Ellie remained crouched out of sight, clutching tightly to their weapons.

"Jodi, the towel. I can't reach it."

"Sorry," she said, grabbing the white cloth.

It was more grey than white. But it would do in a pinch. He took it and waved it over his head where the men could see. A white flag. Surrender.

They cheered. The pair with the grappling hooks launched them, and they landed on the back of Damo's boat with a teeth-rattling crash. Funny to think that just two weeks ago, he'd have been really bloody upset at the damage to his paintwork. He felt nothing about it now. They were close enough for him to make out individual faces and details.

They looked hard.

Again, Damian Moloney had worked in some of the worst places in the world. He was used to dealing with hard men. He recognised them when he saw them. And he knew that if you were going to cross them, you did it fast, and you made sure they couldn't come back at you. Ever.

The man at the wheel of the pursuit boat gestured to him to shut down his engines. Instead, he idled them, and the Reef slowed, starting to drift. It was enough. The two men hauling them in with the grappling hooks were joined by two more, both of them packing what looked like military weapons. The sort of thing that could hose down Damo's boat with hundreds of rounds in a couple of seconds. He could feel Jody's terror coming off her in waves.

"Steady on there, Jodes. Keep it sweet. Show them your pretty smile. In fact, why don't you walk out there where they can get a good look at you?"

She started to move towards the stern, but he stopped her with a gentle hand on her elbow.

"Better leave the gun here, Darlin'. Just put it at your feet. No sudden moves."

She was shaking, but she did as he told her.

"When it starts, you drop to the deck as quickly as you can, okay?" Damo said quietly.

"When what..."

The two vessels thumped into each other, and all four men standing at the bow of the other boat started to crabwalk forward, meaning to jump across.

"NOW!" Damo roared.

Ellie and Karl stood, each racking a round into the chamber of their shotguns as they did so. The boarding party seemed genuinely surprised. One of them even threw up his hands. Another, one of the men with an assault rifle, tried to raise it. Karl got off three shots in the time Ellie squeezed out two.

The one man they didn't cut down with gunfire was the pilot of the vessel. He dived over the side of the boat and started swimming for shore.

Karl covered the bodies of the other men while Ellie threw off the grappling hooks.

One of the bodies rolled into the water. None of the others moved.

"Jesus, Damo. What did we just do?" Jodi said, her voice shaking.

"Better them than us, mate," he said before calling back to Karl, "Are we clear back there?"

Karl gave him a thumbs up, and Damo fed a little power back into the engines, moving them clear of the drifting vessel.

"You better go look after Max," Damo said. "Poor little bugger is probably pissing his pants down there."

13

INTERLUDE

Lucy Harkins scanned the darkened seas with a powerful pair of binoculars; now and then, she would lower her PVS-14 monocular for a look around as well. The Commander had ordered a double deck watch; the fire-shot night was alive with malign intent. Her ship, the *USS John Paul Jones*, was slowly cruising between Long Beach and Catalina Island. Their mission was fucked-up; they were to intercept any threats from the People's Liberation Army Navy. The Arleigh Burke-class destroyer was the best that could be managed in a very compressed time frame, but they would throw themselves between Los Angeles and whatever appeared over the horizon.

She shook her head as she looked around once more. The shore was alight with fires and occasional tracer fire; it looked more like Yemen or some other dump than anywhere in the US should. At this rate, she thought, there wouldn't be much left to defend. The city seemed to be tearing itself apart; she was too far out to hear much, but her mind filled in the explosions and the rattle and pop of gunfire.

Lucy's job was complicated by hordes of yachts, sailboats, and anything that would float. The piloting skill of the various watercraft reflected the eclectic mix on the water; some ships stayed carefully out of the destroyer's way. Others seemed not to notice her at all. For those that got too close, there was a spotlight, followed by warning flares and finally, warning shots. The Rules of Engagement were clear; a ship that was perceived to be a threat would be fired upon. No second chances.

Everyone remembered the *USS Cole*. As she played her binoculars over the far shore, she shuddered. It must be pure hell in LA, she thought. A speedboat sped vaguely in the *Jones's* direction to starboard; she keyed her radio.

"Oscar, this is Watch Five."

The officer answered. "Send it, Five."

"Be advised, speedboat to starboard, eight hundred meters."

"Roger, we are tracking."

"Five out."

She could hear the M242 25mm Bushmaster behind her whining as it tracked the boat. Before anyone so much as hit the speedboat with the spotlight, however, she veered off. Lucy let out a breath. This was hairy as shit, she thought. People were gonna get themselves killed out here. Lucy wondered how the wider war was going; she wondered about friends who were stationed out at Pearl. They had to be going nuts out there, just like 1941.

Lord knew there was plenty of panic on board, she thought. The *Jones* had been dispatched with haste from San Diego. The mission brief had been terse, rushed. The crew had been preparing for yet another deployment cycle, so at least they were at full strength, unlike some ships sent forth with haste from the USN's main west coast base.

And now they were here, defending a riot-torn Los Angeles from a real-world Chinese attack. Supposedly.

Lucy spotted something odd through her binos, but the flickering shadows of the coastline were messing with her ability to see what exactly it was. She lowered the binoculars and hit the lever on the NVGs.

She saw a greenish-grey, slightly grainy nightscape with some flaring light sources, appearing as fuzzy, glaring white dots in her field of view. One obscured what she wanted to look at, so her night vision was worthless as well. She knew there was something out there, though. Something small, moving slowly. She lifted her Harris radio again and pressed the ribbed call button.

"Oscar, this is Watch Five."

"Go ahead, Five." The words were clipped. Terse. Lucy wondered how many of these calls he was fielding.

"I've got something at maybe four hundred meters, starboard, about three o'clock. Can you see anything with thermals?"

"Give me a minute, Five."

Lucy said nothing. She waited, peering into the flickering dark. Something was out there. She knew it for sure. The seconds ticked by.

"Looks like a rowboat of some sort, with four souls aboard." A pause. "Good eye, Five."

"Roger, Oscar." Lucy flipped up her night vision. It wouldn't do to look at the target with NVGs when the spotlight came on. She was just in time, as the powerful light speared through the darkness like a laser. It searched the waves for a moment, then fixed its target. Lucy could see the little boat clearly. She could see its occupants, too. Looked like a man and two kids; they were waving frantically and pointing at something. Something in the boat that Lucy couldn't see. What was it? These people didn't look like a threat, but maybe the suicide bombers who attacked the Cole didn't, either. The man started to row furiously toward the bobbing destroyer, and through her binos, Lucy could see his determined grimace. They were damn good binoculars, a pair of Steiners with a reticule. Lucy imagined that she could hear the man pant as he heaved on the oars. What the hell, she wondered, would bring a man to risk the sea at night in a row boat? Hell, with the chop, it was a miracle that he'd made it out this far. She shook her head. The rowboat kept moving, inching in the destroyer's direction.

He was within three hundred meters when someone aboard fired a flare. Lucy scanned her sector and then returned to the rowboat; it continued to come. Slowly but steadily, the man pulling on the oars was making headway.

Lucy knew the next step was a loud hail and warning shots. Her radio crackled.

"Five, this is Oscar. You watching that boat?"

"Yes, Oscar."

"Is it a threat?"

Lucy's armpits tingled as they pumped out cold sweat. Her mouth went dry. She keyed the radio.

"Probably not, Oscar."

"Yes or no, Five."

She needed to pee. Lucy took a deep breath. What if that dinghy was packed with explosives? Did that man look Asian? So what if he did? And she thought of those kids. The Bushmaster would turn them into so much loose meat. There was no time. The boat was getting closer. She keyed the mic.

"No, Oscar." She let out a breath. Whatever happened, it was her responsibility.

"Roger, Five."

As the *Jones* searched the sky for ballistic missiles, the little boat approached. Lucy saw Marines covering the rowboat with a machine gun and rifles. Someone hailed them with a megaphone, but she was too far away to hear the response. The man at the oars looked weary unto death. Lucy could finally see down into the rowboat: there was a woman, her torso stained with blood, lying at the bottom.

What the fuck was happening ashore?

Lucy squared her shoulders and maintained her vigil. She had made the right decision.

She wiped her sweaty palms on her dungarees.

But the night was still young.

JENNIFER HADN'T MINDED her transfer to the ICU. Floor nurses generally had a low opinion of the life: demanding doctors, families insane with fear, and the constant life-and-death demands at every moment. There was a high turnover rate from burnout, but that's exactly why Jennifer didn't mind. She burned out on the hypochondriacs in the outpatient clinic. A shift in the ICU was never dull. This is what she had gone to nursing school for.

Even the set-up of the Mercy General unit had impressed her. A central station surrounded by six glass-enclosed bays so the two nurses on duty could see everyone at once. You could almost run things without moving from the station, seeing that everything that happened with the patients was displayed in real-time on the station's screens. Even ventilators and IV drips were wired for remote control from the station. Bay Central was at the cutting edge of tech. Someone still had to go in and check on the patients, but really, it was the tech that made the staffing ratio work. That's why everything was going so wrong.

They told her that Sacramento was different. It was protected now, a stronghold city. There weren't just Marines and Army guys everywhere. Doctor Volker, who was an Army Reserve Colonel, told Doctor Ludgrove on the Board that the Cyber Command had even moved units into the city. The shit that happened everywhere else would not be happening here.

Except it was, and to Jennifer's patients.

Mrs Castile was 82 and vent-dependent. She would only be able to breathe on her own again if the pulmonary swelling from her pneumonia lessened. Then they could wake her from the medically induced coma she needed to be in on the vent. In the old days, it was unheard of to go to such lengths at Mrs Castile's age, but she had still been playing tennis every week before she got a chest infection that went bad. Her immune system couldn't fight it off, and she hadn't sought help until she was pretty ill. Her family was lovely, still visiting every day, even after they'd been assigned to work gangs. And always brought flowers and even cookies for the staff.

The cookies were appreciated because of the rationing.

So the vent was keeping Mrs Castile alive. But the vent wasn't working any more.

An hour after Jennifer's shift started, the four ventilators currently serving six patients had started to glitch. The computer system was supposed to control the rate, gas mix and pressure. Once you set the vents, they ran by themselves, protecting the patients from too much pressure on their lungs. But now the computers were acting up. Alarms tried, warning that the pressure was spiking. Jennifer, as the lead on shift, had no choice but to turn them off and manually bag the patients. That, of course, was why, instead of two nurses and four aids staffing the unit, there were currently three people in each of the four vent-dependent bays.

She had pulled staff from the emergency department, which was now calling them back. Administrators were on the phones trying to get more staff in, but Jennifer needed those spare hands now.

They told everyone that Sacramento was different.

This place was supposed to be safe.

Mrs Castille's heart rate monitor started to ping an alert.

"Cardiac arrest!" Nurse Tabbard cried out.

Jennifer moved.

There was no time to wonder whether the computer was glitching or if it might be something worse.

She had a patient to save.

DANTE PHELPS HATED HIS SHOES. They had seemed like a good choice when he started his trek; they were a stylish but comfortable-seeming pair of basketball trainers with red accents. Now, they chafed his heels with every step. The blisters on the bottoms of his feet squished and burned as well, but he couldn't stop.

Not if he valued his life; that much was clear. Those who stopped lay all around him. And they wouldn't be getting up again. An old woman with an oxygen tank. A hugely fat man, his face grey and featureless in death. A young mother with a gaping, ugly gunshot wound, her children screaming beside her body.

There was a carpet of corpses strewn between, and sometimes under, all the tightly packed, stopped cars on the US 87 through Yonkers. They were stinking, bloating: the broad highway was a sunny charnel house.

Twenty-four hours ago, he'd never seen a gunshot wound. But during his escape from his stuffy and waterless apartment in Corona,

Queens, Dante had seen a battle's worth. In a city where gun ownership was supposed to be tightly controlled, he'd seen way too many of them.

The route to the RFK bridge had been absolutely packed with people when he decided to leave. It was like New Year's but murderously worse. The only police he saw were dead, and with all the fires burning out of control, he thought the firemen must be gone, too. One wise decision he had made was to climb up on the rails and use the Hell Gate Bridge to cross over the East River. Thinking back, that had probably saved his life. For now.

He heard another gunshot, then a flurry of them. He ducked behind a car and hurried forward, his eyes stung with the black, acrid smoke that hung like a funeral pall over the highway leading north. Dante wore nothing but a checkered short-sleeved shirt and a pair of Tsubi jeans; he wished he had a flak jacket. He clutched his precious half-full bottle of Evian in his hand, his two chocolate-chip Clif bars squished in his pocket. Someone had stolen his daypack with its precious, if meagre, supply of organic quinoa protein balls hours before.

Dante was breathing fast, almost panting. His mouth was dry. He looked along the highway for some sign of the shooter or shooters, but he couldn't see anything. Please, God, he thought, let me get away from here. I don't want anything but to get out to the country and get some food.

As he crouched and rushed forward, he had the vague mental image of a black and white cow, like the ones pictured on milk cartons. The cows always seemed to be smiling, eager to be used as food.

Dante sure wasn't smiling. He swore if he lived through this, he would never smile again. He kept moving forward. His body tensed for the bullet that would strike home with a whisper, a curious noise he had heard for the first time that morning. In the crowds, the bullets never missed. Someone always seemed to get hit. They would fall underfoot and be smashed to a pulp by the human tide.

He was crushing a child's body at that exact moment, in fact. He felt a squishy feeling, like stepping on a crunchy water balloon. He made the mistake of looking down. Dante moaned. His shoe was planted firmly on the child's ribcage, and filth leaked from her dead mouth.

Oh God, oh God, oh fucking God, he thought.

A bullet plinked into the car beside him.

Dante made his shoes move.

14

INSTAGRAM BALLER PIRATES

Damo was saying something, but Ellie Jabbarah wasn't really listening.

She'd just killed a man. Maybe two.

She'd sure as shit pulled the trigger on at least one of them. But everything happened so fast. And Karl had been standing right next to her, blasting away, and the bodies had been coming apart and dropping hard...

"We really gotta move now," Damo said.

Ellie shook her head, trying to escape the fugue state that was stealing over her.

Am I in shock?

"Hey, baby? You did good. I was so proud," Jodi cooed, wrapping her arms around Ellie and squeezing, but not too hard.

"You okay, El? You need a moment, mate?" Damo asked.

Why was everyone talking to her like she was a child?

She looked for Maxi. He might know. But he was nowhere to be seen. The sun glinted fiercely off the waters of the Tract. Silver bursts of light exploded from the polished chrome trim of the pirate boat, which was connected to Damo's by a bright orange rope.

Ellie frowned. She thought she had cut the lines to the speedboat.

"We should get in out of the sun," Karl said. "Miss Ellie, she looks a little pale to me. It's a helluva thing, killing a fella. Even if he was trying to kill you."

"I'm fine," Ellie said, struggling to find her voice. "I'll be fine."

She had done more harrowing days than this. She would do harder ones yet.

The other boat, still draped with dead bodies, all of them leaking blood into the water, bumped up against the stern of the *Lassiter's Reef*.

"We should put a little distance between us and these arse clowns," Damo said.

"You don't want to check their boat for salvage?" Karl asked him. "Maybe siphon their fuel?"

Damo seemed to consider the question seriously, but then he looked at Ellie. He wasn't sure what he saw in her eyes, but he shook his head. "We can always come back later, clean up then. Come on, let's get out of the sun. And out of here."

"No," Ellie said, forcing her voice out through numb lips. "Check their boat. Strip it for anything useful. Weapons, ammo, food, fuel. Take it all. They'd have done the same to us."

"You sure?" Damo asked, frowning.

She nodded, and Jodi hugged her again.

Karl and Damo were twenty minutes ransacking the other vessel, and half of that was taken up with Karl siphoning as much of their fuel as he could. They left the bodies and took everything they could transfer. It wasn't much compared to what they had on the Reef. But Ellie supposed that explained why these guys had come at them. They were jackals.

Jodi kept a lookout while they made the transfer. Ellie, who was possessed of a ropey, tenacious strength, helped Damo and Karl loot the other vessel. She noted with a sort of dull surprise that they had a lot of primo shit in crates and boxes. Jars of caviar. Tins of cassoulet. A fucking case of Veuve Clicquot. These guys were like Instagram baller pirates.

But of course, she thought.

That was the sort of shit Damo had in his storeroom.

These mopes had been hitting luxury yachts all over the Bay and probably up and down the coast.

That's why they looked so well-fed.

Or why they *had* looked so well fed.

Now they were just fucking dead.

The salvage piled up at the transom of the *Reef*. A lot more than she had first thought. She was already thinking in terms of nutrient stacks, by how many calories for how many people they had just fattened up the margins of their survival math.

It helped. Meant she didn't have to think about what she'd just done.

"You good, Miss Ellie?"

"Huh?"

That was Karl.

He threw off the line, still holding them to the other vessel, and waved up at Damo in the wheelhouse.

"Good to go, chief."

The deck thrummed beneath their feet as Damo spooled up the engines.

She felt better as they moved away from the scene of the...

What was it? A killing? Murder?

No, it was self-defence, Ellie assured herself. Those assholes shot first. They came at her Jodes and little Maxi, meaning to do them harm.

"Miss Ellie. You should sit down in the shade. Have some water. Seriously."

Karl again.

"What?" she said.

He made a face at her. Pointed at himself.

"Miss Ellie. Look at my serious face. Listen to my serious voice. You've had a real shock here. It'll pass. I promise you that. You're tough. I rarely seen anyone with more grit than you. But we all got only so much as we got, and you need to give yourself a rest now."

"You're right," she admitted. "Some cold water would be nice."

"Maxi!" Karl called out. "Where's that water for your other mom?"

The boy appeared with a bottle of Perrier. It was chilled and beaded with condensation.

"I put a lemon in. Like a chef!" Max announced as he proudly handed it to her.

Ellie laughed. A nervous, ragged sound. But a real laugh nonetheless.

She rubbed the boy's head and climbed up the steps to the open bridge, where she sat on one of the padded leather stools, gratefully drinking the icy cold water. Jodi came and draped her arms around Ellie's shoulders again, but it was hot, and Ellie felt sticky and uncomfortable. She also worried that she was covered in blowback from the shotgun blast. She eased her girlfriend loose and said quietly, "I'm okay, baby. I just need to sit by myself. Also, I'm fucking gross. I need a shower."

Jodi kissed her temple but backed off.

"I'm so proud of you. Maxi, too."

"You done real good," Karl affirmed.

Ellie looked at him.

"Karl. You told us you were a driver in the army. But you... you..." She was lost, looking for the right words.

"Ain't the first time I been shot at or had to shoot another, Miss Ellie," he testified.

It sounded just like that, too. As though he'd put his hand on a bible to deliver a sworn oath.

"Got ambushed four times in Iraq. And once in Utah! That was a whole thing, let me tell you."

The expression of astonishment freshly remembered upon his face was so real she laughed out loud. And with that laughter, a stoppage somewhere between her heart and her soul unblocked, and before Ellie Jabbarah could get hold of her feelings, they erupted from within. A sudden and furious outpouring of tears and great gulping draughts of air and cruel, bitter laughter at the madness of having survived a for-fucking-real fight to the death, and more tears and hugs from Ellie and Max, and a firm squeeze of the old shoulder by Karl, and a "You right, mate?" from Damo up at the wheel.

A few minutes of that, and she was done with being fucked up by everything she'd been forced to do.

"I'm right, Damo," she said. And she did not lie.

Because those men had made her kill them.

Damo cut the motor back as they left the narrows behind them and entered a confluence of at least three riverine systems. It was so confusing in the Delta. Ellie had no idea how he managed to keep track of it all.

She wiped the last of her tears away and promised herself she would not lose it again. Ever. She could see some of the other vessels far across the water, much further away than they had been earlier that morning. It had all changed so quickly. They had settled into something of a rhythm here. Alternating watches. Fishing off the back of the boat. Even swimming occasionally. It had been quiet. Pleasant. But, of course, it couldn't last.

"So I reckon that fuckin' tears it," Damo said. "Dunno where those fuckwits came from. Dunno why they chose us..."

"Cos we were the best and biggest target," Karl suggested.

"I guess they liked nice things," Ellie said, pointing to the salvage they had taken from the dead men's boat.

"Yeah, I guess so," Damo conceded with a shrug. "But they won't be the last. It's been a week or so since the sticky fucking faecal matter hit the rotational air cooling device. And there's no sign it's getting any better. People must be bloody desperate by now."

All four adults stood on the flying bridge. Ellie was spotted with blood, but not her own. Karl looked super chill, sitting directly across from her, behind a pair of Damo's mirrored shades, still cradling his shotgun. Jodi hovered nearby, tending to Maxi, who was begging to hear stories of the pirates and how they had beaten them.

Damo kept them in the middle of the channel, feeding a little power to the engines now and then, adjusting the wheel to hold their station.

"It's not a good look," he said. "Those blokes just sailed in here, had a look around, and decided they'd have a red-hot go. Fuck that for a game of two-up. Tells you everything you need to know about what's been happening back in the city. Cos that's where I reckon they came from. They looked pretty fucking well-fed to me. And pretty bloody sure of themselves, too. They probably been pulling this stunt or something like it since everything turned to custard. So we need to make some choices and be fuckin' sharpish about it."

"You should do what you think is best, Damo," Jodi said.

"What about you, Karl? What you reckon?" he asked.

Karl Valentine shook his head.

"I'm just grateful to be here, Damo," he said. "Was nothing good happening when we left town. Looks like it got a lot worse."

Frustrated by that non-answer, Damo threw his hands in the air.

"Mate, I want to know what you think we should do. I want everybody to tell me what they *think* we should do. I'm not the captain of this ship. All right. Get it through your thick fucking skulls. I'm just the bloke who wrote a big fucking check for an orgy boat a long time ago. And to be honest, I never had any fucking orgies worth writing home about, and now that I can't write any more cheques to make my problems go away, I've got no fucking idea what to do about them. So I'm asking you, Karl, all of you, what do you think we should do?"

It was Jodi who spoke, surprising everyone. She was the least assertive among them, the most likely to keep her mouth shut in any discussion. Mostly, she took care of Max and looked after Ellie, who had stepped up to keep them safe. They all took turns standing watch. But Ellie, as she had just proven, was willing and able to stand up with Damo and Karl if it came to a fight.

"I think..." Jodi started. She stopped and seemed to search for the words. "I think you're probably right, Damien. Those men thought they could just come in here and take whatever they wanted, and that's what it's like everywhere now, I bet. They're just like that guy who mugged me for my camera. And they won't be the only ones. There's a lot of men like that. They make it bad for everyone."

Nobody said anything for a moment. Eventually, Karl broke the silence.

"That's usually how it goes," he said, with no further explanation.

"What about you, Ellie," Damo asked. "You think we should stay here, try to get back out through the Bay, maybe head up or down the coast, or what..."

She cut him off. The shock she'd felt earlier, and the guilt that rode in behind it, that was gone now. Washed away by that flash flood of tears. This was just like handling Damo when they overbooked lunch and had rumours of a *Gourmet Traveller* writer spooking about.

"You had a plan, Damo. We hit a roadblock, that's all. We couldn't get upriver. Into Sacramento, or past it or whatever. But that was more than a week ago. Things have changed. Probably got much worse, like Jodi and Karl said. Maybe nobody's even guarding the port anymore. But we won't know unless we head up to Sacramento and find out. Let's try that."

Damo weighed it up, speaking slowly. "They still have a working government up there," he said. "Got that stronghold thing going for them."

"Well, that can go either way, I imagine," Karl said.

"They weren't letting anybody in before," Damo said. "Don't know why that'd be different now."

The breeze, which had been wafting across the lake all morning, stiffened, drying the sweat on Ellie's skin. She blinked away a strobing image of the one man she knew for sure she had killed.

Fuck him.

"They're not letting people in," Jodi said. "But I'll bet they're letting them out."

Everybody turned to her.

"What do you mean, Miss Jodi?" Karl Valentine asked.

"I mean, if they're short of food like everyone else, I'm sure they would be grateful if we offered to take some people with us. You know, to Damo's farm."

The big Australian looked at her as though she was nuts, but then his expression changed.

"Shit, mate," he said. "You might be right."

15

CREAM OF GROUNDHOG STEW

Tammy wasn't sure how many times they'd broken camp after that crazy shit in Ohio, but it seemed to her that they'd been on the road for an eternity, and now they were so close... but Elkins might as well be on the far side of the moon, as far as she was concerned.

She stared at the Rand McNally again, ignoring the bloodstains which always made her a little queasy. They'd scavenged the precious road atlas from the wreckage of a massive pile-up on a backroad an hour out of North Georgetown. No earthly reason she could figure out why seven cars would just decide to drive into each other like that. But it had thrown a lot of stuff clear of the impact, and the road map book had been only a small part of their haul.

That was days ago, though, and they'd run out of the food they'd salvaged. Things were getting tight again.

"Gotta be a back road around Dryfork, a way we could get into Elkins from the side," she muttered to herself.

Roxy was leaned up against the car next to her, watching the kids play on an old tire swing hanging from a tree in the front yard of a farmhouse. There was no prospect of anyone from the homestead taking offence to them pulling into their patch. It had burned down some time ago. Smoke still curled up slow and lazy from the embers.

"That book ain't so good at the little roads as the big ones," Roxarne said.

Tammy blew out her cheeks.

"Yeah, but we can't use the big ones no more. Man, I really fucking miss the GPS," she said. "Ain't no getting past that roadblock at Dryfork, and our gas is pretty much just fumes now."

It was their third tank, and it had cost her most of what was left of their cash. To think they'd ever dreamed of going all the way to Canada.

The two families had spent more than a week and a half trying to reach Roxy's people, and Tammy was determined that a bunch of hilljack assholes hiding behind some thrift store barricade weren't going to stop her. If they had to, they would ditch the Olds and hike to Elkins, but only if they had to.

At least it seemed the heat of summer was behind them. The hundred-plus days they'd endured back in Dillonvale were a lousy memory, and the mercury mostly now hovered around a very pleasant eighty or so. Maybe it was because of all the factories that shut down, Tammy thought. They stayed the hell away from the main roads and big cities now, of course. Only a fucking idiot would venture out where millions of other idiots had already brought themselves to a bad end. And tracing a long and wandering route north through the backcountry had, in a way, been the adventure she'd promised the children.

They slept out under the stars most nights, with Rox and Tammy taking turns to stand guard. Even Bobby Jr had volunteered to stand a watch, but proud as Tammy was of him, she wasn't about to entrust their safety to a twelve-year-old boy. And she sure as hell wasn't about to hand over the pistol to him neither.

They'd recovered the gun, which looked to her like an old-fashioned police revolver, from the same place they got the road atlas. That massive pile-up outside of Georgetown. It was in the glovebox of a little two-door that'd been crushed between a big-ass pick-up and a Volvo SUV. It was Tammy who searched the car because the owner was still wedged in behind the steering wheel, and she had been there some time. The poor woman—Tammy was almost certain it was a woman—had been on the hefty side when she was alive, but in death, she was enormous. A giant, bloated balloon of flesh, swollen, taut and fit to burst.

That wasn't the sort of thing would normally invite a close inspection, and they had indeed kept all the children well back from the wreckage. But supplies were tight, and for an honest to goddamn miracle, none of those vehicles had burned. Probably cos they were as low on gas as the Oldsmobile. So there could be road food. Twinkies or even Pop-Tarts. It would have been rank foolishness not to check for stuff they could salvage. Their carefully hoarded stash was running low. What she would not do for a fishing pole and some lures, she thought. Or a .22 rifle for squirrels.

Tammy had been sure of finding food in the dead woman's ride. She looked to have been the type to drive and snack. But instead of the potato chips or melted chocolate bars, she prayed she might find, the woman's glove box gave up the revolver. It only had four bullets, but even so, Tammy felt a whole helluva lot better to have the protection.

"We could maybe try going through that big park there," Roxy suggested, pointing at a large green chunk of the map.

"The Canaan Valley Wildlife Refuge," Tammy read out.

She recognised 'Canaan' as a Sunday School word. Sort of place the Pharaohs or Israelites hung out back in the day.

"If there's wildlife, maybe we could shoot a deer or something," Roxy said hopefully.

"Maybe," Tammy said cautiously. "Or maybe the place would already be full of people camping out and shooting deer and maybe shooting each other by now."

It was so hard to know what to do.

"Hey!" Roxarne said suddenly. "If it's a national park, there could be rangers there. And they got to help people. It's their job, right?"

Tammy frowned, unconvinced. But, thinking about it, maybe Roxy did have a point. It had been some days since they'd seen anything like a policeman or a state trooper, and Tammy had gone from dreading such an encounter—even though they'd spent all the evidence of her grand larceny on fuel and food—to dreading the idea that she might never see another cop again.

What the fuck had happened to them?

"Well, I guess there would be camping facilities, like showers and stuff," she conceded. "And maybe a ranger place where they could give us directions and some fuel? We're just two women and four kids, and we're in some trouble here."

None of it sounded convincing as it came out, but she worked hard to convince herself anyway.

"I reckon we got enough gas to make it, and I can't see where else we could go."

"Then let's go," Rox said, settling it.

They wrangled the kids back into the Olds and pulled out onto the road again. Forty minutes later, the car coughing and dying, Tammy steered them into a road stop with a few picnic tables and a barbecue setting. They were out of gas and a good few miles short of the park proper.

But there was a water faucet, and so they made the best of it.

Roxy got a fire going with some twigs and junk the kids hunted up from around the site. Bobby Junior pitched the Dora tent, and Tammy took stock of their supplies. They had a packet of fig newtons, two bags of cheese and onion potato chips, some beef jerky and half a dozen of the mystery cans from under the sink back in Dillonvale.

It wasn't much, but Jakey and Wynona came running up to report that they had found a dead groundhog on the road, and it didn't even smell. Bobby Jr. was sent to investigate, brought the critter back and confirmed that it was indeed fresh roadkill. There weren't even ants yet. Tammy and Roxarne exchanged a look. Her friend shrugged and grinned.

"I ain't too proud."

None of them were.

Half an hour later, with the sun low in the west, Tammy looked around their little camp in something akin to wonder. The kids and Roxy had gotten really good at this. The older kids slowly added fuel to the barbecue until there was a decent little blaze going and a thick bed of coals building up. Two of the mystery cans had given up a pint of creamy mushroom soup, and Roxy broke down the fresh groundhog for a couple of fistfuls of clean meat. Gamey and tough, to be sure, but clean, she avowed.

Roxy was no Girl Scout. But her useless shitstain of an ex-partner had been a hunter, and she was used to dressing everything from squirrels to wild hogs. Tammy hoped the mushroom gravy would cover most of the taste. Roxy seared the groundhog bits in their precious five-quart camp pot, and for greens, they had cattail hearts and dandelions. Nothing great, but it was better than many folks were probably eating tonight. Times was damn tough, Tammy thought, as her mouth watered at the prospect of squashed varmint in tinned gravy.

As Tammy stood in the gloom watching Roxy cook, she prayed. But only to herself. She had never been one for happy clapping or anything. But she had been doing a lot of quiet praying to herself of late. Because if some miracle didn't happen soon, they would be on foot headed to Elkins, and a bad situation would get worse. Everything they owned would be on their backs or left behind.

Tammy heard the heavy motor lugging its way towards them before she saw the headlights in the dusk.

She and Roxy both froze.

"Shit, Tammy, should we run?"

"Where to?' Tammy shrugged. 'And we'd lose the food. I'll get the gun."

She fetched it from the car.

The kids instantly noticed the change in the mood of the grown-ups.

"Mommy, what's happening?" little Jakey asked, running to Roxarne.

"Ain't nothing, Jakey," she assured him.

Bobby Junior got to his feet and stared into the gloom. For a moment, he reminded Tammy of his father, achingly so. He had Robert's fiercely handsome profile when he stood, jut-jawed like that.

But those looks had not been good for much beyond trouble.

"Take it easy, Bobby," she warned. "In fact, you kids, get over by the car. Roxy and me will see to these folks."

Bobby led the other three little ones over to the Oldsmobile.

Both women watched as the vehicle came into view around the bend. It was a camper. Tammy let out a breath.

Maybe they were older folk, then.

But no, turned out it was just a very large camper with some stupidly fat guy at the wheel and some skinny dude riding shotgun.

The camper pulled in behind them, close enough that they'd have a hard time getting out, and the kids who had been half hiding in the car, abandoned it to run back to their moms.

As the children sheltered behind their guardians, Tammy stood with her hands on her hips. The gun was tucked into the small of her back. The groundhog stew was starting to boil.

The skinny one got out of the camper, and he was followed shortly by the fat fellow. It was the thin man who spoke first.

"Hey, don't mean to interrupt y'all. We just needed a place to park for the night."

Tammy replied. "Couldn't get by the roadblock by Dryfork?"

The man frowned.

"Nah, we ain't been that far yet, but thankee for lettin' us know." He smiled. "Cute kids."

Bobby Jr. spoke up. "Don't go askin' for our food 'cause we ain't got any extra."

"Bobby!" Tammy scolded, but without much heat in the scold.

He was right, though: the big fella looked like he could eat all of their stew and most of them before he was full.

The thin man put up his hands and grinned.

"I would not dream of such a thing."

His grin got wider.

"In fact, we would be pleased to dine with y'all if'n you would care to share some of our supplies. All we ask is good company. That ain't so easy to come by these days."

Tammy saw Roxy's eyes go narrow. These guys would want something else, for sure.

Her friend spoke quietly but firmly. "Maybe we could work something out."

The fat one smiled. He looked like a chunk of carved lard. He
called into the camper's door.

"Yo, Darrell, come on down. It's dinner time."

16

THE TINY WOODEN HAMMER OF POWER

The playing fields of Silverton had a name once. Mullan Park. Just over two hundred yards from end to end, the park was bounded on one side by a small, nameless rear lane that provided access for commercial deliveries to all the businesses on the northern half of Main Street. Carved out of a rare plot of level ground on the high side of town in 1861 and never developed for housing or commercial needs, the fields had endured as a public good thanks to the drawings of John Mullan Jr.

Explorer, soldier, civil servant and road builder, Mullan initially surveyed the site for the Northern Pacific Railroad, setting aside the tiny parcel of conveniently flat terrain for a railway goods yard that never materialized. Loggers built a camp and then a village in the space cleared by the railwaymen, who never returned to lay their track through the dense alpine forest. Over time, the park became a de facto commons, tended to by volunteers and used by all of Silverton's private clubs and school students for everything from kite-flying festivals to log-throwing competitions. In 1953, the State Supreme Court ruled that the land had been alienated from private ownership by 62 years of non-payment of local government charges. It was now the property of the County Council and, through that Council, of the people of Silverton.

As Jonas Murdoch, Chad Moffat and Brad Rausch drove into town through the Cascade Gate, towing a bullet-holed Jeep behind Rausch's truck, the once green and pleasant Mullan Park opened up to their right as a weird, almost medieval barrens tilled by bent-backed serfs in Nikes and baseball caps.

"Putting in the pumpkins today, I reckon," said Rausch as he manoeuvred the tow truck around the back of Doc Cornwell's surgery, the last business on the north side of Main. "Too late for that, you ask me. Not that nobody ever does, of course."

He punched the horn, scattering a work crew who'd been taking a break, leaning on their shovels. They hurried aside with scowls and muttered curse words, but Rausch had a free pass from the Emergency Committee, allowing him to drive through the fields – as long as he stuck to the flagged path leading out to the barricade, which sat about thirty yards in from the forest. The semicircular fortress wall of old cars and some new ones salvaged by Rausch enclosed the freshly planted fields, protecting them against intrusion or attack from the forest. It was a makeshift structure but impressive nonetheless, and it could not have been assembled without his help.

"I'll get out here," Jonas said when they were behind the County offices. He could see a small group gathered around a whiteboard, probably taking instructions from Jacques Loubert on where to plant their pumpkin seeds. Loubert wore a straw hat with a comically wide brim and stood on a wooden table to address the volunteers. As Jonas alighted from Rausch's truck, Loubert nodded to him, smiling in thanks for his earlier help with the generator.

Jonas winked back at the grinning idiot before turning to Rausch in the cab on the tow truck.

"I'll see about getting us some more gas and diesel," he said.

"Thanks. Diesel's the bigger problem," Rausch said. "Just so you know."

Jonas nodded and walked quickly past Loubert's group, and slipped into the County building through the rear entrance to the Sheriff's station, which adjoined it. He passed through Muller's squad room and into the County annex via a discreet doorway behind the reception counter.

Dale Juntii was the first person he saw in the crowded room.

Dale smiled in his weird, almost lipless way when he caught sight of Jonas.

"Murdoch," he said.

Jonas barely heard him over the uproar.

The connecting door from the sheriff's office opened into a large, featureless committee room that served as the meeting chamber for the County selectmen twice a month under normal circumstances. The current circumstances being about a thousand fucking miles from normal, the Council, rebooted with a couple of extra members as the Emergency Committee, met in here every day. Often more than once.

Jonas had parlayed his note-taking skills from the Florida bar into an occasional role taking, the minutes, a task which tended to fall to him when everything turned to shit. On those days, it was not unusual for the warring factions of the committee to draw on his proven skills as a mediator. Looked like he'd be taking some notes and mediating the shit out of this motherfucker today.

He almost smiled. Anything to add to the myth of his usefulness and indispensability.

Instead of letting his pleasure show for these blue pill fuckwits, however, Jonas furrowed his brows in theatrical concern. He caught sight of Selectwoman Bohenski across the room, and she gestured helplessly, all but imploring him to do something about the fight that had erupted between Darren O'Shannassy's faction and whoever was fronting for Dave Muller and Howard Wetsman today. The county Comptroller, Wetsman, did not like to inject himself into what he characterised as 'purely political contretemps'. Sheriff Muller had no such qualms, but he wasn't around. Muller made it his rule to walk the perimeter of the town at the change of shift for his deputies every day. No matter what. He was somewhere out on the edge of Silverton right now, checking on the defences and taking the temperature of the citizenry while he was at it.

He would totally put it like that, too. Sheriff Muller was a man who thought in terms of his 'responsibilities to the citizenry'.

The pompous asshole.

Still, Jonas hadn't slipped sideways into the complicated power structure of Silverton by openly taking sides. He was still here and still welcome because of his jailhouse facility for playing one faction against another and not getting caught at it.

"What's going on?" he asked Dale. The ex-marine rolled his eyes. Unlike Jonas, Dale was not one for subversion or deceit. He preferred to go right at a problem.

"Fucking same old shit for a brand new day," he said. "Forward defence or fortress Silverton."

Fuck me, Jonas thought. This bullshit had been rolling since day one. Just another way for Muller and O'Shannassy to have at each other.

"Got it," he said.

He strode forward through the milling crowd. Dozens of people had squeezed themselves into the room. Assholes should be out sowing their fucking crops or something. It was hot in the room, with no power to run the air-conditioning. The county offices did have solar panels and even a Tesla battery, but that precious supply of juice was strictly for first-order priorities, such as keeping the sheriff's office walkie-talkies charged and the town's dwindling supply of medications refrigerated.

The roaring mass of voices did not diminish much as he took his place next to the chairman's seat at the head of the meeting table. But they shut the fuck up once he started banging the gavel and yelling at everybody to be quiet. Howard Wetsman gave him a look that floated somewhere between relief and apprehension, and he heard Darren O'Shannassy's unmistakable growl cutting through under the receding tumult.

"It's about goddamn time."

Jonas banged the gavel another four or five times to establish that he was the boss of making all the noise around here, and once he sensed that he had control of the room, if only for a second, he projected his courtroom voice into the suspended commotion.

"Good morning to you all," he bellowed with bogus cheer. "I, for one, cannot wait to find out why everybody is in such a good mood today."

A small ripple of laughter circled the room, not loud and sounding more relieved than amused. Jonas held up the gavel, arranging his face in a lopsided grin.

"As you can see, I have the tiny wooden hammer of power..."

He paused, scanning the entire room, letting his grin grow wider, before speaking again, putting just a bit of grunt into his delivery.

"... And you do not."

A few more weak but appreciative chuckles. People were glad not to be in each other's faces for a moment. They were also, he knew, quietly pleased that somebody had stepped up and taken charge.

"So do not make me swing the tiny hammer in defence of Robert's Rules of Order and the dignity of this august chamber."

He got some genuine smiles at that as he gestured around the unremarkable meeting room with its spartan fit-out and bare walls. There were no windows, or picture of the president or photographs of old Silverton to break up the institutional sameness.

"Alrighty then. Everyone sit down who can sit down. Ladies and old-timers get first dibs, and let's try to do that without any pushing or shoving."

The room filled with the sounds of chairs scraping and banging together and the low mutter of people arranging themselves at last. There were far too many observers for everybody to have a seat, but most of the able-bodied men did move to the sides and back of the room, freeing up the limited seating for the older folks and a handful of moms with younger kids. Jonas took advantage of the moment to lean over to Howard Wetsman.

"Dude, let's get this party started. I'll take the minutes if you like."

The comptroller nodded gratefully. He had an RSI, which forced him to strap his right wrist when the pain flared up, and the wrist was wrapped in a dull, discoloured bandage this morning.

"So," Jonas boomed out in his courtroom voice, "Do we have an agenda?"

"We do, but there is an item without notice we need to discuss," Howard Wetsman replied.

Jonas looked to O'Shannassy to see if this was some kind of power play, but the store owner nodded brusquely. He, too, was in favour of ditching the agenda for whatever exciting new development had forced itself onto the docket.

"The chair recognises Comptroller Wetsman," he roared.

"Thank you," said Wetsman, almost sighing before gathering himself and going on in a much louder voice for the benefit of the whole room. "At four-thirty-five this morning, we received a communication by radio from Fort Lewis. The army units there have been ordered by the president to pull back into their barracks and to secure those facilities for the duration of the emergency."

The room exploded into turmoil, and Jonas had to hammer the gavel and roar "Quiet" a few times before things calmed down again. Wetsman thanked him and went on.

"We don't know whether this order was specific to Fort Lewis and Seattle or whether it was a general directive for the whole country."

"Doesn't matter," Darren O'Shannassy growled. Jonas cracked the gavel down, but only once.

"Sorry," O'Shannassy said.

"Mister O'Shannassy is correct in one sense," Howard Wetsman conceded. "What matters here is what happens here."

And here, Jonas thought, *it comes.*

"And we need to hunker down," a new voice boomed from the back of the room. "We're on our own now."

It was Sheriff Muller, back from his patrol.

JONAS ONLY NEEDED two heavy blows with the gavel to restore order to the room, which was a shame cos he was almost getting his wood on, banging away with that thing. But Sheriff Muller helped calm the room down with a quieter gesture, gently patting the air in front of him and repeating, "Settle down everyone, just settle down," as he made his way to the conference table. Jonas took command of the room before anybody else could.

"Howard," he asked, raising his voice. "You got any more details from the army guys? Any current information about the situation in the city? Maybe the military pulled back because the feds are getting things under control?"

Jonas didn't believe that for a second. Didn't want to believe it, truth be known. But he also knew he had to turn down the heat on this bubbling ass-casserole or risk a boiler. A simple query for more information was a good start, especially from Howard Wetsman. The county comptroller could make a three-way in a hot tub sound duller than a double math class on a high summer's morning.

Wetsman shook his head.

"I didn't take the call. That was Deputy..."

He looked to Muller for help.

"Deputy Treacy was monitoring the radio room," Muller said, projecting his voice to carry all the way to the back of the room. "Fort Lewis wasn't calling around for a deep and meaningful encounter group session," the Sheriff explained. "They were simply alerting all functioning state and local authorities that they would not be able to render further aid to the civil power. Bottom line, we have to look to our own defense."

The angry buzz that greeted that was completely bipartisan.

"Let's keep it nice, people," Jonas called out. "The Chair recognises Darren O'Shannassy, who looks fit to burst with his need to constructively contribute to the public discourse."

"We need to mobilise and meet this threat head-on," the store owner growled, and for him, that really was about as constructive a contribution to the public discourse as you could hope for. At least with Dave Muller on the opposite side of any argument.

Half the room moaned. The other half cheered. Howard Wetsman rolled his eyes, and Sheriff Muller grumbled, "What? You want to invade China, now?"

But only Jonas heard that. And maybe O'Shannassy himself.

"We don't need to hear any more about what's happening in Seattle or anywhere else," O'Shannassy said. "We know everything we need to know. The army's given up. We're gonna have a million starving survivors coming at us from the city. We can't hold out against those numbers. They will overrun us. We need to push out and meet them in the passes, where we can bottle them up. Hold them off."

The cheering finally overcame the groaning and booing. Jonas banged the gavel and was about to call on Sheriff Muller to reply, but the big man was already on his feet, patting the air with his hands again, putting noticeably more volume and power into his command voice this time.

"That's enough, that's enough, just settle down," he boomed out, and the hell of it was that they did. Until Muller spoke again.

"I agree with Mister O'Shannassy..."

The turmoil returned, this time as a tumbling roar of confusion.

Muller pitched his voice to be heard over the top of it.

"... Up to a point," he bellowed. "Up to a point. Now, hear me out."

Jonas banged the gavel. Muller gestured for quiet. And even Darren O'Shannassy waved at a couple of his more vocal supporters to shut up.

Selectwoman Bohenski leapt to her feet and pleaded with the room.

"Please, can't we just all be civil?"

O'Shannassy got back to his feet and bellowed, "Shut the fuck up. Everyone."

Gasps and hissing answered him, but the explosive outburst had the effect of stunning the worst of the yammering fools into silence. Gradually, the room stilled itself. It was appreciably hotter and stuffier than when Jonas had arrived, and when the din finally died away, he could hear the rustling of paper as some of the spectators tried to cool themselves with improvised fans.

"Sheriff," Jonas said, nodding at him to go on.

"Thanks. It seems things have not improved in the city," Muller said, "and likely will not improve any time soon."

A few of the fans fluttered with increased vigour. A few more fell still. Jonas watched Doc Cornwell at the end of the conference table, frowning at some of the more animated older folks in the audience.

She clutched at her medical bag, which she'd brought to every Emergency Committee since old Brian Pumfrey had keeled over from a heart attack in the second meeting while yelling at Leo Vaulk to stop acting like a damn Nazi.

"We might have a day to prepare," Muller went on. "Maybe more, possibly less. But prepare, we must. The last good information we had from Fort Lewis on conditions in Seattle was not encouraging. The army had secured a number of food wholesalers, but gridlock on the city's road networks badly disrupted all the evacuation plans. Most folks could not get their cars out. As you know, plenty tried walking. A lot did not make it up the hill."

Jonas scoffed at the euphemism. He'd ridden up more than a thousand feet of incline to reach Silverton by the end of that first day. He was young, fit and strong and even he'd had a tough time of it. Your average couch potato woulda gassed out after a couple of miles. Lots of them probably died of heat stroke and heart attacks on the road behind him, and he hadn't even known.

"We need to understand the scale of what's coming," Muller went on. "The population of the greater metropolitan area was just under four million as of two weeks ago. Fort Lewis, FEMA, and the city council agreed on a casualty count of a hundred to a hundred and fifty thousand in the first week of the crisis."

A murmur went around the room.

"Initially, that was all about road trauma, power failure, that sort of thing. The immediate death toll was large but not significant. Not what the Army calls significant, at least. A couple of thousand people died in motor vehicle accidents. Hundreds were trapped in high-rise elevators. Still are, but they're gone now too. No water, you see. Kills folk a lot quicker than starvation. Three or four days at most."

The room had gone completely silent. Muller's voice was low but steady.

"We've had some rain the last few days, of course. But not enough to make do when the power failed to the Public Utilities. We got access to the springs up in the hills. The city didn't. The taps going dry was when we got that first real big surge of refugees. The ones we tried to reroute via the Skagit hydropower access road."

More murmurs greeted that, and a darker elemental growl of people recalling the moment they realised everything was not just going to sort itself out.

"Yeah, and how'd that work out, Muller," O'Shannassy said, but in a low voice, so only a few people heard the comment. The Sheriff ignored him.

"Casualties down the hill piled up pretty quickly then," he said to the room. "Mostly from dehydration and exposure as folks tried to hike out of the city. Fort Lewis said they started taking their first casualties from urban pacification at the same time. Gunfights, basically. With the army, if you can believe it. Over food and water. And we seen some of that up here, too, with folks trying to break in through the cordon."

"Anyway, bottom line, ten days in and we got somewhere up over a hundred thousand dead in the greater metro area, and now there's more'n three and half million people not so far southwest of us, who just found out they are on their own. Mister O'Shannassy is right. At least some of them will be headed this way. But I don't believe we can meet them in the passes. There's not enough of us for an expeditionary group. Too many will get past any pickets we post, and too few of us would remain here to secure the cordon. We need to throw everything we got into hardening our defences at home."

Muller paused and looked directly at O'Shannassy.

"The Gates. The Wall," he said deliberately. "We will either hold them at our strongest point or not at all."

Darren O'Shannassy had had enough of listening politely. He jumped to his feet.

"Dave Muller is doing what he thinks best," he said, confusing a few of his supporters. "But he almost lost the town in the first week..."

The room erupted again; this time, it was Muller's people shouting down his old foe. Jonas pounded away with his little wooden hammer as the meeting fell into chaos.

Not his finest hour, he had to admit.

He was tempted to knock a few heads together, starting with Muller and O'Shannassy, but in the end, he didn't have to.

Howard Wetsman brought the meeting back to order.

Howard fucking Wetsman.

Can you even believe it?

The County Comptroller was talking with Deputy Milfull, who had come spooking in through the connecting door to the Sheriff's office. The two men leaned in close together and conferred in low voices as though the chaos around them wasn't happening.

Howard Wetsman surprised the hell out of Jonas by climbing onto his chair and then, with Deputy Milfull's help, onto the conference table around which the Emergency Committee had been sitting.

"Excuse me, excuse me," he said, waving his bandaged arm high.

"Oh Howard, do be careful," Doctor Cornwell cried out.

Jonas could barely hear them over the crowd, but the sight of the staid civil servant standing astride the agenda papers, his tasselled loafers very close to kicking over a water jar, was bizarre enough to quickly capture the attention of the whole room.

"Excuse me," Wetsman said again, a little louder and with more success this time.

The tumult died away.

"Deputy Milfull has just come from the Seattle Gate," he said. "A large group is demanding entrance to the town. They have weapons. They look like some sort of motorcycle gang."

17

BLOWBACK

"I can't believe you're telling us this."

Mel Baker's voice wavered somewhere between distress and outrage. Another unseasonably cool night had fallen on the Canaan Valley, and she shivered inside her thick padded jacket. She hadn't expected to need it. Hadn't expected to need many clothes at all when it was just Rick and her planning a weekend away. But then things had gone wrong, and he'd warned her that even in summer, the high country they'd travel could turn bitterly cold at night.

"You can't believe what I'm telling you? Or that I'm telling you at all?" Michelle Nguyen replied. Her voice was flat and almost devoid of emotion. Her eyes were unfocused, as though she was looking into another world, not necessarily one better than this. Just different.

"Both, I guess," Mel conceded. She folded her arms, hugging herself against the chill.

James said nothing. He'd been quiet since Michelle had confessed her fears about the BBC's report of a pandemic in China.

"And you... worked on this?" Mel said.

Michelle gave her a look.

"I didn't brew up the virus, no. I didn't even know it was a virus. I just did threat vector analyses for blowback in scenarios like this. We had a generic code for it. Plan Jericho."

James's mouth twitched.

"For when the walls come tumbling down."

"Something like that, yes," Michelle said. "Probably some Pentagon asshole with an Old Testament hard-on. You'd be surprised how often you get that."

"No. I wouldn't," Mel said.

They all went quiet again. Rick was gone for the night, patrolling the forest approaches to the campsite. Nobody suggested going to look for him. It would be stupidly dangerous for a whole bunch of reasons. Instead, the three campers sat on logs around the old tree stump, each hunched over, examining their thoughts.

Michelle had identified herself as some sort of intelligence analyst when they'd met back in Darnestown. She didn't look it, with the blue-black hair dye and all of the high-concept tattoo ink. But Mel was familiar with her type from working around DC. Michelle had surely behaved as though she was plugged into the government at some deep and fundamental level.

No, Mel corrected herself. Not just the government — The State.

Or what some people had taken to calling the Deep State the last couple of years.

Governments built libraries, handed out food stamps, and wrote you your parking ticket when you were a bit thoughtless of your fellow citizens. As a copper, she'd been the strong arm of government back in London.

She'd been a guarantor of civilisation.

The State was different. To her mind, the State was a vast, black machine for doing violence to the world.

A cool breeze reached up from the valley floor, cleaning out the last smells of the cooking and campfire. Near the edge of the plateau, Nomi chewed on a bone. For a little while, the sounds of her gnawing on the bone were the only noise in camp. Mel stared across the Canaan Valley, trying to lose herself in the grand sweep of the wilderness. The sun had fallen below the mountains in the west, and although it was not fully dark yet, the lowland reaches were disappearing into shadow. Night birds sang to each other, and here and there, a few tendrils of smoke rose into the sky from isolated cooking fires. The punters sitting around those fires would soon have to put them out.

"Are you in danger?" James asked, breaking the reverie.

"What?" Mel asked, looking back, assuming he was talking to her.

"I meant Michelle," James said. "If she was at risk? From this virus?"

The young woman shrugged.

"I don't know. I don't know what sort of package they sent..."

"Package?" James asked.

"Sorry," Michelle replied, subdued. "It's just... you get used to thinking about things in certain ways and to talking about them that way, too. If there were a package—she sketched a pair of air quotes with her fingers—"it would've been a tailored virus, something with a recent history in the region, like bird flu or something. But they would have tweaked it to target a host population defined by some genetic marker."

"What?" Mel shot back. Her temper was finally slipping the leash. "Like slanty eyes? Or the wrong skin colour."

"Don't be offensive," Michelle said, but without much heat. "No, nothing in the phenotype. It would have been something to define a significant cohort of Han Chinese into the catchment population while defining out everyone else. Or as many people as they could exclude."

Mel stood up, unable to stay seated any longer.

"You're telling me they built a killer flu bug, but just for the Chinese? It fuckin' sounds like a white man's dream weapon," she said. "Smallpox in the blankets, that sort of thing."

Michelle smiled sadly at her. "I'm not a white man."

"And Rick is," James added. "But he's not responsible for this, and neither is Michelle. Please, Mel, sit down and let's deal with this. Let's get all the information we can for a start."

Mel nearly turned away and started to stomp off into the dusk, but there was nowhere to go. Just the forest and the edge of the plateau.

And anyway, Michelle Nguyen's empty, hollowed-out expression cut across her disgust and anger.

"I don't know anything about the specifics of this Plan Jericho outcome," Michelle said in a small voice. Even so, Mel could hear the capital letters marking this Jericho thing as a big deal. In her mind's eye, she saw buff-covered folders stamped with TOP SECRET in red and the words PLAN JERICHO in plain black letters, six inches high.

"I don't even know if they went ahead with a plan," Michelle Nguyen continued. "We would have retaliated for the Chinese attacks, for sure. Not just for the cyber strike but for the military attacks on Vietnam, the Philippines and the rest. We have alliance responsibilities. You were there for that, James. You saw what was happening in those meetings."

The investment guy nodded, first to Michelle and then to Mel Baker, as if to confirm the story just for her.

"Looked to me like they were getting ready to drop bombs," he said.

"Bombs and missiles, for sure," Michelle confirmed. "But the Chinese were still denying they had anything to do with Zero Day. They only fessed up to the stuff we could actually nail them for. Sailing their fleet south, attacking Vietnam and Thailand and Malaysia, shooting the shit out of anyone who even looked sideways at them. Last I heard, they were still denying they had anything to do with the drones that crippled the Seventh Fleet. They were calling out rogue North Koreans or some shit. Like there's any other sort."

She looked at them as if for support. Nobody said anything.

Michelle Nguyen went on. "So I'm guessing we played their game. Deniable counter-value strikes. They killed millions of us. We kill millions of them. Nobody admits anything. And we all go down together."

"Jesus Christ," Mel said, finally sitting down again, or really just collapsing as her legs folded underneath her. "You're sure? This is madness, girl."

"Of course, I'm not sure," Michelle snapped before apologising. "I'm sorry. This is hard and really awful. But I had to tell you. Because... I don't know... I just..."

She ran out of words.

James O'Donnell reached across and took her hand, squeezing it gently. Michelle laid her head on his shoulder.

Mel wondered whether they were sleeping together. They had seemed so close when they stayed over at Rick's, and she had found them under the same blanket on the couch the following day. But there seemed a distance between them, even now.

"Right then. I apologise for getting angry," Mel said shortly. "It's just that there's so much trouble right now, and this just seems to have no purpose but to add to it."

"It had a purpose," Michelle replied. She took her hand from James. "To make sure they didn't win. There'll be other plans, too. For the Russians. The Iranians. All of them."

An awkward silence followed, and James eventually stepped into it again.

"Do you have any idea how tightly targeted the virus would be? You know, assuming it was targeted at all."

Michelle shrugged.

"Not my area of expertise, James. Maybe they focused on something like an enzyme deficiency, like an inability to digest dairy or something. Maybe some mad fucking scientist in a bunker in Nevada somewhere sequenced out a specific Y-marker that differentiated 99.94% of Han Chinese exclusively. I just don't know."

"For somebody with no expertise in this shit, you sound like you got a lotta fuckin' expertise," Mel said, but not in accusation as much as resignation. Of course, things would get worse. Millions of people had probably died of hunger and thirst in America already. They were probably lucky nobody had decided to fire off a bunch of nuclear weapons and be done with it.

James stood up and stretched. He walked off a few paces, turned around and came back.

"All right," he said. "Let's look at worst-case scenarios. This bug, or whatever it is, gets back here somehow. What then? Is it gonna be like a Stephen King novel or something."

Michelle shook her head.

"No. There'd be no point to that. Jericho was all about selective mass causalities. A discerning apocalypse, if you like."

"I don't like, no," Mel said.

Michelle ignored the retort and went on.

"If and when it gets here, anybody with the wrong gene marker is going to get sick and die. That's it. That's all. You guys will be fine."

"And you?" James said, sitting down next to her again. He reached for her hand, and Michelle let him take it, but she did not return his grip.

"I have no idea," she said.

RICK BOREHAM GHOSTED through the Eastern Hardwoods in the blue-black dark, all five senses so keenly attuned to the surrounding world that, in concert, they achieved a sort of transcendence, all five becoming one. It was not a new sensation. Not to Rick. But it had lain dormant within him for so long because he had not dared to wake it.

He crept through pooling shadow and pale moonlight, taking long pauses to drink in the night. He smelled the loam and dustiness of earth, the slow rot of dead leaves, and on the gentle breeze, the merest whiff of an extinguished campfire, not his own. These few wandering molecules of smoke and ash carried with them the scent of tinned beans and a sweet tincture of roasted marshmallows. He heard the scuttling of raccoons and, above, the cry of a screech owl among the rustling leaves and creaking hardwood. A fallen twig bent but did not break beneath his carefully placed step. The night was dark and pregnant with terror, but he was that terror which came upon the wary and the unwary alike, and thus, he did not give himself over to fear but instead to meditation.

A killer's meditation.

Once upon a time, when he was done with killing but found that killing was not done with him, the doctors at the VA had taught Rick Boreham to still his panicked thoughts and slow his racing heart by measured breathing and quiet focus. But this was not that. This was, in some ways, the opposite of that.

Rick's breathing was slow and deliberate, but instead of telescoping his focus on some singular mental point, he unsealed his mind to a vast pouring flood of stimuli. So much rushed in through watchful eye and heedful ear, through the living parchment of his skin and the subtle filigree of fine hairs that covered it, through taste and smell and the tenebrous vibrations of earth and air, that collectively, they became something weird and extrasensory. An otherness that Rick had come to think of as a third eye, the one that perceived everything precisely as it was.

This was how a killer meditated upon the world.

And in his arms, he cradled another killer, the captured M-4. Rick held his weapon at the low-ready, his thumb on the safety and his right index finger resting on the cold trigger housing. Standing silent in a thicket of fir trees, he tasted instant coffee at the back of his throat, sweetened just slightly by the scent of sap, sticky and oozing from the rough bark a few inches from his face. He read the darkened Valley below, relaxed but alert, his nerves quietly humming with the old mortal song. *This we will defend*, they sang; *his friends, his woman, his life*.

Three small fires, widely spaced, burned in the marshy lowlands, but many dozens more campsites held fast down there unseen. The points of light he could see were probably newcomers. Nobody who had been here when tracers lit up the night would be foolish enough to draw attention to themselves now. He did not wonder from where the newcomers had travelled. Such considerations were for the daylight hours and, to be frank, for others to ponder. He had simpler endeavours to be about.

Content for the moment with his survey, Rick took a step away from the edge of the plateau. He inhaled deeply, slowly. He listened and waited. He had never been to this place before, but it was as though he had never left. The Canaan Valley. Iraq. Afghanistan. It was all the same to him. Jihadis, bandits. Whatever. He would kill them all to protect his own. He was about to step off, to resume his track through the woods when he heard a metallic clink, a sound so unnatural and out of place that his senses at once narrowed from a wide band scan into a tight beam, concentrated on the source of the disturbance.

He was so long waiting that he had begun to wonder if the strange acoustics of the Canaan's vast rocky bowl might have transmitted the sound from miles away or from his camp in some weird recursive loop when the crack of a single gunshot, followed by a burst of crackling fire collapsed all those possibilities into one dread reality.

Danger was close.

For an instant, he was pulled into two directions; toward the threat, which he now perceived lying some distance to the northeast, a mile or so further along the ridge line, or back toward the camp and the three souls he had sworn himself to protect. Four, if you counted Nomi. And he did.

Rick did not move immediately. He gave himself another minute to gather what observations he could. More shots. And cries of fear, followed by shouts of anger and warning. The cries were too distant to make out individual voices or words but not so cryptic that he could not tell immediately that a number of men moved in pursuit of one or two women. Muzzle flashes, hidden between folds in the upland terrain, revealed themselves as bright, unmistakable beacons when the shooters, at last, climbed free of the natural trench line and fired into the air.

He saw that clearly. Saw too that four men, or four shooters at the very least, hurried to capture or recapture whatever quarry they sought. They were firing to arrest headlong escape, not to destroy the escapees.

Freed of the imperative to immediately defend the camp or to directly engage this unknown enemy, Rick Boreham allowed himself the luxury of another half-minute's surveillance. He counted two shotguns in the armoury of the hunting party and two rifled long arms. He saw no return fire from their prey. He calculated that if the shooters did not catch up with the women they were chasing, the whole company would overrun his campsite in fifteen to twenty minutes.

That decided the issue for him.

Rick Boreham made his choice and experienced it as a moment of free fall, of weightlessness. Like launching from the door of a C-130.

He moved towards the guns.

18

INTERLUDE

Lieutenant-Colonel Petrov sat atop his armored beast and waited. He chewed upon a tasteless pork patty from his ration pack and listened to the command net on his tanker's headset. The leather stank of his dried and stale sweat.

The net was silent. Andrei Pavlovich Petrov could hear his jaws work at the meat; he struggled to swallow. His mouth was so dry. He took a swig from his canteen and washed the protein lump down into the acidic mess of his stomach. He had the worst heartburn; no amount of charcoal or Gastal seemed to help.

He sighed and took another drink. He would have dearly loved a shot of vodka from his flask just to take the edge off, but he didn't dare. Not yet.

Andrei and his T-14 tank, Number 623, were at the very spearpoint of the army that had passed seemingly without notice and at great speed through Belarus. His command, a battalion of the 1st Guards Tank Army, waited in a forest of birch trees close to the highway that led to Bialystok in Poland.

Bialystok, he thought. He rubbed his eyes and pinched his nose. He took another swig. *Gavno*, he thought. Shit. The world had gone crazy. Everything was shit. Everything. His hurried departure from his family. The frantic mobilization of his command. The loading and unloading of his equipment and men. His arrival in Belarus, which was a complete shock, was rivalled only by the orders he had received via courier only a short while ago.

He burped and regretted it immediately. Bile stung the back of his mouth, and he nearly puked. Instead, Andrei made a face, raised himself in the hull, moved his boom mic, and spat. The spittle didn't make it to the ground; it splashed against the tank's reactive armor.

"Blyat!"

Colonel Petrov's driver spoke up. "You said something, sir?"

Andrei shook his head. "No, just clearing my throat."

"Yes, sir."

Andrei tapped his hand on the thick steel of his hatch as his intercom fell silent once more. He could smell the violated earth and chewed-up vegetation. Diesel fumes. The sweet smell of munitions. Live munitions, of course. His tank carried the full forty-five rounds of 125mm, along with other, lesser killers. The forest was crawling with his tanks, and he wondered for how long this had been planned.

"This" being the invasion of Eastern Poland, of course. This fucking madness, Andrei thought. It would kill them all.

A week or so ago, he could not have been sitting by the highway to Bialystok like this, of that he was sure. It would have been suicide. American satellites would have seen him; drones would have been hummed invisibly overhead. Heavy blocking forces would have moved into position, and a steel rain would fall.

But not now. Not since the world's eyes had been put out. Now armies could once more move in darkness, and his army had.

From what little he knew for sure, the Yankees were fucked. They would not be coming, and the few that were here were blinded, distracted, and utterly bereft of support. They would be easy meat, or so his superiors said. He grunted to himself. His superiors, of course, were a thousand miles away. They were almost certainly enjoying a chilled vodka as they contemplated what was about to happen.

But here and there, icy cold vodka or warm, spit-heavy canteen water, both Andrei and his superiors would soon find out how the Poles would fight this time. It was not 1939 come again. The wretched little mazuriks would not charge his T-14 on horseback. It would be with Javelin and Hellfire missiles and their own Leopard tanks - ironically supplied by the damned Germans.

Andrei stared at the trees. It didn't matter to him. His duty was clear. But still, he had to pee. He was just about to lever himself out of the tank and piss off the deck when the command freq crackled.

Andrei's heart rate shot up, and he held his breath.

"All Black Cat Elements, this is Falcon."

Falcon was the commander of the Tank Army. This was like hearing the voice of God.

"Execute Pechka. I say again, execute Pechka. Forward for the Rodina and for our great President! Falcon out."

Andrei waited a hair. His radio crackled once more.

"Blue, this is Raven." Andrei was Blue, and his regimental commander was calling.

"Go ahead, Raven."

"Blue, move immediately to Phase Line One, assault objective Bravo Three upon command."

"Moving, Raven."

"Good luck to you, Blue. Raven out."

Andrei heard a sound like freight trains speeding past as he buttoned up inside Tank 623. Artillery, he thought. Lots of it. The Red Army had always prided themselves upon the professionalism and deadliness of their fires. And so fucking what, Andrei thought before he keyed his mic, if we are no longer officially called the Red Army? He was proud to be a soldier of Russia, no matter what.

He pushed the transmit button and spoke with his soldiers in a level, businesslike tone.

"Third Battalion, this is Blue with a combat alert. Be advised, we move immediately to Phase Line One in attack order, as briefed." He paused. "Commanders report your status in sequence."

One by one, his company commanders called in. His battalion was ready. It was time. There would be no turning back.

Even nestled deep within Tank 623, Andrei could still hear the deafening roar of artillery, the red King of Battle. He looked through his vision blocks; his machine would crush the lovely thin birches.

He felt a brief pang of sorrow for the ruination of this forest, for the devastation he would leave in his wake. *Nichevo*, he thought, it couldn't be helped.

He pushed the mic.

"Move out, Third Battalion."

The army of the Rodina rolled west.

WIETSE CONSIDERED HIS FRIEND JELLE. They were both junior policemen, and they had been told to control traffic and keep an eye out for looting along the road to Silvolde. Someone was *niet goed in de hoofd*, crazy, thought Wietse. This was a job for a dozen or more, with full support.

Jelle spoke. "OK, just please, indulge me. Tell me again who we are supposed to stop, and for what reason?" Jelle regarded the scene strung out along the road and shook his head. Wietse put his hand on his chin; then he covered his eyes for a moment. He rubbed at his eyelids. He was already tired.

One little provincial road, the Ulftseweg, was jammed full of cars, pedestrians, and bicycles. There was a wreck somewhere on the N317, the main local highway, and Wietse imagined that this traffic had attempted a detour.

"I don't know," Wietse said.

As he answered his friend, he controlled his annoyance, but really, he wanted to tear out his hair. No one knew quite what to do, and no one could communicate. Cell phones? Junk. Radios? Crypto didn't work, and something was jamming them. Television? All the digital signals were scrambled all across Holland. He wanted to jump up and down.

Everything electronic was *kapot*, broken. Useless.

This morning, his Sergeant had told the pair to take some motorcycles and head out to a position a little south of the village. The mission seemed simple enough. Since this, this... war, incident, whatever, had started, no one had enjoyed a moment's rest. None. The simplest tasks weren't simple anymore. Control traffic, he thought.

Prevent looting.

Wietse watched as an elderly woman plucked a cabbage from the field right before them; she was one of dozens busy stripping the immature crops. What were they to do? Shoot the hungry old folk? Everyone knew that Albert Heijn's food distribution network wasn't working. What hadn't made it to the news, but Wietse knew, was that GPS was down, utterly shot, and government logistics and command were haphazard at best.

He spat. *Verdomme!* He didn't know who had thoroughly destroyed the NATO and civilian cyber infrastructure, and he guessed it didn't matter. No doubt NATO had retaliated. Although he wondered whether a country as primitive as Russia would be much inconvenienced by anything short of an old-fashioned invasion.

And who would be so foolish as to try that at the end of summer? Even with all of the global warming?

God, he thought, it was like one of his Great-Grandma's tales of the infamous Starvation Winter of 1944-45. Except this time, there were a lot more people and a lot fewer farms. It would happen much faster this time.

Wieste sucked in air through his teeth. Disaster.

A red-faced man with a shovel approached the pair.

"Policemen! Thank God!"

Jelle turned to address him politely. "May I help you, sir?"

"Yes!" The man gestured at the field. "You can start by chasing those people from my fields! And arrest the thieves. They are taking everything!"

"Perhaps we should shoot them?" Wietse deadpanned.

It was cheeky and would probably see him reprimanded, but he'd had enough.

The farmer threw up his hands; his face was nearly purple. "Yes! I don't know! Something!" He started to repeat himself. "They are taking everything!" He leaned his shovel up against a fruit tree, wiped tears from his eyes, and wrung his hands. "Can't you help? Please?"

Wietse looked around. There were hundreds of people moving about, dozens in this field alone. Everyone looked intent on their mission. He heard both German and Dutch spoken. Of course, there would be Germans, he thought. Not far from the border, and the Ruhr Valley was home to millions.

Millions of mouths, and they all needed to be fed.

He didn't doubt that some of them were here, in this field.

He felt the weight of the pistol on his belt. It felt like a lead brick. He supposed this poor man was right; he had to do something. He looked at Jelle. They had a job to do.

"What do you think, Jelle?"

"It's like bringing water to the sea."

"Yeah." A woman hurried by with an armload of cabbages. Wietse furrowed his brows. One, he could understand. Maybe even two. But an entire armload? Maybe she was selling them, he thought. He shot out his hand and seized the woman; she tried to pull away, and her cabbages fell. Some people saw the commotion and rushed over to claim the fallen produce.

Jelle called out. "Stay back!"

The people ignored him. Someone pushed at the young police officer, then snapped and hit him. Jelle tripped and fell. Wietse struggled with the woman. She kicked him in the shin and grabbed for a cabbage. Someone tugged at his service pistol.

Enough was enough.

Wietse kicked the woman in the gut and delivered a vicious downward blow on the hand that tugged on his pistol. The woman folded like a cheap umbrella, and the would-be pistol snatcher grunted and attempted to run. The young police officer drew his weapon and aimed it at his assailant's centre of mass.

"Halt!"

The man kept running. Wietse cursed and eased off on the trigger. The man was going to get away. But he couldn't just shoot someone in the back. This was a civilised country, and he was responsible for keeping it so.

His partner called out. "Shoot this fucker!"

Wietse looked down. Jelle was wrestling with a large man, and he was losing. The fellow looked as if he slung armloads of bricks for a living, and he was trying to beat Jelle's head against the fruit tree.

Wietse hesitated for a split second. Was deadly force necessary?

If he didn't act, it seemed Jelle was dead. He raised his weapon, but he couldn't get a clear shot. His bullet would go through the man into Jelle. His eye caught the farmer's shovel, still resting against the tree.

He put his pistol back in its holster and grabbed the spade. The construction worker was on top of Jelle... Wietse brought the shovel down flat on the back of his head. With prejudice.

It made a curious *bong-thump* sound.

The attacker fell lifeless to the ground.

Jelle wheezed.

Wietse panted.

After a moment, he reached down and helped his friend up. Jelle's nose was bleeding.

The farmer was gone; more pickers had come. They paid no mind to the unconscious man or the police officers.

After a moment, Jelle spoke. He sounded as if his mouth was full of cotton.

"I'm not dying for cabbage."

Wietse nodded.

"You speak the truth."

19

STRONGHOLD

As they motored upriver to Sacramento, Jodi sat out with Max on what she thought of as the fishing deck. It was at the back of the boat where Ellie and Karl had fought off the pirates. There were half a dozen little swivel chairs out there. Really nice ones with padded cushions in hand-stitched leather. Now that they were on the move again, now that they seemed to have a plan, it was lovely to sit out in the sun and the breeze with her little boy, watching the countryside slip by. It was mostly countryside out here. She knew they were heading towards a big city. Just as she knew that San Francisco was less than an hour's drive away in the opposite direction. But you wouldn't know it out here on the water. It was so quiet.

It was also good to get away from the lake and what had happened there.

On both banks of the river, deep green fields marched away in regimented formation. Jodi had no idea what sort of crops the farmers had planted in those fields, and she thought it was crazy that people were going hungry, even starving to death and killing each other for food, when there was so much of it in the ground so close by. Ellie's boss piloted the big boat upriver at little better than a walking pace. Ellie said it was because they didn't have charts, and Damo didn't know how deep the water was. He didn't want to run up on a sandbank or something.

"Mom, are there going to be more pirates?" Max asked. "Will Ellie and Karl have to shoot them, too?"

"I don't know, babes," Jodi said and quickly regretted it. She should have just said, *'No'*. She didn't want to worry her little boy. But Max did not seem worried at all. If anything, he seemed to be the only one on the boat who was enjoying himself. He had a colouring book and a box of Crayola from somewhere, and he was concentrating fiercely on filling in a castle. His brow furrowed, the tip of his tongue poking out through his lips. It was almost as though he'd forgotten the morning. Jodi was momentarily seized by a fear that he actually might have, that Max may have been so traumatised by the attack and the violence needed to repulse it that he had somehow blacked out the entire event.

But of course, he hadn't. He'd just asked her if there would be any more pirates. She forced herself to take a couple of slow, deep breaths. The kid was coping with all of this a lot better than she was. He'd been dealing with it since they picked him up from his father's place, and Karl had shot Chad's roommate dead. Gunned him down right in front of Max, right out in the street.

The things her child had seen.

Jodi shaded her eyes against the afternoon sun. The yacht was slowly sweeping around a long bend in the river. She wasn't even sure which river. There were so many of them here. And they all had different names. The Delta was a sprawling patchwork of farmland, wilderness, strange straight-arrow canals cut through remnant forest and open fields, and occasionally, worryingly, small villages and isolated real estate developments. They came around a tight hairpin bend at one point, and Damo had almost rammed into another yacht tied to the end of a pier in front of what looked like a golf course. Or a real estate development meant to look like a golf course. There were long rows of townhouses, all of them identical, all of them buttoned up tight. Their lawns were brown and patchy. Here and there, a broken window stood out starkly, and a sports car lay half in the river and half out. As though someone had driven it there on purpose, maybe drunk or something

"Nah mate, that's a Tesla," Damo explained when Maxi pointed it out. "It got hacked and drove itself in there."

There were long stretches of water where they saw nothing and no one. Just wilderness. Karl said this had been a state reserve or a national park or something, and Jodi could believe it. It was a beautiful landscape in its natural form, but it felt desolate and haunted as well. The boat made noise, of course. Not just the engines but the splash and ripple of water. And there was birdsong, too. And the whispered passage of the wind. But Jodi was used to the quiet roar of a great city, and this felt eerie to her.

"Maybe you and Max should come in off the deck," Damo called down from the little wheelhouse.

Ellie appeared from out of the shadows. She had gone down below to shower and change. She waved them inside.

"Come on, we better do as they say," Jodi said. She saw why when she stood up.

There was a small settlement up ahead on the left bank of the river. People with guns stood on a boardwalk observing their approach. Max was still sitting, colouring in his castle. With no time to argue, Jodi just gathered him up in her arms and carried him inside.

"Hey," he protested. "My castle."

"I'll get it," Jodi said as she deposited him inside and out of sight. "You stay here, please. Do as I say."

He attended to the change of tone in her voice.

"Yes, Mom," he said.

Jodi hurried out to grab the colouring book and Crayola. She stayed bent down low, but none of the people on the bank raised their weapons or moved much at all. They swivelled their heads slowly as the *Lasseter's Reef* swept past at a stately pace.

"Scouts or an outpost, I reckon," Karl said, coming up next to her. "See, they're calling it in."

He pointed out one of the watchers talking into some sort of backpack radio set.

"Probably giving the folks up ahead fair warning."

Damo's voice came down from the wheel deck.

"Hey Karl, can you hop down to the radio room and see if anybody's trying to raise us?"

"Sure thing, buddy," Karl said.

Jodi followed him down there. When the FM and AM radio stations had gone quiet, and all of the satellite TV links dropped out, they had still been able to use the boat's maritime radio to collect a few snippets and nuggets of information about the outside world, mostly from ham radio operators.

The comms room, as Damo called it, was a small cupboard-sized space full of electronic equipment of such dense and confusing complexity that Jodi worried she might screw something up just by walking too heavily past the door. Karl didn't seem bothered at all. He swung himself into the small swivel chair in front of a tall stack of receivers or transmitters or whatever they were, pushed a few buttons, twiddled a few knobs, and took up a black plastic handset that reminded her of an old-fashioned telephone.

"Don't intend to say nothing unless someone says something to me first," he explained.

The words were only just out of his mouth when the radio crackled into life. Karl frowned and fussed about with the dials, eventually finding what he wanted.

A male voice, distorted by static, crackled out of the speakers.

"Unidentified marine vessel, you are approaching a federally designated stronghold zone. Please reverse your course."

Karl put the handset up to his mouth. "Sorry, can't do that, sir," he said. "I'm just the hired help. The fella you want to talk to is up top, driving the boat."

The other voice came back.

"Unidentified marine vessel, please reverse your passage upriver. This is Sacramento border control. You are not authorised to enter the city."

"Well, son, we're not looking to enter the city," Karl replied in a drawl. "We're just sort of looking to slide on through if that's all right with you."

"Unidentified marine vessel, you will be stopped and boarded by armed officers."

"Sacramento, we ain't unidentified. You can call us *Lasseter's Reef.*"

"*Lasseter's Reef,* you will be stopped and..."

Karl wasn't paying attention. He covered the handset and leaned over to Jodi.

"Miss Jodi, could you run up to Damo and let him know what's going on?"

She nodded and hurried back topside to tell Damo.

"Karl's talking to someone from Sacramento," she called up. "They say we have to turn around. Or stop. And they say they're going to board us."

"What? All three?" Damo asked. But he kept moving them forward.

Jodi didn't know whether to stay with Damo or return to Karl. In the end, she stayed. If Damo wanted her to go back down and relay messages, he would ask. The countryside had changed again. On the left bank, she could see paddocks and fields and rows of dark green leafy crops stretching away. Dozens of people worked in those fields. Maybe hundreds now that she looked.

On the other side of the river, however, a golf course hugged the banks. Sprinklers spat jets of water high into the air, keeping the greens lush and healthy. Right next to the golf course, though, a vast open scar lay upon the land. The soil there was grey and lifeless, and she could see the giant trunks of fallen trees scattered across the wasteland. Maybe it was another housing development?

"Here we go then," Damo said, dragging her attention back to the river.

It felt like so long since Jodi had seen the city or even more than a handful of people at one time that her mind locked up at the sight before them. A bridge reached over from one side of the river to the other. It was one of those old mechanical drawbridges where an operator could raise or lower the midsection to allow river traffic through. At the moment, it was low, and there was no way Damo's boat was getting through there. He didn't seem bothered by this in the way he had been instantly on edge this morning when those guys had turned up at the lake. He pulled a few levers on his control panel, flicked a few switches and eased the engines back until they were merely idling.

Two speedboats in the livery of the Sacramento Port Police Department had blocked the approach to the bridge. One of them began to motor toward Damo's boat.

"They reckon they're going to board us."

It was Karl, just up from the radio room.

"Figure as much," Damo said.

Ellie came back from the front of the boat. Her expression was sombre, except for a small crease at the corner of her mouth.

"I guess shotguns aren't appropriate this time."

"Not unless you want to get picked off from the bridge," Karl said, ducking low and pointing up.

Jodi followed his gesture, her heart skipping a beat when she saw two teams of riflemen on the bridge.

"Snipers," he explained.

A voice crackled through a bullhorn.

"This is the Sacramento Port Police. Prepare to be boarded. If you are armed, lay down your weapons. If you are carrying weapons, we will shoot on sight."

Damo patted the holster at his hip. He took out the pistol and laid it down. The shotguns stood in their rack just behind him. Nobody was armed.

"Ellie, mate, we got no front-of-house staff," he said. "You reckon you could go greet our guests?"

She smiled, a genuinely warm expression, and Jodi found her heart melting. It was the first time Ellie had smiled since the horror of the morning attack. If she could smile, Jodi told herself, everything would be all right. It might take a while, but it would be all right. In the end.

"Where's Maxi, she said suddenly, terrified that he might try to repel the boarders as he had seen Ellie and Karl do earlier.

"I'm here, mom," he said.

Jodi spun around. The trip-hammering of her heart slowed as she spied him sitting in a corner of the wheelhouse, colouring in his book again.

"Okay, good. Just... stay there, okay. It's not pirates this time."

He rolled his eyes at her.

"I know that, mom. It's the police."

Jodi turned to Karl and Ellie.

"Do you think... Do you think we might be in trouble for this morning?"

Karl shook his head.

"Nope. I think these fellas got bigger fish to fry than us, Miss Jodi.".

The police boat came alongside, and an officer threw up a rope, which Ellie caught and tied off. A second rope came over the side, and she did the same again. Jodi sighed, her heart swelling with pride. When had Ellie picked up these skills? She moved as naturally around the decks of Damo's boat as she did through the chaos of a working kitchen. Jodi, meanwhile, was only good at taking photographs and being a mom, and there were plenty of days when she doubted herself on both of those.

The policemen climbed over the side of the boat. They were dressed up like soldiers in battle helmets and black body armour, and they carried very heavy-looking weapons.

One of them, a woman, barked out a question.

"How many people on board?"

That surprised Jodi. They all looked the same in their bulky armour, and they all wore dark or mirrored sunglasses.

"Four adults, one child," Damo said.

He was still at the wheel.

"Drop anchor," the woman ordered, and Damo did as he was told, pressing a button that released the anchor chain. It rattled away and hit the water with a loud splash.

"Now cut the engine."

Again, he did as he was told.

The silence that came over them felt massive.

Boots thudded to the deck, and more police officers climbed on board. They were all pointing weapons, and without thinking, Jodi moved in front of Max to shield him.

"Who's the captain?"

Damo raised his hands and very carefully came down to meet the boarding party.

"That's me. Damian Moloney. Master and Commander of the *Lasseter's Reef*."

"You were told to turn around."

It was the same woman, and she did all the talking. She must be in charge, Jodi thought.

"We don't want to go into the city," Damo said. "We just want to go through and keep going out the other side."

"Not possible," the woman said. "Sacramento is a federally mandated stronghold. Only authorised personnel in."

"And out?" Damo asked.

The woman looked annoyed, but Damo pressed on.

"I mean, would you let us pass through if we offered to take a few punters with us? A few hungry mouths you don't have to feed any more."

The woman said nothing.

Damo opened his mouth to speak again, but she held up a hand.

"Just shut up for a moment, Crocodile Dundee," she said. The police officer stepped as far away as she could, walking all the way down to the back of the boat. One of the other officers went with her. They huddled together and talked for a few moments.

She spoke to somebody on her radio. Conferred with the other cop some more. And returned.

"Right. The boat stays here. You come with us," she said, pointing at Damo.

"I want to take someone with me. My sous chef."

"Your what?"

"Ellie. I want to take Ellie with me," Damo said.

20

THE HORROR CLOWNS MCGUIGAN

When she tripped and went down, running in the dark forest, Tammy Kolchar had Wynona thrown over one shoulder, and Bobby Jr. tucked under her arm. "*No, mommy, nooo,*" her daughter called out, and everything turned treacle slow and scary movie terrible. As if it hadn't been scary enough before, with the horror clown twins and their retarded cousins Darryl and the other Darryl chasing them with guns and crazy big knives. One second, she's running through the forest, holding onto her little ones for the love of sweet life itself, trying to keep up with Roxarne and her kiddies, who were all big enough to run for themselves. And the next second, it's like she's taken this step, and the world itself wasn't there any more. Just a big hole for her foot to go into and then her leg, and then she's falling and falling and falling in the dark and holding tight onto Bobby Jr. and Wynona, and then starting to let go because she's worried she's gonna land on them and crush them dead. Just like Rudi Kanetski did playing football with his toddler two years back. And then Tammy is holding tight on to them anyway, like with mad retard strength, because she's remembered they were running on top of a hill and there was a steep fall away into a valley, and if she lets the kids go, they'll fall for sure and she'll never see them again and...

She hit the ground, and it was mercifully soft, almost squishy, except for a small rock or something that punched into one hip like a stone fist. Both children wailed in fear and shock but not in pain. A mother got to recognise the different cries she heard from her children, and the good Lord knew that Tammy Kolchar had heard plenty this last week or so.

Falling drove all of the air from Tammy's lungs and made her whole body ring like a bell, if a bell could ring with pain, and as she tumbled through the dark, it was all she could do not to wonder what the fuck had she'd been thinking when they lit out like bandits from Dillonvale?

Turns out she didn't know from bandits and outlaws. Not one little bit.

Things had gone sideways hard in the 'vale, and then things had gone the same way pretty much everywhere, and it had been a matter of some perplexity and regret to Tammy—and probably doubly so to Roxarne, who got dragged along with her—as to whether they had done the right thing or not. It was Roxarne who kept her sane. She always said that no matter how much trouble they seemed to be in, it couldn't be as much trouble as she had when the Blockbuster closed down and she lost her job, and her useless fucking boyfriend stole the last forty-three bucks they had and got drunk and gift-wrapped a light pole with his Honda. The light pole fell down and crashed through the front window of the Dillonvale county offices, and of course, the Honda wasn't insured for shit, and even if it had been, he'd been stumble-ass drunk, so that was that.

"And that was real trouble, honey."

Or at least such was Roxarne's understanding of it until they camped in the little roadside park half an hour outside of Dryfork, West Virginia, them not being allowed into Dryfork proper on account of the townsfolk there standing off all comers, and doing so with guns and no small measure of bad manners. That was a hell of a thing that had been happening more and more, too. Tammy could understand why, shivering whenever she recalled that dead city and the vast plain of a million broken people where they'd almost come to their end. Things were hard all over, and folks would keep to their own if they could.

Tammy Kolchar surely would, but they had almost no gas, and the Oldsmobile got real thirsty as the needle dropped down that end of the gauge. Their money was all but gone, but that didn't matter so much as the hard truth of having almost nothing to spend it on anyways. Nobody anywhere had stuff to sell. Not at any sort of reasonable price.

There was a coin-operated gas fire barbecue in the little park and a shower block, which was a mercy. They could at least clean up and stay warm on the unseasonably chilly night. But they had been hungry and tired and running out of all hope when the camper van pulled in, and the McGuigan twins stepped out. Followed by the cousins Darryl and Darryl.

Those McGuigan's were a sight.

Giant beach ball-shaped fellas, each with a shock of red hair that'd terrify Ronald McDonald himself. Their mobile home rocked on its axles as they stepped down and introduced themselves. And their cousins, the double Darryls, they weren't any easier on the eye, but they were as thin as the McGuigans were not, and they had an unsettling air of outlaw skeeviness and meth-lab cunning about them.

But they also had food, they said.

Steaks and burger patties and, for a wonder, not-too-stale bread, which they were of a mind to share with fellow travellers, wanting nothing in return.

"Men always want something," Roxarne muttered to her an hour later as the children gorged themselves and the McGuigans told of their adventures on the road since the Chinese "attacked the Navy and the Walmarts".

And Roxarne wasn't wrong. But where Tammy and Roxarne might have contemplated enduring the usual slobbering grunts and dogged thrusting if it meant keeping their little ones safe and well fed, the McGuigans and at least one of the cousins Darryl soon enough revealed that they did not possess the carnal appetites of normal men.

It happened during the dessert course, for which one of the Darryls produced a Sara Lee poundcake from the refrigerator of the mobile home. Two of them, in fact, which was not a surprise on account of those McGuigans looking the sort of boys who could inhale a whole poundcake each on their own.

"Hey kids, who wants cake?" the Cracker Barrel Darryl asked as he reappeared from the darkness with a foil tray full of butter cake held in each dirty paw. Tammy thought of him as the Cracker Barrel Darryl because that was the T-shirt he was wearing. His cousin, the other Darryl, was definitely the more stylish of the two, seeing as how he wore a proper collared shirt, although he had torn off the sleeves to let out his ropey little arms, and for that, she detracted a few dress-up points. They both wore camo pants, which was of no never mind to her because half of Dillonvale did too.

The kids were mad for the promise of cake, naturally, except for Bobby Jr, who had been quiet and careful all the way through dinner. It reminded Tammy of the way he got when his daddy, the bigger Bobby, got his drink on and let his temper loose.

But neither McGuigans nor Darryls were serious drinkers, not like Bobby's old man had been, and they had no temper to speak of. If anything, the shared dinner was a little weird and uncomfortable because of the way they kept making each other laugh at their own jokes. The little kids thought they were hilarious, and Jakey almost threw up, he was laughing so much when the slightly bigger McGuigan lifted his shirt and made a face of his enormous belly, with his belly button doing for a mouth. And, of course, upon discovering he had an appreciative audience, he just had to take his shirt off all the way and make the children almost sick with hysteria by grabbing up each jiggling man boob and turning them into fun-time characters as well.

"Who would like to eat me?" The bellybutton asked.

"Oh no, we're full," replied man boobs one and two.

And they all fell about laughing. The little ones and the McGuigans and fashionable Darryl, at any rate.

Not Tammy and Roxarne, though. Roxy had been nudging her in the ribs all the way through the pulled pork rolls.

"What?" Tammy asked in a low, strained voice.

"He keeps looking at me," Roxarne muttered, nodding at Cracker Barrel Darryl, who was sitting almost opposite them on the other side of the campfire.

Tammy glanced through the flames, and sure enough, he was grinning like a fiend at Roxarne. Like she, too, had just flashed a few acres of boob.

That particular Darryl winked at them.

"Excuse us, gentlemen," Tammy said as sweetly as she could manage, which she calculated was sweet enough on account of her having learned to sugar talk her way through a hard shift at the Dollar General.

"Where y'all going now?" asked the big shirtless McGuigan.

"Secret lady's business," Tammy said, standing up and hauling Roxarne up with her. "Come on," she said with some urgency and haste.

"We cain't leave the kids."

"We ain't doing that. Come on."

"Mom?" Bobby Jr said, sounding worried.

"Ain't nothing," she smiled back at him. "Look after your sister."

Tammy and Rox walked out of the firelight, huddling together about twenty yards away in the dark. The night sky was cloudless, and a billion stars shined with hard brilliance.

"We need to settle on which of us is going to ride the Cracker Barrel over there," Tammy said, "if it becomes needful to do so." She hurried on before Roxarne could reply. "And I volunteer it to be me because God knows I dragged us all out on this hell trip, so it should be me that pays the price."

"But he's been looking at me, Tammy," Roxarne protested.

"That don't matter," Tammy shot back. "You know what men are like. They think they want one thing until they get another, and they're happy enough to make do with that rather than nothing. So it's gonna be me. I'll do it."

"That don't make any sense at all, Tamara," Roxy said, and

Tammy knew she was getting worked up because that Tamara thing was always a tell. "And even so, that's only one of them," Roxy added. "What about the other three?"

Tammy looked back across the little camping area and into the small circle of light. Both McGuigans were giggling and jiggling, and all of the kids, save for her little Bobby, were rolling around in delight.

"I think those big ones been taking their pleasure at the bottomless buffet so long they've forgotten how to find it anywhere else," she said. "As for the sleeveless Darryl, I don't get any sort of vibe off of him. Maybe he's a gay redneck."

"There ain't no gay rednecks," Roxarne insisted. "That's just the way of things. But maybe he lets his brother do the talking, and he just picks up the leftovers."

"I thought Cracker Barrel Darryl was his cousin," Tammy said, confused.

"No," Roxarne said. "The Darryls are cousins to the McGuigan's but brothers to each other. That's why they look so much the same."

"Huh," Tammy said. "I did not realise that. Do you think they're like the Sheridan brothers? Word was those boys would not date a girl unless she would date them both."

"Oh, gross," Roxarne winced, firming in her resolve. "You cain't do it, Tammy. You cannot pull a train full of Darryls. Not even two of them. Not for any reason."

"Honey, we got four good reasons sitting over there. If I have to do it, I will. You notice the way they parked us in. We can't even get out of here without their say-so."

Both women regarded the scene around the campfire with real distaste. None of this felt good.

"Maybe they'd go for a hand job," Tammy suggested.

After a pause, Roxarne agreed, if reluctantly.

"A handjob for a pulled pork dinner seems a fair trade. I guess."

It did not come to that, however. When they returned to the campfire, the Darryls had gathered up all the plastic plates and camp cutlery and taken them inside the trailer for cleaning. Big shirtless McGuigan was off at the edge of the forest, urinating massively and groaning as though very pleased with himself to be doing so. The other McGuuigan was nowhere to be seen, but all four kids were still sitting around the fire, so Roxarne rejoined them, and without thinking on what she was doing, Tammy Kolchar went to the motor home to offer help with the dishes. Or a quick wristie if such should be required in lieu of payment for their dinner.

That was both a bad step and their deliverance, for approaching the entry to the motor home, she overheard the Darryls in animated conversation about what was to come next. Roxarne had been right about Cracker Barrel Darryl, who was fixing to have his way with her, whether she fancied such a thing or not. He almost seemed to hope not.

"I do love it when they fight," he said.

But they were wrong about all the rest of it. Turns out the others were not to be repaid with anything as wholesome as a freely given hand job. Turns out the objects of their lustful intentions were not the women at all.

Not grown women, at any rate.

"Help you, ma'am?"

Tammy shrieked and jumped.

The missing McGuigan was standing behind her. Where he had sprung from, she did not know. But she could see from the grin on his face that he had heard what she had just heard. Or enough to make no difference. His grin was sick and wrong. Electrical shocks coursed through her body. Just under the skin, but all over. The world began to fade away at the edges. Going dark and pressing in all around until she took hold of her foolish senses and shouted "NO!" and kicked the McGuigan so hard in the balls that her boot sunk into his groin like he was a monster made out of swamp mud.

AND SO IT was that Tammy Kolchar came to be running through the West Virginia wilderness in the full dark of night, carrying her children, pursued by four perverts—or perhaps three and a plain rapist —when she stumbled on the rough ground and tumbled headlong to her end.

This had to be the end, she thought as she gasped, winded, and groaned at the bright, white explosion of pain in her side, even as she pulled a crying Bobby and Wynona close to her as if that might protect them from what was coming.

"Keep running, Roxy, keep going," she cried out, although she barely had the breath to whimper, and what she wanted most was for her friend to double back and sweep them up somehow and carry them away. Roxy and her two, Jakey and Liana, were such a long way ahead of Tammy that she didn't imagine they'd even heard her.

But then Roxy was always good at miracles. Small ones, anyway. Like fashioning fairy princess costumes out of bubble wrap for the wings, or building whole castles from the cardboard boxes Tammy brought home from work for Bobby's ninth birthday party. It was Roxy who'd got her the job interview at Dollar General when Tammy's husband took off to the fracking and then took up with that waitress there. And, of course, it was Roxy, always Roxy, who kept them moving this last week or so whenever Tammy had just wanted to pull over to the side of the road and give up.

It wasn't Roxy who appeared out of the nighttime forest, though.

It was a Darryl. And then another Darryl. And what seemed like an eternity later, the huffing and puffing and cursing McGuigans. They were all swearing at her. All promising the most awful reckoning. Her babies wailed and trembled in her arms.

"Y'all are gonna regret that," one of their hunters panted and gasped, but Tammy never did find out which one because Roxy came back, and they all died.

ONE WOMAN and two children crashed through the undergrowth towards Rick. They ran without pause or obvious direction, just trying to put as much distance between themselves and their pursuers as possible. The second woman — wait, was there a second woman? Or had he mistaken the cries of one of the children for another adult?

A shotgun blast, aimed into the treetops, lit up the ridge line ahead of him, and he saw in the bright flash of light that there was indeed another woman, and she was down.

Everything happened quickly then, but not so quickly that Rick Boreham lost track of the sequence.

First, a young boy and then a girl of about the same age ran past the tree behind which he had taken cover. The girl kept moving swiftly, but the boy, perhaps alerted by his heightened senses, stopped and turned to call to his mother.

He saw Rick, a dark silhouette, entirely still, and he cried out in alarm instead.

His mother—at least Rick assumed she was his mother —called back.

"Keep going."

But she ran past the same tree and, looking for her son, saw Rick.

She gasped and turned tail. Literally running back from where she had just come.

"Keep going, Jakey," she called over her shoulder, and Rick could not help himself.

He smiled faintly. Almost fondly.

Some mad maternal instinct, buried deep in her animal hind-brain, had switched on, and she was trying to lead him away from her children.

He didn't move from cover.

Instead, he raised his weapon and waited on his target.

The first one appeared over the crest, a thin man. The tree line was spare, and he blocked out enough stars for Rick to lay the iron sights on his centre mass.

A small voice cried out behind him.

"No!"

It was the boy.

He thought Rick was going to fire on his mother.

Tiny feet crashed through the undergrowth toward him as another figure appeared in outline above.

The woman was halfway back to her friend when the last of the pursuers struggled into view. They were much bigger men, and Rick fancied he could hear their laboured breathing as he squeezed the trigger.

Two rounds took the first man in the chest.

Another two dropped the one beside him.

The boy, just a few steps away now, wailed in distress.

Rick had almost no time left to make the final shots.

He killed the nearest of the big men with a clean hit, but the boy slammed into him, ruining his aim on the last.

The gun roared, but he was confident the rounds did not find their mark.

21

MERE ANARCHY IS KICKING ASS

Jonas heard the engines as soon he was clear of the building. A heavy metal thunder that he could feel in his chest. His hand dropped to the pistol at his hip, but he made a conscious effort to leave the gun alone. Instead, he followed Muller and O'Shannassy as they marched the quarter mile from the county offices to the Seattle Gate. It seemed to Jonas as though half the town had joined the group by the time they reached Big Al's place. These fucking idiots were going to get themselves killed if they were heading into the sort of trouble he suspected was waiting outside the gate.

He couldn't break away, though. Not without being noticed. He wasn't a pussy or anything. He was just being rational. While everybody else was swinging their dicks and losing their minds, Jonas seemed to float above it all. And nothing he saw from up there gave him good feelings. Hundreds of dumbass locals hurried onto Main Street, many of them armed, but not all with firearms. Some carried shovels and pitchforks like an angry mob from some bullshit black-and-white movie. His guys joined him, hurrying toward the Seattle Gate and the deep, industrial growl of the engine noise; Leo Vaulk, cosplaying The Punisher (if The Punisher had really let himself go to seed), and Dale Juntii, who carried an assault rifle taken from a raiding party. It would have been hard enough sneaking away with those two flanking him, but as they passed the sidestreet that ran up next to Al Barrett's diner and out into the fields of Mullan Park, Brad Rausch and Chad Moffat appeared at the head of a dozen or so men and women who'd been working on the Wall.

So, how many of these losers had stayed behind to actually stand guard out there? Jonas thought.

He'd seen Joe Wolfenden's militia crew earlier, but there was no sign of them now. Part of him wondered whether they might have got smart and bugged out. But no. That wasn't Wolfenden's style. The man had accepted the shelter of the town in return for aiding in the defence, and he hadn't shown any sign of reneging on that deal. (A deal Jonas had brokered, in fact). Anybody lucky enough to find themselves behind high walls and strong gates was probably there for the duration now.

The engine roar grew louder as they approached the Seattle Gate. The makeshift structure had always looked imposing despite its hasty construction and improvised design. But to Jonas, it now resembled a child's plaything, a fort glued together from matchsticks and tooth-picks. Goose flesh stood out on his arms as the massed iron choir of —what, a dozen?— powerful motorcycle engines began to resolve itself into the savage roar of so many individual machines. He was no expert on big-ass bikes, but he could tease out the weaponised double-shot report of a big squad of Harley-Davidson's from the continual volcanic rumble of Japanese and European rides.

His boss in Miami had ridden a Harley. Jonas had learned to hate the sound of them.

"This is it, boys," Leo Vaulk said. "The dim and bloody tide is loose."

"The fuck you saying?" Dale Juntii asked. His voice was tight, and his lips barely moved.

"Our man Leo is a poet," Jonas said, trying for a calm, detached tone and almost choking on his spit. How the hell he could do that when his mouth was drier than Death Valley, he didn't know. His legs felt light but leaden at the same time, as though he might float away or collapse with the effort of dragging their impossible weight forward one step at a time. Walking beside him, Juntii looked like a human tractor, gearing down to push through whatever lay ahead.

"The blood-dimmed tide is loosed," Jonas recalled aloud. "And mere anarchy is, fuck, I dunno, kicking ass all over the world or something. It's a poem. Right, Leo?"

Leo Vaulk rolled his shoulders and hefted the shotgun he was carrying as if to test the weight. He wore three handguns around his body. One at each hip and another in a shoulder holster. The black composite handle of a fighting knife poked out of some weird sort of neoprene holder he'd Velcroed around one of his biceps. It looked like the sort of thing you might stick a big-ass phone in if you were going out for a run, but Leo had jammed this gigantic pig sticker in there. He looked ridiculous. They all did.

"This'll be the Angels," Leo said, before adding, "The Hells Angels." Just in case there was any doubt. "I've dealt with these assholes before. We need to put them down and put them down hard."

Dale Juntii chuckled.

"Leo, you're a security guard. The only time you dealt with these assholes was when you held the door open for them to come into the bank and make a big cash deposit."

"Fuck you, Dale," Leo said, but without any real venom.

It was all just a monkey dance, Jonas thought. A bunch of apes screeching and beating their chests, hoping to avoid any real violence and damage. He'd seen plenty of it, repping for the sort of lower-tier douchebags who couldn't afford a top-shelf Jew from Harvard.

"Jesus Christ, is anybody actually standing guard anywhere?" Jonas asked, mainly for the sake of moving his jaw and stopping his own screeching monkey brain from running wild with visions of everything turning to shit and blood. The rolling thunder of engine noise and the growing buzz of frightened, excited exchanges between the heavily armed but anxious residents of Silverton meant he had to raise his voice to be heard. He squinted and blinked a trickle of stinging sweat from his eyes. The sun seemed to have climbed high overhead in the space of a few short minutes' walk from the county offices. The reek of body odour, his own and everyone else's, was overpowering. A few steps ahead of him, Sheriff Muller strode towards the gate as though he was merely rambling along Main Street to take the morning air. His light tan uniform shirt, however, was stained with sweat. Two dark patches under his armpits were quickly spreading across his back and down towards the heavy leather utility belt he wore loosely under his gut. He spoke into his walkie-talkie as he advanced on the gate, but Jonas could not make out a word of the exchange.

"I don't know how many guns they got left on the Wall," Juntii said, raising his voice to answer Jonas's primarily rhetorical question. "I saw Wolfenden and a few of his guys heading out through one of the breaks."

"Probably getting the fuck out of here while they still can," Leo groused.

"No," Juntii said. "I reckon they were gonna work their way around the flank. Take some high ground."

The crowd, maybe three or four hundred strong, bunched up as it approached the Gate. The fortifications here were much more substantial than those guarding the approach from the Cascades. Most of the traffic they'd had to turn back came from the city, after all.

Boasting two towers, instead of the single one that commanded the Cascades Gate, a firing platform accessible by three separate ladders and running across the entire width of the road, the town's main defensive works – if you didn't count the improvised steel breastworks of the Wall – pushed another 25 or 30 yards toward the forest on both sides of Main. The construction was mostly of pinewood, but Wetsman's engineers had reinforced the barrier in front of the firing platform with sandbags, a few steel plates and I-beams scavenged from the half-renovated shell of the former Silverton Ironmongery. It had been halfway towards being rebuilt as an artisan bakery and cheese shop when the Chinese launched their cyberattack.

Standing just beyond the last structure at the southwestern end of Main Street, the gate enclosed the tiny park where Jonas had left his roommate's stolen mountain bike on that first crazy fucking day back in August. As Sheriff Muller hauled himself up the main ladder, followed by Deputies Milfull and Tilly, and a little more slowly by the county Comptroller with his bad arm, the good people of Silverton gathered in loose clumps and knots behind the gate. Nobody issued any orders not to group together, but with so many people carrying so much edged metal and firearms and blunt instruments, people naturally gave each other a little bit of elbow room.

Jonas would have happily stayed at the back of the crowd, ready to dive for cover if and when everything went sideways, but he felt a strong hand gripping his arm, pulling him forward through the loose crush of townspeople. It was Dale Juntii.

"Come on," he said. "I want to see what's happening."

It did not seem to occur to Dale that Jonas had zero interest in joining him on the platform. But the former Marine and Leo, the walking gun locker, virtually carried him forward, assuming that he, like them, wanted only to be in the thick of the action.

Fucking idiots.

The thick of the action was where all the bad shit happened. Jonas had a reputation to maintain, however, and any reluctance to face up to danger now would inevitably eat away at his standing later. There was nothing for it. Unless he wanted to end up on the wrong side of the gate, Jonas Murdoch had to play his role. If he was forced to show willingness, then it was best he showed himself to be the most willing motherfucker on the mountain.

"Better hurry up before old Howard bores them to death," he said, loud enough to be heard not just by Juntii and Vaulk but everyone around them. A few of them laughed. Someone cheered. Selectwoman Bohenski, protected from the morning sun by an outsized floral bonnet, clapped all three of them up the ladder.

Jonas set his jaw and tried to banish any fear from his face. Armed only with his pistol, he was able to ascend the ladder hand over hand and climb onto the platform before Sheriff Muller could start talking. Juntii followed closely on his heels, his assault rifle secured on his back by the strap. Leo Vaulk, ten or maybe fifteen years older and at least fifty pounds heavier, was much slower. His face was purple and sweating when he pulled himself up and joined the others at the parapet.

The road outside Silverton was a hell of a sight.

It had been a few days since Jonas had pulled duty on the Seattle Gate. He always seemed to manage an assignment patrolling well inside the town. Since he'd last stood on this platform, the county's engineering crew, under supervision from Dale Juntii, had constructed a herringbone blockade out of salvaged and abandoned motor vehicles, preventing any vehicles or foot traffic from a direct approach to the main gate. Bullet holes had punctured some of the car bodies. Most had shattered windows. Two sat on the rims of their tyres, blown out by gunfire to judge from the pockmarks in the panels around them. Two signs affixed to steal pickets borrowed from Alex Tewes, Silverton's long-time realtor, warned outsiders to proceed no further. Jonas couldn't see the hand-painted lettering on the outside of the gate, but he knew that it warned, "LETHAL FORCE IS AUTHORISED AGAINST INTRUDERS BY PRESIDENTIAL EXEC-UTIVE ORDER 14101."

Work crews had felled and cleared trees and bushes on both sides of the road, creating a free-fire zone a hundred yards out from the gate. Nobody in town was keeping count anymore – Howard Wetsman had given up after the raid that killed Brian Chillmaid and wounded Cathy Tranent – but Jonas knew dozens of bodies had been dragged away from that killing field over the past week and a half. Unlike some in town, he had zero problems with that.

Even so, more striking than all of the defensive works and the damage they had sustained was the small group of men – they were all men – who now challenged those defences. Jonas counted nine motorcycles, four of them Harley-Davidsons. Despite the balls-out craziness and mortal hazard of all this shit, he was quietly pleased that he'd been able to identify the machines simply by their tell-tale double-shot report. The engines, all of them, were hugely, powerfully noisy. Even sitting and idling, they destroyed the stillness of the morning.

Which was the point, he knew.

"Lookit these fucking assholes," a new voice said just off to his left.

Darren O'Shannassy.

Muller turned slightly towards his old rival, clocked his presence, but pivoted back to the men outside the gate.

"I count nine in the open," said Juntii.

"Nine confirmed," Vaulk responded.

Juntii gave Vaulk a sceptical look and took up a firing position on the platform between Dave Muller and Howard Wetsman.

These nine men were trouble. Jonas recognised them. Not as individuals but as a type. He'd pleaded out a couple of low-level soldiers for the Pagans motorcycle gang in Florida and appeared for members of a rival club, the Outlaws, in Tampa. It was all petty bullshit. A domestic assault, some street violence, a minor dope charge for the guy in Tampa. Jonas never did graduate to Hondo's A-list clientele.

But because of that, he knew these rimjobs like they were brothers.

The nine stood about a hundred yards away, all of them armed with military-grade weapons and all but one shrewdly placed where they could best take advantage of the protection afforded by the herringbone blockade. The one man who wasn't ready to dive into tactical cover was striding forward, weaving his way through the blockade, the ghost of a smile on his face. Jonas didn't recognise his colours or patches. He wasn't close enough yet to read the insignia sewn into his leathers.

Didn't matter.

He could tell they were from a couple of different outfits. And that was the worst news of all. These motherfuckers would've been murdering each other for market share and criminal bushido just a fortnight ago. Now, they had banded together.

Jonas drew his sidearm carefully, keeping it below the line of the parapet as he squeezed in next to Juntii.

"You recognise any of the colours?" he asked.

The ex-marine shook his head and squinted.

"The guys on overwatch? Nope, too far away. This asshole coming at us looks like Hells Angels. He's got the wings patch, I think."

"Told you," said Leo.

"Nah, you just guessed good is all, " Juntii smiled. In a louder voice, he went on, "Anybody got a pair of binoculars? Or a working phone with good zoom? Be good to get a look at these assholes. Figure out who they are."

"Their order of battle," Leo added, raising his voice too.

Juntii shook his head and sighed to himself, "Save me, Obi-Wan, you're my only hope."

"The spokesman is a full member of the Hells Angels. He's got the four-piece crest and Dequiallo patch," Sherriff Muller said, not loudly, but with enough projection to be heard over the engines.

Jonas didn't know what the fuck a Dequiallo patch was, but he supposed it made sense that Muller would.

The man approaching them through the last couple of cars in the barricade was not physically imposing. If anything, he seemed wiry, and his face was a little hollow and drawn. Most of the bikers he'd represented had been fat, bearded fuckwits. A sense of genuine menace came off them in radioactive waves, but mostly because of what they were plugged into, not who they were as individuals. The biker who had now cleared the barricade somehow managed to transmit a visceral threat on a very personal wavelength, as well as carrying with him the promise of something worse because of what, not who, he was.

He didn't even bother coming armed. Although that hardly mattered. His backup had enough firepower between them to kill everybody on the Gate before starting in on the crowd behind it.

"That'll be close enough, I reckon," Sheriff Muller called out. His voice was steady and commanding. The man took a few more steps anyway before coming to a halt about thirty yards out.

He stood with his hands at his side, his knees slightly bent, his back straight.

He called up, "You in charge around here?"

Muller waited before replying. Waited long enough for it to become uncomfortable.

Finally, he spoke up.

"Sorry. Didn't catch that, son. Kinda noisy because of all those garbage wagons."

He said nothing more.

The scout or the sergeant at arms or whatever the hell he was actually smiled. He made a small gesture with one hand, and one of the other riders, but only one of them, stepped away from cover and wandered back to turn off the motorcycles. He did not hurry. The two sides were at least two minutes waiting for the last engine to go quiet. The silence that suddenly flooded in from the mountain forests was an almost physical presence. The man standing in front of them smiled again.

"You good now, Sheriff? You need a hearing aid or something?"

"Just a name," Muller lobbed back.

"My name is Renken," the biker answered. "And you never did tell me if you're in charge here?"

"I keep the peace. That's all."

The man's grin grew wider.

"Well, that's excellent," he said. "Because we would never seek to disturb the peace of your fine town. We are just looking for passage through to better days."

"Then you're out of luck, asshole," Leo Vaulk yelled out. "Because you won't be coming in here, or through here, or nothing."

"Put a sock in it, Leo," Muller hissed.

Jonas had to agree with the cop, even if he did so silently.

Read the fucking room, Leo, he thought.

"Yeah, shut the fuck up, man," Dale Juntii muttered.

Howard Wetsman stepped up to the parapet. His voice shook a little when he started to speak, but he increased his volume until it wiped out the slight tremor.

"I am the senior administrative officer for Snohomish County," he called down. "The Mayor and Deputy Mayor were in Seattle on business the day of the attack. They haven't come back yet. I am County Comptroller Wetsman. I have authority for the duration of the crisis."

The smile on the man called Renken became positively vulpine.

"That's awesome, man. Good for you. So you can tell the Sheriff here to open the gates and let me and my friends pass through. We'll be no trouble. We just headed on down the road."

"I wouldn't open those gates, Howard," Jonas found himself saying.

"Never gonna happen," Sheriff Muller said quietly. In a louder voice, he went on to Renken. "Comptroller Wetsman chairs the committee in charge of things around here for now. But I'm in charge of security. It's my say-so whether you come through or not. And I say no. You can all just back up a ways and take the Skagit Dam access road. It's well-signed. It forks north to Skagit County and west to Chelan. Happy trails, Mister Renken."

"Sheriff, please," Renken pleaded, or more accurately played at pleading. "You can see our vehicles. Damn fine pieces of American industrial design for the most part." He threw a look back over his shoulder. "Except for the rice burners. But they are not designed for off-road travel, and that dirt track is in even worse shape than normal. I know because we tried it. I'm afraid we're going to have to insist on our right to pass through."

"Insist all you want," Muller replied. "But only residents of the town are allowed within the town limits for the duration of the Emergency. We have the legal authority to deny you passage."

"Wasn't aware I woke up in Russia this morning," Renken smiled.

"Wasn't aware they still existed," Muller said.

Renken laughed. It seemed a genuine, good-natured whoop of amusement.

"Oh, you are the witty one, Sheriff. But seriously, now, we need the road."

Darren O'Shannassy's voice boomed out.

"Then you are shit out of luck, scumbag!"

"Yeah, fuck off!" Leo Vaulk added helpfully.

It was all Jonas could do not to facepalm.

Muller did not turn toward either man, but he addressed them both out of the side of his mouth.

"If you two do not get off this platform right now, I will have my deputies arrest you, and you can spend the next week in the cells."

"You can't negotiate with these people, Sheriff," O'Shannassy said, loading up the last word with a sneer.

"I'm not negotiating," Muller said. "I'm trying to avoid a bloodbath."

Down on the tarmac, standing among the leaf litter and brass casings of expended rounds, the biker looked bemused.

"Mr Comptroller, it looks like you have a plurality of views as regards how best to handle this. Perhaps we could come through and discuss it. Just a small number of us."

Howard Wetsman didn't even bother replying. He just waved his good hand as if dismissing the biker.

Jonas wondered where the hell this Renken guy had been to know how to use shiny five-dollar words like 'plurality'.

Down behind them, people were growing restive. The buzz of conversation and the sharp discord of emerging arguments drew Jonas's attention back there.

Jesus fucking Christ. Was everybody in town all jammed up behind the gates now? He could see Rausch and Chad down there on the edge of the crowd. Natalie Bochenski's stupid floral bonnet stood out among the baseball caps and a couple of bicycle helmets.

"Sheriff," Renken called out, looking bemused that everybody's attention had somehow slipped away from him. "Scouts honour, we'll be less trouble than those two gentlemen currently aggravating your ulcers."

"That's right, you'll be no trouble at all, Mr Renken," Muller replied, "because you will not be coming through this town. Not you, or any of the men behind you, or any of the two hundred more you got parked around the bend in the road back down the mountain a ways."

For the first time, Renken's smile faltered. He glared momentarily at Muller before rearranging his features back into the serene mask he had worn up until now. Standing next to Jonas, his weapon pointed directly at Renken, Dale Juntii smiled.

He leaned across to Jonas and said quietly, "That'll be Wolfenden. He's out there somewhere doing recon."

Howard Wetsman conferred with Muller, asking, "How do we get them to move on, Sheriff? If there are that many of them?"

"As long as nobody starts shooting," Muller said, "I'm pretty sure I can talk them around. They can tell we won't be easy to push over."

"Maybe they really do just want to pass through?" Wetsman said.

Both Jonas and Muller replied to that together.

"No," they said in unison.

Muller glanced over at Jonas as if seeing him for the first time. He nodded and then went on, "I don't know what they want, Howard. But I don't want to find out by letting two hundred of them through the gate. Once they're inside, even if we have guns on them the whole time, they could take this place apart. They're not like the others we've had to see off. They were just desperate people. These men are killers. There's a couple of hundred more of them out there, where we can't see them, and they are very heavily armed. They're not coming in. Under any circumstances."

"Finally," O'Shannassy said. "You're talking sense."

"I say we send a message," said Leo Vaulk. "Put a few of them down and..."

Sheriff Muller jabbed a finger into Leo's chest.

"You pull a trigger, and you better be pointing that gun at me because otherwise I will kill you. Understood?"

The threat fell into a moment of quiet.

Leo glared at Muller. Darren O'Shannassy squared his shoulders and jutted out his jaw but said nothing more. The whole thing reminded Jonas of the first-day confrontation between O'Shannassy and Joe Wolfenden. He'd secured his place in town by mediating that showdown. He saw his chance to do the same again.

"Listen," he said. "Sheriff Muller is right. You can't have these shit-heads coming through, not in a group that's, what, two hundred strong? But I don't think they're gonna back down. Guys like this, they can't. They'd get eaten alive by their own. Maybe we could trickle them through, three or four at a time? Keep them under armed escort the whole way. Posts sentries and snipers on the roof line along Main Street."

Muller at least seemed to consider the option briefly, but then he shook his head.

"Nope," he said. "Too dangerous."

Darren O'Shannassy butted in.

"They wouldn't have got this far if you'd listened to me about pushing our defences further out and down the mountain," he said.

"I think we'll table that agenda item for discussion at a later time," Muller said testily.

"Yo! Still waiting down here, gentlemen," Renken called up. "Not going anywhere. That's a promise."

"Fine by me," shouted Darren O'Shannassy. "You can curl up and die out there like the rest of them."

"Jesus Christ," Muller said quietly.

Renken's posture and attitude changed. It was as though somebody had tightened a crank somewhere inside him, pulling taut a bunch of wires.

"Pretty fucking sure we could force our way in if we wanted," he said.

Jonas saw Dale Juntii crouch a little lower over the iron sights of his weapon. But Dave Muller seemed to stretch himself up, standing about two inches taller.

"And I'm pretty sure you couldn't," he said. "I do not advise you to try, sir. Nobody needs to get hurt today."

Renken was moving now, but slowly. Withdrawing towards his comrades.

"No, they don't. All we want to do is pass through, Sheriff," he shouted, raising his voice as if to project the message over Muller to the hundreds of people gathered behind the gate. "Why don't you talk it out among yourselves? Take as long as you want. Canvass all the issues. And then, if you're smart, you'll open the gates and let us through. Before we just come through anyway."

It was Leo Vaulk, naturally, who said exactly the wrong thing.

"Why don't you try then, you fucking faggot? Cos you're scared, that's why."

The bikers' guns came up with unexpectedly tight discipline.

Jonas never did figure out which of the men out there shot first, but he did know who opened up from the defender's firing platform. He was standing right next to him.

Dale Juntii had done two tours of Afghanistan and one in the sandbox. He had not survived the experience by being slow to recognise a threat and pour fire on it. His gun barked three times. A discrete burst of fire chewed through one of the bikers, packing a fat-barrelled combat shotgun of some sort. Everything slowed down to a strangely serene, almost abstracted timelessness, and Jonas found he was lost within a vast and terrible whirlpool of everything and nothing all at once.

For the longest time, he stood, not moving.

Next to him, Dale serviced the targets below. A workman doing his job. As the assault rifle crackled in short, three-round bursts, the hot brass casings flew up and away. One bounced off Jonas's cheek, burning him. Causing him to flinch. He turned towards the other men of Silverton, now stood fast on the Gate. Sheriff Dave Muller, drawing his sidearm calmly, without flourish or pretension. Comptroller Wetsman, both hands gripping the top of the parapet, even his bandaged hand, the muscles jumping and twitching all along his jawline as he ground his teeth together. Darren O'Shannassy, all the arguments with Muller put aside for the moment, as he stepped forward, pushed Wetsman down out of the line of fire with one meaty arm as the other brought his shotgun to bear. And further down the firing platform, other men, some of whom he knew and some he did not, all reacting in their own way at their own pace. Some fired back, standing tall. Others crouched and trembled but did their best.

Bullets chewed through the parapet, turning rail sleepers and house timbers into deadly splinters. More bullets caromed and sparked off the car bodies of the blockade and crashed into the few unbroken windscreens and windows, shattering them.

Jonas had no idea when he'd started shooting, but his gun was out and kicking in his hand.

He fired again and again.

Fuck knows at what. He just wanted to make sure it wasn't his ass getting blown into protein confetti.

Reality kept coming apart and putting itself back together in weird and extra forms. It shattered into mirror shards of things he saw and things he knew and disconnected moments of utter mayhem and absurdity.

Somewhere, people screamed.

Dale Juntii, flexing at the knees, fired with the regularity of a

Swiss clock, even as a dark, wet stain spread from his crotch down both legs of his jeans.

Dave Muller, side on, like an Olympic pistol shooting champion, was taking careful potshots with his service revolver.

A revolver?

Like a cowboy.

That was odd.

Screams punctuated rock music from a ghetto blaster.

Leo Vaulk, on the far side of Dale, cursing and rolling around on the raw pine planking, shot wildly from guns he held in both hands, but he fired high into the air, directly above them, making Jonas wonder if bullets came back to earth at the same speed that they left it.

That would be dangerous.

But not as dangerous as the terrible, thumping explosions which seemed to shake the entire structure of the Seattle Gate as though a Norse God had come down from Valhalla or fucking Midgard or wherever they hung out just to punch seven kinds of shit out of the world. Two of the car bodies lifted up and fell with a crash. Another explosion seemed to shove one sideways. Men screamed. Jonas felt his knees go weak. Why had he climbed up here? He honestly could not remember. Surely not because he was afraid of somebody thinking he was afraid? As if that made any sense, which it totally didn't. So he just kept his head tucked in and kept shooting and waited for it to be over.

And then it was quiet again.

"All clear," somebody yelled.

The somebody turned out to be Sheriff Muller, who helped Jonas to his feet, clapped Juntii on the shoulder and gave Leo Vaulk a kick in the ass by way of celebrating the unexpected fact of their survival.

They were alive.

Jonas could not explain it.

What the hell just happened?

He could not tell from all the screams and shouts behind and below them. Although what anybody safely tucked away behind the gate had to scream and shout about, he didn't know. It wasn't like the bikers had been lobbing mortar rounds over the...

He stopped.

His reasoning ability suddenly returned from the cloud cuckoo land where it had fled.

His legs were rubbery but firm enough to carry him back to the parapet, where he looked out over the herringbone blockade of old car bodies and was stunned to find them in smoking, ruined disarray. Men in camouflage uniforms moved swiftly through the wreckage, occasionally stopping to deliver a double tap or a three-round burst to some shivering corpse on the ground.

"Fucking grenades," Juntii said with something almost like glee in his expression. "Out-fucking-standing, man."

Jonas slowly put it all together.

Joe Wolfenden's militia outfit had flanked the bikers by taking a path through the woods. They had fired down on the attackers from above and slightly behind. And they had thrown grenades. Or maybe fired them from a launcher. At least three that Jonas remembered.

The shock of the explosions was still reverberating through him. Numbing and exhilarating all at once.

"You're bleeding," someone said.

One of the interns from Doc Cornwell's surgery.

"Huh?" Jonas grunted.

"Flesh wound," the young man said. "Maybe a splinter. Hang on. Let me clean it."

Some things happened with cotton swabs and disinfectant. It hurt. Stung. But he was alive, and he could enjoy the stinging and throbbing and frantic euphoria of not being one of the bodies down there on the tarmac.

A single shot cracked out.

One of Wolfenden's guys making sure of a kill.

"Dude," he said to Dale Juntii. "You pissed yourself."

Jonas wasn't judging. If all the protein bars and powder hadn't given him constipation, he totally would have shit his pants.

Juntii laughed. "That's how I know I'm good," he said. "Every fire-fight, I piss myself. And then I get to wash my shorts cos I'm the motherfucker whose heart is still beating. Every time. The day I don't piss myself, I'm a dead man."

Jonas finally thought to check for casualties among the defenders. Oh.

Howard Wetsman was dead.

Doc Cornwell was raging and hammering at him, trying to punch some life back into his heart. But Jonas could see it was hopeless. He'd caught a round, a big one in the chest, right over the heart. He was done.

Cornwell was crying and seething all at once.

"You idiots. You fucking idiots," she cried. She was covered in Wetsman's blood.

"Where's the others?" Jonas asked.

"What?" Juntii said.

"The other bikers?"

"We got 'em all, partner."

"No. No, we didn't," Jonas said. "There was more. Muller said there was more."

Or maybe Wolfenden said that?

He tried to remember who had said there were more bikers somewhere.

He was sure of that, just not who said it.

Two hundred of them.

Was it him?

Had he said that?

Jesus. Why couldn't he keep a thought straight in his goddamned head?

22

INTERLUDE

Private Kewayne Mosser looked imposing in his battle-rattle, but he was starting to shake, and he really needed to pee.

The plaid-shirted, red-faced man across from him was yelling. "Hey motherfucker, why don't you let us get what we need?"

Kewayne said nothing. His grip tightened on his rifle, an M4A1. He glanced to his left and right, the guys in his squad flanking him. At least there was that, he thought. He wasn't facing these pissed-off civilians alone. He had gone through combat training out on Yakima Range, where his squad was tasked with clearing villages, but the role players there always yelled in Arabic.

This was a lot like that, except no one here was dressed in bedsheets, and this was no drill. The crowd of hundreds, maybe more, surged in front of him in the parking lot. The people wanted into the Walmart off of Bridgeport Way, a little south of Tacoma. His platoon had been ordered to secure it against looters; the Lieutenant had briefed them as if it were a combat operation. Kewayne was new to the service, but he didn't have any trouble feeling the ugly vibe of the crowd. Their shouts were a roar; a powerful animalistic smell assaulted his senses. This was bad.

Kewayne's hands were clammy, and his pulse raced. Some plaid-shirted dude got in his face, shouting. Almost screaming at him. Spittle flecked Kewayne's protective goggles.

"I'm getting in there, asshole, and you can't do shit! You got rules. I'll fuckin' bet your gun ain't even loaded!"

The man advanced on Kewayne as if to shove him over or perhaps to brush him aside. Kewayne did as trained. He jabbed the man in the sternum with the muzzle of his rifle.

The plaid-shirted man cried out and clutched at his chest. He fell. Kewayne had struck him with full force. Another man bent down to help him.

Kewayne knew this second man, a priest. His mind flashed back to a detail when he had first arrived at Fort Lewis. Kewayne had helped pass out donated toys to needy children. This priest had supervised the giveaway. He was a nice man.

Someone screamed. The man writhed on the ground. The crowd recoiled for the briefest of seconds, and above it all, Kewayne heard a hoarse command. One he had never seriously expected to hear. Not even on a battlefield. It was Sergeant Kominsky.

"Fix...Bayonets!"

Automatically, Kewayne undid the snap on the sheath, and with a tug, the M9 knife came free. Mechanically, he snugged it into place. A firm pull produced a metallic click as the squad's naked steel was exposed along the line. He tried not to think about what he was doing. Better just to do it.

An unnatural silence fell as the crowd glowered at the soldiers. Kewayne could smell their hot sweat mixed in with his own stink and the diesel exhaust of the idling Stryker fighting vehicles behind them.

Kominsky called out again, this time addressing the crowd. "You will disperse! We have orders to secure this facility!"

Someone called back, "What, so you can eat while our families starve? Fuck you, fascist!"

Another shout, high and panicked. "Weapon!" It sounded to Kewayne like Peabody the SAW gunner.

Kewayne saw it, too. Without thinking, he moved his safety lever to "fire," shouldered his rifle and covered the target. A man in gaudy urban fatigues filled his sights. The tip of his red targeting chevron rested upon the target's head. A woman partially obscured him. The man disappeared in the roiling crowd before Kewayne's trigger finger could find its rest.

He had no idea who fired the first shot.

But someone did.

An icy hand seemed to reach down and grab the young soldier as a series of images played across his field of view. A woman in a yellow shirt falling. A man's head wrenched violently to the side, his glasses spinning through the air. Someone trying to turn and run, shot down. He registered a flash, a whisper past his ear. Return fire. These people were trying to kill him. The thought slammed home in capital letters, and Kewayne started to engage targets, too. Shiny brass flipped from the side of his weapon.

Horrible screams, grunts, the roar of gunfire. Kewayne knew that they would die if the crowd overran them. He reacted, along with his squadmates. Within seconds, they had suppressed the incoming fire. Kewayne changed magazines, concentrating on the task. Not thinking about why.

From behind, he felt a hard smack on his body armor. Kominsky screamed in his ear.

"Fuckin' cease fire!"

"Yes, Sergeant!"

Someone was babbling. "Jesus Christ! Jesus fuckin' Christ!" Over and over again.

Kewayne watched the civilians run away. The lucky ones, anyway. In front of him, a pile of dead and wounded heaved and writhed or lay still; their bodies twisted unnaturally, their faces slack. The ones he could see, anyhow.

His eye settled on one victim as he heard the Lieutenant yelling at someone, maybe into a radio.

With a terrible certainty, Kewayne knew he had shot this man while trying to get the urban camo dude. It was the priest. The man had stepped into the line of fire, holding his hands aloft as if in prayer. As if he had been blessing the men who threatened him and his flock. Dark blood stained his cassock and clerical collar. His arm jumped and twitched as his soul raced to eternity.

And Kewayne had pulled the trigger.

MAHMOUD SAT in his tiny office in the back of the stifling tailor shop. The days when tourists would drop in were over for good. The tourists had disappeared, along with businessmen searching for a stylish ensemble at a reasonable price. Mahmoud rubbed at the *zebibah* on his forehead, then sighed when he heard more gunshots outside. It would not do to rush into the street and attempt to flee, as so many were trying to. That simply added to the chaos out there, of which there was already an overfull sufficiency, in Mahmoud's opinion.

No, he would stay in his shop on the Al Madbah, here in downtown Cairo. It was a humble establishment, but it was his. For fifty years, with his own hands, he had measured, sewn and cut his way to a modest sort of security.

Ha! Security?

What was that?

The distant and muffled chatter of automatic weapons fire mocked the clacking of his old sewing machine. It reminded him of his one awful year as a conscript when he was but a youth, a stupid boy in a bunker facing the Jews. How glad he had been to leave that madness behind. He had made suits for Jews in the decades since. Americans mostly, but some Europeans. An airline magazine once listed his little shop as one of the secrets of old Cairo, and he had feasted on the profits of that for many years. He did not care how anyone worshipped their God if they were true to themselves and their faith. Even the Jews were people of the Book, after all.

Mahmoud sighed again and lifted the cup of tea to his mouth. He took a sip, savouring the taste of the black leaf, then placed the cup back on the piecework table. The old tailor regarded the cup; the liquid within was the last water in the shop. The machines that pumped from the Nile had stopped, along with all the other ephemera of civilization. It was all so fragile, he thought. So easily taken. And they had been such fools to trust it.

Cairo was thousands of years old when America was born. It had not lived or died by some light switch or computer back then. But now it was to perish because such things no longer worked? It was madness.

But Mahmoud had always known this. All were dependent upon the will of God, and if he withdrew his favour from this world, then he did. What would happen would happen.

A gunshot caught his attention; it was close. He heard someone screaming. Outside on the street, the rumbling, thumping sound of heavy foot traffic was constant. Everybody was trying to get somewhere, some refuge, anywhere but Cairo. Without water, the massive city by the Nile was a necropolis in waiting.

Mahmoud knew this.

He had witnessed for himself the impossible traffic snarl on Cairo's already famously clogged streets. Where, he wondered, did the people think they were going to go? To Alexandria, to get on a ship? Perhaps to Suez, to cross into the barren Sinai. Downriver? He shook his head. A flood of people would be stripping the farms along the river bare. And after the farms were gone?

Nothing. Red land, as far as the eye could see. Egypt lived and died by the Nile, and Cairo, with its dead pumps, sat at its head, the delta that reached toward the Mediterranean.

Mahmoud picked up his cup again and thought of the sea. He tapped the delicate glass with its few remaining drops and thought. He prayed. His son had begged him three days before to pile into the family car and head toward Port Said with the others. He was firm in his refusal, and as he pointed out, he was old. It was only fitting that he give up his seat for a child to have a chance. A strong grandson like Omar, that boy was the future of the family. Not Mahmoud. He was the past, and he trusted that God would know his own.

He sipped carefully, then he picked up his prayer beads and ran them through his fingers, going through the *dhikr* without really concentrating. Mahmoud thought that perhaps he could be forgiven for thinking of his absent family and the two hundred kilometres to the sea. Two hundred kilometres under normal conditions, that is.

Another gunshot outside. Closer.

Although the narrow front of his shop's steel roller curtain was down, he could tell from the quality of the light through the cracks that sunset was coming. Usually, it would be time for the evening prayer, and Mahmoud would either go to the mosque or spread out his rug in the shop. The imam's voice reached all corners through the loudspeakers on the street.

He shook his head. Today, there would be no loudspeaker. There was no electricity. And getting to the mosque would be impossible. Too many people, too much violence. An old man like him wouldn't stand a chance. What did it matter that he was a hajji, or that he had memorized the Holy Quran?

His mouth twisted. Of course, it counted, he thought, and he cursed himself for a fool. Prayer mattered more to him now than ever, even when he was under the guns. They were not even Jewish guns. Instead, the Iranians had come and all of their hirelings. His fleeing family, they were in the hands of God. It was the least he could do to pray.

Mahmoud spread out his mat, took off his sandals and knelt in the direction of Mecca.

He prayed.

When he was done, he rolled up the humble rug and put it away. He returned to his seat in the near darkness and felt for his precious last sip of tea. He allowed himself a drop. He could tell from the weight of the cup that it was nearly gone.

His wife was gone, too, long before. And now his family as well.

He heard laughing and swearing. Things breaking. He furrowed his brows. What, would the jackals come into his shop as well? There was nothing worth having unless the thieves wished to be well-clothed.

Even though Mahmoud was a man of immense faith, his mouth still went dry when he heard the sound of the padlock on his rolling steel curtain being cut. The curtain slammed upwards, and a brick flew through the plate glass window. A harsh beam blinded him.

He did not fear death. But he did fear the dying.

———

BENNY MA'S vision exploded in black blooms and stars. He tasted blood; his body twisted and fell. He was distantly aware of hitting the ground. He heard a noise like thunder and screaming. Swearing. Someone stepped on him and wrenched his arms behind his back. Something sharp wrapped around his wrists, and he heard a "z-z-z-i-p" sound. His nose burned with pepper spray, his mouth filled with vomit and leaked onto the blacktop and cobbles.

A policeman swore and struck him again with a truncheon. Benny wet himself and screamed, but it was a weak, pathetic cry. Someone hauled him to his feet and dragged him away. His vision greyed out from the pain. Nothing seemed real. He suffered a high-pitched keening in his head, mixed in with the roar of the crowd at the Yee Woo crossroads, directly in front of the Sogo department store. He was hustled along to a black armored vehicle. There were dozens of them parked in rows.

All this for me, he thought. He grinned. Another cop saw his expression and slapped him across the face with his open hand. It stung, and he felt dreadfully humiliated. Benny spat blood. His guards ran him up the steps into the paddy wagon, where another pair of cops waited. These policemen, who wore different uniforms from the Hong Kong police, jammed him onto a narrow steel bench and chained him down.

Benny was stuck. He tugged a little at his restraints, but only a little. They were tight, and they hurt. Within a few seconds, another prisoner, a girl, was jammed in next to him. A few minutes passed, and a woman called out.

"We're full! Close the door, and get ready to go."

"Yes, Sergeant."

"Start processing these enemies of the people."

Benny heard that phrase and thought it overly dramatic. Seriously. Who talked like that? All he had wanted to do was to hang out with the hot girl from his economics class. She had insisted it was essential to make a stand against the mainland's warmongering. She had virtually dragged him to the protest. But she was hot, so Benny had gone along. Perhaps afterwards, she might drag him to her bed?

Well, he didn't see her in the paddy wagon. And he was starting to doubt the wisdom of making his highly principled but obviously pointless stand against the evil old goats who ran the Chinese Communist Party and who thought they ran the world.

His thoughts were suddenly disrupted by somebody jerking his head back by the hair and shining a light in his eyes.

"Prisoner, look without blinking into the light."

Benny heard a strange whirr. The guard spoke.

"Scan complete."

Benny blinked.

"Open your mouth."

He obeyed, the guard jammed a cotton swab into his gums, rubbed it around, a most uncomfortable experience, and finally withdrew the intrusion.

"State your full name, identification number, and address."

Benny did so. He thought for a moment about lying, but only for a moment. He was pretty sure the government already had his DNA, and they had just taken it again. He really didn't feel like another beating. His wrists burned, and the zip-tie restraint was tight. His stomach was sour; it was sinking in. He was an Enemy Of The People now. All because he wanted to get laid. Or maybe even just a hand job. Surely the people could forgive that? The paddy wagon lurched and moved with a snort.

A Sergeant standing in the back of the vehicle spoke up.

"Prisoners of the People's Republic! Look at me!"

Benny tried, but he had to contort himself painfully to look at her. The Sergeant waited patiently and flexed her knees as the paddy wagon moved.

"Do I have your attention? You there, look at me!"

She pointed, and another guard yanked the prisoner's head up.

"Good. You can all hear me. This is important."

She sneezed, which somewhat detracted from the intimidating effect she'd been going for. And she sneezed again, ruining it completely.

The woman sniffed, rubbed her nose and glowered at them. "You are scum. You have no rights now. You will never see Hong Kong again."

Someone moaned, and another man cried out. The Sergeant flicked her hand dismissively, and a subordinate kicked both men, one after the other.

"If you do not do exactly as we say, you will not survive the trip to re-education." She paused and sniffled. "Not a word from any of you until we get to the camp. And when we do arrive, I will have absolute obedience. Understood?"

Benny said, "Shi!"

They all did.

The Sergeant nodded, and the paddy wagon rumbled on. Benny sat and suffered. After what seemed like hours, during which the only noise was the sneezing of the sergeant and the hacking cough of another guard, the wagon finally stopped. Great, Benny thought. He was totally going to catch their filthy colds out of this. One by one, the prisoners were unshackled and led from the back. Benny heard screams and blinked into harsh lights. His turn came, and he was hustled up and out. He could barely stand; his legs had fallen asleep.

The guards didn't care. Someone struck him with a club, and although his legs were numb, it still really hurt. Dogs barked and growled. They made him run; blows came from all directions. He fell; more blows and kicks rained down. Someone turned on a hose and sprayed him. Choking and crying, he crawled to his feet once more.

Eventually, he stood in a brightly lit building with many others in a rough formation. A few officers sat at a table in front while guards with stubby QBZ rifles stood every few meters around the shivering and bleeding prisoners. Every couple of minutes, a guard barked out a name and a prisoner would be prodded before the soldiers at the table.

It took Benny a few minutes to figure out what was happening.

His head started to throb in waves.

It was a People's Tribunal. Like in the Cultural Revolution.

The three officers were passing sentences.

"Hard labor."

"Re-education."

"The Highest Punishment."

After the sentence was passed, the defendant was taken away

immediately. There was to be no second chance. Benny started to hyperventilate. What had he done? What sort of fool was he to have followed that girl down to the stupid protest? Idiot!

It took a couple of repetitions for him to realize they were calling him.

"Ma, Bo! Present yourself!" He was used to his nickname, Benny. Nobody called him Bo.

"Here!" he said.

Two guards rushed in and seized him by the elbows. Another stood behind him with an assault rifle. They duck-walked him forward. He tried to look at the judges, but his vision blurred. They looked at one another, at their tablets, and murmured. He couldn't hear what they said. Finally, the soldier in the center nodded and signed his tablet.

The three judges looked at him. Their faces looked like granite slabs. The judge in the center raised his voice, but it was croaky. He had a bad cold.

"The Highest Punishment," he coughed.

Benny sagged and cried out. "No! I just wanted to... I just..."

But it was pointless. They did not care.

The judge in the center turned to the officer on the right.

"Have we reached the quota yet?"

"No, sir," the officer replied. "We will need more of the youngest ones. They are best for harvesting."

23

AM I A BAD PERSON?

James came awake with a start.

Shit! He'd forgotten to send out his newsletter.

The momentary surge of panic recalled exactly the waking nightmares he suffered from three months after finishing his MBA, waking up in a flop sweat of fearful desperation because he was convinced he had a ten thousand word essay due and he hadn't even finished his reading list.

He had finished the list, of course. And submitted his essay early for an A+

Just as he hadn't forgotten to send out *The Acorn*, his newsletter.

He'd chosen not to because the world no longer existed in which MBA graduates could profitably write investment advice for a monthly fee of fifty bucks (one month free with a yearly subscription, paid up front). The last copy of *The Acorn* had pulsed out from his server a few hours before the Chinese attack. There would be no more editions.

He was not that guy anymore. He hadn't woken up in his apartment in Baltimore or the hotel room in Washington. He lay on a thin camp mattress, in a sleeping bag, in a tent. Michelle Nguyen lay next to him in her sleeping bag.

"James?"

She was awake and had noticed him stirring.

"Hey," He said quietly. "Can't sleep? You worried about something?"

She laughed at that. And he had to laugh, too. It was a superbly stupid question. James propped himself up on his elbow. They were lying close together, but they were not actually *together*, if you get the difference. He had always been that way with women. Letting them make the first move. It felt safer that way. Surer.

Not that there was anything safe about this woman. Michelle was... different. It was not just the midnight blue hair and the acres of tattoo ink staining her skin. She was simply unlike any other human being he had ever met. He couldn't quite say why, if you insisted on asking him. It was just a truth he felt in his core. He seemed to have known this woman his whole life. Or at least known she would arrive in his life at some point.

And right now, he knew, she was hurting and scared, possibly even terrified.

"James," she said. "Can I ask you a question?"

"Sure. What?"

A heartbeat passed. Then another. He heard her intake of breath. Like she was standing at the edge of a cliff over a water of uncertain depth.

"Am I a bad person?" she asked.

It was dark in their tent, and he could not see her face, but he could hear the need in her voice. She really did not know the answer. She did not know herself.

"Are you crazy?" he scoffed. "No way."

"I didn't ask if I was crazy," she said. "I asked if I was a bad person. I think that Mel thinks that I am. Because of the..."

She didn't so much trail off as she choked mid-sentence. It was as though, having divulged the secret of Jericho earlier, probably breaking about a hundred different laws in doing so, she could not bring herself to talk about it again.

"Hey," he said gently. He reached out for her in the dark and accidentally smacked her face with the back of his hand. It was not exactly the reassuring gesture he was looking for.

"Sorry," he said quickly, feeling like a complete fool.

But she took his hand, squeezed it and kissed the back of his fingers. The feeling of her lips sent tingling waves up his arm.

"That's okay," Michelle said. "I'm sorry. I'm just feeling very fragile and, I dunno, overwhelmed or some shit. It's not like me."

"I'll bet it's not," James said. "I doubt anything could really overwhelm you."

They kept their voices low, even though they knew Mel would be awake and on guard somewhere around the camp, probably sitting with Nomi under the stars. Everybody preferred to sit out with Rick's dog when they had guard duty. She was a good companion and much better at keeping vigil than any of them.

"Michelle," James said, holding onto her hand in the darkness. Her fingers felt small but strong. At some point, she had taken off all the rings she wore when he'd first met her back in Washington. James wondered where she'd put them. "I don't have any doubt that you are a good person," he said. "None at all. And I know you were doing good things in your job. Remember, I'm the one who sought you out after reading your stuff. I know what motivates you, Michelle. You want to help people."

He could almost hear the smile in her reply.

"And you need to remember, James O'Donnell, that I'm the one who reeled you in with bullshit promises of hot scoops for your newsletter so that we could recruit you for our nefarious ends."

"Your promises weren't bullshit," James said thoughtfully. "And I'm not worried about any of that, but I am worried about you, Michelle. This flu bug they released. It's just... I can't..."

He struggled to find the words.

"I don't want you to get sick," he said at last, in a rush, opting to keep to simple. "I don't want you to die."

She leaned into him and wrapped her arms around his neck, holding on tightly.

"I'll probably be fine," she said. "But... but so many people...all dead..."

She trailed off.

James wasn't sure who she meant. Americans? Chinese? Everyone, probably. He didn't ask. He just held her for as long as she wanted to be held.

It was a cool night, but not cold. The light material of the tent bellied in and out on a gentle breeze.

He felt Michelle lift her face to his and her hand grip the back of his neck, pulling him down to her. She kissed him and sighed. Her breath was hot on his neck.

"It's all fucked up, isn't it?" she said.

"I liked the kiss," he said. "But yeah, I know what you mean."

"Do you think they were wrong to do it?" Michelle asked. "The plague, I mean. Or the flu, whatever it was."

"Do you really think they did it?" he asked, deflecting a question he didn't much want to answer. "You don't know that it's not just happening because it's happening. You weren't in the room when they made the decision. Were you?"

She shook her head.

"I wasn't. But I think Panozzo might have been. And I can't raise him."

"You can't get anyone," James reminded her. "The satellites are toast, remember?"

She shrugged. A very small movement.

Her lips found his. A light kiss. James was aware of how bristly he must be. It had been days since he'd shaved.

"I think it was wrong," Michelle said. "They shouldn't have..."

She didn't finish the thought.

Nomi started barking, a loud warning bark and a voice called out, "James! Michelle. Get up. There's people coming. Lots of them."

The flap of their tent suddenly reefed back, revealing a silhouette against a brilliant star field.

It was Mel.

"Come on," she urged. "Get your pants on."

James was already wearing his pants.

He was up and out of the bag with just a few quick, economical movements, another payoff from all those years sleeping out on the range back home. Grabbing his rifle, he climbed out of the tent and waited for Michelle. Out under moonlight, he could see Nomi bounding about. The tone of her barks had changed. No longer the deep, almost snarling roar of the hell-hound, she was now excited and happy to greet her master on his return.

Rick's voice reached them from the forest.

"Nomi. Friends!" he called out.

James calmed a little. His heart, which had been hammering at the inside of his rib cage, slowed. He took a moment to breathe slowly and deeply as Michelle crawled out of the tent. She stood up and slipped her pistol into the holster at her hip.

"What is it?" she asked Mel.

"Don't know," Mel replied. "It sounded like trouble at first. I heard gunfire about half an hour ago. Just the usual stuff, I thought. A few pops before it went quiet. Then I heard lots of punters heading straight for us, but that's Rick for sure, and Nomi's okay now. So I don't know."

All three of them stood by the small tent, waiting. James could hear voices. Lots of little voices. And two women talking loudly. Not arguing, but not bothering with any sound discipline or stealth. For a second, he wondered whether Rick had wandered down into the valley and gathered up that school group still camped out by the pond, and then four children burst out of the forest and ran towards Nomi. She barked excitedly and turned in small, tight circles, wagging her tail.

"Nomi!" Rick called out from somewhere back in the woods. "Friends."

The children, two of them young teens or tweens and the other two, small enough to be in their first years of schooling, fell on the dog. They squealed and laughed, and James imagined that the whole of the Canaan Valley must be able to hear the commotion. He started walking over to where they had emerged from the edge of the tree line. They all did.

"This doesn't feel like the best moment to sit down with Rick for a long chat about biological warfare," Michelle said.

"Agreed," Mel said. "But we do need to talk about it. "

"Agreed," Michelle conceded.

James almost returned his rifle to the tent but then thought the better of leaving a loaded firearm around with four children loose in the campsite. Rick appeared from the scrub at the same time as the two women he led into the clearing.

"These better not be Tinder dates," Mel said. She sounded dead serious, but James was getting attuned to her sense of humour.

They approached the newcomers cautiously. They approached all newcomers cautiously these days. James scanned the wider night, searching for signs that anybody else might be coming, perhaps somebody using all of this confusion to sneak up on them. He saw Mel doing the same thing. One of the women broke away and joined the children playing with Nomi. She told the children to have a care, and he was pretty sure he heard the deep twang of Kentucky in her voice. Rick led the other one over to the big tree stump, where they had eaten dinner. James could still smell smoky fish oil in the ashes of the campfire.

"Might need to put on some coffee and make up some hot chocolate if we still have any," he said as Rick came up. The woman with him looked young, maybe somewhere in her mid-20s. It was hard to tell in the dark. She had long hair and a slim build, and she was dressed practically. Jeans, heavy boots and a hoodie.

"Everyone, this is Tammy Kolchar," Rick announced. "Tammy, this is Mel, my girl, and our friends James and Michelle. They'll make you welcome. You and the kids will be safe here."

24

I THINK LIKE A BULLET

Doctor Cornwell was covered in blood, but it was the blood of others. She examined Jonas for minor wounds, his second check-up in just a few minutes, while he leaned back against the parapet and stared out over the retarded goat rodeo of Main Street. He was dizzy. What a supermassive fucking shit show. Half a dozen fat-fingered muppets had shot themselves or their neighbours in the shock and terror of the firefight. A lot more had been injured in a scramble to get the fuck gone from harm's way. Even though they had a giant fucking fortified wall between them and danger. Jonas had seen none of it go down. All his attention had been focused on the assholes trying to kill him, and they were all outside the gate. But now, leaning back at his leisure, zoned out while Doc Cornwell fussed around with triage, he was able to appreciate precisely how fucked up Silverton's first general mobilisation for the common defence had been.

This wasn't like previous raids or showdowns at the Gate. The raids had been small, and most often at night, and the immediate response had fallen to the sheriff's deputies, or Joe Wolfenden's militia guys, or even to a patrol of the Town Watch, bolstered by at least few veterans like Dale Juntii or Paul Tisevich. That old fart hadn't picked up a rifle since getting home from Vietnam in 1967, but there was no denying he had a cast iron pair of danglers. Tisevich had legitimately clubbed some dude half-dead the previous week. Just some hungry fucker he found trying to sneak into the old bakery when there wasn't even a stale crust to be had there anymore.

"Jonas, how many fingers am I holding up?" Dr Cornwell asked.

"Two, Doc," he said. "V for victory, yo."

He started to chuckle at his own wit.

She folded one away, leaving only her index finger in the air. Jonas stared at the latex glove she wore. It was stained with blood.

"Please follow the movement of my finger with your eyes," she said.

He grinned.

"Be a hell of a lot easier to do that if both of you stopped moving around, Doc."

"Try not to be a jerk, okay?"

He couldn't promise to do that, but he had no trouble tracking her finger. It wasn't like he'd been hit in the head or anything. Not like her friend Wetsman. Jonas could see she was barely holding it together. Her eyes were red with tears, but she had a job to do. Tough bitch, then. He'd give her that.

"Can you stand up?" Cornwell asked. "Don't rush it if you can't. Wouldn't be any point surviving this mess to break your neck falling off the damn platform."

Oh yeah. That's right. He was on the firing platform, way up high.

"I'll be okay, Doc, but thanks," Jonas said, pulling his legs underneath him. "Best you go see to someone who needs it, I reckon. I'm just lazy. Any chance to sit on my ass, I'll take it."

She didn't smile at all. Stripping off rubber gloves and quickly putting on another pair, she moved on to Dale Juntii, who had also sat his ass down. He was enjoying a smoke. He put it out before Cornwell checked him over. Jonas was not a smoker, and he wondered whether the town's supply had been rationed.

"I'm fine," the ex-marine said. "Just pissed my pants is all, Doc. Perfectly natural. I'll take a beer on prescription if you got one. Otherwise, I'm good to go."

Doctor Cornwell played no more heed to his macho bullshit than she had to Jonas's.

"I want you to come and see me, both of you, immediately if you suffer any symptoms like cold, clammy skin, rapid, fluttery heart rate, nausea, vomiting, fatigue…"

"Doc," Jonas grinned, "it must be a while since you've read your Camus. Nausea, vomiting, fatigue, that's just the human condition, man."

She shook her head, and maybe she was trying to grin, but it came out as a grimace.

"It's not the time for jokes, Jonas. Not even smart ones."

She had been crouched down next to Dale, and she struggled to get back to her feet. Jonas rolled to his knees, stood up, took a deep breath to ward off the dizziness, and helped her up by the elbow. There wasn't much to her. She didn't weigh nearly as much as a flatscreen TV back at the old fulfilment centre. Dale came to his feet with ease. He smelled terrible, like an old wino, but he didn't seem to care. Cornwell moved on down the line of defenders, pointedly ignoring Leo Vaulk, who was standing, smoking near the guard tower at the far end of the platform.

"You did okay, man," Dale said.

"Thanks," Jonas replied. His eyes swept the scene below. "Don't know you could say that about everyone."

"Nope," Dale agreed. "Not everybody's meant for this shit."

It looked as though the whole town had been drawn to the Seattle Gate. To secure the defences or to see to the wounded. But not in any organised way. Most of these assholes were just fapping around. Some were running to and fro like they had important shit to do. Some women wailed over bodies on the ground. Some guys sat with their legs splayed out in front of them, crying like grown-ass babies. It was a mess. You couldn't tell who was in charge, most likely because nobody was.

Jonas spied Dave Muller down at ground level, conferring with Joe Wolfenden and some of his guys. They had stripped weapons and ammo from the corpses of the bikers outside and salvaged what they could from the packs and panniers on the motorcycles themselves.

He saw Tomi Yates moving through the crowd, looking lost. But hot. She was wearing cut-off jeans and a T-shirt, and even though it was only a couple of hours since he'd banged her that morning, Jonas felt his cock growing hard again. Dale saw him looking at her and grinned.

"Yeah, it comes on like that sometimes. And this is a hell of a lot better than the fucking sandbox. I know for sure I'm gonna get laid today. You should go put it to her, man. You got the scent on you right now."

"Huh?" Jonas said.

Dale smiled. "Blood and battle, man. Just a little dab. Nothing hotter to a bitch. You should go for it."

Jonas nodded, and he'd never wanted to stick himself into anything more than he wanted to fuck Tomi Yates right then, but he shook it off like a dog coming out of a cold lake and said, "Maybe later. Yeah, later. But I wanna know what Wolfenden's telling Muller. Those guys we killed, they were just the scouts. Like the advance team or some shit. You remember? There was more riders away down the hill or something."

The question seemed to bring Dale Juntii back to earth.

"Yeah," he said. "I remember that. They weren't the main force. Just reconnaissance. Let's find out."

They both climbed down from the platform using the same ladder they'd gone up earlier. It felt like something that had happened years ago, somewhere else. Jonas was surprised to find it easier going down than he had climbing up. The strange, contrary heaviness and floaty feeling were gone. Instead, he felt utterly both in and of the world. As though he *was* the world, every fucking rock and tree and all of that shit raised to fucking consciousness. Again, he didn't smoke, didn't do drugs, but this was a trip. Tomi came running over as he headed toward Muller and Wolfenden. She had been crying. She ran at him so fast and hit him so hard, throwing her arms around him, that she almost knocked him over.

"Oh baby, I thought I lost you. They told me you were shot, everyone was shot, and there were like gangsters and shit and..." she said it all so quickly it was like a crazy word salad she just tossed into his face, "and... and... they said you got shot and..."

"Whoa, now. It's cool, T," Jonas said. "I just got a scratch, is all." He pulled her in tighter and nuzzled her ear as he squeezed the small, tight mound of her ass through the cut-offs. "Nothing like the scratches you put on my back this morning, so let's do that again. But I got some shit to get done first, baby."

She tried to argue with him, tried to drag him back to the cabin right there and then, but Jonas patted her on the rump and pushed her away.

"I'll be there soon, honeybunch," he promised. "And I'll need to clean up. Go fill the tub for me," he grinned. "You can scrub me down."

"Oh god," she said, her lips brushing his ear. "I'm gonna fuck you like you were meant to be fucked."

She turned and hurried away. They both watched her go.

"Man, you are one lucky son of a bitch," Dale Juntii said. "That fine piece of ass belonged to Todd Jozniac."

"Yeah, I heard all about him," Jonas said. "And his trial with the Longhorns. Don't reckon he's coming back from that."

"Nope," said Dale. "Likely not."

They moved aside for a couple of guys who were going up onto the platform to recover Howard Wetsman's body. That was gonna be a hell of a job. Jonas would've just rolled the dude off the platform, but it looked like they were going to try and bundle him into a sheet and carry him down with dignity or something. That promised almost as many lulz as a really decent Hold My Beer video, but Jonas turned away from the entertainment, heading instead for Muller and Wolfenden.

The self-styled militia captain stood in front of the Sheriff, his combat boots shoulder width apart, thumbs hooked into a webbing belt from which hung a small arsenal of reloads, handguns, fighting knives and even one hand grenade. That had been a hell of a surprise. Jonas hadn't realised the Wolfpack had loaded out like a fully operational Death Star. The town had supplied a lot of the firepower the four surviving militiamen carried now, adding to their armoury after they agreed to stay on and help with the defence – in exchange, naturally, for food and shelter. Turned out those were in much shorter supply than assholes with guns.

Wolfenden, like Jonas, an outsider, had, also like Jonas, proved himself remarkably adept at negotiating the sometimes treacherous channels that ran between the town's contending factions. But as far as Jonas could tell, he hadn't played any games. Wolfenden was more your straight-arrow sort. "I think like a bullet," he would say, but he wasn't much of a talker. Not many incels were when you pulled the plug on their modems. But when he did run his mouth, he tended to talk in bullshit euphemisms such as "I think like a bullet."

Still, the Wolfpack had proven themselves. They were the ones who regularly patrolled way out into the forests, pushing miles down the mountain back towards Seattle, reconnoitring the road up from the city to provide early intelligence of any significant groups of refugees who'd need to be turned around or, more likely, redirected along the Skagit Dam access road. And, of course, warning of smaller, more dangerous groups of potential attackers or marauders.

"... they pulled back all the way to the turnoff," Wolfenden was saying when he saw Jonas and Dale approaching. "Hey. You get some?"

"Yeah," Dale smiled. "It was a good day."

Wolfenden looked at the urine stain on Juntii's pants but said nothing.

"What's this about the other bikers?" Jonas asked.

Wolfenden checked with Muller, who shrugged.

"Hell, they'd be coming over the wall if it weren't for these two."

Wolfenden chewed on it for a moment, nodded and spat onto the ground.

"Tony, one of my guys, he cut around the northwest ridges, got a good lay-up point where he could see the Seattle Gate and the main force unit."

"The bikers, you mean?" Jonas said. He wasn't being sarcastic. He wanted to be sure.

"Yeah. Tony worked in a chemical supply joint down in Algona. Had the feds in all the time wanting to know if any biker types came through looking to buy equipment or precursors for cooking up meth. Gave them a handy little chart of club colours and patches and stuff. These guys do love to play dress up."

Jonas had to force a smile off his face at Wolfenden standing there cupping his balls through those camo-pattern man-panties dissing on someone like Renken for playing 'dress ups'.

"So, anyway," the militia captain said, rocking back and forth in his spanky fucking combat boots, "Tony reckons he eyeballed chapters from the Bandidos, the Outlaws, the Vagos, the Mongols and the Hells Angels."

"Oh man, that's a helluva tea party," Sheriff Muller sighed. "The Vagos aren't even from in-state. They must've ridden up from Oregon."

"A lot of people come in from even further," Jonas said. "Chad Moffat, a guy we got helping Brad with the heavy lifting on the Wall, he got out of San Francisco. Came up the back roads looking for his kid."

He looked around to see if Chad was nearby but could see no sign of him in the milling crowds.

"That guy had a kid? "Wolfenden said. "I thought the steroids woulda shrivelled his nuts."

"He has a little boy," Jonas said. "Reckons his wife turned lesbian and took off for Canada with some New York dyke. Kid sent him a text when that was still working. And there's that dentist who's working for Doc Cornwell now. He fetched up here from Santa Monica or somewhere. Didn't ride a chopper to get here, either."

"No," Wolfenden conceded, "folks are on the move all over, I guess."

Jonas wondered if perhaps he should be on the move. Shit was getting real in Silverton, and it might be time to pull out. He'd always figured that was gonna happen at some point. Aloud, he asked, "So how many of these pricks?".

Out of the corner of one eye, he saw Howard Wetsman's body lowered from the platform. Six men and Doc Cornwell had joined in the effort.

"Tony counted about two hundred and change," Wolfenden said. "But that's give or take a dozen. Plus the ones we just killed."

"Jesus," Jonas breathed. "That's like a couple of infantry companies, isn't it?"

Dale nodded. "Call it a deuce. Maybe they brought the admin platoon as well."

Muller grunted and shook his head, turning the gesture into a slow scan of the chaos still roiling around them. Jonas didn't need to ask what he was thinking. He could see it all on the lawman's face. They weren't ready for this.

"How are they armed," Jonas asked. "Some of those shitheads with that Renken guy looked like they raided a military base or something."

Muller was interested in the answer, too. He turned sharply back toward Wolfenden. Likely, they hadn't gotten to that part of his briefing when Jonas and Dale rolled up on them.

"He didn't see any rocket launchers or crew-served machine guns or anything like that," Wolfenden said. "But they're comin' heavy. Lot of the gear we stripped off them wasn't street legal."

The sheriff took off his hat and wiped the sweat from his brow with a handkerchief that was already soggy and dark. The sun was high overhead now, and Jonas could feel sweat running freely under his shirt. He was really gonna have to soak in that tub. He hoped Tomi put enough hot water in there. They had solar at Al's, so she had no excuse.

"Outlaw gangs wouldn't need to go looking for weapons," Muller said. "They got their own caches. Mostly to protect themselves from other gangs. But the way things are going out there, I figure they probably loaded up along the way, too."

"I don't suppose we have any idea where they're actually headed?" Jonas asked. "Or if they're even headed anywhere?"

Like Muller, he turned around and took in the aftermath while speaking. There seemed to be nobody organising anything here. Everything was in flux.

"Sorry. Can't do human intelligence and signals intercepts," Wolfenden said with an apologetic grin.

"They're probably foraging for now," Dale suggested. "Like old-time cavalry. Living off the land."

"More like raping and pillaging everywhere they go," Muller said. "But yeah, I think you're right, Dale. They have mobility. They have firepower. They are a coherent force. They can move around and take what they need while it's still there for the taking. Probably got out of the city as soon as the army moved onto the streets. Maybe they'll head back there now that Fort Lewis has pulled back inside the wire."

"Doubt it," Jonas said. "They need to eat, like everyone else. And there's nothing left in the city."

He almost let slip that he'd heard the soldiers on the radio at Brad Rausch's place discussing the pullback to barracks and their orders to clean out the last of the food warehouses on the edge of Seattle. He swallowed his words. A small slip like that might not bring him undone, but it could make for some uncomfortable questions. Sheriff Muller, however, offered up pretty much the same information.

"Dan Treacy was on the radio when Fort Lewis warned us they were withdrawing. He kept scanning for chatter. You can learn a hell of a lot more from just listening in on the guys out in the field than from taking the word of the higher-ups."

"Amen to that, brother," Dale Juntii grinned. The piss stain on his pants had spread so far now you couldn't really tell they were stained. He still didn't seem bothered by it.

Jonas was grossed out by the smell.

Muller nodded before continuing. "Dan reckons the city's been picked bare. Panic buying emptied the shelves on the first day or so. Rationing didn't even have a chance to take hold. People probably ran down whatever stores they had in the pantry at home within four or five days. It must be hell down there now. The army isn't just shooting looters or rioters. They're firing on civilians who are coming directly at them. Armed and dangerous. God bless the Second Amendment."

"It saved our asses today!"

Oh no. Jonas almost winced.

It was Leo Vaulk. And Darren O'Shannassy was with him, cleared by Doctor Cornwell and ready for his next go-round of the octagon with Muller.

"I warned you this would happen," O'Shannassy seethed, jabbing one thick finger at the sheriff. "I told you we had to push out and meet these threats as far away from the town as possible. But no. You had to have your way. You had to build your little kingdom. And now Wetsman is dead. You killed your friend, Muller. You good with that? How does that make you *feel*?"

O'Shannassy had been careful not to actually lay a hand on Muller. But the sheriff stepped right up into his space, taking the next finger jab in the chest. His voice, when he spoke, was low and threatening.

"It makes me feel like you and this moron should be in chains," he growled, jerking a thumb at Vaulk. "You started that clusterfuck. We were just lucky more people weren't hurt or killed on account of your stupidity."

He pushed O'Shannassy's hand aside and leaned in so close to him that he could have kissed the man on the tip of his nose. A drinker's nose, Jonas noted. Heavily bloodshot.

"And if you dare speak the name of my friend again," Muller said quietly, "other than to offer up a prayer for his immortal soul, I will shoot you in the mouth before whatever steaming horseshit you were about to cough up comes out and soils his memory."

Naturally, Darren O'Shannassy wasn't one for backing down.

"The hell you will, you fat slob," he hissed. "I'll have that tin star off you before this day is done. And then this town is gonna organise its defences in a sound and rational manner."

"What? By sending Leo down the hill on a search and destroy mission? I'll admit the idea of pushing him out the gate does appeal."

"We should be turning you out of the gate," Vaulk shot back.

"Try it," Muller growled.

Vaulk stiffened and stepped towards him, but before the two could come to blows, Jonas intervened.

"Whoa, now. Settle down. Leo, be cool. Sheriff, I understand why you're angry, but that standoff was always going to end badly. You and me, we know those guys. They'll be back. And Leo here..."

Jonas turned a cautionary frown on the security contractor, warning him without saying so to shut the fuck up.

"… He might've run his mouth. But he wasn't alone. And I did see him get the dude who killed Howard. Dude straight-up murdered Mister Wetsman, and Leo settled with him for it. Drew down and waxed that motherfucker."

Muller looked sceptical and chagrined, but he took Jonas at his word. After all, his word was good in Silverton.

Leo Vaulk, meanwhile, was staring at him with undisguised amazement. He'd spent the entirety of the firefight curled deep in cover, squeezing off rounds high into the air. If he hit anything, it was most likely a bird passing far overhead.

He was smart enough to shut up and let Jonas speak for him, though.

Muller decided to let it go.

"Just keep him out of my sight," he said. "Vaulk, you should probably man the other gate from now on."

"Oh, that's just great," O'Shannassy protested. "Take one of our best fighters and banish him to the outfield. Are you trying to get us all killed? We need to seize the initiative here."

And they spooled up their engines again.

"We need to secure the town," Muller snapped. "What we don't need is to go off on one of your sniper hunts and foolishness. You're just gonna get even more people killed."

"Couldn't do any worse than you have so far," said O'Shannassy.

"Shut up!" a woman's voice cried out. "Shut up, the pair of you!"

Doctor Cornwell stomped up to Muller and O'Shannassy and whipped at them with the earpiece of her stethoscope.

That did indeed shut them up.

Howard Wetsman had descended from his last watch on the Seattle Gate, and his funerary party now carried him away to…

Well, to be honest, Jonas had no fucking idea. He'd never bothered to find out what happened when you caught one in Silverton. Not if you were on this side of the gate. Cornwell's eyes were red-rimmed and wet with tears.

"You should be ashamed of yourselves," she glared. "Both of you. The best man this town had on its side is dead of this madness, and all you can do is bicker about the size of your dicks. Well, let me put you out of your misery. I'm your doctor. Both of you. They are nothing to brag about."

"Hey now," O'Shannassy protested. "That's not so."

But Dave Muller blushed and found something fascinating to inspect at the end of his boots.

"Sorry, Doc," he said quietly.

O'Shannassy, too, then underwent a moral collapse.

"I'm sorry too," he said.

They both watched as friends and neighbours carried Howard Wetsman away, wrapped in white linen stained red with blood. The colours of the Hells Angels.

Somebody started to sing in a fine, sweet voice, and Jonas was surprised to discover it was Dale.

Singing *The Streets of Laredo*.

The young Marine Corps veteran stood smiling sadly, a strange light in his eyes. He reeked of urine, but he was transported to some better place where he sang beautifully, almost an aria, of a poor cowboy, now wrapped in white linen and as cold as the clay that would soon close over his mortal remains.

Nearby townspeople stopped whatever they were doing and fell silent. Sheriff Muller removed his hat. Darren O'Shannassy hung his head, and Doc Cornwell suppressed a quiet moan of grief.

Jonas shivered as Dale bade them all to beat the drum slowly and play the fife lowly.

He hadn't realised it until now, but Dale Juntii was authentically mad.

25

_____

HASHTAG, BLESSED

Leo Vaulk took his banishment to the far end of town with unexpectedly good grace. He'd so fully embraced the myth of his courage and warrior prowess in the fight at the Seattle Gate that Jonas could see the dude was starting to believe he really had stood into the face of the enemy's fire and that he did totally and personally lay the vengeance of the town upon the killer of Howard Wetsman.

Jonas had cooked up that bullshit on the spot to dampen Sheriff Muller's ire and redirect his ill will away from Vaulk. Leo wasn't much of a man, but he belonged to Jonas now. One of the guys he figured he could count on if it went bad here.

And make no mistake, podcast listeners... it was some hard fucking times in Silverton.

Jonas had the same uneasy feeling he remembered from Florida right before Hondo fired him and ratted him out to the Bar Association, weirdly enough for screwing up a gig with the Outlaws motorcycle gang. Man, he'd never expected to cross those assholes again. He pled their guy out, as agreed, but there were some, you know, irregularities with invoicing the shelf company the bikers used to wash all the funds sluicing into the club from their off-the-books revenue streams like gun running, loan sharking and, of course, drug trafficking.

That was all ancient history now, he told himself, as he stalked back up Main Street, heading for his cabin at Al's and hopefully for a hot bath and some desperately needed high-intensity jungle sex with Tomi Yates. His cock still hadn't gone down. It was literally high on life.

"What're you laughing at?" Dale Juntii asked, intrigued to know whatever had just made Jonas giggle like a pantomime fiend.

Jonas looked at him as they passed the Farmer's Mutual, where he'd rescued Al Barrett.

"Tomi," he said.

Dale snorted.

"Testify, brother."

Leo Vaulk walked on the other side of him.

Banished by Sheriff Muller, he'd chosen to stick with Jonas rather than cleave to Darren O'Shannassy, who was trying to round up the votes for an extraordinary session of the Emergency Committee.

He struggled to keep up with the younger, fitter men. Vaulk was at least twenty years older and a lot chunkier, and he still carried a heavy load of armaments and reloads. His colour was high, and his receding hair was plastered with sweat, but he double-timed it anyway to stay in contact with Jonas and Dale.

As they put distance between themselves and the Seattle Gate, the street scenes gradually returned to normal – for a fucked up, half-apocalyptic tiny Asian penis value of normal. Jacques Loubert was leading his gardening crew back to the fields, escorted by half a dozen of the town's designated hunters, all of them carrying rifles. Picks and shovels crunched into the black soil of the town common, turning over the sod, readying the earth for seeds, fertiliser and water. The sun glinted off the glass panels of the hothouse where Lachie Saunders had promised everyone he could grow asparagus spears at the rate of nearly a foot a day, given the right conditions. Sheriff's deputies and Wolfenden militia shouted at squads of the Town Watch, directing them to man the Wall or the Gates.

"When do you think they'll come back?" Jonas said, directing the question at Dale.

"The bikers?" he replied. "If they're smart, late tonight. Like, really late, when everyone here is exhausted and strung out from watching out for them. An hour after that. That's when I'd come."

They crossed over Main, passing through the ever-growing garden beds of the town common by means of an improvised footpath constructed of wooden pallets salvaged from Darren O'Shannassy's supermarket and broken up for a rudimentary boardwalk. Nobody stopped them to ask to help with the planting. Jonas was smeared with his own blood from the shallow splinter wound he had taken. Dale carried himself with a serene detachment that didn't invite interjection. And Leo looked like their fat, asthmatic gun bearer.

"I got the bastard who murdered poor old Howard," he said for no apparent reason at all.

Except there was a reason. A good one.

Leo's eyes darted to Jonas and then to Dale before he dropped his gaze. Jonas could have let him squirm. They both knew he'd done no such thing. But he did not leave Leo Vaulk swinging from his dick in the breeze. That was not the smart play here.

"You did that, Leo," he confirmed. "I don't know that you meant to, the way you were just spraying that bullet hose of yours around, but yeah, you got him. I saw it."

"It's a weird place, a battle," Dale Juntii said, mostly to himself.

"Well, I got him," Leo insisted.

"And I will tell anybody who asks that you did," Jonas said, clapping him on the shoulder.

They passed out of the town common and onto the tarmac of Main Street's divided road on the other side. Leo looked like he was trying to say thank you, but he couldn't look Jonas in the eye.

Jonas smiled.

"I used to be a lawyer," he said. "Did you know that, Leo?"

The contractor's weapons clanked and rattled as he shifted on his feet. His face was covered in a thin, greasy sheen of sweat. "I think I heard that, yeah. Somewhere back east, right?"

"Florida," Jonas said. "I did a lot of criminal work. Defended the sort of guys your company was hired to defend other people against."

He smiled as though they shared some inside joke. Dale had gone back to beaming at the sky with his eyes closed.

Leo looked like he had some difficulty unpacking what Jonas had just said, but finally, he got it.

"Right," he said. "You represented the bad guys. In court and stuff."

Jonas beamed.

"Yes, yes, I did. I did a lot of time in court. Took a lot of witness statements. Cross-examined a lot of people in the dock. You know what I found out, Leo?"

"No," he said, not looking as though he wanted to find out, "What?"

"Every event is infinitely describable. And every person who was there saw it differently. Sometimes so different that you wouldn't believe they were talking about the same thing. But they all believed that they saw what they saw. You understand?"

Leo Vaulk managed to hold his eyes for a few moments this time.

"I think I do, yeah."

Jonas grinned.

"Not my scumbag clients, of course," he said. "They were a bunch of lying assholes. But I know what I saw today, Leo. I saw you cover yourself in glory, man. You walked into the guns. The gate held. And Howard's killers are dead. That's all anybody is ever going to hear from me."

Dale Juntii looked as if he'd fallen asleep on his feet.

"What about you, Dale?" Jonas asked. "You good with that?"

Dale opened his eyes and blinked as if surprised to find himself alive.

"Hell," he yawned. "I don't remember anything after pissing my pants. That's how it goes for me, bro. It's a gift."

"I can see that," Jonas said. "Hashtag blessed, man."

"Yeah, I am," Dale said. "But I fucking reek. I gotta go wash down and change. Later."

He left them standing on Main Street.

"I should get cleaned up too, Leo," Jonah said. "I'll see you down at the other gate. We need to talk about some shit."

Leo Vaulk reached out and gripped Jonas by the arm before he could break away.

"Thank you," he said. "I won't forget this."

Jonas smiled.

"Hashtag blessed, man."

TOMI WAS WAITING for him in the hot tub with cold beer. A six-pack of Old Schoolhouse IPA from the back of Big Al's walk-in cold store, which was now running on a diesel generator. She rode him hard but ruined everything when she started crying after he came, blubbering that she thought she'd lost him. Jonas was in no mood for that shit, so he carried her to the unmade bed, turned her over and fucked her into shutting the hell up, at least for a while. He wasn't sure he had that last one in him, but... turned out that almost getting his ass shot off was some horny fucking goat weed for the soul. When he was done, he smacked Tomi on the rump, telling her to grab the last of the beers. He needed some thinking time.

She complied. Happily, he assumed, since she'd stopped blubbering. One of those bitches who measured herself by how much you wanted to put it to her. And he'd banged her five times today. So even if he was shooting dry at the end, she had that dick-drunk afterglow now.

"Baby, don't go out again, okay?" she said, kissing him lightly and dancing her fingers over the dressing on his cheek. "You did your bit today."

They lay in the tangle of damp bedsheets. Jonas leaned up against the padded headboard, Tomi on her stomach next to him, one long leg draped over his. The TV was on, but the screen was just white noise. He had the volume down. There hadn't been any network or cable coverage for nearly a week. Maybe the fake news giants had folded up like a cheap Chinese umbrella in a typhoon. Or perhaps the Chinese or Russians or some merry prankster from Gab had hacked the delivery channels. Jonas didn't know and didn't much care. He was still breathing and fucking, and that was what mattered.

If he was straight up with the truth of it, he could die an old and happy man, never again having the experience of some asshole trying to kill him. And indeed, with his head buzzing from three heavy ales on an empty stomach and his cock all but numb from pussy burnout, he was a little surprised to find himself... happy.

When had he last been truly happy? Like genuinely content?

That morning, he found out his podcast had cracked the front page of iTunes?

Probably not.

He sipped at the Old Schoolhouse and kneaded Tomi's ass because it was such a perfectly sculpted piece of vanilla booty it legitimately demanded the attention. He hadn't been content, as such, when his podcast, *The Centurion,* had exploded. He'd been stoked, jacked up, hungry for more. But that wasn't happiness.

"Baby, did you hear me?" Tomi said

"Huh," Jonas grunted.

"I said you shouldn't have to go out again," she pouted. Kissing the visible ridges of his abdominal muscles. He'd always been cut, but the hard physical labour and reduced rations of the past week—and all the bootleg protein bars he'd scarfed—had really stripped the last softness from his frame. He was probably down to low single-digits in body fat. Tomi traced a feather-lite trail of kisses up his sternum, throwing her leg all the way over him and settling herself atop his lap, where she squeezed his hips between her thighs and gently rubbed her snatch into his groin.

Jesus Christ, this bitch was insatiable.

"I need to reload, baby," he said, gentling her off him but giving her a friendly butt-slap to testify to her infinite hotness.

She looked like she might start sulking, but he scoped her body and smiled, growling, "So fucking hot," and that was enough to chill the bitch out.

She joined him back in the hot tub. Big Al's ran to industrial-scale solar tanks, and the water was still pleasantly warm. Jonas soaked his muscles and let Tomi scrub all the sex off him.

"Are we going to be all right?" she asked before quickly adding, "If those guys come back? The bikers."

"*We* are gonna be fine, baby," he answered, leaning into the promise of their future.

"But what if they come back?"

"Oh, they'll come back," he said. "And they'll come heavy too."

Tomi stopped sponging his pecs.

"Honey, they're fucking animals. Do you think we can fight them off? I mean, look at what happened when that greaser attacked Al. Everyone just stood around. Except you."

Jonas smiled.

"Except me, yeah."

Then he shrugged.

"Someone else woulda done something eventually. Sheriff Dave or one of his guys. Dale Juntii if he'd been there. For sure. Maybe even Leo."

Tomi snorted at that.

"As if."

"Yeah," Jonas conceded. "Okay, that's a long shot. But that was then. This is something else. People here, they been schooled in some hard truths since shit went dark. The cavalry's not coming, T. Not the army, the state troopers, National Guard. None of them. What is coming are more fucking animals, like you said. Cos they're the only ones fit to survive this crash. Gangs, criminals, fucking taco bandits like that spick who bashed Al, the whole fucking evil clown show. Shit, maybe even the gooks. They started this...." He paused to think about it before going on. "Probably not them, though. Pretty sure we could still nuke Beijing if we haven't already."

He almost felt as though he was back on his pod, riffing quietly but fiercely into his mic in the dark hour before dawn. Tomi looked worried, and he smiled and pulled her into his lap.

"Doesn't matter who comes, though," he said, nuzzling into her neck, chewing on the earlobe. "We'll kill 'em all."

She groaned and started to move against him.

Then she stopped.

"But what if we can't?" she asked, pushing back. "What if they just swarm us? I heard there were hundreds of them."

Thinking back on it later, Jonas had to confess to himself, if nobody else, that she caught him at a moment of weakness. Almost unbelievably, his cock started to stir again. The beer, the hot tub, the lips of her hungry little minge folding around his shaft, he lost the usual iron grip he kept on his thoughts.

"If they come over the wall or through the gates, I'll get you out," he murmured into her neck, feeling through his lips and tongue the strong and quickening heartbeat pulsing through her carotid.

"Will you? How?" she breathed.

He should have stopped, then. Should have just bullshitted her, but Tomi had reached down to cup his balls in her hand, and she was gently rolling his nads through her fingers and, well, what the fuck would you have done? Jonas told her about the getaway plan.

Seriously fucking stupid. Like, fatally dumb.

But he did score the best blowjob of his life out of it.

26

ALL THE TRUTH YOU NEED

R ick had killed three men in the night. A fourth lay wounded in a dry gully that looked to James as though it might be a natural watercourse in the wet season. The deadfall littering the tiny ravine was tinder dry, but a couple of inches beneath the surface, the loamy soil was damp and soft. The injured man was also kind of damp and soft. He was shirtless. Lathered in rank, stale sweat, he had also wet his pants. Rick had cut away the camo-patterned material where a bad leg fracture had torn through the skin, exposing an obscenely white bone shard to the air. The limb was bent at a terrible angle. The man moaned and shuddered, partly from shock, mostly in pain.

James had trouble looking at him. Every time a tremor ran through his body, the whole vast and naked bulk of it shuddered like meat jelly.

"I say we just leave the sumbitch here," the woman said.

"We can't do that, Tammy," Mel said, but without conviction.

She was standing closest to the man, but not so close that he could lay hands on her if he tried to. She wore an anxious, deeply disturbed expression. Rick Boreham sat nearby on a fallen log, cradling his assault rifle, drinking coffee from a thermos they had brought back from the campsite. He seemed unaffected. The sun was up now, and the nighttime chill was gone. Going to be another scorcher, James thought. The wounded man would not last the day.

The three bodies lay where they had fallen nearby—or where Rick had dropped them, to be perfectly honest—all painted in blood from gunshot wounds. Flies swarmed in black, humming clouds around the corpses. James wondered how long it would be before they started to smell. It was going to be a hell of a job burying them if that's what they ended up doing. One of the dead guys was enormously fat. Easily as big as the wounded man. Maybe even more so. They were obviously related. Possibly even twins.

It almost seemed a waste of time and energy to bury them. There must be millions of bodies lying around the country by now, he thought. Jesus, what would it be like in places like New York?

Hell of a thing, though, just leaving people out to rot.

Off in the distance, he could hear the faint but happy cries of children and the barking of a dog. Tammy Kolchar's friend was back at the main campsite with Michelle and four kids. James was pretty sure Tammy was the mom to the older pair. She wasn't attending to her children at that moment, though. She was zoned in on the fallen man with furious intensity. Her rage was all the more impressive for being so tightly reined in.

McGuigan was the name on the man's driver's license. Francis McGuigan. Mel had retrieved his wallet when Rick cut away the leg of his pants.

He was, according to Tammy Kolchar, a pedophile. They all were. Or some of them were. Ms Kolchar hadn't been entirely lucid on the topic when Rick brought her into camp with the kids and her friend Roxarne, and she hadn't really got her shit together in the time since. Fair enough, he conceded, if her story was true.

Mel was trying to sort it out, but Tammy seemed less interested in helping with any investigation than she did in straight-up executing its subject.

"They were gonna kill us and mess with our kids. We heard them talking about it," she hissed. "I was listening to them in their camper. They was almost squealing like pigs they was laughing so much at it."

"But not all of them?" Mel said.

Tammy rolled her eyes at the stupidity of the question.

"I already told you that! Cracker Barrel Darryl wasn't no child molestor. He's just a rapist. He was gonna take Roxy."

The dying man's protest grew louder. He moaned, "No, no," but James couldn't tell whether he was denying the allegation or simply giving voice to the agony of his shattered limb. Mel gave up on her witness, turning instead on Rick. Her tone was mild, but she still sounded like the cop she had once been.

"Why did you think it was necessary to open fire on them?"

Rick shrugged. Pushed back.

"Why do you think it's necessary to ask?"

Mel opened her mouth. Closed it. And opened it again.

"Rick, we can't just go around shooting people. Not without cause."

"Oh, he had plenty of fuckin' cause," Tammy butted in. "Don't y'all worry about that."

Mel held up one hand to forestall further interruptions. She said nothing more to Rick, but it was obvious from her expression that she expected some explanation from him. He sipped his coffee, screwed the lid back on, and stretched as though waking from a long slumber. He resettled the assault rifle in his lap.

"I heard the shots, as you did back at the camp. I heard the women and the children screaming. I saw four armed men in pursuit of Tammy and her friend. And the children," he added. "Maybe two weeks ago, I would've looked for a cop. But that time has passed, Mel. And we need to figure out what to do with this gentleman now."

Rick nodded at the wounded... what? Prisoner? Were they in that line of business now? James tried not to look at the grotesque wound to the man's lower leg. No bullet had done that. He'd seen similar fractures on horses that had lost their footing at speed. This guy had fallen over, probably when Rick put his friends under fire. It spared him a bullet, but he was going to die of it anyway. His whole considerable weight had come down on his shin bone at an angle. It was hard to look at. Neither Mel nor Rick, who had probably seen more than their fair share of such things, seemed bothered by it. And Tammy

Kolchar looked as if she wanted to stamp on the broken bone a couple of times before shooting McGuigan in the face. It spoke to the genuine loathing she held for him and, with it, the integrity of her story. But neither of the other two were of a mind to allow her to do that, at least not yet.

James carried his Ruger on a shoulder strap, and he found his free hand straying to the weapon as if for reassurance. He made a conscious effort to stop caressing the rifle. It was of no use now. His stomach growled. He'd made breakfast for the kids and coffee for the two women, but it was more than fifteen hours since he'd last eaten. The screech of cicadas was almost loud enough to drown out the buzzing of the flies feasting on the dead. James felt dizzy with the heat of the morning, his empty stomach, and the sticky horror of the scene.

"Tammy," Rick said, surprising James and Mel, too, judging from her expression. "Do you know how long you've been on the road? How many days and nights?"

The question seemed to draw the young woman out of her angry fugue state.

For the first time since they had returned to the killing scene, she turned away from the wounded man. Rick sketched a smile for her, his expression kindly. It seemed to short-circuit the intense fury she had focused on McGuigan.

"I don't know," she said. "Sorry. We sorta lost track."

"When did you leave your hometown?" Mel asked, picking up the line of questioning.

"That was late on the day of the big computer attack," Tammy said with greater certainty. "I remember that because all our point-of-sale shit went down. And it was just after the distributors called to say they had warehouse trouble, and we had nothin' coming' for the weekly restock anyhow. So I guess we been on the move since then."

Rick nodded.

"Twelve days," he said. "You've done very well. You kept your kids safe. You should be proud of that."

Tammy Kolchar stared at Rick as though he had grown a second head. Her expression was utterly blank for at least a second. The morning light, dancing through the forest leaves, played across her face. She had big racoon eyes from lack of sleep, but she finally nodded as though affirming what he had said. Yes, she was proud of that.

"It weren't easy," she said. "I thought we could hang out at my brother's place. He has a farm. Or he worked on one anyway. But he wasn't there. Nobody was. And turned out it wasn't a real farm anyhow. There was no food a kid could eat, so we kept going."

"Do you remember the names of any of the places you drove through?" Mel asked. Her voice had softened noticeably.

James wasn't sure what they were doing, but he was sure that they were working together. Rick passed the thermos to Tammy, and in one of his pockets he found a protein bar, which he also gave to her.

"Doesn't taste the best," he said. "But it'll help if you got the head spins."

"Thanks," she said in a small voice. "We ate a lot last night, but I vomited everything up when we ran. When I knew what was happening. I'm hungry."

Rick nodded.

Tammy tore the wrapper from the protein bar and stuffed half the length into her mouth.

"And you ended up at the roadside stop because you couldn't get into Dryfork, is that right?"

Tammy stopped chewing to answer him around the mouthful of food.

"Yeah. There was like a police barricade, but no police." She held up one finger. Finished chewing her mouthful, swallowed, and went on. "There was just heaps of people with guns and stuff. They told us we weren't local and we had to keep driving through. We couldn't stay there. There wasn't enough food for outsiders they said. That's how we ended up at the rest stop. It wasn't even really a campsite. More like one of those places to pull off the road and break the trip, you know?"

"I do," Rick said. "And that fella there and the ones he was with, they pulled in after you, right?"

Tammy answered after biting off a piece of the protein bar and washing it down with a swig of coffee.

"Yeah, they had food. Lots of it. And it was fresh, too, but I don't know where they got it. No way anybody in that town sold it to them."

"No," Mel Baker agreed, her voice thoughtful.

The wounded man groaned. Louder than before.

"Water, please, I'm thirsty," he said in a feeble rasp. James was about to step over to him with a canteen, but Rick raised a hand and shook his head.

"Don't waste that," he said.

"Rick, the man needs water," Mel said.

But Rick just shook his head slowly, almost regretfully.

"No," Rick said. "I'll wager the man needs putting down."

"Please," the man croaked. His body spasmed, sending blubber waves rolling through the mounds of fish-white belly.

"You shut the hell up," Tammy spat at him. She picked up a rock and threw it at him. It missed a wide margin and went on to disturb the thick cloud of flies around his dead companions. The dense black swarm broke up for a second but quickly descended on the bodies again. James half motioned for her to stop, but she had already backed off, her arms folded tightly across her chest.

Mel took a few steps toward Rick, lowering her voice.

"Rick, no," she said.

"I'm sorry, babe, but it's the best thing for it," Rick said. "I don't like it at all, but even if we could look after him, and we can't, what are we gonna do? Bandage him up, give him our antibiotics, and tell the cops? You think anybody's coming up from Dryfork for this guy? That sheriff back in Aurora, you think he'll hike up here? Despatch an air ambulance?"

James couldn't let the man, whatever his sins, go without a sip of water.

"It's not decent," he said quietly, mostly to himself. He took the canteen over to McGuigan, knelt, unscrewed the cap, and lifted the bottle to his lips. The man drank greedily, spilling water down the thick folds of pink flab around his neck. James kept the water up to him, and nobody made a move to intervene. He tried to ignore the foul stink coming off McGuigan, but his throat closed up against it. He gagged.

"I know what I saw, Mel," Rick said. "Four men chasing these women and their children intent on murder. That's all the truth I need to know."

"So?" Mel said. "What are you going to do? Shoot him?"

"No," Rick said, keeping it low and slow. "It would be a mercy, but it'd also be a waste of a bullet we might need later."

"James is right," Mel said. "This is not decent. It's not us, Rick."

Her frustration was plain on her face. She stepped up to Rick and placed a hand on his arm.

"You were a soldier. I understand what that means. My brother was too. But I was a copper. People think they're almost the same thing, but they're not, Rick. You understand that. Soldiers break things down. They fuck shit up. Because sometimes you have to. But all my life, Rick, I have been about helping people hold things together. I've always tried to stop the world from coming apart, and that's what's happening, not just here. Everywhere. We still have choices, Rick. We're not animals. We can fuck shit up, or we can hold it together. It's up to us."

"No, it's not just about us," Rick said quietly. "It's how things are now, Mel. I don't want this. I don't want any of it, but there is worse than this. I've seen it, Mel, when things fall apart. You're right that we still have choices, but they're all hard. And if we don't make those choices, good and decent people are gonna get hurt."

"Well, he ain't decent," Tammy said, pointing at McGuigan. "That's for damn sure."

"I can make it quick," Rick said. "Painless," he added. "Without wasting ammunition."

"No," Mel said, shaking her head. "You do that, Rick and there's no coming back from it. Not for you. Not for us. This isn't a war. And you are not a soldier any more. And even if you were, you wouldn't just slot this bloke."

"No," Tammy agreed, but with a very different tone. "He don't deserve that. He should fuckin' suffer."

James stood up.

"Enough," he said firmly, so loud he surprised even himself. "Let's at least check out this whole story. If these characters have been up to no good, it'll show. There'll be evidence. Probably in the camper van."

He looked to Mel for support.

She didn't seem convinced, but she agreed in the end.

"Sure, okay. If it means we don't just murder this git. I'll check it out. See what sort of shit he and his mates were into."

She turned on Tammy.

"But even if it turns out he's a complete villain, it doesn't mean you get to just kill him."

Rick nodded.

"Sounds like a plan. I can stay and keep an eye on him. I promise not to put his lights out. But I'm not of a mind to waste our supplies on him either. I believe Miss Tammy here, her little ones, and their companions were in mortal danger from this man and his comrades."

"Fine," Mel sighed. "I'll go with James. I will check out the van and Tammy's... allegations."

"Weren't no allegations," Tammy said. "They was gonna kill me and Roxy and have their way with our children. You'll see if you really was a cop. You'll see."

Nobody said anything for a moment.

Finally, Mel spoke up.

"Yes," she said. "I will."

27

INTERLUDE

Wilson, Kansas, wasn't terribly close to any major cities. With a population that hovered a little south of eight hundred souls, times were usually pretty quiet. The years and the seasons would come and go, and very little changed. Most around these parts preferred it that way.

It had been a rude shock then when Route 70, the major highway that passed to the north of town by about a mile, started vomiting cars filled with distraught, desperate people into the main street of Wilson. The out-of-towners came looking for something, anything they might eat or drink or simply stack into the back of their expensive SUVs and sedans. At first, the merchants of Wilson had been more than willing to help out and, of course, to profit. Nothing wrong with making good by doing good. But the last ten days had made a difference. No trucks had arrived to restock the shelves at the Stop 2 Shop or the Krogers. Gasoline tankers did not top up the pumps at Ray Camden's Texaco, out by the off-ramp.

The TV news had gone bad. And then had just gone altogether.

Train tracks pierced downtown Wilson like an arrow, but the trains themselves? Stopped days ago. Maybe for good.

For a short while, there was the radio.

But now that had mostly gone silent, too, save for a couple of single-handed operators, clearly religious nut jobs, who appeared to have gone mad beneath the unforgiving sun.

That same sun beat down on John Mathers as he walked along Old Route 40 in a pair of faded Army pants. He had a lever-action Marlin in his hands; it wouldn't do to sling it. His eyes cast nervously from side to side. He was headed for the Stop 2 Shop, his wife having sent him to see if he could find some beans or better yet, a bag of rice. Mathers shook his head as he walked past the World's Largest Czech Egg; he did not spare the famous local curiosity a glance.

The streets of his hometown had been transformed—in nothing flat, it seemed to him—into a landscape of threats and strangers that would make a Dali, or maybe that Munch fellow, proud. As he scanned around for threats and problems, he marvelled at the way he recalled the names of those painters from an art class in High School so long ago. Then he marvelled at his own foolishness in letting his thoughts wander.

His sleepy hometown had turned kind of nightmarish in a little over a week. Not quite a war zone, as he knew only too well, but not a nice or healthy place, either. Not the quiet, pleasant town he'd come home to after his war. It had quickly become a thing that happened in Wilson that anything not guarded or chained down would walk off or get plucked clean. His neighbour Rich Atterbury's prize pear tree got itself fully stripped on the evening of the third day, and the pear thieves hadn't even woken Rich's dog, Sophie. Imagine that. She was a notorious barker.

It was every man for himself, John thought, as the convenience store came into sight. When he saw the store, though, he simply shook his head and cursed. As he had feared, the trip had been a dangerous damn waste of time. There was a crowd of listless refugees hunkered down there; one person lay on the ground. Maybe he was sleeping, John thought, but he didn't look any closer to find out. He glanced over at Wilson Wine and Spirits; the store's shattered glass windows glittered like fangs in the white-hot sun. It had been robbed the second day. Out-of-towners for sure. Nobody local would have done that.

The Stop 2 Shop's parking lot had hosted an impromptu bartering spot for a few days the first week of the trouble, but it looked as if that was done for now, too. Torn tarps and collapsed stalls spoke to a bad outcome there. John shrugged and turned back north to 23rd Street, where his humble little split-level waited. He seethed again at the bad luck, the sheer terrible timing of that Zero Day thing on the radio news. While there had been radio news, of course.

It had struck right before his payday, and they never kept a real stock of food in the house; they weren't Mormons or anything.

His wife was going to be pissed. But what could he do? Go out to the field and steal ears of corn? Raid the grain silos? His mouth pressed into a thin line. It was going to come to that; Scotty Plater was already talking about how Anderson's farm had no diesel, and this crop of soybeans and wheat would mostly rot.

John still thought of himself as a postman; he had been a rural letter carrier since he left the army seven years ago. On his hopeless mission to the center of town, he had stopped by his workplace again. The brick, glass and blue-painted Post Office on the corner of E Street and 24th was shuttered. That sight really caused his balls to shrivel. When the postal service was down, the whole country was down. No doubt about it.

And pretty soon, the only thing to eat this winter would be wheat and corn. His mouth twisted into a sour expression. That was not an exactly balanced diet. John Mather knew a little about balancing his diet because he'd let himself get fat about five years earlier and it was true what they said. Losing weight was eighty per cent diet and only twenty or even less how much you burned off moving around.

John was worried they were all gonna find that out for real before too long.

He crossed the railroad tracks and took in the sight of the tall grain silos to the west. From somewhere behind, there came the sound a gunshot. And another. It was fairly distant, but John quickened his pace; there was more cover along 26th Street.

This is just awful, he thought. I'm thinking of tactical cover in Wilson. He furrowed his brow as he cleared the field by the tracks. Thinking of cover and wondering about nutrition in the middle of some of the world's most productive farmland in the world. Seriously?

He snorted and sweated. This computer war business was as serious as a goddamned heart attack.

More gunshots cracked out behind him, and the staccato picked up until it sounded like a string of firecrackers going off.

Cold sweat stained his blue labourer's shirt, and his grip tightened on his rifle. The gunfire seemed to be back at the Stop 2 Shop. He was sure of it. His breathing picked up as he power-walked north. He began to breathe easier when he was definitely out of line of sight from downtown, and the gunfire died down as well. If he never heard another gunshot in his life he would go to his rest a happy man. He took a deep breath and walked along Wilson's grid-patterned roads, and eventually, his own tan and brown house came into view.

No one was outside anywhere in the street. This was new, too. Before Zero Day, there would have been kids messing around, people mowing the grass, couples going for walks, or headed to one of the many local churches. Not now. As he approached his house, a curtain moved in the living room window.

It was Mary, and he knew she would have the family's .38 close by as she watched. As he climbed the front step, he heard the deadbolt click. The door opened, and there she stood, revolver in hand. He ducked inside with no greeting; she shut the door.

His wife spoke. "No luck, huh?"

John shook his head as his daughter peeked around the corner and hurried to him. "We heard shooting, Daddy. We were scared."

He gathered Anna in and looked at his wife. If he could run and take his family anywhere, he would. Somewhere, anywhere else. But he could read a map, and he knew his car had a quarter tank of gas. In Kansas, it might as well be empty. The first place stripped bare, of course, was the Texaco out by 70. And who said that any place else would be better? This same situation was everywhere. Even worse in the big cities with all those people packed in on top of each other.

John Mather set his rifle down, and he ran his hand through his greasy hair. The village water pumps had failed. From here on out, it was rainwater or bust, and it hadn't rained in a while.

Mary crossed her arms and looked at him. She put down the revolver.

"Post office still closed?"

"Yeah."

Her blue eyes looked sunken and hollow, "It's been ten days."

Mary's lips set in a thin line. John regarded her silently.

"No one's coming to help, are they?"

"No."

She threw up her hands. "Well, ain't this some shit!"

"Honey, not in front of..."

She put her hands on her hips. "We are going to starve to death in the middle of the world's biggest fucking farm!"

He couldn't disagree.

Anna started to wail.

MUHAMMAD COULD HEAR the truck long before he could see it. The valley was strange like that, the way some noises echoed and reflected and rolled around the long, snaking folds of the gorge. His body glistened with sweat in the stifling heat. A monkey screeched in a nearby tugaar tree, and the young man flinched as the creature laughed itself out of the canopy, thudding to the ground and noisily chasing away a rival. Muhammad's shirt was soaked through; his useless cell phone was heavy in a breast pocket.

Maybe, he thought, maybe it would make a difference if he showed the phone to Ali, the screenshot he had taken, the message that said in both English and Arabic that his funds weren't available. But when he thought about it, he only wanted to cry out in rage and panic again; thousands of American dollars, all gone. Disappeared. The money his village was to pay for this next shipment of khat that his clan would take to the markets in Mogadishu.

This arrangement with Ali and his people had been respected through generations; through wars and invasions, it had remained a constant. Ali would bring the product to the village; the young men would make sure it got safely to the markets in the city. It was, or had been, foolproof.

Muhammad's mouth was dry, his vision blurry with the sweat that ran into his eyes. Maybe with tears, too, if he was being honest with himself. The money was gone, probably stolen by the foreign devils who wrote the phone app. Gone. He should have stuck to cash.

The truck's motor grew louder, and he saw for the first time a cloud of dust rising from the curve in the wadi.

What would Ali say? Muhammad had no idea.

Movement caught his eye; the banged-up blue Toyota came around the bend into the village's sole, unpaved street.

The usual groups of playing children and gossiping women were nowhere to be seen. The old men did not squat by the well as was their custom. Muhammad stood ready to receive the visitors on his own. Where had everyone gone?

Also, there was more than one truck. Usually, Ali would come with just a driver and some guards riding in the bed. The men would be armed, of course. That was only natural. In this part of the world, a man leaving the family hut picked up his rifle as casually as he pulled on a pair of Chinese flip-flops to protect the soles of his feet from jujube tree thorns and the baking heat of the red earth. Men with guns were only to be expected. But on this day, Ali rode into the village with more guns and more men than Muhammad had ever seen. Three trucks arrived in convoy.

The Toyota, riding low from the weight of the khat. And two escorting vehicles, both technicals: the gun wagons you saw every-where in Mogadishu. They spread out. One of the technicals had mounted a Dishka. Muhammad could see the belt with the huge bullets snaking into the gun. A fuzzy-haired Ajuraan man in a brightly coloured vest pointed the heavy, long-barrelled machine gun directly at Muhammad and behind him at the village. His home.

His bowels felt as though cold water was sluicing through them. He did not doubt that with even the briefest pull on the trigger, he would be swept away in a storm of blood and the huts behind him reduced to sticks.

The big gun drew his attention, but it was a long way from being the only weapon bristling in Ali's convoy. The man must have brought his whole crew with him, Muhammad thought. His legs were leaden, although his feet were oddly feather-light, almost as if he might yet fly away on them. But it was too late to flee. Much too late.

The passenger door of the Toyota opened with a squeal. The panel was dented, and the door did not sit squarely within the doorframe. Ali climbed out slowly. He looked at Muhammad and grinned. But that lazy, gold-toothed smile did not reach the man's coal-black eyes. Ali held no weapon. Muhammad's Star automatic was tucked into his waistband. The hammer dug into his stomach. He sucked at his sweaty upper lip. The little pistol might as well lie in a crater on the dark side of the moon for all the good it would do him.

The men on the trucks regarded Muhammad in silence, their flat, empty expressions amplifying his growing urge to run. Someone charged a weapon; the noisy clatter of a bolt chambering a bullet breaking the silence.

Ali spoke. "Do you have my money, little brother?"

Muhammad opened his mouth, but no words came out. His chest felt as if a great pile of rocks had been heaped upon him or an invisible giant held him fast in his grip.

Ali tilted his head to the side; his eyebrows came together.

"What is wrong, brother? You cannot speak?" Ali waved toward someone. "Maybe I can help you find the words."

Muhammad heard a scream. A woman's voice, one he knew well.

An abrupt movement to his left revealed a pair of men dragging Muhammad's wife, Astur, into the street. Astur fought briefly until one of the men brought a gleaming knife to her throat. Her eyes pleaded with Muhammad. Do something, husband. Make this go away.

Ali spoke in the most reasonable tone, as though they discussed nothing of importance.

"Muhammad. I know your money has disappeared." He held up a phone. Muhammad did not recognise the model, but it looked very new. Ali would, of course, have the best. "Your little phone has betrayed you, yes?"

Muhammad ran a shaking hand through his hair. He could not look Astur in the eye. But he did finally find his voice.

"Ali! I do not know what has happened! Wallahi—I swear to God —Your money was there, the Prophet witness!"

Ali looked at Astur. Then he turned slowly and looked at the truck. The Toyota loaded down with heavy bundles of khat. Over a thousand American dollars' worth.

Muhammad trembled and fumed, but Ali held up his hand.

"Do not utter the Prophet's name to cover your lies and excuses. Do you see that even when the machines failed, I managed to harvest the plant as always?"

"Yes, but..."

Speaking slowly, as if to a small child, Ali said over the top of Muhammad's protests, "So why is it that you do not have my money? The Chinese and Americans did not make a pile of all the cash in the world and set fire to it, did they?"

"No, but..."

"I have just come from the village of Ibraahim al Galgala, and he paid me in cash, as he has always done."

"But Ali, please, the Barakaat Bank has your money, my brother! They are responsible for this, not me!"

Ali shook his head. When he spoke, he sounded dejected but mockingly so. "Kullaha, Muhammad, you have no money, but you will still pay."

Ali smiled at Astur and nodded to the man holding her. It happened so very quickly. The sharp knife opened her throat with shocking ease. Astur's eyes went wide as she jerked in sudden pain, her life's blood jetting out of the wound.

Wordlessly, Muhammad screamed, and his hand scrambled for the Star pistol. Everything was diamond clear to Muhammad in that instant. The monkey screeched in the tugaar tree. Ali's face shone with sweat and a sort of delirious glee. Astur's body slumped to the ground. Muhammad tried to raise his pistol, expecting to die before he could put a bullet into Ali's stupid, grinning face. But his arm would not move. Strong hands gripped him. Someone kicked out the back of his knee. His useless Tokarev pistol fell from his waistband to the red dust. Somebody forced him to his knees. He shut his eyes and prayed. This wasn't happening. Not to his wife. Not to his village. Small stones dug into his kneecaps. The smell of blood was rich and cloying at the back of his throat.

"Muhammad, open your eyes."

Something hard tapped him on the back of his head. He opened his eyes.

He saw his wife's body and the spreading pool of blood. Tears blurred his vision, but he could hear that the flies were already buzzing around her. And then he blinked away the swirl of colour and saw his family. His father. And mother. One of his brothers. Aunty Ahlaam, who was holding his son. His nine-year-old daughter.

Muhammad puked and wailed, then puked again.

Ali waited for him to finish. Then he spoke.

"I knew you had lost my money, Muhammad. You were never half the trader that Ibraahim is. You are soft and foolish. But you still have things of value here."

Muhammad wheezed wretchedly. "What do you want, Ali?"

"Al-Shabaab needs warriors and servants. The time to rise against the infidel is now."

28

A WALK IN THE FOREST

With all of his years on the family ranch, James was the most comfortable navigating through the light forest and occasional patches of open grassland, and he took the lead. For a while, he carried his rifle at the ready, but somehow, that felt wrong and, even worse, an affectation. He was not a soldier like Rick. So he went back to carrying the rifle on his shoulder again.

"James, are you all right? Are you having trouble with that? Do you want me to carry it?"

He paused in his headlong march along the rim of the valley. The sun had climbed high overhead into a cloudless sky, and the full heat of the late summer's day beat down on them. It was hard to believe the valley had been so cold just before dawn. Mel, who had been a good eight or nine paces behind, caught up. He could tell she wasn't lagging from lack of fitness. She was breathing easily, and unlike him, she wasn't sweating much. As she joined him, her head swivelled left and right, constantly checking their surroundings. They had dropped down and away from the ridge line overlooking the vast open arena of the Canaan to follow a shaded track through open woodland. The trees and the undergrowth in this part of the National Park had not grown to an impenetrable density, but you couldn't see much further than fifty or sixty yards in any direction. When he thought about the scene they had left behind and what they were possibly moving toward, he shivered just a little.

"No," he said. "I just feel a bit... I dunno..."

He trailed off.

"You and me both, brother," Mel said with genuine sympathy. In her London accent, the last word came out as 'bruvver.'

James joined her in scanning their surroundings. Leaves rustled, branches and tree trunks creaked, and small creatures skittered unseen through the deadfall. Mel Baker's face was unreadable, but he guessed that she was no more at ease than him.

"I guess I just don't know the rules anymore," James admitted. "A couple of weeks ago, walking along this trail, if you bumped into somebody, you'd have said hello, maybe stopped to chat. But now it's like... Well, I don't know what it's like. Rick probably did the right thing shooting at those guys as soon as he saw them."

"He didn't just shoot at them, James," Mel said. "He shot and killed them."

She sounded despondent.

James shook his head, but not in denial. You couldn't deny what Rick had done, but could you deny the necessity of it?

"I still think he probably did the right thing. I mean, after what Tammy and her friend told us, and the kids..."

Mel frowned.

"I know," she conceded, but she didn't look happy about it. She interrupted her continual scan of their surroundings to look directly into his eyes. It was not a pleasant sensation. After a while, she said, "That was our first fight, you know. The first time Rick and I have disagreed about anything."

She sighed and shrugged.

"We should've been arguing about what movie to see tonight, or where to have lunch, or whether the toilet seat gets left up or down. You know, stuff like that. Not about whether it's legit to straight-up murder a bunch of kiddy fiddlers in the woods or to leave one of them to die of shock or sepsis. Or exposure, or... I dunno. I really don't know anything anymore, James."

She had retreated so far into her thoughts that she seemed oblivious to the broader world and its dangers, and James felt the need to take over her continual surveillance of the forest.

Nothing had changed in the short time they'd been talking.

Towering conifers stood sentry, dark and mute. Starflowers and marsh marigolds bathed in patches of late morning sun where a break in the canopy let the light stream down. Somewhere nearby, he heard ducks and the honking of geese.

"We should keep moving," he said.

"Yeah," Mel nodded.

They resumed the trail, following the directions Rick and Tammy had worked out between them. It could not be far now. Maybe another five minutes.

They did not resume the conversation as they trekked on. Without remembering how it had got there, James found himself cradling the Ruger in his hands. Mel's pistol was still holstered, but when they finally hit the two lanes of blacktop slicing through the nature reserve, she undid the clip, securing the weapon at her hip. They stood by the side of the road, listening.

There was nothing to hear or at least nothing of human civilisation. No engines, no planes in the sky. Nothing. Just the rustle of leaves and the low, eerie murmur of the forest around them. That was unnerving because they knew there were plenty of people hiding out in the reserve. But everyone was laying low.

"This way, you think?" he asked, inclining his head to the north, where the blacktop curved around a gentle bend. Leaf litter and deadfall had covered the road, but not completely. He could see it was starting to build up. There had been little or no vehicular traffic through here in over a week.

"Reckon so," Mel said, and this time she led off. Her hand drifted to the pistol at her waist, but she did not draw the weapon.

James forced himself to ease up his grip on the rifle. He was tense; they both were. Their footsteps seemed very loud in the stillness as they strode along in the dead centre of the road. Once or twice, he looked down and saw the solid white line of the median divider beneath his boots. It was another data point marking a greater change. Two weeks ago, he would never have done this, no matter how remote or deserted the route. The chance of being mowed down by a speeding car, perhaps by a fast-moving, almost silent electric vehicle like one of the high-end Teslas, would be too great.

Now, it seemed not just unlikely but impossible that any car might appear. He wasn't sure whether he wanted one to or not.

"What do we do?" he asked, causing Mel to turn around but not to stop. "Like, if we meet someone," he added.

"If we meet up with anybody, and they're friendly, we can be friendly," Mel said. "But that doesn't mean we let our guard down, James."

She stopped talking for a moment but kept walking, resuming a few steps further on, "Honestly, mate, if things feel bad to you, you can be pretty sure that's because they are. And if that happens, we do what we got to, right?"

She did stop then, coming to a halt in the middle of the tarmac.

"You gonna be right with that? If you have to point that thing at someone and use it?"

She nodded at the rifle.

James did not answer straight away.

"I don't know," he said, eventually. "I couldn't tell you until it happened, Mel."

She surprised him by smiling.

"That's the right answer," she said. "But I reckon you'll be okay."

They set off again.

THE CAMPSITE, a roadside rest stop with some basic facilities like a coin-operated barbecue and a small toilet block, was another few minutes' walk away. As soon as they caught sight of the big, white RV and Tammy's very well-maintained Oldsmobile, they both slowed. Melissa drew her weapon then, motioning for James to fall in behind her. She advanced in a cautious shooter's stance, almost crab-walking sideways, with the pistol held low in both hands. James tried to imitate her obviously practised gait, but he felt like an idiot. His breath sounded like the bellows of a dragon in his ear, and every foot-fall seemed to crash down like an elephant's stomp. His limbs felt loose, and every inch of his skin prickled with sweat like he already knew he was going to screw this up.

To his surprise, she increased the speed of their approach as they got closer, eventually hurrying to take cover behind the solid concrete fortification of the barbecue. He rushed in behind her, his heart speeding up and a weird, sort of flattening effect seeming to press all of the depth out of the world around him.

Was this how Rick had spent all of his years in the Army, he wondered. He honestly didn't know how anybody could endure this as part of their everyday life.

Next to him, squatting down on one knee, peering at the campervan as though through x-ray eyes, James could see Mel was doing that thing that Michelle did so often: threat assessment. Her eyes swept over the campsite, traversing it from end to end and peering into the woods beyond before returning to the two vehicles.

The Oldsmobile was secured, the doors closed, and the windows rolled up. The RV's driver-side door stood open, and two swing doors at the back of the vehicle had been thrown wide the previous night and left that way. James started to pay attention to his other senses, smelling the rank, foetid stink of meat gone bad in the sun and the bitter, hoppy tang of spilled beer. Something rattled in the back of the RV, and they both dropped down out of sight. James's mouth was dry, and his heart hammered with force enough to make him dizzy. Mel pressed one hand down on his shoulder, indicating she wanted him to keep his head down. Neither of them moved for nearly a minute. James was beginning to doubt he had heard anything when a metallic crash from inside the van, louder than the first, set his nerves to jangling. Mel risked a peek around the corner of the barbecue, snorted, smiled and stood up. She still held her pistol in a shooter's grip, but she advanced on the vehicle with confidence. James took a deep breath and followed her, just in time to see a raccoon darting out of the back carrying what looked like a heavy, metal soup ladle away in its jaws.

"There's nobody in there," Mel announced.

She didn't drop her aim any further, and she advanced on the RV with all of the caution she had displayed previously, but she was not putting out the same furious, dangerous waves of dark energy she had emitted on their first approach. She raised the gun as they drew closer, and James finally thought to bring his weapon to bear. At least he didn't sweep her with the business end of the barrel. His father had taught him that much.

"Anybody in there?" Mel called out. "You can come on out now. We are armed, but we're not dangerous. We don't mean you any harm."

Nothing. No movement, no sound. Nothing.

With the departure of the raccoon, the whole site had taken on the air of a truly abandoned place. James kept his rifle at the ready, still not sure he could shoot anybody with it.

"Mate, can you keep a lookout while I have a poke around inside?" Mel said. "I reckon it's clear. That giant skunk or whatever it was wouldn't have been making off with the silverware otherwise."

"Sure," he replied.

Mel approached the rear of the RV as though a gang of armed robbers could be hiding in there, slowly, quietly, gun ready to snap up and start laying down fire. James tip-toed the short distance to a picnic table, stepped up onto the bench seating, and then the table-top, thinking it would give him coverage of the surrounding area. He quickly hopped down when he realised that all it did was expose him to the fire of anybody lying in ambush.

Jeez, this stuff was hard.

He tried not to get distracted by the scatter of items lying around. He did not have a trained eye for these things, but he could see a few kids' toys lying in the dust. Mel would undoubtedly be able to put the whole story together for them.

He heard her moving around inside the RV, opening and closing doors, searching for... whatever.

He forced himself to turn through three hundred and sixty

degrees, scanning for movement or colour or whatever the hell he was supposed to be looking for. But there was nothing. Just a warm breeze and bird song.

Did the birds mean they were alone here?

He never finished the thought.

Mel's scream cut him off.

29

A DEEP-FRIED
CLUSTERFUCKTURDUCKEN

Of course, it was Leo Vaulk who spoiled everything, pounding on the door of the cabin while Tomi was still sucking down the last few drops of Jonas Murdoch's much-diminished supply of love yoghurt.

"Jonas? You in there," he yelled. "You gotta come, man. You gotta come now."

"Too fucking late for that," Jonas sighed, but happily, almost chuckling.

He was done.

He pushed against Tomi's shoulders and stood up from where he'd been sitting on the edge of the tub. Truth be told, he was kind of glad to escape the ravenous bitch and was starting to understand why her boyfriend had taken a football scholarship on the other side of the country. She was like something out of a Grimm's fairytale porno. Ignoring Tomi's protests, Jonas wrapped a towel around his waist and answered the door.

Leo was briefly taken aback to find him wet and mostly naked, and he couldn't help trying to catch a sneak peek of Tomi as she climbed out of the tub. Jonas moved to block his view. No fucking way was that skeevy douchebag testing the video quality of his imagination by jerking off to any gash belonging to Clan Murdoch.

"Help you, bro?" he asked pointedly.

Leo came back with a shake of the head.

"Yeah, Jonas. Get dressed, man. There's a big meeting. O'Shannassy's moving on Muller like a bitch."

The fat security contractor tried again to catch a glimpse of Tomi in the cabin, but Jonas was having none of that shit. He'd been holding the towel closed, but now he let the towel fall, freeing his hand to move Leo away from the door gently but firmly.

Jonas stood at least four inches taller than Leo Vaulk, and he massed out at well over two hundred pounds of hard-packed muscle and thick dinosaur bone. He didn't have to shove. Standing there naked, laying a closed fist on one of Leo's jiggling man-boobs and simply pressing while smiling was enough to send him shuffling backwards.

"Thanks, man," Jonas said, keeping it pleasant. "Appreciate the heads up. Just let me get dressed. But wait for me. We'll go together."

That seemed to please Leo almost as much as nearly copping a peep of some quality bush. The sort of quality he could only imagine.

Closing the door on him, Jonas plucked a relatively fresh pair of jeans from the pile of clothes on the floor and buttoned himself into one of the shirts Tomi had given him. Her boyfriend, Todd, had left them at her place when he left for college.

Big dude.

Tomi liked 'em big.

"Sorry, babe," he said. "I gotta do this. Some shit about O'Shannassy and Muller feuding again. Gonna punch it out, Leo reckons. Like right now."

Tomi was pulling on yoga pants and a sports bra. She seemed a lot more settled than before.

"Coolio," she said. "Don't go getting into something you can't get out of, though. That Darren O'Shannassy's a prick, but Dave Muller's no pussy-ass bitch neither. You side with one of them, and the other will remember."

Jonas showed her his open hands.

"I'm an outsider, T. Just passing through. On which matter…"

He stepped over and put his hands on her shoulders, digging the fingers in just enough to make her wince before easing off.

"That thing we talked about before," he said. "That's between us. Don't go yapping to anyone else about it."

She shook him off, annoyed.

"I'm not an idiot, Jonas."

"Not saying that, babe. I'm saying shit is for real now. It's dangerous. Not just here. Everywhere."

"I know," she said. Softening and stepping back into his arms.

She hugged him.

"Be careful. Find me later."

He didn't think to ask where the fuck she might be going.

Too busy planning his next move to see Tomi's.

BEFORE JONAS MURDOCH launched *The Centurion* into America's top fifty podcasts, he had another show, much more conventional and much less successful, which attempted to explain the political moment. Specifically, he was trying to unpack that moment for the great mass of his fellow citizens who couldn't be fucked pulling themselves out of a bath full of blazing hobo liquor to escape third-degree burns if it meant they might also have to drag their lazy asses to a voting booth. Jonas had this stupid plan to capture that hundred million-strong demographic of broke-dick sloths and sell it to political consultants from both parties — but the pod tanked after three episodes and forty-seven downloads.

One of those eps, however, Jonas did recall fondly. He'd thrown together a short, potted history of the American town hall meeting - only he'd collected the worst, most disastrous examples, such as the gathering of 1837 in Barnstable, Massachusetts, during which somewhere between thirty and fifty feral hogs crashed through the slab-walled hut that served as Barnstable's Meeting Hall, gored the chief constable and carried off the good lady wife of Deputy Mayor Purchase Dunderland, never to be seen again.

It sort of reminded Jonas of this deep-fried clusterfuck-turducken right here.

Most of Silverton had crowded into the small park just inside the Seattle Gate. The green patch was not as well suited to being dug up for cultivation as the main stretch of the town Common, being shaded by three giant trees, two Big Leaf maples and an Oregon White Oak. Jacques Loubert had pronounced their extensive root systems too strong and deeply entangled to make the effort of digging them out worth the calories the labor would burn. An old fountain, which had stopped working twenty years ago and had never been repaired, took up more of the space, but a concrete table next to a coin-operated gas barbecue did provide a convenient platform for speeches. Darren O'Shannassy was roaring like a bear over the heads of the eight or nine hundred onlookers.

"It's not business as usual; it can't be business as usual, but Sheriff Muller is trying to pretend that nothing has changed. That deputising a couple more folks to walk the beat will keep us safe when those animals come back here and try to take the town."

The ragged roar that greeted this was half outraged, half spurring him on. Muller, standing on the stone table but as far away from O'Shannassy as he could without falling off, rolled his eyes theatrically. He was carrying a shotgun and wearing a ballistic vest. He hefted the firearm and lifted his shoulders as if to demonstrate that nothing about this was business as usual.

"We get one shot at this," O'Shannassy thundered. "And if we screw it up, we're dead. All of us."

The roars were louder this time, both the catcalls and the jeers.

Weaving his way around the edge of the gathering, leading Leo Vaulk like a lost dog, Jonas anxiously checked on the lookouts manning the Gate. He counted seven, including two of Wolfenden's militia guys, all of them armed with some of the heaviest weapons the town could supply. That was good, but half of those morons had turned their backs on the road coming up the mountain to follow the action at the rally. He also worried about how many guns they had on the Cascade Gate and strung around the Wall. If those bikers could see this shit, they'd roll on the place now and take it apart like a road-house chicken.

A sudden, disturbing thought occurred to him. What if they had a drone?

He craned his head back and scanned the airspace over Main Street. Nothing but blue sky and a few wisps of cloud.

The cellphone networks were still down, and he wondered if you could even use a drone for surveillance without phone cover.

"We need to stand up the Watch," Darren O'Shannassy shouted out, dragging his attention back to earth. "Three shifts, fully manned, heavily armed, and aggressive patrols out to a mile beyond the wire. We can't have them coming up on us by surprise."

More cheers but also more booing.

Jonas saw Dale Juntii at the rear of the action, leaned up against a post outside the Savings and Loan, smoking a hand-rolled cigarette. He'd changed his clothes and now wore a ballistic vest like Muller, except Dale's looked as if it had done a few laps around Fillinthe-blankistan. All the way around. Jonas was impressed that he could still snap it closed. A lot of guys went to seed when they got out of the service, but Juntii looked as tough as a two-dollar steak and cold with it. Like one of those private military contractors you saw on the news. Or in that movie about Benghazi.

Those guys had their shit tight.

"Hey Leo," he said out the side of his mouth. "I reckon these idiots might have left the back gate open. I can't see anyone standing watch. You reckon you could check the perimeter? Assess the exposure. You're the pro here."

"Sure," Leo replied. "You're right. This looks like a wide open shit-house door on a sinking tuna boat to me."

"Thanks," Jonas said. "I'll meet you at the Cascade Gate in about fifteen."

Vaulk saluted him like a perfect assclown and trooped off to inspect the defences, freeing Jonas to join Dale Juntii in the shade under the awning of the S&L.

"Hey," he said. The mercury was trying to break the century

again, and it was a merciful relief to get out of the sun. Cooler away
from the close-pressed body heat of that crowd, too.

"What d'you think about this?" Jonas asked.

At this distance, it was difficult to make out what O'Shannassy
was yelling over the crowd noise.

Dale shook his head.

"Can't be fucking around when you got Haji at the wire," he said
quietly. "They'll cut your head off and piss down your neck-hole
before you know what happened."

"Testify," Jonas said quietly. "You think Muller's got this?"

That shake of the head again.

"Don't matter, bro. This is going bad. If it's not the next attack, it'll
be the one after. There's no command chain. No resupply. No chance
of reinforcement."

Jonas held his breath. He hadn't told Dale about his escape plan.
Only Brad Rausch and Chad Moffat were up on the deets.

Oh, and Tomi, of course. Having literally sucked it out of him.

He was planning to bring Leo Vaulk into the program before the
end of the day, if only because the dude was sure to have a stockpile
of guns and ammo that he was keeping to himself.

Dale though, he'd be an asset.

Jonas was actually dry-mouthed, worrying about whether he
should trust him. The two men said nothing more for a while,
watching as Muller took over the speaker's table from his rival. He
had the booming command voice of a man who used it profession-
ally. He started by pointing out that having more people on guard out
patrolling the forest approaches meant less working on food produc-
tion, but he pivoted quickly to the vote.

"Before we even take this poll," he bellowed, "we need to settle to
who gets a say."

That brought forth competing choruses of applause and abuse,
but Muller just rode on over the top of it all.

"We got some hundred and thirty folks from outside the town, all
of them here because we let them in to serve our ends. Doc Cornwell's medical staff. All outsiders. Joe Wolfenden's men, who walked

up the first day and have stood watch over Silverton every minute since. Them too."

Just as Jonas was wondering if he might get a shout-out, he did.

"Jonas Murdoch," Muller called out, even pointing him out over the heads of the crowd, "who saved Al Barrett's life on day one and who stood up at the Gate this morning."

Muller referenced a few more outsiders, including Chad Moffatt for helping Brad Rausch with constructing the Wall, and some Professor Boylan, who Jonas had never heard of, for advising Jacques Loubert's group on the best seeds to plant for fast-growing returns.

"Since these folks have been working as hard as any one of us and sharing the same risks, it's only fair and proper that they get a say on how we meet those risks," Muller shouted.

Dale laughed softly, leaning over to be heard.

"This is how he beat O'Shannassy last time," he said.

For the next three minutes, Dave Muller argued passionately in favour of a bigger tent, a larger pie, to be shared by everyone he personally welcomed inside. Jonas could only nod in admiration for some really impressive grassroots populism. O'Shannassy tried to argue against giving anybody but registered voters in Silverton a say, but even his supporters went quiet at that. Many of them had been treated by Doc Cornwell's interns, stood watch at the Wall, or even been trained in basic fire and movement by Wolfenden's militia. Jonas almost laughed when he realised he had been used as a pawn or maybe a prop. He saw Al Barrett, still sporting a few bandages, pointing him out to other voters and speaking animatedly, almost certainly in favour of Sheriff Muller's proposition. Barrett waved to him, and Jonas gave him a thumbs up.

When the vote to enlarge the town's franchise was put, it passed quickly on the voices.

"Game over," smiled Dale.

And it was.

Muller carried the next vote on the voices, too, riding to victory on the backs of the newly enfranchised.

"Reckon we're done, here," Dale said, as the crowd broke up.

"What was the point of all that?" Jonas asked.

"What's the point of anything?" Dale replied. "If you're smart, Murdoch, you'd get out now."

Jonas said nothing for a moment.

Then, "You bugging out?"

"Dunno," Dale said. "Don't have transport. I could hike out, I guess. But I haven't got the gear or supplies. I gave most of my shit to the emergency committee."

Jonas chose his words carefully.

"Would you get out if you could?"

Dale looked at him.

"Five minutes ago."

30

A PASSAGE TO CANADIA

One of the first jobs Ellie ever had in the restaurant trade was also one of the worst. Dish pig at an *Outback Steak-house* on 19th Street, Sacramento. She had only been there for three months, but they were an intense three months. Ellie thought she remembered the city well, for better or worse. But this was not Sacramento as she knew it.

"Where the hell is everyone?" she asked, leaning forward in the back of the police patrol car.

"Curfew," said the cop behind the wheel.

"Lean back, please," his partner said.

"And gardening," the driver chuckled to himself.

"Yeah, and gardening," the other cop snorted. "Now lean back."

Ellie had no idea what they meant by that, and these guys weren't giving up any more information. At least not to a couple of outsiders.

"I think they've got people working the farms," Damo said. He sat next to her in back of the patrol car. They weren't restrained. The cops hadn't slapped handcuffs on them or anything. But they were caged in, and there were no handles to open the doors.

"I don't know whether you saw them as we were coming up the

river, but as you got closer to the city, there was lots of people working out in the fields. Fuckin' thousands of them."

Ellie had seen that but hadn't thought much of it. She'd adapted to the idea that the cyber-attack had melted down so much technology that it seemed only natural that things like tractors and combine harvesters didn't work anymore either. But now she thought about it, that was bullshit. Those things were sturdy analogue brutes. They ran on diesel, not software. Or at least she assumed not.

"Did they used to navigate the big tractors with satellite links or something?" she said.

"Some big places back home, yeah," Damo confirmed. "Dunno much about the local setup, though. You ever deal with any of the growers from around here?"

She shook her head.

"No, not much. It's all big agro-industry combines. Our suppliers were all small indie producers."

Damo leaned forward and rapped on the cage dividing them from the cops up front.

"Where are we going, mate?"

"Convention Centre," the cop on the passenger side said. "Refugee resettlement runs out of the convention centre. They got 'em all in there."

Ellie went back to staring out of the window. Flashbacks to the morning still haunted her. It was surreal. She had killed a man, and now she was riding along in the back of a cop car, but not because of that. She wasn't quite sure where they were going or what they were supposed to do when they got there, but nobody had asked them about the bullet holes in Damo's boat or the blood splatter on the hull.

Nobody here seemed even remotely interested in anyone or anything that wasn't from here. Still, neither she nor Damo mentioned the fact that they'd gunned down three or four people just a couple of hours ago. That was not the smart play here.

Ellie wondered what'd happened to the asshole who'd been steering the boat, the one who'd taken a grazing shot and jumped over the side, swimming away. Had he bled out? Drowned?

"You right, mate?" Damo asked.

"I'm good," she said tightly.

Fuck those guys.

There was some traffic on the streets, she saw. Military vehicles, of course. They were everywhere. But there were buses and trucks, too, all of them full of people heading out of the city or empty and driving back in. Everyone looked tired.

As much as she had not enjoyed her first time in Sacramento, she did remember it as a beautiful city with some nice, well-kept public spaces. It was apparent, as they neared the centre of the state capital, that nobody was bothering with shit like rubbish collection anymore. Or maintaining the parks. Litter collected in drifts against the side of buildings and in the gutters. Manicured lawns had been allowed to grow ragged and weedy. Cars that had obviously been damaged in collisions had been pushed out of the way.

They pulled up next to the curb outside the Convention Centre, and it was a shit show. A tent city. A couple of thousand people had been corralled inside temporary fencing patrolled by heavily armed soldiers.

"What if they just tossed us in there and drove away?" she said quietly, leaning across the rear seat to whisper to Damo.

"Mate, if they wanted to play silly buggers, they'd have done it back at the boat. Knocked us on the head and took all our shit. No, they want something."

The cops climbed out first and opened the doors for them. One stayed with the car, taking the chance to enjoy a cigarette. The other ordered them to follow him. They walked the length of the block. The smell from the tent city was gross. Way worse than the bins in any restaurant she'd ever worked. The cop took them in through the front entrance to the centre, led them through a crowd and up to a trestle table where half a dozen harried-looking civilians worked with ring binders, notepads, pencils and paper. Most of them were busy trying to process hundreds of people who remained docile and compliant under the stony glares of military policemen. Their uniformed guide led them to the end of the table, depositing them in front of a balding middle-aged man in a white shirt that hadn't been properly laundered in a couple of days. He looked up with red-rimmed eyes, and when he spoke, his voice was exhausted.

"What now?"

"Couple of squirters from the river," said the cop. "I got told to bring them to you. Lieutenant de Stasi said to give you this."

He handed over a slip of paper.

They waited while the man read the hand-written message.

He looked like he would have been surprised if he had the energy for it.

"Right, okay. I remember this," he croaked. "Thanks. I'll take it from here."

The cop left them without another word. How were they supposed to get back to the boat? But before Ellie could say anything, the man behind the trestle table stood up, grabbed a plastic cup and told them to follow him.

He took them through a door into a small windowless room.

Another man, for sure another exhausted civil servant given his beaten-down pallor, was leaving the room as they entered. The two men exchanged tired fist bumps.

"Sit down and grab a cup of coffee if you want," their guy said. "I'm afraid it's shit. And there's no milk or creamer. Or anything. But you can have all the shitty instant coffee you can handle until it kills you. I'm drinking so much that it won't be long now. It'll be a merciful release."

"We're good," Ellie said.

The man topped up his brew, tapped out a cigarette, and offered the packet to them. Neither of them was a smoker. He shrugged and lit up anyway.

"Please, sit down. My name's Paul Fenton. I'm the refugee resettlement coordinator."

"We're not refugees," Ellie insisted.

"Yeah, I know," Fenton snorted. "If you were, you wouldn't be here talking to me. You'd be locked up in the big open-air cage out there. Come on, sit down."

They joined him at the small table in the middle of the room. It was full of newspapers and magazines, none of them recent. Empty takeaway boxes, junk food refuse, and other detritus covered the surface. It didn't seem to bother Fenton.

"Where did you come from?" he said.

"Australia," Damien Moloney deadpanned.

Fenton snorted again.

"You should go back there... mate," he said, mangling Damo's accent. "As long as the Chinese don't nuke them, they'll probably be okay down there. Lots of kangaroos to eat."

"We came up the river. From the state park, the lakes," Ellie said, cutting in on him.

"Been there long?" Fenton asked.

"Since the first night," Ellie said. "Why?"

Fenton took a long draw on his cigarette and leaned back. He closed his eyes. For a moment, she thought he'd fallen asleep, but he came back to them with a start.

"Sorry," he said. "I haven't had a break. I owe you one for that."

"You can pay us off by telling us what's going on," Ellie replied.

Fenton smiled, or rather, he tortured his facial muscles into something approximating a smile.

"That's easy," he said. "You're gonna go back to your boat. They're gonna raise the bridge. And you will sail on through, do not pass go, do not collect $200, do not even think about setting foot in Sacramento again."

Damo smiled.

"Sweet as a nut. But what else?"

Fenton nodded.

"I can see there's a reason you're still alive. Okay, the *quid pro quo* —you remember when we got all worked up about them? Ha, good times—well, the *quid pro quo*, the favour you're doing for us, is that I've got some Canadians nobody wants to feed any more and no way of getting them back to the magical land of Canadia. Or at least I didn't until you rolled up. I give them to you, you take them off my hands, you got your pro, and you most assuredly got your quo. Am I clear?"

"How many of them?" Ellie asked. She was already thinking about their food supplies.

Fenton smiled, "You're in luck, there's only two. Both children. But they're special."

"Shit," Ellie said. "What happened?"

Paul Fenton's ragged smile disappeared completely. He stood up, went to the coffee maker, poured himself another cup and sat down again.

"These two belong to the Canadian finance minister. She was in town for business, brought the kids with her to go to Disneyland afterwards, and got caught down in San Francisco."

"Why weren't they with her?" Damo asked.

"She was only expecting to be down there for a couple of hours. She put them into the kids' club at the hotel here. Rang on the first day. Said she'd get herself back. We haven't heard from her again. But we have heard from Ottawa. Dad is a big old hunk of Moose cheese in the Mounties. He wants them back. Congratulations. You're diplomats now. Or couriers. Yeah. Diplomatic couriers, that sounds good. I wish you the best of luck in your new career. Soon as I finish my coffee and maybe have a little nap, I'll get you the kids. You can get back to your boat and be on your way. Just get them to the border, hand them over to the nearest Mountie, or lumberjack, or to be honest, whoever the fuck you want. I just really want these kids off my books and Justin Trudeau off my ass. I wouldn't have thought Canadians could be such a persistent pain in the ass."

"That's it?" Ellie said. "You don't want to know about us? We could be, like, child slavers or something."

Fenton sipped at his coffee.

"We still have some capabilities," he said. "The cops who stopped you on the river checked the registration and ownership of the boat. That's you, Damian Moloney. Australian-born, naturalised American citizen, resident of Chestnut Street, the Marina, and proprietor of Fourth Edition, described by the Chronicle as an abso-fucking-lutely fabulous Temescal bistro. And you would be his infamous and heavily tattooed chef, Eliza Jabbarah, resident of Oceanview, San Francisco, where you share a two-bedroom bungalow with your girlfriend, unemployed photographer Jodi Sarjanen."

Ellie gave him her stone face.

"She's freelance."

Fenton snorted.

"Yeah, we're all freelance now."

Damo jutted out his jaw but said nothing. Fenton raised his hands as if in apology.

"Look. The government is going through a few things at the moment, but we can still do a basic background check. The phone system still works. Did you know that? The old copper landlines that is. And the State Department, which okayed this arrangement, has better networks than I can access. So we know who you are. We know where to find you. Get the kids home, and we'll raise the bridge."

Ellie sketched a thin smile.

"Well, if we're helping you out like this," she said. "What about some fuel and food and..."

Fenton shook his head.

"Don't even bother. We've got nothing for you but clear passage, and you should be glad of that. I don't think you understand what's been happening here."

Damo said nothing.

"We've been out of touch," Ellie explained.

"Yeah," Fenton said. "I can imagine. San Francisco is a disaster. LA a complete write-off. The fact you're even alive and you got yourself here tells me you've been hunkered down somewhere far away from the real world."

They both nodded carefully.

"Yeah, the world," Ellie said. "Can you tell us what's been happening out there?"

Fenton rubbed at his bloodshot eyes.

"Well, we're at war with China. Did you know that?"

They both shook their heads.

"Figures, I guess," Ellie conceded.

"Yeah, so that's a thing now. Congress did that. Voted for it from some secure and secret location last week. Anyway, I got no idea how that's going. There's no cable or network news at the moment. We think Russia fried them. We're not at war with Russia, but most of Europe is. South East Asia is a free-fire zone. And, here's this year's

Oscar winner for delicious irony: Mexico has closed the border and deployed its army and paramilitary police to stop any American refugees getting in."

"What about Oz?" Damo asked.

Fenton shrugged.

"I think they declared war on China after those missiles fell on Darwin. Otherwise, I got nothing. Sorry. What I do know is the Feds declared a dozen cities mandated strongholds. They got military resources. They got funding, such as that is. They got priority for resupply, but there's not much of that. And if you're stuck outside a stronghold, you're on your own. For now. When things stabilize, the plan is to push out and pacify."

He leaned back in his chair, stretched his back and groaned slightly.

"We got lucky. Port of Seattle has been a basket case for years because it can't handle container traffic. But it does sit in the middle of a gigantic food bowl. And all that stuff comes through here. It meant Sacramento could still feed itself. Small population, at least a quarter of which flew out in the first week when everyone was freaking over a nuclear war. Lots of nutrients in storage at the port. Lots more waiting to be plucked from the fertile earth. So we're a stronghold. We'll probably pull through. Probably."

"Especially if you can get rid of outsiders, extra mouths, that sort of thing," Damo said.

Fenton nodded.

"So, you up for this?"

Ellie and Damo exchanged a look. They both shrugged.

"Sure," Damo said. "It'll give little Maxi someone to play with."

THEY PICKED the kids up half an hour later. Pascal and Beatrice. A boy and a girl. Twelve and fourteen years old, respectively.

"Maybe not such great play pals for Maxi then," Damo conceded as they filed into the office where Fenton had left them under guard.

The children looked scared when he told them they would be going home with Damo and Ellie.

"Back to Canada," Damo hurried to explain. "Not Australia."

"Our mother said she was coming back for us, and we weren't supposed to leave the hotel until she got here," Beatrice said. 'She works for the government, and you'll be in trouble if you don't do what she says.'

"See what I mean," Fenton said out the side of his mouth. "Good luck."

Ellie tried to smile reassuringly. She perched on the arm of the couch where the children sat, thought better of that, and got down on her haunches so that she was at eye level with them.

"My name is Ellie," she said. "I don't know your mom, but my friend Jodi has a little boy I help to look after, and I know that the thing your mom would want most in the world is to get you safely home. She's tough, I'll bet, your mom, isn't she."

They both nodded. Pascal seemed to be holding back tears.

"Well, a tough lady like that and mom who loves you as much as she does, there's a reason she can't get back to you straight away. She must be handling some pretty hard stuff where she is."

"She's in San Francisco," Beatrice said, making it sound like an accusation.

"Yeah, and we just came from there a week or so back," Ellie said. "So I know what she's dealing with."

She gave Beatrice her serious face.

Just like Karl had done for her back on the boat.

"If your mom could get here, she would, Beatrice. But she can't, so the thing she would want most in the world is for you to get to your dad. We can do that. If you want to come along. It's your call."

Fenton started to interrupt, but Ellie shut him down with a fierce, warning expression.

"I want to go home," Pascal said, and the tears came.

Beatrice held out a little longer, but not too long.

The army provided a Humvee and driver to get them back to the river where the Lasseter's Reef was anchored.

Before they cast off, Karl asked if he could have a couple of minutes to talk with the soldier who'd driven them.

A couple of minutes turned into an hour, and the Port Police controlling bridge started to complain. But a sergeant in combat camouflage took them aside and chilled them out. When Karl returned, he was carrying a faded green duffel bag.

"Goodies," he said when Ellie asked him what was in the carryall.

Damo took up his station at the wheel. A whistle blew, and the deck of the bridge climbed slowly away from the water.

He fed revs to the propellers, and the boat slipped forward, heading north.

31

SILVERTON ON THE EVE OF THE GREAT BATTLE

Jacques Loubert and Lachie Saunders seal the last panel of glass in the hot house they have just finished building at the northern end of the town Common. A small party of volunteers, mostly kids from the small Silverton Consolidated High School, clap and cheer as Loubert holds aloft a caulking gun, waving it like a winning pennant before an appreciative homecoming crowd. With the summers so hot and drawn out these days, it will be a few weeks before the first hard frost lays on the ground. Still, the high school science teacher promises he can tease eleven or twelve inches of growth a day from the almost magical green spears of any asparagus planted right away.

Watching from across Main Street, Bob Shapcott, ninety-something years young, sits on his park bench smoking a Pall Mall. They moved his bench last week, during all the fuss and bother about the computers. Bob used to sit under the statue of John Mullan Jr., but peas and potatoes are growing there now, and the wooden bench where Shapcott has long enjoyed the guilty pleasure of watching others work hard now sits on the sidewalk out front of Edwin Fholer's pharmacy. In Bob's experience, the feeling of guilt is always more pleasurable when other folks are hard at work on a fella's behalf, and he is looking forward to seeing how them taters fry up when they are good and grown. There are pictures in the county library from the town's early days, and they show Chinamen in black pyjamas and conical straw hats tending to market gardens around about where Frenchy Loubert has built his greenhouse. The irony is not lost on Bob, who has himself contributed to the commonwealth by handing over his four prize chickens—known locally as the Gang of Four—to Selectwoman Bochenski. Natalie, granddaughter of Vic Bochenski with whom Bob jumped into France back in '44, is in charge of wrangling foodstuffs and other necessaries, which is another one of them historical ironies because of how her grandad was well known as the champion scrounger of the 101st back in the day. Or maybe it's more coincidence than irony, Bob Shapcott thinks as he takes a long drag on the Pall Mall, closing his eyes and enjoying the rich but gentle burn of the cigarette smoke as it fills his lungs. Bob has always enjoyed the crossword and finding the right word is important to him. So much so that the difference between coincidence and irony is the last thought he ever has, sitting on his favourite bench with his eyelids closed against the late afternoon sun. In a left-handed gift from the Almighty, the gossamer-thin walls of millions of blood vessels in Bob's parietal cortex burst under pressure, caused in part by decades of overindulging in fried potatoes and Pall Malls. The hemorrhagic stroke kills him swiftly but softly. The butt of his cigarette falls to the concrete sidewalk and burns out. It appears to passersby as though Bob Shapcott has dozed off on his favourite park bench.

Selectwoman Natalie Bochenski smiles as she crosses the Common and catches sight of old Mister Shapcott counting sheep on a wooden bench recently moved under the awning in front of Fholer's Pharmacy. A guardsman armed with a shotgun stands watch over the premises, which houses the town's dwindling supplies of medication. A shadow flits over her carefully cheerful expression as she recalls that the supply of Mister Shapcott's heart medication is getting low. So, too, with Andy Elridge's cancer meds and the insulin that so many of Silverton's older folk (and a few younger ones) rely on. As the manager of the town's critical supplies—or supply shortages, she thinks mordantly—Natalie Bochenski is all too familiar with the hopeless math of trying to eke out the minimal store of pharmaceuticals that Fohler's had in stock on Zero Day. She knows that even with severe rationing, supervised by Doctor Cornwell, the situation will soon be untenable. A cold word that; untenable. Not really descriptive of what will shortly happen.

With an effort of will, Selectwoman Bochenski turns her thoughts away from the imagined darkness of the near future. Instead, she reminds herself that after the ugly madness and violence at the Seattle gate that morning and the unpleasant showdown between Darren O'Shannassy and Sheriff Muller that followed, it is lovely that the town can still provide for moments of grace like this; old Mister Shapcott enjoying the warmth of late afternoon sunlight. Bob looks so peaceful, snoozing and no doubt snoring away, she thinks, before suddenly losing her train of thought.

Why? Because Jonas Murdoch has appeared as if from nowhere with his lazy smile and those deeply dreamy blue eyes, and it is all that Selectwoman Bochenski can do not to flutter utterly away on the wings of her delight and surprise. Jonas Murdoch, in her opinion, could pass in the dark for a very believable Jon Snow, and were she ever lucky enough to get him into a dark room, she would be more than willing to do a thorough compare and contrast between the handsome outsider and the King in the North.

Jonas Murdoch is aware of the effect he has on Bochenski, which is why he approaches her seeking an extra thirty gallons of gas, ostensibly for Brad Rausch's tow truck, which has been put to hard use all day, reinforcing the outer wall. Brad Rausch also has an effect on Natalie Bochenski, but that is because he looks more like Ser Gregor Clegane in his late Zombie Mountain period than Jon Snow busting out the tastiest abs in the Night's Watch. Better to go with Jonas for this part of the plan, they agree. With tiny, crooked smiles and a darkly promising twinkle in his eyes, Jonas quickly extracts a signed, handwritten chit for the gasoline, winking at Bochenski, "You're my favourite," when she hands over the precious voucher. He does not see Tomi Yates observing the transaction from across the street, where she is conspiring with her besties, Lisa Dees and Trudy Smith, but he would not much care even if he did see her. Jonas is no pussy-ass bitch, and he will not be led around by the dick.

Leaned up against the pole outside Gary Kemble's barbershop, Tomi Yates does well to keep the smirk off her face as she thinks how easily she's led Jonas around by the dick. It is, admittedly, a very nice dick, and he does know how to use it. But so does she. She sees him over there, charming the grandma panties off that dried-up old dyke Bochenski. She knows he's scamming her for gas to top up the Mazda back at Rausch's place. And if they have to get the fuck outta Dodge, Tomi is taking the Mazda, and she's rolling with Lisa and Trudy. Helen, her wackadoodle stepmother owned a CX5, and Tomi knows that model of car intimately. Like literally. Helen threw her ass to the curb for fucking Tyson Garrett in the back seat. And the front seat. And on the hood, where she left a dent. When everything turns to shit, and Tomi is a realist about such things, she's not waiting for anybody's say-so that it's every bitch for herself. She's taking that car and burning her name in the motherfucking road.

Lisa Dees is, like, shittin' kittens, even though Tomi says she's got this sitch' locked down. Lisa was actually in the city when the Chinese hacked everything. Lucky for her, she'd been on the edge of town, chasing an internship at Redmond. Even luckier, the slave labour gig wasn't with Microsoft, but at the Redmond Ridge golf club a couple of miles to the northwest, just close enough to the outskirts of the greater city that after two days of gridlock and madness, she was able to escape by stealing an electric golf cart at four in the morning and driving across the river at the 124th street bridge. From there, it was only another two-day hike up into the foothills to get back home. Although that'd been hairy as hell. Not just the trek but not getting shot when she approached the barricades that would become the Seattle Gate.

To Lisa, this looks like the craziness down in the city when peeps started to realise that shit was legit fucked up. The shelves were empty at Walmart, and UberEats wasn't coming to the rescue. She is desperately thankful that Tomi has included her in this escape plan because she saw some shit on the way up here, and she would run a thousand miles never to have to see that sort of thing again. But unlike her friends, Lisa Dees has family here in Silverton, and she can't just leave them behind. She says she can, of course. Because Tomi Yates can be a stone bitch when the situation demands, but Lisa is pretty sure that if they really have to get out, and she just turns up with her mom and her little brother, Adam, that in the rush of the moment, Tomi will be cool. Like that time Lisa brought Chrissy Ellus to Coral Smith's house party even though Coral was like, strictly no try-hards. So Lisa nods and says she will totally keep Tomi's plan secret, and they all agree to meet at the Cascade Gate if the church bells start ringing to signal the Wall or the other gate has been breached. But the first chance she gets, Lisa is gonna tell her mom to pack a bag full of tinned food and, get Adam into his summer camp gear and just be ready to go.

Adam Dees, twelve years old and a talented artist who can rip out a sketch of any of the major Marvel characters, except for Black Widow, who he finds hard to draw, sees his big sister with Tomi Yates and Trudy Smith. He wonders where they find the time to stand around talking shit when everyone else in town has jobs to do – but Adam also has a job to do, and he ignores them to follow Lachie Saunders back to the county offices. Lachie is super cool, which is what you would expect of the town's legally licensed cannabis grower, even though he's not growing the good smoke anymore; now he's all about salad vegetables and greenhouse design.

That's where Adam comes in. Turns out he's even better at drawing blueprints for Lachie's greenhouse project and Mister Joubert's planting maps than he is at doing Ironman. There is no electricity for photocopiers, so every map for the planting teams has to be done by hand. Mister Corney, the head of the high school art department, has personally recommended Adam for the job. How about that?

He did volunteer to draw up some bitching designs for much better defensive walls and gates than they had at the moment, but Mister Wetsman had said they'd have to make do with what they had. Adam's unfailingly bright mood dimmed somewhat when he remembered the county clerk, who was dead now because the Hells Angels had murdered him. Maybe if someone had just listened to Adam about the need to build everything bigger and gnarlier, like his Helm's Deep fortress design, Mister Wetsman would still be alive. He tries to forget about that and about how scary it is that everyone is getting ready for the Hell's Angels to come back tonight, and he hurries to catch up with Lachie, who's fired up a big joint and is like just openly smoking it.

How cool is that?

Lachie Saunders has been waiting all day for a smoke, and since they are done with the first glasshouse, and there is no chance work will resume until tomorrow, he feels he's earned a quick toke. And hey, maybe there'll be no tomorrow anyway. Not if those shitheads come back tonight like everyone is saying they will. He can't hardly believe any of this shit is even real, and for a moment, he stares at the choice fatty he's just lit up, wondering if he's been betrayed by his special blend.

But no.

There's that Wolfenden guy, the militia captain, and he's stalking up Main Street looking like all sorts of bad news, and it's a wonder to Lachie that they got guys like this walking around openly, toting fucking machine guns and shit and people are like totally cool with it.

Joe Wolfenden isn't cool with anything, of course. He hasn't been cool since they had to leg it out of Seattle with half of their unit and most of their materiel stuck back in the city. He's lost even more guys since then. Simon Hall took a bullet in a bullshit little skirmish on the second night in. No idea who got him. Just scavengers probing the edge of town. And then Vallon Davis went out on a long-range patrol and never came back. That shook Joe more than he cared to let on. Davis had a tour of the sandbox to his credit. He wasn't some amateur, and he knew how to keep himself safe. But the forest just swallowed him up all the same.

Wolfenden takes a long drag on a cigarette. A real cigarette, not one of that Saunders guy's hand-rolled specials. He laughs bitterly. Five years he's been off the coffin nails, and he starts smoking again at the very moment he can't even buy a new pack. He's a fucking idiot. He throws the butt away, angry with himself, but he can't hold onto the self-loathing. Chances are they'll all be dead before daybreak tomorrow, anyway. He doesn't doubt the bikers will come back in force. Maybe they'll sack the town. Perhaps they'll take it over for themselves. It's a good, defensible position if you have the personnel to defend it.

Which Silverton doesn't.

He sighs as he reaches the Sheriff's office.

He honestly cannot say whether he made the right choice to stay in town.

Maybe he saved his men.

Maybe he doomed them.

Who can say?

Sheriff Muller is standing at the top of the steps, waiting for Joe Wolfenden. He hitches up his pants. They are loose on him these days, what with all the work he's been doing and the tight rations. So, at least there's that. Muller sketches out a tired smile for the militia captain, who looks even worse than he does. A good man, he thinks. They're lucky to have him.

As Wolfenden climbs the stairs, his head hanging low, Muller takes a moment to survey the town.

It's busy as the late afternoon slips toward twilight. It seems almost everyone is out preparing the defences or working the fields. Well, everyone except old Bob Shapcott over there, who's taking a nap outside the pharmacy. Fair enough, though, at his age.

It's noisy, too, he thinks. Hammers and saws fashioning new pieces for the gates. The distant crunch of metal as Brad Rausch adds another car body to the Wall. Music from a speaker somewhere in the vegetable fields.

Batteries, Muller thinks idly. They'll run out of batteries soon. They really shouldn't be wasting them on music players.

But then he thinks about what's coming, and he knows they have bigger worries.

32

A CHANGE OF MIND

J ames O'Donnell had never experienced terror. Not true terror; the elemental, organic shock of a living soul suddenly confronted with its violent end. Like most people, he knew of the fluttering stomach or a sudden lurch of the heart in life's small anxious moments. The big speech. The job interview. The dry mouth that made asking Laura-Marie Lawson to the Senior Prom such a choking humiliation.

But when Mel Baker's cry pealed out of the seemingly empty RV to shatter the morning stillness in the quiet rest area, James felt the floor of the world drop away from beneath his feet and a dizzying, head-spinning rush of disorientation that robbed him for an instant of any idea of where he was or what had happened.

But it was Mel.

She was screaming.

James tripped on the two left feet that had somehow swollen to the size of giant novelty balloons, lost all feeling, and utterly betrayed him as he tried to run towards her.

He fell, landing heavily on the rifle, a painful shock running up one arm. Pins and needles in his fingers.

Mel was still crying out as he tried to regain his footing, but now she was yelling obscenities, or just one obscene word, over and over again— "*Fuckfuckfuck*"—and he could see her backing out of the RV clumsily, but at speed. Her gun hand hung limp at her side. Her other hand was clamped over her mouth and she was shaking her head emphatically. *No. No. No.*

Hundreds of birds, disturbed by the uproar, took to the wing from the dark forest canopy, adding their shrieks and calls of alarm to hers.

James got his feet underneath him again and jerked the rifle back and forth, looking for targets. He was no longer unsure of whether he could pull a trigger on another human being. It was all he could do to stop himself just blasting away at nothing.

Thankfully, he did not. He probably would've shot Rick's girl-friend, who was advancing on him, in a half-stumbling half-run, waving her hands at him, shaking her head.

"Don't shoot," she trilled out in a shaky voice.

And he did not, to both their relief.

James was shaking when Mel rejoined him, and she was not much better. Violent shudders ran through her upper body, and when she tried to speak, she couldn't. Instead, she bent over to vomit, and having nothing in her stomach to bring up, she simply dry-heaved and swore in a strangled, choking retch.

"What is it? What happened?" he asked. The birds had flown away on a storm of furiously flapping wings, and the silence of a fallen world rolled back in over the rest area.

Mel shook her head emphatically, and for a second, he thought she wasn't going to tell him, but she held up her hands, squeezed her eyes tight shut as though trying to force a terrible image from them, and shook her head again, this time as though in denial of some unspeakable truth.

And then Melissa Baker told James O'Donnell what she had found in the camper van.

THEY WERE NOT LONG GETTING BACK to the spot where they had left Rick and Tammy with the wounded man. He still drew breath, but his efforts were laboured, and a wet rattle accompanied every exhalation.

Fear and loathing hastened their return, but James had no trouble retracing their path along the rim of the Valley. They followed a hiking trail for most of the way, and the only fork in that track was signposted with a National Parks Service marker, which indicated the direction to the picnic area where they had made camp at the old tree stump a few days before.

They did not speak much on the way back, each lost in their thoughts. James carried his rifle at the ready the whole way, and once or twice, he called out directions to keep them on track. Mel replied with one-word answers.

"Yeah."

Or, "Okay."

Before leaving the scene, James did not venture into the campervan to verify what Mel had found. That first scream of outrage and horror was all he needed, and she advised him against going in there, anyway.

"I won't stop you, mate," she said quietly. "But if I was you, I wouldn't."

So he did not.

By the time they rejoined Rick and Tammy, James had stopped shaking from fear and instead started shaking from a weird sense of violation and possibly from exhaustion. He had not eaten in nearly sixteen hours, and they had burned a lot of energy in a short time. He did not feel hungry, though.

He saw the first dead man before he saw Rick, who had killed him.

One of the Darryls had rolled a good way down the slope from the ridge where Rick had shot him. He lay on his back, sightless eyes staring through a break in the overhead canopy directly into the late morning sun, arms flung high over his head. His sleeveless, red checked shirt had ridden up, exposing a fish-white belly. Ants and bugs swarmed over the corpse, and James could see that a few larger scavengers had already taken small bites from the flanks. He found that he did not care. The thing on the ground was not a man to him anymore.

"Mel and James, coming in," Mel called out, and Rick's voice came back from somewhere over the rise.

"Acknowledged. You're good to come on."

James wondered if she and Rick had worked out that little call-and-reply thing before or if that was just what people like them did. They were different from him. Maybe not so much from Michelle, who seemed to view the world with the hard eye of somebody waiting for it to turn on her. But definitely different to a naive little farm boy who'd gone off to college to study accountancy. James wondered where that guy had gone.

He scrambled over the last rise, past the other dead men. He noted that the thin corpse must have been the one Tammy Kolchar referred to as Cracker Barrell Darryl. You could tell he was wearing the t-shirt despite all the blood. The bigger body was just another McGuigan.

James and Mel climbed carefully down the treacherous slope of the dry gully where Rick and Tammy waited a short distance from the lone survivor of the hunting party.

That's how he thought of them now. A hunting party.

But it was too weird, and James shook his head in unconscious imitation of the gesture Mel had made when she emerged from the RV.

He was trying to unsee what she had seen.

To unthink what he already knew.

As they came into the gully, Mel lengthened her stride and pushed past James. Not forcefully, but firmly.

"Whoa, now!" Rick called out but to little effect.

She pushed past him, too, drawing the pistol at her hip and levelling the weapon at the wounded man, who lay shivering and sweating in the dirt before her.

"You fuckin' animal," she spat out at him.

He was delirious with pain or maybe shock.

He muttered, "No, no, don't," in a weak voice, but James didn't think he was actually talking to Mel. He wasn't talking to anyone.

Still, Mel Baker did pause in her rush towards whatever decision she had made.

She turned around to look at Tammy, who was watching her with wide eyes. More fascinated than frightened.

Mel let the gun fall before checking it, perhaps to see if the safety was engaged. Satisfied, she walked the few steps over to Tammy.

"You were right," she said. "I'm sorry. These men would have killed you and your children."

She handed her the gun.

"I'll do it if you want. I used to be an officer of the law. But..."

Tammy cut her off.

"No. It's for me to do."

She took the small, black handgun and checked it over like she knew exactly what she was looking for.

She took a few steps to get around Mel and James, flicked off the safety, raised the gun and pulled the trigger without preamble.

The report was loud but not as loud as James was expecting. He still jumped every time she fired.

Three times in all.

The man's body arched up, and he groaned when the first bullet struck him in the chest, but he absorbed the second and third bullets in stillness and silence.

Nobody said anything.

James was surprised to find he felt nothing.

He hadn't really felt anything other than a sense of creeping desolation since Mel had told him what she found in the RV.

A freezer full of human body parts.

Tiny human body parts.

THE BIG FELLA they called Rick led the way back to their camp. He was the quiet type, a lot like Tammy's dad had been.

He didn't say much while they were waiting on the other two to get back. The black English girl and the college boy, but Tammy wasn't much fussed by that. She was used to men who were no good with words. And this guy wasn't exactly like that anyhow. She got the feeling he would know exactly what needed to be said if the situation arose, but it wouldn't be much, and it wouldn't be loud.

The college boy, James. He was a talker, she guessed. Or he would be if the cat hadn't got his tongue, chewed it good and then swallowed the damn thing.

Cats will do that.

He was cute, too, even all dirty and sweaty like he was. He would scrub up nicely, she thought.

The English woman, Mel: she said she was a cop or had been.

She didn't look like no cop Tammy Kolchar had ever dealt with, but she supposed they did things different over there.

English cops wore those funny hats, after all. And they carried little back billy-clubs instead of guns.

Nobody said much of anything on the way back to the camp. But it wasn't a hard silence. It wasn't like they wanted her to go away or anything. Not like those assholes back in Dryfork. Tammy thought these folks had suffered themselves a little shock, just like she had at the door to the McGuigan's RV. It could put the world into a new light, something like that. Make you see things you could not see before.

Which was all a blessed relief as far as Tammy Kolchar was concerned because if these folks would have her and her people, she reckoned she might have found her some guardian on the long trek west.

That's where they were going, Rick said.

West.

33

THE BATTLE OF SILVERTON

Dale Juntii was right. The bikers returned in the dead man's hour. Silverton's defenders stood ready to receive the enemy, but they stood tired, strung out and fearful. As the night fell, it seemed all the terrors of a dark and dying world gathered close around. Jonas, assigned to the Seattle Gate, armed with his own pistol and a Remington bolt action rifle from the village armoury, was both exhausted and wired. He couldn't stop yawning, and his bladder felt tight, even after pissing half a dozen times.

"Gotta go again," he groused to the other watchers on the platform. Six men all up. Besides Jonas and Dale, the night's watch consisted of Andy Eldridge, who ran the town's major camping supply store. Alex Tewes, the realtor. Dan Meehan, retired master carpenter. And Mark Sangwin, a sales clerk at the arts and crafts shop. Indeed, Jonas was the only one without some sort of military or law enforcement background. Alex Tewes had gone into real estate after ten years as a facilities manager for the Navy. Dan Meehan first picked up a hammer and saw for the Army Engineering Corps. And Sangwin and Eldridge had nineteen years between them as a military cop and a state trooper, respectively.

They all peered into the night, looking down the road to Seattle.

"Son, for a fella with such a big pair of cast iron balls, you got the littlest bladder on you," Andy Eldridge chuckled.

"I have the biggest bladder, Andy," Jonas lobbed back. "Everyone says so. The best bladder. And I keep it that way through regular care and maintenance."

Somebody chuckled, but in the dark, Jonas couldn't tell who.

Nothing moved out there besides the tops of the trees in a light breeze. The bodies from the firefight had all been cleared away, but nobody had gotten around to rebuilding the herringbone blockade of old car bodies.

Too busy with all the panty-bunching psychodrama of Darren O'Shannassy's tilt at Sheriff Muller.

"I'll come with," Dale said, shouldering his assault rifle.

"Hey, can you stop by Elaine's and refill the coffee pot?" Alex Tewes asked.

The realtor passed Jonas a Thermos, shaking it to show that just a few drops remained.

"And maybe get some cookies, too," Sangwin put in. "We should get something for pulling the graveyard shift."

"Sure," Jonas said. Just what he needed, empty carbs and sugary shit and even more coffee to piss up against a wall.

He climbed down from the firing platform to the use toilets near the barbecue area where Muller and the shop owner had argued their cases the previous day.

"Watch out for the wire," Dale warned.

"Huh?" Jonas grunted, but he caught himself before he walked into the trap.

Juntii and Dan Meehan had strung baling wire across Main Street, fixed tightly to one of the maple trees in the picnic area and a lampost outside of the S&L. It was just the right height to take the head off any motorcycle rider who came blasting through the gate. A few yards further on, the county engineers had dug a small trench across the road, and Jacques Loubert's gardening crew had stretched a tarpaulin over the ditch, scattering dirt and leaves on top to disguise the pitfall.

Jonas blinked away the cobwebs in his mind. Might be that he really did need that coffee.

The two men pulled into Elaine Chang's knick-knack store to top up the thermos. Elaine wasn't there, and the knick-knacks had all been replaced by boxes of ammunition and medical supplies, but Natalie Bochenski and Melanie Drake were on hand to top up the coffee and cookie rations. Selectwoman Bochenski was sleeping in a fold-out cot when Jonas and Dale arrived, meaning they were able to fill their order and get gone without a long and winding conversation, for which Jonas was grateful.

He was just stepping out of the picnic area's toilet when it happened.

A sudden crack of gunfire from the forested hills that surrounded the town.

The ground rushed up to meet him, and he hit the sidewalk awkwardly, winding himself in the fall. Part of him thought he'd been shot. But he realised Dale had kicked out his legs and crash-tackled him to the ground, even before Jonas had realised they were taking fire.

It was just after 3.34 in the morning.

The sharp crackle and pop of small arms escalated to a bullet storm centred on the defenders of the Seattle Gate. Streaks of orange and red tracer zipped in from the darkened slopes. Sparks burst where the bullets struck. Dale was already belly crawling towards cover, the concrete picnic table where Muller and O'Shaughnessy had given their speeches. Jonas followed him as quickly as he could. He risked a couple of furtive glances in the direction of the gate, looking back toward the men on the firing platform. He saw one body lying at the foot of the ladder they'd climbed yesterday to confront the bikers. Another man was writhing around on the platform, screaming in pain. It sounded to Jonas like Dan Meehan. The animal pain of the man's screams made him feel nauseous. Frightened. Meehan was a tough old bastard but he was screaming like a stuck hog.

"Gutshot, sounds like," Dale said. "Come on, follow me."

Jonas was struggling to breathe. Mostly from being tackled by

Dale, but also from terror. The hills strobed with seemingly hundreds of muzzle flashes. He couldn't believe the number of guns firing at them. Couldn't believe that he hadn't been hit. How could anyone live through this shit?

Dale Juntii hadn't just lived through the opening onslaught, though: he seemed determined to crawl through the worst of it to lay his actual fucking hands on their attackers.

Jonas would have been paralysed by fear had he not been even more frightened of Dale leaving him behind. The once-upon-a-time marine seemed to be the only one around there who knew what was happening and what he needed to do about it. Jonas struggled manfully to gain some sort of conscious control over his arms and legs, which seemed made of quivering jelly, and he forced himself to belly crawl along behind Juntii. Mostly, he kept his face buried in the dirt. Occasionally, a stray round sparked off the road surface nearby or crashed into a shopfront, shattering glass. But the attackers concentrated their fire on the gate, chewing away at the improvised structure like some mad, crowd-sourced wood chipper.

Jonas heard shouts and return fire coming from the roofline all along Main Street. Muller had stationed riflemen on top of the businesses, which offered the best cover and firing solutions. He put most of the local hunters up there, behind the thick stone crenellations atop the Farmers Mutual and the Savings and Loan. Another team worked behind sandbags on the roof of the county building. Some of them would be the same men Jonas had watched breaking down a deer carcass the previous morning. A few had night vision scopes, but he had no idea whether they'd be of any use.

Dale swore under his breath before scrambling up into a crouch, grabbing Jonas by the collar and dragging him violently away from the Gate.

"What the fuck, man?" Jonas protested. They had almost made it back, after all. But he didn't protest too much.

Instead, as he gave in to the animal need to just get the fuck away, as far away as possible, from the thing that was trying to kill him, he became aware of something that wasn't the sound of gunfire. It was a steady, growing thunder. A snarling, industrial rumble that he mistook for the massed engines of dozens, maybe hundreds of motor-cycles. But it wasn't. Jonas knew it was something else when he heard something big crashing through the scattered remnants of the herringbone barricade outside the main gate. The metallic crunch took him back to the first day of the Emergency and the hundreds of road accidents he'd seen back down in Seattle. But the deep, rumbling bass of a massively powerful engine was even more famil-iar. He knew it well from working at the Amazon warehouse. It was a truck. A big one.

Somebody had put the pedal to the metal and was driving directly at the main gates. His bowels let go in a liquid rush, and he groaned in disgust and self-loathing. Also, in terror.

They were going to ram the gate.

It was almost as though imagining the possibility conjured up the reality. Jonas and Dale made it to the cover of the ancient Oregon White Oak, which shaded the barbecue area, when the whole of the mountain seemed to heave and shudder underfoot.

Everything slowed down. The gate structure flexed. And exploded inwards, throwing off a lethal shower of splinters and metal shards. He saw bodies launched into space, limbs grasping at noth-ing. A weird, abstracted part of his mind thought calmly, '*Hey, I know those guys.*'

He even recognised one of the tumbling, flying defenders as Alex, the real estate guy. Jonas had been standing next to him just five minutes earlier. The weird, slow-mo effect suddenly snapped back to real-time as flying debris smashed into the trunk of the oak they were sheltered behind. Jonas did not need Dale to pull him into cover this time. He cringed away instinctively. But as he squeezed his eyes shut, an after-image burned on the back of his retinas. The front of a huge, powerful truck wedged into the shattered remains of the Seattle gate. The attackers, the bikers, whoever the fuck they were, had done something to it, engineered some form of armour or dozer blade to the front to create a sort of spearhead, a metal ram. Jonas could hear shattered timbers squealing and screaming as the driver of the vehicle crunched through the gears to throw it into reverse. The diesel engine wheezed and shrieked. Timbers groaned and cracked.

And still, the barrage of incoming fire swept in from the hillsides, except now a few lines of tracer had shifted their aim, moving away from suppressing the gate defenders, feeling through the dark, seeking out new targets. The snipers on rooftops. The fire teams on the upper floors of solid brick buildings. Isolated defenders like Jonas and Dale.

None of it stopped Juntii. Not for a second. He leaned into the trunk of the oak tree and methodically serviced target after target. Jonas had no idea who he was shooting at. But to judge from his fixed, unsmiling expression, and the fierce concentration in his eyes, the small mechanical adjustments he made to his stance and aiming point, Dale obviously knew what he was doing.

Jonas didn't. He'd lost the rifle he'd been assigned earlier and had to scramble to draw his pistol from the holster at his hip.

He loosed off a couple of shots at the truck. It was the only thing he could see or think to shoot at. One round appeared to spark off the windshield and he stupidly wondered what sort of trucker equipped his rig with bullet-proof glass.

He risked a peek around the tree. Amidst the uproar of gunfire, explosions and shouting, he could still hear the screaming of the diesel as it tried to free itself from the ruins of the gate. He saw then that whoever had fixed the gigantic steel arrowhead to the grill had also thought to weld some kind of shield in front of the driver's side window. It was probably just a steel barbecue plate, something to give the driver a little extra chance of surviving his suicide run at the gate. The truck engine howled, tyres smoked, and finally, the great beast freed itself with a lurch, bringing half the gate down with it. He thought he heard cheering.

"Time to go," Dale said. "Come on."

Jonas was perplexed to find he couldn't move. He couldn't make his legs work. Part of him wanted to see what came through the breach in the gate.

"Come on!" Dale hissed, smacking him upside the head and dragging him away by the collar. Jonas finally got moving. But his legs were jerky and unreliable beneath him.

"That's not the main attack," Dale said.

The fuck you say, Jonas thought, but nothing came out of his mouth save one strangled obscenity.

"Look," Dale said, hitting him again, directing his attention to a side street between Big Al's diner and the boarded up façade of Ginger McCauley's *Get Fudged* storefront. He was running now, panting and out of breath, and it was dark, but he could see what was happening over at the Wall. Even more gunfire and explosions. Not the dirty concussive blast of hand grenades like Wolfenden's men had used. Something else. Something exotic and fiery,

"Molotovs," Dale said.

Oily blossoms of orange-yellow flame erupted up and down the length of the Wall. Tracer fire reached down from the hilltops, raking across the fields where schoolchildren and seniors had planted green beans and potatoes. Jonas forced himself to turn away from the spectacle. It was enthralling and terrible but something worse was coming up behind them. He recognised the sound of dozens, maybe hundreds of big motorcycles. They were heading for the breach in the Seattle gate.

"JONAS! DALE!"

Sheriff Muller called out to them from the steps of his station house. He was carrying a shotgun and clad in body armour. He had some sort of night vision goggles strapped to his head but the monocular lens was flipped up, pointing to the stars above. Muller looked grim. Both men stopped, their flight interrupted by the command in his voice.

"They're coming through the gate," Muller shouted.

"And the wall," Dale shouted back. "You need to bring up the reserve from the Cascade Gate, Dave."

Deputies Millfull and Tilly appeared behind him, hurrying out of the station carrying rifles and ammunition. They looked as though they had just woken up. Probably had, Jonas thought. Half of the town's watch was stood to, while the other half rested and waited.

Gunfire crackled and the roar of bikes grew closer.

"They'll hit the traps soon," Muller shouted, just as the volcanic rumble of chopped hogs and Japanese super-bikes gave way to a confused heavy metal crash.

Jonas flinched. He looked back over his shoulder towards the Seattle gate, which was now aflame. The burning structure gave off enough light to see that the first wave of attacking riders had hit the wire and the hastily dug trench line about twenty yards inside the shattered fort.

Big bikes clattered and fell, sending up showers of sparks.

He saw one machine, eerily piloted by a headless rider, veer left and avoid the pitfall, carrying on for at least thirty yards before hitting the gutter outside *Get Fudged* and flipping high into the air, coming down with a bone-juddering crash.

The trench was not deep, three feet at most. Nor was it very wide. But that didn't matter. When the wheels of the motorcycles passed over the edge and onto the camouflaged tarpaulin, the riders were instantly unseated and thrown clear, creating a chaotic pileup. Defenders poured deadly fire into the tangle from both flanks. Most fired from cover, but one went striding, or rather staggering, down Main Street holding an oversized revolver in one hand and what looked like a bottle of Jack Daniels in the other. Everyone's favourite town drunk, Colin McFarland, had somehow laid his hands on a live weapon and an open bottle – neither of which he was supposed to be anywhere near. Muller and his deputies and Jonas and Dale stood gape-mouthed as McFarland unsteadily advanced on the interlopers, chugging lustily from his bottle, bellowing drunken defiance, and popping off shots.

"Fill your handsome bitches," he roared, or rather slurred at maximum volume, before correcting himself, "I mean sumbitches... I mean... Fill your hams..."

Whatever he meant was lost in the mouthful of liquor he poured down his throat, all the while continuing to blast away with the old cavalry pistol.

It was enough to sow confusion and a temporary panic among the attacking bikers, adding to the train wreck just inside the gate. Jonas stood with his mouth hanging open, slowly shaking his head. The bikers were in utter disarray. Their machines piled up on top of each other. Men—they were all dudes—scrambling over the broken, twisted metal and the bodies of fallen or crippled comrades to escape. If you looked closely enough, you could start to make out different club colours. He recognised the wings of the Hells Angels on some of the men's riding leathers.

"Colin! No!" Muller cried out. But too late. One of the bikers laid his sights on the stupidly brave, disastrously shitfaced drunk and cut him down with a burst of fire.

Dale Juntii brought up his own weapon, the one he had used to kill Renken the previous day, and returned fire, dropping McFarlane's killer. It was enough to break the strange, suspended moment. Muller and his deputies got moving again. They hurried across the street to the Red Apple, where a dozen or more of Darren O'Shannassy's supporters were holed up, taking advantage of firing slits cut into the heavy steel shutters that secured the building.

"Get reserves from the other gate," Muller cried out. "Plug the breach."

"Will do," Jonas called back, flinching as Jacques Loubert's glasshouse shattered into thousands of crystal shards when a biker road directly into it. Loubert appeared from the darkness, running at the man, holding a shovel over his head. He charged into the wreckage of his treasured project, swinging the heavy spade like a mediaeval axe. Jonas heard it strike home with a sick wet crunch.

"Jesus Christ," he muttered.

A massive explosion to the north-west lit up the whole town.

"The wall," Dale said, as though that explained everything. He suddenly spun and fired blindly into the darkness to the east, where the terrain dropped away precipitously.

"They're climbing up the rock face," he said matter-of-factly.

That was enough for Jonas.

"These fuckers are coming from everywhere," he shouted.

And they were. He could see it. Could see where this was heading. Bullets sparked and flashed off the road surface just a few feet away. Jonas and Dale started to run again, but sprinting this time. Towards the Cascade fort, or simply away from the Seattle Gate, he had no freaking idea. All he knew was that he was running, he was still alive, and if he stopped running, he would probably die.

He heard music. Fucking music! And he recognised it. *Let the Gods*

Decide. By Manowar. It wasn't fair. He fucking loved that album, and now these assholes trying to kill him had chosen it as their battle hymn. It just wasn't right. So he ran.

Dale ran with him. That made him feel better. If a stone killer like Dale Juntii knew it was time to rip and run, who the hell was Jonas Murdoch to second-guess him? They charged the length of Main Street, sprinting past the Farmers Mutual, Wells Fargo, Tewes Realty, the statue of John Mullen Jr, the neatly planted beds of winter vegetables, the shuttered shops and darkened windows of the local retailers and Dr Cornwell's surgery, finally reaching the Cascade gate where a dozen men waited with longarms and worried expressions. The sounds of battle from the far end of town were growing louder, more chaotic.

The small cluster of residents at the Cascade Gate had been detailed as a Quick Reaction Force, which would have been laughable if Jonas was in the mood for lulz. Leo Vaulk was down here, of course, having been banished from Sheriff Muller's presence after yesterday's fiasco, and Leo was by far the most combat-ready of Silverton's Quick Reaction Force. Next to him, Paul Tisevich leaned on his WW2-era rifle, using it as a walking frame rather than a weapon. Professor Boylan, a retired agronomist, held a pitchfork at port arms. And a clutch of old Bob Shapcott's checkers crew shuffled about looking as though the excitement might hurry them on to rejoin Bob long before the barbarians at the Seattle Gate did.

They all looked massively relieved to see Jonas and Dale run up.

"What's happening?" Tisevich demanded to know. "We moving up the line?"

His martial spirit was not in doubt, but his sense of balance was, and he nearly fell over when he tried to come to attention.

"Are we out of here? Are we bugging out?" Leo Vaulk wanted to know. Leo looked ready to jump off the gate and go tear-assing into the mountains on his own.

"What do you mean bugging out?" Tisevich protested. "We're moving up the line."

Jonas stood dumbly in front of the small crowd of armed yokels, lost for what to do next. He had assumed they were cutting and running as soon as Dale had... well, cut and run. But confronted by this last line of the town's defenders, he realised with horror that they were all looking to him for leadership.

What the fuck was he supposed to do? Cry havoc and lead a column of walking frames into the breach?

Even Juntii was staring at him, panting for breath, waiting for orders.

The roar of motorcycles, the bark and snarl of weapons fire, and the music pounding out of a mobile sound system, the crashing din of it all shattered and scattered his thoughts into a thousand jagged shards.

"Shit," he said. "Come on."

He meant, *'Come on. This isn't fair. Find someone else.'*

But they heard his plaintive "Come on," and that was enough to get them moving.

Perhaps they might have shuffled into battle and allowed him to quietly slip away in the confusion. But as the Quick Reaction Force moved out, they ran headlong into another, larger group moving at much greater speed for the Cascade gate.

Not the marauding bikers.

Tomi Yates and her besties.

And their families. And their friends. About thirty peeps in all.

Shit, he'd forgotten all about Tomi. But she hadn't forgotten about him or his escape plan.

"The fuck are you doing?" he asked her, his voice raised to be heard above the din.

"Getting the fuck gone, Jonas. What d'you think? Open the gates now. We gotta get to Rausch's place."

Tisevich and his crew came to a confused halt.

"We're falling back to Brad Rausch's place?" he asked. "But that's a mile out of town. We can't fight them from there."

The furious noise of the gun battle at the far end of town seemed to spike up fiercely, and everyone crouched lower. A heavy industrial din, crashing and discordant, rolled over them from that direction. Jonas peered back along Main Street. His balls contracted.

Two pick-ups had forced their way through the shattered gate structure. The attackers had mounted heavy machine guns on them.

"Fuck me," Dale Juntii barked. "Technicals."

"Jesus. Okay. Just the women and children through the gate," Jonas improvised. "It'll be safer at Brad's place."

Tomi actually smirked. Jonas could have slapped her. The gaggle of mean girls she'd brought with her were too terrified to notice the exchange.

"Open the gate," Jonas ordered. "Get the women and children out."

It was completely fucking crazy, of course. Tomi's raggedy ass band of bitches and all their hangers-on wasn't going to fit into the three vehicles Rausch had ready to go, and they were in no shape to hold off a siege of the auto repair yard if the bikers chose to try one.

But what the fuck was he supposed to do? Everyone was looking to him. Even Dale.

Some kid started to unlock the little postern door, causing a rush to the gate.

Dale looked at Jonas with a confused and questioning expression and Jonas could only shrug.

The whole debacle might have collapsed into panic and rout had not Sheriff Muller come running up at the moment, puffing and red-faced, sweating like a wheel of cheese and barely able to speak.

"Where's..." he started, before bending over to catch his breath, "...reinforce..."

Paul Tisevich pushed through the crush of refugees.

"Ready to move out and kick ass, Dave. We were just coming up with Jonas and Dale when the women folk and kiddies turned up."

"What?" Muller asked with a confused, breathless gasp.

He ducked, and they all did as the gun wagons started to service targets on the roofline of Main Street. The children screamed and their carers didn't do much better. Most of them sheltered under the firing platform of the Cascades Gate.

"Later," Jonas said. "It's not important."

"Keep that gate closed!" Muller shouted at the kid who had been about to unlock it. He sucked in a deep draught of air and spoke again, forcefully but not as loudly this time. "They're... trying to flank us...All round. They'll be out there."

Anxious protests flew back at him, but the gate stayed shut.

"We need to hit back hard, right now," Muller said.

"You need to take out those technicals," Dale said, nodding at the up-gunned vehicles about four hundred yards away. Long ropey streams of tracer fire licked out of the mounted weapons, raking at the topmost brickwork of the Savings and Loan. No return fire answered the attack.

Muller sucked at his lower lip. He cast a sceptical eye over the so-called Quick Reaction Force and shook his head.

"Dale, Jonas, it'll have to be us. O'Shannassy's guys are pinned down. Joe Wolfenden is in the forest trying to dig out the shooters on the high ground. If we can get up on top of Ginger's fudge shop, we can fire down into those pickups from behind."

"I lost my rifle when they hit the gate," Jonas confessed. Not mentioning that he'd left it on the parapet when he went to take yet another piss. Also, not mentioning that the last thing he wanted to do was drag his ass back into that unholy shitfight at the far end of town.

"You can have mine," Leo Vaulk said, handing him an assault rifle that looked like a fucking prop from a video game. "You familiar with any military-grade systems?"

"I go to the range," Jonas said. And he had when he could afford to. That felt like a million years ago.

"Well, that's an FN SCAR battle rifle," Leo said proudly. "Only serving military and licensed security professionals can load out with these bad boys. Gas-operated, self-loading. Full auto, 7.62mm. You take this one. I got some other toys in the bag I been wanting to break out."

He jerked a thumb over his shoulder back toward the Cascade Gate.

Jonas forced a rubbery smile onto his numb face as he stepped up to take the weapon. You had to admire Leo. A legitimate Hell regiment of apocalypse bikers overrunning his hometown, and he could still find a moment to give his dick a little squeeze over a centrefold in *Guns & Ammo*.

"Thanks," Jonas said, and then more quietly. "You be ready, Leo."

Vaulk nodded.

They stepped away from each other.

"Safety selector is on," Leo said. "You flick it off like this."

"Got it," Jonas said.

His eyes shifted to Dale Juntii.

Dale was waiting to see what Jonas did.

"We should sneak around the back way," Jonas suggested. "Less likely to get our asses shot off in the alleyway behind those shops than charging down Main."

Muller nodded.

"Good idea". He turned to Paul Tisevitch. "Paul, can you get these kids to shelter? Right now."

"I'll wrangle them into Doc Cornwell's place," the old soldier said. "Be careful, Dave, you boys."

Jonas was about to leave with Muller when someone gripped his arm. Tomi. She dragged him aside, just far enough away that nobody could listen to them. Not that anyone did. They looked like a couple in the torrid throes of an *affair da-fucking-amour*.

"What about me? What about our deal?" Tomi hissed.

Jonas leaned in close and glared, "You fucking broke it, you dumb bitch. Who the fuck are these cripples? Why'd you bring them?"

Tomi narrowed her eyes.

"That was Lisa, not me," she hissed. "She told her stupid mother and her mom brought all these other assholes. I couldn't get rid of them, baby. Not with everyone watching."

Shit.

This was getting worse by the second.

If Lisa Dees and her mother knew Jonas was looking to cut free, half the fucking town would know by now and the rest by morning if they survived.

"You want to get out of this. You need to get rid of them," Jonas said through gritted teeth.

"Problem, Jonas?" Dave Muller called out. He was clearly pissed. He and Dale had already stepped off and moved towards the nearest side street - a narrow walkway between Doc Cornwell's surgery and Kinsella & Fetterly's Secondhand Bookstore.

"Nope, coming now," Jonas shouted back.

Jonas peeled Tomi's thin, strong fingers off his bicep.

"You keep your shit together and your mouth shut," he said quietly through clenched teeth. "We are done here, and you are done if you can't rid of your little entourage."

He could see from her expression that she was this close to dropping a dime on him to Muller and making a run for it anyway. On her own.

Treacherous fucking bitches.

How did they always find their way to him?

He finally started using his brain instead of his dick.

"Get rid of all the old women and children. Your bitches can ride along. We got room for them. Nobody else."

Jonas didn't have time for any more, and Tomi seemed satisfied with that. He didn't doubt she would find some way of ditching them. She was a devious whore. The heavy automatic weapons fire from the back of the pick-ups had moved on. The gun trucks poured it into the front of Darren O'Shannassy's Red Apple now. Two ribbons of tracer fire, yellow and green, snaked across Main Street, painting the storefront in a spectacular, pyrotechnic display. He turned away from the light show and followed Dale and Muller into the darkness.

"I'll get these women and kids to safety, Sheriff," Tomi called out.

Dave Muller waved in acknowledgment but did not turn around.

The alleyway fed into loading docks at the back of the retail strip. Beyond the unsealed back lane, which serviced the bays behind the shops, the recently ploughed fields of Mullen Park lay under the dancing, eldritch light of Molotov cocktail fires along the Wall. Muzzle flashes and small explosions traced the arc of the battle out there, where the attackers seemed to be having a harder time breaking through and overwhelming the dug-in defenders.

"Least that's holding," Muller grunted as they turned left and hurried through the shadows back up towards the Seattle end of town.

"Wolfendens's guys trained those fire teams," Dale said.

He sounded like he approved.

He also sounded happier and maybe even content now that he had something to do.

Even though it was taking him back into danger and away from the possibility of escape.

Jonas kept his mouth shut and concentrated on not tripping in the dark.

The uproar of battle out on Main was terrifying.

When you thought that every gunshot you heard could end your life, and there were hundreds of them, maybe thousands of rounds a second... well, it was better not to think about it.

Especially now he had to figure out what to do about Tomi and her dumbass friends unleashing a bitchkrieg on his getaway plans. Jonas gripped Leo's big-ass gun closer to his chest. He could just turn the thing on Muller now. Cut him down. Dale, too, if he had to.

But chances were, he'd be dead a few minutes later when some asshole biker shot him in the face.

Or one of those redneck technicals ran him down in Main Street just for fun.

No, he had to survive the next five minutes before he could think about tomorrow or the day after. All he knew for sure was that he was done with this place.

They made the rear of the shuttered fudge shop. Climbed a wooden staircase to the roof, a flat expanse of tar paper, wind scoops and a brick chimney. The wooden facade overlooking the street would afford them no real protection against high-powered gunfire, but it did mask their approach to the edge of the roofline. All three men dropped to their bellies and snaked across the rough, sticky tar paper. Wooden beams of doubtful stamina flexed and creaked beneath their weight.

"Jesus Christ," Jonas muttered, imagining himself falling through.

A short burst of random gunfire crashed through the thin boards of the building's prow, reducing a carved wooden cornice to hot splinters and dust. A couple of seconds later it would have killed Jonas and Muller for sure. The Sheriff kept crawling forward. Jonas stopped, but only for a moment. Dale came up beside him, punched him on the arm and said quietly, "Come on."

"You pissed yourself yet," Jonas asked, more derisively than he'd intended.

Dale just laughed.

"Oh, I did that as soon as they blew the gate. Shit myself too."

Jonas realised with a grimace that he wasn't lying. He could smell the guy's stool.

The clamour and din of battle had not abated. The attackers must have fully infiltrated the town by now, but the good folk of Silverton were still standing to their guns. Still hammering back at the intruders.

Jonas found himself crouched low, almost curled into a foetal position at the edge of the roofline, behind a mere foot or so of flimsy, peeling clapboard shot through with ragged bullet holes.

Dale, lying on his back, produced a small handheld mirror and raised it briefly to scope out the scene below.

Jonas couldn't see anything in the compact reflector and Juntii did not hold it aloft for more than a second or so. But that was all he needed.

"Directly below us," he said. His voice was low, rather than whispering.

"They got some support. I'll take the ones on foot and the Ford Ranger with the two-gun mount. You guys concentrate your fire on the Toyota. Jonas, you rake 'em. Sheriff, you should pick off the driver. Stop 'em redeploying to bring those guns to bear on us. I think you got a good shot into the cabin. Just unload on that sucker, then switch to clean up. Count of three."

"Count of three," Muller confirmed.

Jonas didn't have time to object or equivocate.

Dale counted out, "One-two-three…"

And they were up, all of them drawing down on the vehicles below.

It was a hellish scene. The store front of the Red Apple had been chewed into scrap metal and debris. Smoke and flames poured out of the wreckage, but also the occasional gunshot. Jonas was surprised and even a little freaked out to see at least a dozen fighters on foot, surrounding the pick-ups, supporting them like infantry alongside tanks in a war movie.

Dale's assault rifle clattered and spat bright fire right next to his face, almost blinding him.

Muller squeezed off shots from his service pistol with a businesslike rhythm, an almost metronomic pulse, before holstering the hand weapon and swinging his shotgun to bear.

Jonas squeezed the trigger of the FN and cursed when nothing happened.

He frantically sought out the sector Leo had shown him, flicked it so hard he almost tore off a fingernail, and swept the muzzle back down to bring his target into the sights.

He pulled the trigger, and his heart leapt as the weapon roared in his hands, jerking up in his grip. He'd set the selector to auto and the first burst mostly missed as the kickback pulled his aim astray. By the time Jonas had re-centred his sights on the rear tray of the Toyota, Muller had killed at least two of the men fighting in back, and Dale had reduced the other vehicle to a broken meat wagon.

Jonas fired again.

This time, the big NATO standard rounds hit the pick-up like a steel tsunami, tearing apart vehicle and humans in a terrifying squall of violence.

He squeezed the trigger once, twice, and it was done. Smoke and flames poured from the engine block. Nothing moved in the rear tray.

The foot soldiers had already scattered, and Dale was chasing them with fire. Muller's shotgun boomed and clicked as he worked the rack. Boomed and clicked.

Silverton's surviving militia emerged from hiding up and down Main Street, engaging the foe.

It looked, just for a second, as though they might even win.

A single shot cracked behind them. Another followed quickly and Muller slumped with a grunt. Jonas looked at him stupidly. Dale spun and fired at the man who had come up the staircase behind them. He cried out as the short burst stitched him up, tumbling back into the night and landing somewhere below with a crash.

Jonas and Dale both crouched low again, remembering how exposed they were.

Dale moved quickly to check Muller.

The big man was writhing and groaning.

Jonas was shocked. Firstly, at how close he'd come to getting nailed. But also at how much relief he felt to see the sheriff cut down like this.

If they got through the night, he was going to have to answer some hard questions about what he'd been planning to do with the cars and supplies at Rausch's place.

"Looks bad," Dale said. "One round straight through the vest. Edge of the plates. One under the armpit. Be lots of damage and bleeding in there."

"Go get the doc or one of the interns," Jonas said without thinking. "I'll stay here. Look after him. Make sure you let me know when you're coming back up. I'm gonna shoot anyone who comes up those stairs without warning me."

"Okay," Dale said. "I won't be long."

He hurried off, bent low.

Jonas crouched where he could keep an eye out for any further sneak attackers coming up onto the roof.

"Fuck it hurts," Muller breathed.

"You had a bulletproof vest," Jonas said.

"Bullet... resistant," Muller croaked. "Not the same," he groaned.

"No," Jonas said. His mind was racing.

Part of him hoped that Muller would bleed out before Dale got back.

Part of him didn't want to be left alone up here. The fighting still raged below.

He took Muller's shotgun and laid it down where he could snatch the weapon up if needed. The sheriff tried to fumble for extra shells. Jonas took them from him. Muller's fingers were trembling and sticky with his own blood.

"That shit... at the gate, what was that?" he asked, his voice weak and panting.

"Just Tomi and the cheerleaders freaking out," Jonas lied. "Keep still."

"Lot of... people."

"Lot of idiots," Jonas ventured. He thought he heard the distinctive hammering of Dale's weapon down in the street blow.

"You... you planning to go?" Muller asked.

He spoke so softly that Jonas had to lean in to hear him.

"Not planning anything, no," he answered.

And he wasn't.

He didn't plan to kill Dave Muller. There was no premeditation when he placed his own big, strong hand over the sheriff's mouth, pinching off his nostrils between thumb and forefinger.

He knew what he was doing as the dying man started to jerk and buck about under his grip. But it wasn't planned. He understood the consequences of leaning in the man's upper body with all of his own considerable mass and strength, driving the last few gasps of air out of him, chocking off the man's airways so that Muller could not breathe. Jonas was just sort of... reacting.

He was simply in the moment. Doing what had to be done.

And then it was done. Surprisingly quickly. And Muller was dead. And Jonas Murdoch was free to move on again.

FAIL STATE IS DONE. The story will continue in *American Kill Switch*.

John Birmingham

PO Box 437

Bulimba, Queensland 4171

Australia

 Created with Vellum

ALSO BY JOHN BIRMINGHAM

The *End of Days* series.
Zero Day Code.
Fail State.
American Kill Switch.

The Axis of Time.
Weapons of Choice
Designated Targets
Final Impact
Stalin's Hammer
World War 3.1
(World War 3.2 & 3.3 coming in 2024)

A Girl Time in Time.
A Girl in Time.
The Golden Minute.
The Clockwork Heart (coming in 2024)

The Cruel Stars series.
The Cruel Stars

The Shattered Skies
The Forever Dead (2024)

Dave vs the Monsters series
Emergence.
Resistance.
Ascendance.
A Soul Full of Guns.
A Protocol for Monsters.

CHEESEBURGERGOTHIC

Hi. It's me, JB. If you liked this book and you'd like more of the same, sometimes for free, please join me over at my blog/book club/dive bar on the internet.

At the moment, it's hosted on Substack, but it kind of moves around, and wherever it ends up, it's *always* called CheeseburgerGothic.

Just throw that into el Goog or whatever AI chatbot runs the world now, and I'm sure they'll hook you up. I give away free stories there at least once a month. And my faves—everyone who signs up at the Burger is my favourite—get steep discounts on new releases.

Everyone else? Well, my friends, don't be like them.

I look forward to seeing you there.

www.ingramcontent.com/pod-product-compliance
Lightning Source LLC
Chambersburg PA
CBHW060434030726
47495CB00003B/869